THE LAST DOLLAR PRINCESS

A Young Heiress's Fight for Independence in Gilded Age
America and George V's Coronation Year England

Linda Bennett Pennell

Black Rose Writing | Texas

The author grants the final approval for this literary material.

Second printing

This is a work of fiction. Names, characters, businesses, places, events, and incidents are either the products of the author's imagination or used in a fictitious manner. Any resemblance to actual persons, living or dead, or actual events is purely coincidental.

ISBN: 978-1-68513-031-2 (Paperback); 978-1-68513-245-3 (Hardcover)
PUBLISHED BY BLACK ROSE WRITING
www.blackrosewriting.com

Printed in the United States of America
Suggested Retail Price (SRP) $22.95 (Paperback); $27.95 (Hardcover)

The Last Dollar Princess is printed in Sagona Book

*As a planet-friendly publisher, Black Rose Writing does its best to eliminate unnecessary waste to reduce paper usage and energy costs, while never compromising the reading experience. As a result, the final word count vs. page count may not meet common expectations.

For Jackie with all my love.
May your independent spirit lead to a lifetime of success!

THE
LAST
DOLLAR PRINCESS

CHAPTER 1

1910

Pisgah, North Carolina

Dawn's rays kissed the mountains, turning the blanket of mist hanging about their shoulders to spun silver. From her bedroom window, India stared at the scene as though it might fade away without warning. Her chest tightened and tears welled up. She had loved this view all her life. These were her mountains, all her own. She never tired of them. In winter, their peaks glistened with snow. In spring, wild azaleas, laurel, and rhododendron painted them in vibrant pastels. When summer temperatures rose in the valleys, they provided respite, but the grandest time of all was autumn. In that most glorious of seasons, the peaks and hollows of the Blue Ridge Mountains blazed with amber and crimson shades finer than any artist ever put to canvas. It was then the words of her old nurse came back to her. "You was borned and bred in these here mountains and mountain folkses has always knowed where they's gonna be buried. It's what makes us'uns different from them flatland ijots." Descended from fierce "Scotch-Irish" ancestors, Nanny Gordon truly believed she had second sight.

India rested her forehead against the glass and squeezed her eyes shut. The Falls had always been her home. She had known no other. While she prayed Nanny Gordon was right, Mother's plans portended a very different path.

A soft knock at the door broke the spell. India turned to find Althea, her lady's maid, entering with creased brow. "Mrs. Ledbetter says you better come downstairs right now." As India drew near, the maid leaned in and whispered, "She's not in a very good mood, so look out."

Luck had been with her the day she discovered Aletha dressing another maid's hair, a ladies' magazine opened on the long oak table in the servants' hall. It hadn't taken much persuasion to entice Althea out of the parlor and into her bedroom as lady's maid. Mother had first been appalled, then skeptical, and finally jealous.

At the top of the grand staircase, India paused and gazed at the scene in the foyer below. Mother, Mrs. Robert Ledbetter to most, Petra to a select few, stood at the base of the stairs tapping her foot while shouting last-minute orders to the butler and his minions. Given the diminishing pile of traveling cases and trunks, a casual observer might be forgiven for thinking the Ledbetters were leaving never to return. India rolled her eyes and sighed. Mother had plans for their stay in New York and woe be unto anyone who got in her way. India squared her shoulders and began her descent.

Mother spun around. "It's about time you appeared." She scanned India's tweed ensemble. "I suppose that will have to do. Trains, like tides, wait for no one, including you, young lady."

India swallowed hard. Summoning her most charming smile, she attempted a soothing tone. "I believe an hour to travel the mile to the Pisgah Depot should be sufficient. Since Papa had the driveway paved, getting down the mountain has not been a problem." India scanned the hall and frowned. "Is Papa not coming with us?"

"No. He and I agreed he would stay in North Carolina."

"But won't his absence seem odd?"

Mother's lips curled in a sneer. "Perhaps, but you know how he hates New York. He is also still complaining of his chest."

India's heart grew heavier. "Is Papa so ill? Maybe we shouldn't go either."

"He's not really sick. He just likes to complain. One of the many reasons he should stay here. Furthermore, it is my wish. His presence would only complicate matters. We will say he can't get away due to business concerns."

Mother couldn't be let off the hook so easily. India drew a breath and released it in a rush. "He has no business concerns, which everyone in New York surely knows. Other than meeting with the estate manager once a week and agreeing to whatever he proposes, Papa is really rather idle." India hated the brutality of her comment, but that did not change the truth. As much as she loved Papa, he gave in to Mother too often. His failure to stand up to her could be infuriating.

"That is beside the point." Mother jabbed her index finger in India's direction. "Your father indulges you in your fantasies, so he would only be an encumbrance. Your future is at stake and I will ensure that no mistakes are made. At nineteen, you can hardly go on as you are." With a final survey of the foyer, she continued, "Let's go to the auto without further delay." Glancing over India's shoulder, Mother continued, "Althea, ride on the second baggage wagon and make sure that driver takes care not to jostle our things."

India followed her mother into the first cool air of autumn and into the waiting vehicle. Through the Pierce-

Arrow's window, India soaked in the final views of home with Mother's words haunting each yard they traveled. Her future? No one had considered what she wanted. Given her druthers, she would have continued her education at Davenport Female College in Lenoir, where she would learn how to run a boarding school for the mountains' needy children. There were plenty of them deep in the surrounding hills and hollows. Mother insisted time spent at such an undistinguished institution would be ludicrous given India's prospects. She suggested a Swiss finishing school, but India objected so strenuously that for once Mother had given up.

They drifted in stalemate for months until now they were headed to the life Mother had known as a girl before she married Robert, only son and heir of Wall Street and oil tycoon Thomas Jefferson Ledbetter.

As they passed the waterfall from which the estate took its name, India leaned from the window and craned her neck for a final glimpse. She sucked her lower lip between her teeth and tilted her head back to prevent the tears rolling down her cheeks. Mother had won this battle. India would go to New York and endure a debut season, but no matter what happened there, the war was far from over.

CHAPTER 2

India stretched and rolled her shoulders. Lifting the shade, she gazed at the sun-washed New Jersey countryside speeding past the train window. Leaves in shades of red and gold swirled in the gusts created by the train's wheels while dairy cows on a hillside pasture nodded and blinked at the noise. The scene reminded her so much of home.

India pinched the inside of her upper arm to forestall tears. For better or worse, they would be in New York within the hour. Massaging the back of her neck, she sniffed her underarm. A long soak in one of the clawfoot bathtubs was in order as soon as they arrived at Grandmama's. Despite the luxurious appointments of the family's private car, twenty-five hours being jostled on a train had left her tired and cranky. Mother had elected to breakfast in the dining room, but India couldn't eat. It was too early, and the car's rocking left her slightly nauseated. She could wait until luncheon without ill effect. Thank goodness Grandmama was able to keep an excellent cook.

India dropped the shade and scooted back in her seat, a smile lifting one corner of her mouth. Of course, Papa's inherited fortune paid for the cook, the butler, the maids, and everything else that Grandmama enjoyed. It had been part of the marriage settlement. Mother's family, the Van de Bergs, were old money who had fallen on hard times before Mother and Papa married. With what some wags at the time referred to as the merger of the century, the Van de Bergs gained a portion of the Ledbetter wealth and ole Grandpa Thomas Jefferson "T.J." Ledbetter gained some secondhand respectability. India chuckled. Hers was a mixed heritage indeed.

Unfortunately, Mother had never forgiven Papa for being the son of a nouveau riche, social-climbing-nobody from the mountains of western North Carolina. India sighed. The prospect of Grandmama Van de Berg's small circle of society matrons once again inspecting her like she was some exotic insect from the wilds of darkest Appalachia filled her with dread. It happened every time they traveled north, so she should be accustomed to it by now. Nonetheless, it still galled. Dropping her head against the seat, she closed her eyes. If she couldn't sleep, at least she could rest. She needed all her strength for what lay ahead.

The train chugged into Pennsylvania Station at mid-morning. India pulled down the sash and wrinkled her nose at the odor of coal smoke drifting into the carriage. In spite of soot particles lingering in the air, she leaned through the window for a better look at New York's newest homage to the Industrial Age. Redcaps bustled about, assisting passengers with their baggage. Ladies and gentlemen in elegant attire stepped down from carriages onto platforms that shone bright and clean. The station had been open for less than a month.

India shaded her eyes with her hand. Over the tracks and the main concourse were ceiling panels made of glass held together by iron dividers. At the end of the building, a

THE LAST DOLLAR PRINCESS

huge arched window admitted sunlight that gleamed off brass staircase banisters and balcony railings. Wide-eyed, India's head swiveled in every direction as she laughed aloud. Pennsylvania Station was a Gothic cathedral of transportation in glass and steel. Maybe arriving in such a space would make visiting New York feel a little less daunting in the future.

"Get out of that window before you ruin your dress." Mother's voice sounded from the doorway behind her. "It's time to depart for Grandmama's."

India jerked back so fast she banged her head on the window. After rubbing the tender spot raised by the sash, she straightened her hat, then cast a wary eye over her dress. Thank goodness it was unsoiled. She smoothed the wrinkles from her skirt, picked up her handbag, and followed Mother onto the platform.

Once they reached the columned portico, India scanned the cabs and vehicles lining the street. "I don't see Grandmama's chauffeur. Have they hired someone new? I hope not. I always liked James."

Mother's face darkened and her lips thinned. "Your father has decided your grandmother is not in need of a chauffeur. He convinced the trustees to reduce the annuity that paid James's salary and for the limousine among other things."

"But I thought the money was settled for life."

"Oh, no. The actual amount to be paid was not part of our marriage contract. It only specified Mama is to be maintained in style sufficient to her needs. I objected strenuously, but your father seemed not to care. In his opinion, New York has perfectly fine transportation for hire. Furthermore, he believes my mother will not be out about town as she once was, and I quote, since she no longer has a daughter for sale. He can be so vulgar at times. I suppose one should expect no better from the son of a social climbing hillbilly, but I really thought the years with my family had had an improving effect."

"Mother, really. How can you say such things? Papa is very good to you and Grandmama. If he thinks she is capable of paying for her own luxuries, I am sure he is right." India stifled a smile. Papa occasionally roused himself to thwart Mother when she had pushed him too far.

"So says the girl born with a silver spoon who has never wanted for anything. Under no circumstances are you to express such uncharitable views to your grandmother. She, like my dear father until his untimely death, has suffered enough humiliation."

India let the subject of her grandparents' suffering drop. She could recite their misfortunes word-for-word as Mother never wavered in recounting them. Glancing over her shoulder at the porter guarding their baggage, she concentrated on practical matters. "How are we to get to the Square?"

"Your father arranged a hired driver and automobile for the duration of our stay. The maids and luggage will follow by taxi. I believe that man over there is holding a sign with our name on it. Hurry before anyone we might know notices."

The vehicle left the station, traveled east to Fifth Avenue, and turned south. It was a drive India had taken once per year since she was deemed old enough to accompany Mother on her annual pilgrimage to visit Grandmama. As she grew, India came to realize that visiting Grandmama was a euphemism for reconnecting with the social season of which Pisgah, North Carolina was so notably lacking. Mother was in her element for a few short months before the enforced return to the Wilderness, as she called The Falls and the village of Pisgah abutting their estate. India watched with interest as the mansions, hotels, and tall buildings of the central city evolved into the structures of old New York. So much had changed on Fifth since their previous visit, but Lower Manhattan seemed to knock down and build up at a slower pace.

When they reached Washington Square, relief washed through her. Nothing that mattered had changed. The Arch still stood sentinel at the park's entrance. Trees still spread a canopy over the park's paths and would soon flame in full autumn glory. Water splashed into the pool at the fountain's base. She might dread her grandmother, but she loved Washington Square Park. Her happiest memories of New York lay among its grassy patches and under its trees. No matter how full their calendar, she would find a way to spend time there.

The limousine turned left onto Washington Square North. India inspected each house as the automobile rolled past. Thank goodness. Not a single one of the lovely old Greek Revival townhouses of The Row had been altered. When they stopped in front of Number 5, India clasped her hands to prevent fidgeting. The Van de Bergs had lived at Number 5 since it was completed in 1833. She cast a speculative gaze over her grandmother's home. Other than peeling paint on the wrought-iron fence guarding the tiny front garden, the house appeared in good repair. The white columns and trim on the stoop gleamed. The windows shone. The red brick walls stood four stories tall and sturdy as the day they were built.

Presumably the public rooms on the first floor remained as beautiful as ever, if decidedly dated. Their Federal style of pastel green walls, simple white ceiling medallions and crown moldings, and Duncan Phyfe furniture were of an earlier period. India loved the lightness and brightness of those interiors. They were in marked contrast to the heavy furniture and dark wood interiors that were the current fashion. Perhaps she had been born to the wrong generation.

The hired chauffeur opened the rear passenger door and stood at attention. Before exiting the vehicle, India rolled her lips over her teeth and pinched her cheeks. It was always wise to look one's best when entering the lion's den.

CHAPTER 3

India stepped down from the automobile and shook the folds from her skirt. A little flutter played just beneath her breastbone as it did every time she approached Grandmama's domain. She drew a long breath, let it out slowly, and followed her mother through the front gate.

Spencer, the butler, opened the door. "Welcome, Madame, Miss India." The only part of his face that moved was his mouth. Without a smile or any other facial expression, he continued, "Please follow me to the parlor. Mrs. Van de Berg awaits you there."

If Spencer had been German, he would have clicked his heels and made a precise forty-five-degree bow. As he was English, he simply turned and began what could only be termed the March to the Parlor. His posture stiff and erect, he hardly moved above the knees, but he stepped with purpose. India stifled a giggle. Nothing within the house had changed, either.

Opening the parlor door, Spencer announced them and then glided away into the bowels of the service area. India straightened her posture, exhaled slowly, and plastered on her most confident smile. Swishing into the room, she advanced upon the figure positioned beside the fireplace. Just like Number 5 Washington Square, its occupant never seemed to change. Grandmama could pass for a woman of sixty, but her age was closer to seventy-five. Her back was as straight as the brass poker standing among its companions in the hearth tool rest.

The cut and detailing of her ensemble spoke of a slightly earlier style. Not completely outdated, but not of the latest fashion. Its aubergine hue enhanced the platinum highlights in her otherwise snowy hair and the luster of her pale skin. She was not beautiful in the traditional sense, but when she entered a room, all heads turned in her direction. Words India had heard used to describe Elisabeth "Betsy" De Vries Van de Berg arose - formidable, handsome, forthright, a force, but never maternal.

India came to rest before her grandmother, bending to plant the briefest of kisses on her remarkably unlined cheek. Displays of familial affection were expected but must never be excessive. India had learned that dictum as a small child when her exuberant embraces had been rebuffed time and time again. The memory still rankled.

Grandmama received the kiss as her due, then cast an appraising gaze over India. "You appear to have slept in your clothes. I assume you brought other day dresses?"

"You look well, also, Grandmama. And yes, I believe we have packed our entire wardrobes." Did her grandmother catch the hint of sarcasm in India's voice? If she did, she chose to ignore it. A little bubble of satisfaction swelled within India. Score one for the younger generation.

"Good. You will have time in which to make yourself presentable." Turning her attention to Mother, Grandmama continued, "Petra, dear, you look frightful. Whatever are you wearing?"

Mother wilted under Grandmama's scrutiny. This aspect of their relationship never changed. India swallowed hard as a prick of conscience said she should feel some sympathy, but the only emotion presenting itself was a small jolt of irritation. Perhaps if Mother were kinder about Papa, India could muster more pity now. But then, who was she to criticize her mother for observing convention? She was in thrall to Mother's whims, moods, and desires, which is why she was here in New York instead of at home in North Carolina. A silent sigh escaped India as she glanced away from the scene of intergenerational parrying. It never ceased. Women and girls must always bow to the expectations of fathers, husbands, and elder family members in general. It was simply the way things were.

Mother looked down at her skirt and gave it a shake before replying, "I...I thought since we were in our private carriage, I would wear what was comfortable. It was a long journey."

"Be that as it may, one must never give in. Did you bother to consider who might see you on the train platform? You know better, but I suppose living among Indians and hillbillies has tainted your view of what is appropriate. Why Robert insists on living in that godforsaken wilderness is unfathomable."

Mother's cheeks took on a rosy glow. "You know his reasons. He has expressed them often enough. Furthermore, The Falls is a far grander estate than any in New York."

India cut her eyes at her mother. Bravo. For once Mother stood up to Grandmama. It never ceased to amaze that Mother, usually so in charge of every situation, always melted like an ill-prepared meringue in the blast furnace of her own mother's presence. In all probability, most families were complicated, but with her family, it felt like secret battles were constantly being fought beneath a glassy surface of social decorum.

The old woman arched an eyebrow. "Yes, I suppose that is true. Given the obscene amount your father-in-law spent on The Falls, I suppose grand is the word one might choose. Although vulgar ostentation comes to mind, as well." Grandmama was never one to cede a point without exacting a price. Dismissing the subject with a wave of her hand, she said, "We will take luncheon with Lady Clarissa and then go to Madame Osborne for fittings."

"Madame Osborne? But she's…" A withering glance silenced Mother.

India sensed her mother's increasing agitation. Although irritated with the woman, abandoning Mother completely to Grandmama's domineering violated India's sense of fair play. Distraction and redirection were in order. "Grandmama, who is Lady Clarissa?"

Her grandmother took the bait. "She is the daughter of an English earl. She is also Mrs. Jonathan Rivers of 900 Fifth Avenue. The Rivers house is smaller than its neighbors, but it is exquisitely elegant, as one would expect of the English nobility. Lady Clarissa's father was the Fourteenth Earl of Kilnsey."

"My goodness. She sounds mighty grand. Why did she marry an American? Surely, she could have had her pick of earls' and dukes' sons."

Grandmama snorted. "Hardly. The old earl squandered the remnants of the family fortune on horses, women, and games of chance. They say his debts left the estate mortgaged to the hilt. The kindest thing Lady Clarissa's father did before he died of alcoholism was to marry her off to Jonathan Rivers. At least Mr. Rivers is able to keep her in the style she deserves."

"So, how do you know her?"

"Oh, like one does. We have met at various functions since her marriage. The Rivers are not of the 400, of course, but they are perfectly respectable. The new rich can be quite nice when one looks beyond the deficiencies of their pedigrees."

"That is rather uncharitable."

"It is, but I have always believed in being frank among family. It prevents embarrassing misunderstandings."

India opened her mouth to speak, but her mother's hand on her arm silenced her. Petra stepped between granddaughter and grandmother. "Mama, we simply cannot purchase India's ball gowns at Madame Osborne's. She may be well enough for some, but India must make a proper entrance into society. Only Worth will do."

"I did not intend for *you* to purchase from Madame Osborne, Petra dear. I, on the other hand, can afford no better since your husband has seen fit to reduce my allowance. I need new gowns if I am to introduce India properly. At least we have not lost our place among old New York's finest. They are the people who really matter, after all."

Engendering guilt and delivering a social cut in one brief soliloquy. Score two points to Grandmama. Oil was needed on these generational waters. India spread her hands in a gesture of supplication. "I am sure Madame Osborne will do quite well. Worth is lovely, but maybe we should patronize a New York designer. Surely Grandmama's friends would approve."

Petra sniffed. "How little you know. You were born among plebeians. You have no idea what is expected among our people."

The sound of Grandmama's hand hitting the table beside her chair made India jump. "Enough of this inane talk. Call your maids and prepare yourselves for the day."

Clean, refreshed, and wearing an unwrinkled dress, India watched the mansions of Fifth Avenue float past the limousine window. She didn't want to be here, but she was resigned to the inevitable. Her grandmother sat beside her on the third seat while her mother sat facing them on the opposite. The farther north they traveled, the more tension radiated from the two older women. If India allowed it, their anxiety would creep across the seats and grab her by the throat, so she clasped her hands in her lap and concentrated on the passing scenery.

When they reached Numbers 840 and 841, Mother let out a sigh. "Do you remember Mrs. Astor's ball my debutant year? It was the most beautiful event of the season and my dress was the prettiest I've ever worn." A wistful expression softened Mother's eyes. "David Havemeyer proposed to me that night."

A little thrill crawled through India. She glanced at her grandmother and then at her mother. A definite pall had fallen over Mother, while Grandmama simply looked bored and irritated. Unable to hold it in any longer, India asked, "So who is David Havemeyer and why didn't you marry him?"

"Because," Grandmama interjected with a note of derision, "he would not have been able to support your mother in the fashion she wanted."

The whoosh of Mother's breath would have reached the driver had the privacy glass not been closed. A red flush crawled up from her throat. "You mean the manner in which you and Father wanted." She looked at India with glittering eyes. "He was handsome and from one of the oldest families in the city. After Mama and Father made me turn him down, he went to his family's Long Island cottage and refused to come back until the season was over. I was told by his sister that I had broken his heart. I sometimes wonder what life with him would have been."

Grandmama harrumphed. "Decidedly poorer."

India sighed inwardly. Mother had never made it much of a secret that she sometimes regretted marrying Papa, but this was truly unsettling. Poor Papa. Mother always said he was madly in love with her when he proposed. Mother, however, had been less enamored. India now understood why. It seemed that Mother had not quite forgotten this David from the old 400 family.

The automobile began to slow, stopping in front of Number 900. In comparison to its neighbors, it was a moderate sized Brownstone with an elegant stoop and magnificently ornate iron and glass entry. Grandmama led the way up the steps and was met immediately by the butler, who showed them into the drawing room where a lovely blonde woman aged about thirty sat upon a Louis XVI settee.

India stifled a gasp. Lady Clarissa's costume, her furnishings, the room in general were of the most elegant design. The scene did not speak of the current trend, yet no one would say it was unfashionable. Timeless was the word that came to mind. Palest pink walls finished by cream crown molding with a carved formal motif encased a space that held fine French antiques and Aubusson carpets. India tried not to stare, but the effect was quite startling. It was the most beautiful scene she had ever encountered.

After brief introductions and small talk, the trio adjourned to a glass enclosed space housing a small jungle of potted palms, assorted shrubs, and flowering plants. A linen-draped table for four sat just inside the enclosure. Sunlight glimmered over china, crystal, and sterling. The effect was lovely, as was everything about this lady and her home.

Lady Clarissa, seated facing the door, rang for luncheon to be served. "I hope you are not overly tired from your journey. Perhaps we should have postponed until tomorrow?"

Grandmama smiled, but it seemed to India that a slight nervousness hid behind the upwardly curved lips. "My daughter and granddaughter were quite eager to make your acquaintance, dearest Lady Clarissa. They would not dream of inconveniencing you by a last-minute postponement, but you are most gracious to be concerned for their comfort."

Since India had not heard of Lady Clarissa until two hours ago, her burning desire to meet the lady was something of a revelation. India shot an inquiring look across the table, but Mother averted her eyes. A tingle ran down India's spine. There was something furtive in the way Mother refused to meet her gaze. India glanced at Grandmama, whose behavior toward Lady Clarissa could only be termed obsequious. Grandmama rarely bowed to anyone. In fact, India had never once seen her grandmother treat another person as she was treating Lady Clarissa. Mother and Grandmama were up to something. They had clearly been plotting, but to what end could not discerned.

CHAPTER 4

India dabbed her lips with the heavy linen napkin and returned it to her lap. Straightening her posture, she plastered on a smile, focused her attention on her companions, and feigned interest in Grandmama's near monologue. At present, the topic was a ball to be given by someone India had never heard of. Allowing her gaze to shift, she looked at their hostess. Lady Clarissa's eyes held a slightly glazed expression, but Grandmama seemed not to notice and charged on with a description of the ball giver's social status. Not of the 400, of course, but perfectly respectable. Mother nodded and smiled encouragement throughout. Whatever Grandmama's purpose, she was pursuing it with vigor.

India wiggled her toes, then rolled the balls of her feet. The benefit of taking luncheon in the solarium was that the cloth on the table reached the floor, thus hiding her feet. Otherwise, her slender skirt, though stylish, would have betrayed her fidgeting and she would never want to insult such a gracious hostess.

Lady Clarissa had served a sumptuous luncheon of lobster soup, broiled flounder, and root vegetables, followed by a Neapolitan brick cake. Throughout the meal, their hostess had listened to Grandmama rave on without betraying a note of the boredom she must surely have felt. India gazed at Lady Clarissa as she endured Grandmama's unending stream of words. She was a model of social grace. Somewhere in the depths of the house, a clock struck 2:00. Surely manners dictated it time to leave the good lady to prepare for afternoon callers. India shifted in her chair, trying not to glance toward the door.

Her mind must have wandered because a hand on her shoulder made her jump. Mother said, "It has been lovely. Thank you so much and please give our compliments to your cook." Squeezing India's upper arm, she continued, "Dear, we must not impose on Lady Clarissa's hospitality. It is time for us to depart."

India stifled a snort. It was not she who had delayed their departure. Nonetheless, contradicting Mother would serve no purpose. Smiling, she offered her hand to their hostess. "It has indeed been a lovely luncheon. Thank you so much. I hope we shall meet again while Mother and I are in New York."

An ironic smile played across Lady Clarissa's face. "Oh, I suspect we will find ourselves in one another's company quite often. It has been a pleasure to entertain such...enthusiastic guests."

India blinked. She would bet her eye teeth Lady Clarissa's pause had not been a momentary loss of vocabulary. Indeed, a flash of mischief danced in the woman's eyes. Perhaps she was involved in Mother and Grandmama's intrigue or maybe she enjoyed a private joke. India peeked at her relatives. They appeared oblivious, their composure as unruffled as freshly starched linen.

Clasping Lady Clarissa's hand, Grandmama took charge. "Well, my dears, we really must be off. Petra and

India must have new gowns and there is so little time before Mrs. Butler's ball. Will we see you and Mr. Rivers there? It can't be classified as among the best, but she always has an excellent buffet and the room is large enough that one does not feel crowded. Of course, that may also be due to the number who attend. I can never decide if it's the room's size or the lack of attendees. Although she is descended from an old Knickerbocker family, there are those who still hold Mr. Butler's background against him."

Lady Clarissa withdrew her hand. "Yes, imagine such snobbery."

India's eyes widened. There it was again, that hint of mischief. This time, she was sure Lady Clarissa's tone hinted at a hidden meaning. India cast a sidelong glance to judge the effect of the double entendre. Mother and Grandmama remained unperturbed.

Feeling herself the object of scrutiny, she cut her eyes at her hostess. Lady Clarissa responded with a smile, an arched brow, and an almost imperceptible nod. India smiled in return, glowing in the knowledge of a shared secret. Of course, she was not quite certain of the secret's contents, but to be in the confidence of such an elegant, sophisticated person was thrilling.

As they passed through the front door, India's footsteps were lighter than they had been since they left The Falls.

***

Clarissa stubbed out a cigarette and picked up the evening edition of the newspaper. Turning to the international news, she saw that the journalist Edward Mylius had been convicted of criminal libel and was to serve a year in jail. She smiled and lit another cigarette. Served the bastard right for publishing the lie that King George V was a bigamist. It would be hoped the man had learned his lesson. She might be considered an American now, but in her heart she would always be English.

The sound of the front door opening and closing drifted softly into the library. Clarissa put her cigarette in the ashtray and glanced at the mantel clock. It was nearly the dinner hour. Surely Jonathan was finally home. He worked much too hard, but he paid little heed to her entreaties that he delegate more to his vice presidents. The door opened, and he came in to join her at last. She cast a critical eye over him while he poured two whiskeys, adding soda to hers. Dark circles had appeared under his deep-set brown eyes in the last few weeks and new gray shone at his temples. He crossed the room and held out a crystal tumbler.

Taking the glass from his hand, she allowed her fingers to glide ever so lightly over his wrist. "Darling, I'm so glad you are home. How was today? Any better?"

He dropped down beside her on the sofa. "Actually, things are beginning to improve. The bank is recovering now that the nonsense of '07 and '08 is finally behind us. Something really must be done to stabilize the economy and eliminate this infernal cycle of financial panics." He took a long sip and settled back against the sofa cushions. Kissing her temple, he continued, "So, how did your little luncheon go?"

Clarissa chuckled and nestled into the curve of his arm. "Quite well. The grandmother was gruesome as always, but the girl is rather sweet."

Jonathan's fingers traced the line of her shoulder. "I see." His voice held a note of surprise. "So, you think she might do?"

Clarissa looked up at him through her lashes. Men could be so dense. "Of course she'll do. She's pretty enough and her father has pots of money. She does seem a bit naïve, but she's rather quick witted."

"This is old TJ Ledbetter's granddaughter, isn't she? Raised in the wilds of the Blue Ridge Mountains, I believe?"

"You know she is. I've told you often enough. Sometimes I think you pay no attention to what I tell you."

"I'm sorry, my dear. I guess the bank's troubles have rather consumed me for some time." He took another deep sip from his glass. "Do you think the girl will cooperate? Too many of these young women have gotten some rather peculiar notions of late."

"Oh, I suspect she will be easily swayed. In any event, she seems completely subservient to her mother and grandmother."

Jonathan drew back so that he could meet her gaze. "It sounds as though you don't like them very much."

"If they didn't have a part to play, I doubt I would be able to abide them." Clarissa could not keep the contempt from her voice. "They are such frightful snobs. One would think they were related to royalty."

Jonathan laughed. "Well, in a way they are. Mrs. Astor and the Old Four Hundred are the closest New York has to an aristocracy. The de Vries and Van de Bergs have been here since the place was called New Amsterdam. And anyway, isn't snobbery what the English class system is based upon? I seem to recall a few raised eyebrows when we married."

"That was different. We had such a short courtship. Then, our engagement was even briefer. It created speculation."

"Your father didn't seem to mind. In fact, it was he who suggested I propose before other suitors claimed your hand."

"Of course he didn't mind. He wanted me off his hands." Clarissa kissed Jonathan's cheek. "At least he saw to it that I was well settled with someone who could take care of me. Daughters are such a liability to men like Papa. All title and no substance. I adored him, but he had his deficiencies as a peer and as a parent."

"And lucky for me he did. Otherwise, I doubt he would have allowed me within one hundred yards of you."

"Actually, many people would say I am the lucky one. You saved me from the clutches of the odious Lord Simonton."

Jonathan grinned and cocked his head in thought. "Hm. Let's see. I met him several times, and he seemed a nice enough fellow."

Clarissa allowed a small grunt to break through her normally impeccable facade. "You aren't female, and you can hardly claim more than a passing acquaintance. He is an ogre with hands that wander much too freely. Furthermore, if I had wanted to be exiled to the far isles, I would have chosen Lord George. But I really hate those glacial Scottish castles and the North Sea's gale force winds." She patted his knee and grinned. "So much cozier here with you in this lovely townhouse in the city."

His lips brushed hers. "I am glad you approve. After the house you were raised in, I feared nothing I could give you would ever measure up."

"The house I grew up in is a prime example of the aforementioned glacial pile." She heard the derision in her voice. She must not add to Jonathan's stress by being negative. Modulating her tone, she continued, "And anything you give me would be perfect. I don't know how you do it, but you always select the most marvelous gifts. Even when it's something I never suspected I might want."

She cut her eyes upward and winked. "In fact, your gift giving is one of the things I love most about you."

He chuckled and pulled her into a full embrace. "You, my dear, are a greedy little minx, but I love you all the same. So, when does the ship arrive?"

"On the first just in time for Mrs. Butler's ball."

His brow creased and his lips became a thin line. "Butler? I thought we were not attending that one."

Clarissa lifted her fingers to his cheek and let them play upward until they reached the widow's peak that gave him such a distinguished appearance. Letting a finger trace its edge, she said, "I have changed my mind. Or rather, Mrs. Ledbetter and old Mrs. Van de Berg have changed it for me. They are attending with the girl, so we must, as well."

"Oh bother. I had hoped to avoid it."

Adopting her most winsome expression, she looked into his eyes. "You will do this for me? Please?"

He sighed and nodded. "If I must."

"Then it's settled. Mrs. Butler's ball will be our first sortie." Clarissa smiled and kissed his cheek.

CHAPTER 5

India stood before the Cheval mirror in her Washington Square bedroom, turning this way and that so she could view herself from as many angles as possible. The new deep rose ball gown of silk satin was lovely. Its slender silhouette showed her figure to advantage, though her corset's bone stays required to hold everything in place dug into her rib cage something fierce. Tugging on it through the fabric of her gown, she squirmed around until the thing settled into a more comfortable position. Such was the price of elegance.

Light from the wall sconces caught in the silk embroidery and crystal beading that started at her shoulders and cascaded down the front panels to the hem. It curved around to the back to decorate a train stretching a full yard behind her. The overall effect was rather regal. She ran her finger over the strand of pearls Papa had given her before they left home and then flicked one of the matching teardrop earrings. It swung and moved back into place. Pulling on her long, white kid gloves, she took a final glance. Although she really had not wanted to make this trip, she could not deny the self-satisfied tingle the image in the mirror created. Pink was definitely her color. It complimented her dark blond hair and green eyes. Yes, she just might do. Drawing a deep breath and exhaling slowly, India turned and headed for the door.

She found Mother and Grandmama waiting in the foyer. Grandmama cast an evaluative gaze over India. "You really are lovely, Child. Why you resisted the opportunity of a New York season for so long is beyond understanding. You will definitely outshine the other young ladies." She gestured toward the front door. "Shall we?"

If Grandmama had seriously wanted to know the reason for her resistance, India would have gladly given the answer. As it was, the complaint had merely been rhetorical, so she followed her relatives into the limousine and sat silently as the automobile moved out of Washington Square and turned up Fifth Avenue. India watched the mansions of the barons of industry and of wealthy old money families float past the automobile windows until they were almost to Carnegie Hill, where New York's more prosperous Jewish citizens had their businesses and homes. It seemed the Butlers had not settled among the most desirable addresses. Had Mrs. Butler not been of an old Knickerbocker family, Grandmama would surely not have deigned to know her. India grabbed an armrest when the vehicle swayed with a left onto 79th Street. They then cut across Central Park and turned back north once they exited the park. They were definitely headed toward a neighborhood she had not visited on previous trips north.

India peered as the Museum of Natural History's turrets disappeared behind them. A tour of dry, dusty fossils was preferable to what lay ahead. At least they would be edifying. Alas, she bent to Mother's will and Mother bowed to Grandmama's wishes. It was the way they lived their lives. Moreover, it was the way everyone she knew lived. The young were dominated by the old. Women were dominated by their husbands and fathers. Society dominated everyone. Papa was the only outlier. He neither dominated his wife nor bent to her will. He just floated above it all, which sometimes left India wondering if he even noticed what went on around him. Dear Papa. So kind, but so seemingly indifferent. Or was ineffectual the better term? India sighed and straightened her posture. Dwelling on what she could not change was a waste of time and energy. Their arrival at Mrs. Butler's ball was imminent and she must prepare herself to make the entrance Mother and Grandmama expected. Life would be easier in the long run.

The automobile made a left onto 83rd Street and pulled to a stop in front of a beautiful double brownstone. Light blazed from the large second-floor windows. Silhouettes of dancing couples came into view, then whirled away to reappear in the next panes. Showtime was upon them.

India paused on the sidewalk as the others descended from the vehicle. Grandmama's gaze swept over the house. "Impressive, is it not? Who in their right minds but the Butlers would purchase such a house in this neighborhood?"

India cut her eyes at Grandmama. "It looks like a perfectly lovely area to me. Shouldn't we be appreciative of being invited instead of criticizing our hosts' choice of address?"

Grandmama turned and stared at India for a full fifteen seconds before she responded, "You will kindly keep your thoughts to yourself." Frost hung about her words. "Young ladies being launched in society must be above reproach and no one, I repeat, no one likes a young person with opinions. Furthermore, you have little to no experience with New York society and what is expected." She took India's arm and gave her a push. "It's beginning to rain. Hurry."

At the door to the ballroom, Grandmama stopped and motioned India to wait behind her until their entrance had drawn the proper amount of attention. Although she had not really wanted to come, India couldn't help but be a little awed by the scene playing out under the glow of three crystal chandeliers hung from the ornately carved ceiling. Couples whirled to the music of a small chamber orchestra. Floor to ceiling mirrors reflected their movements and that of the lights. The overall effect was rather dazzling. These people may not be what Grandmama considered the top tier of society, but they were stylish and well dressed. India reviewed her ensemble and was glad Grandmama had insisted they buy new gowns.

Within moments, all eyes were upon them. It was then that Grandmama drew India to her side. Smiling and nodding, Grandmama started across the room toward their hosts. Watching the gathering, India noticed a group of older women smiling and speaking to one another behind their fans. Like a tennis ball in play, the women's gazes darted to India and then back over the dance floor to their own group. One might surmise that Grandmama's party was an object of gossip or speculation. India stiffened and smiled directly at them, ensuring they saw her and made eye contact. At least two of the ladies had the good grace to appear embarrassed and quickly looked away. India swallowed the laughter that bubbled up. Point to Miss Ledbetter.

Once India had been introduced to their hosts, Mrs. Butler summoned her sons over and picked up India's dance card. "Let me see. We are about to begin the Chopin, are we not? Oh, it is a mazurka. Do they know the mazurka in North Carolina, Miss Ledbetter?"

India smiled. "Why, yes we do." Arching her brow, she continued, "We have socials with dancing even in the wilds of darkest Appalachia." India felt a trickle of satisfaction as she observed her hostess's reaction.

Mrs. Butler looked slightly flustered, then recovered her composure and laughed. "Well, of course you do. How silly of me." Turning to her sons, she asked, "Now which of you boys will be the first to dance with Mrs. Van de Berg's lovely granddaughter?"

It was not long before India's card began to fill for the first half of the ball. During her third dance, she noticed all eyes looking toward the door. Lady Clarissa, what must be Mr. Rivers, and a young man entered the ballroom. Clarissa looked her way and waved. India nodded in return and watched the attractive trio cross the room. Lady Clarissa had not mentioned attending the ball nor had she mentioned a relative or friend. The young man was handsome in that English schoolboy way. Not a blonde hair was out of place and his cheeks had those rosy patches so lovely on the right person. He was definitely the right person.

As the last notes of the dance faded, Mother rushed over and took India's arm. "Please excuse yourself from your next partner. We must assist Lady Clarissa tonight because she does not know as many people in attendance as we do."

India cast Mother a sidelong glance. Lady Clarissa had thus far given every indication of being perfectly capable of making her way in any social situation and she must surely know more people than India did. However, Mother and Grandmama seemed determined to intervene, so India had no choice but to follow.

As they approached the target group, the younger male companion followed Lady Clarissa's nod and turned toward them. His gaze locked upon India while a slight smile played across his lips. Unless he was an unforgivable snob, India was at a loss for what he found humorous.

Upon introductions, the young man said, "Delighted to make your acquaintance, Mrs. Van de Berg. My sister has mentioned you often."

So, he was Lady Clarissa's brother. India frowned and looked to see if mother had noticed anything untoward in his attitude. Apparently not. India, however, had. She had a good ear for detecting subtleties in people's conversation. The man's words and tone did not quite match. If she had to guess, she would say he was neither delighted to make Grandmama's acquaintance nor thrilled by what his sister had said.

India had read enough novels to know that saying one thing and meaning another was a national pastime among the English aristocracy. And Papa said the nobility were masters of the social cut and verbal gamesmanship. It felt like this Lord Whomever, because he must be a Lord Somebody or Other, had just slighted Grandmama. India gritted her teeth in preparation for her own introduction to the gentleman. She had never taken an instant dislike to someone she had not even met, but Lady Clarissa's brother now fell into that category.

Lady Clarissa moved aside to make space for India. She smiled and took India's hand, drawing her forward. "Let me introduce my brother, Charles Westmorland, 15th Lord Kilnsey."

The gentleman smiled and extended his hand. "We meet at last. My sister has been singing the praises of the lovely Miss Ledbetter." His feigned pleasure and insincere smile did not escape India's notice.

Grasping his hand, she replied in her twangiest North Carolina accent, "Has she indeed? I'm afraid she hasn't said a single word about you."

Mother jabbed India from behind. Stepping forward, she said, "Lady Clarissa has kept your arrival a delightful surprise. We are so pleased to make your acquaintance, Lord Kilnsey. I believe my daughter has an opening on her card for the next dance. She knows so few of the young men here. Would you partner her?" A palpable silence followed the request.

Warmth started in India's chest and crawled upward until it reached her hairline. She glanced at Clarissa's brother. He swallowed and blinked, then smiled. "Of course. It would be my pleasure." Offering India his arm, he led her onto the floor. He placed his hand on her waist and she placed hers on his shoulder awaiting the first strains of a waltz. Lord Kilnsey's dance posture could only be described as stiff and unbending.

If she must dance with this unwilling gentleman, she might as well make polite conversation. Good manners dictated it. India sometimes strained at the bonds of etiquette and this was quickly becoming one of them. She sighed and looked up. "It's been a lovely party so far. Did you arrive in New York directly from England?"

"I did." He made no effort to elaborate.

"What port did you leave from?"

"Liverpool."

"Do you live in Liverpool?"

"No."

With a third attempt at conversation rebuffed, India settled into a seething silence. The man clearly intended to remain taciturn and unfriendly. Whatever Mother had intended, Lord Kilnsey was thwarting her at every turn. So be it. He wasn't so handsome that she would put up with rudeness.

The music started, and they were off circling the floor among other couples who talked and laughed like normal people attending a party. When the waltz finally ended, Lord Kilnsey released India and bowed. "Thank you."

Before he could draw breath for another comment, India gave him a tight smile and replied. "You're most welcome. Now if you will excuse me?" She turned away without waiting for his answer.

Blessedly, her next dance partner flew to her side. She made a show of smiling at him and began an animated conversation. As she and her partner glided by the group made up of her relatives and Lady Clarissa's party, India peeked at the aristocratic brother. Lord Kilnsey looked bored and grumpy. Good. His pleasure and entertainment were not her responsibility or concern. Furthermore, Mother could not accuse her of being inhospitable and ungracious. She danced on with the partners on her card and enjoyed herself.

On the last note of the final dance before supper, servants threw open the double doors to the dining room, and the company moved as a body toward the buffet. In the crowd, India finagled a position so that she became separated from her relatives. The size of the dining room made it possible for her to hide out of sight.

She surveyed the offerings on buffet tables that stretched nearly the length of the room. The multitude of hot and cold dishes created a display that made her stomach growl. From the hot buffet, the fragrance of mushroom stuffed filet of beef mingled with those of scalloped potatoes and roast duck. India went to the beverages first. She needed something cooling. She had not missed a single dance. With all the moving bodies, the ball room had become somewhat over warm. Taking a lemon ice, she made her way back to the buffet.

As she circled the tables, she felt eyes following her progress. Glancing over her shoulder, she noticed a young man to whom she had not been introduced. He smiled and winked. She shot him a withering look, then turned away and hid her smile as she pretended great interest in an ice sculpture hovering above an enormous platter of boiled shrimp. The young man was darned handsome in a cheeky sort of way. Why had Grandmama not arranged an introduction to him?

After supper, dancing recommenced and India's card quickly filled again until the handsome stranger from the supper room came to stand in front of her, having intercepted another young man making a dash in her direction. Mr. Supper Room reached for her card. "May I?"

"I don't see how since we have not been introduced. I do not even know your name."

"How remiss of me." He bowed slightly. "William Connor, Esq. at your service. My friends call me Billy."

She extended her hand to shake his, but he raised it to his lips instead. She choked back a giggle. Feigning a sophistication she did not possess, India withdrew her hand. "How European. Have you spent time on the Continent?"

He looked into her eyes and laughed. Of all the effrontery. She scowled. "Whatever do you find funny?"

An ironic smile lifted the corners of his mouth. "I'm just wondering how many European gentlemen you have actually met on the Blue Ridge." So, he had heard of her. He knew where she came from without being told.

"One or two, *actually*. My father has friends from all over. And it's the Blue Ridge Mountains, not simply the Blue Ridge."

"I stand corrected, but you have not answered my question."

"Which is?"

"May I have a dance?"

She stared at him until he had the good grace to blush. Perhaps he had redeeming qualities after all. "You may."

He took her card and began striking through the names of all the other young men, writing his name beside each dance. India snatched the card back. "You can't do that. It's…it's improper."

"Oh, come on. I've watched you dancing with these guys. You're all smiles, but you're bored out of your mind. All that polite conversation uses a lot of words and says absolutely nothing. Spend what's left of the evening with me. I promise you will not be bored."

"I suspect you are right, but my grandmother would be apoplectic. You may have the dances that are left unfilled on the card." She paused and giggled. "And the next one. You will save me from the regrettable Mr. Webster."

"He of the large feet and famous family tree?"

"That's the one."

He extended his hand. "Well then, shall we?"

And so, they danced and talked and laughed and danced some more until Mother came to her side at the end of their fourth. Placing a hand on India's arm, she said, "I'm Mrs. Ledbetter. You must excuse us. I need to speak with my daughter."

India looked back at Billy and rolled her eyes before gliding away in Mother's wake. Near the back of the room, Mother stopped, wheeled around, and put her hands on her hips. "You ignore Lord Kilnsey and allow that upstart Billy Connor to dominate your attention? Have you completely lost your mind?"

"Stuffy ole Lord Kilnsey is not interested in me nor I in him." India flapped her fan toward the gentleman. "Look at him. He would rather be anywhere else. I guess he finds us mere Americans too far beneath his notice to be sociable."

"And it is your duty to change that."

"Why ever should I? He's nothing to me."

"But he is something to Lady Clarissa, and she has been kind to us. Furthermore, your grandmother expects it."

"Okay. I will be nice if he asks me to dance again, but I will not take responsibility for his enjoyment of the evening."

Mother grabbed India's arm and hissed, "You will do as you are told. Grandmama wishes that you make an effort with Lord Kilnsey, and so you shall." Mother's nature had always been somewhat mercurial. She could go from kind and loving to raging and threatening in a heartbeat. India had learned early the wisdom of walking carefully around her.

India pulled her arm free and considered Mother's emotional state. Compliance seemed the best plan for the moment. "I'll do what I can, but I can't force him to have fun. I need some refreshment. I'm going back to the supper room." Any lie would do to get away from Mother.

Instead of going to the supper room, she fled to the farthest corner away from Grandmama and Clarissa's group. She hid behind a potted palm and slumped onto a chair keeping a lonely vigil against the wall. Conversation drifted to her through the palm fronds.

An older woman's voice said, "It's really a shame, you know. The Van de Bergs are one of the oldest families in New York. If Petra had not married old T.J. Ledbetter's son, things would have been quite different."

A different voice picked up the theme. "Yes, they were once considered the cream of society and were invited to only the best social gatherings. I wonder what will become of the granddaughter."

The first speaker replied, "With that odd father insisting on living down south, it is anyone's guess."

That was enough eavesdropping for one evening. India balled her fists and fled to the safety of the supper room.

The desire to throttle those old biddies eased somewhat with the first sip of Champagne. It disappeared completely by the time she had downed the entire glass.

***

Clarissa watched India's dash from the ballroom and whispered to her husband. "I wonder what has set her to flight. She looks upset."

Jonathan shrugged. "Perhaps the ball has not gone as she hoped."

Clarissa tilted her head. "I doubt it. She has rather been the belle this evening. She certainly has not wanted for dance partners."

Looking at her brother, she said, "You could have been nicer to the girl, you know."

"To whom are you referring?" He leaned against the column around which their party had gathered and took a long sip of Champagne.

Clarissa swatted his shoulder with her fan. Charlie was her little brother. She adored him, but he could be infuriating at times. "Miss Ledbetter, of course."

"Why should she be of concern to me?"

"You know perfectly well why," Clarissa hissed. "Stop trying my patience. We did not bring you all this way for your entertainment. You must take care of the situation and this is the best possible way. You know that."

Charlie's expression did not change from that of the boredom he had shown all evening. "So, she's to be the one, is she? Well, at least she's pretty."

CHAPTER 6

India sat at Grandmama's parlor window, elbow resting on the tea table with her chin upon her palm. Nonstop drizzle since early morning had kept would-be callers at home. The day and her mood had much in common. As she counted droplets running down the panes, a lone pedestrian stepped from the curb. Once on the other side of the street, the traveler stopped beneath a tree and gazed up at the exact spot from which India watched. When their eyes met, a spark of pleasure lit within her. Billy Connor, Mr. Supper Room of the Butler's ball, smiled up at her. He lifted his hand and waved, then beckoned for her to join him. India frowned and shook her head. As dull as the day had been, he could not possibly expect her to dash out into the rain at the wave of his hand. Why didn't he call at the door like a normal person?

A thin smile lifted one corner of her mouth. He must know or at least sense that Mother and Grandmama had already decreed she was to have no association with him whatsoever. India choked back a chuckle. Being afraid of her female relatives made him sort of a coward.

India watched in consternation as Billy laughed and beckoned with greater fervor. She shook her head again. He shrugged and leaned against the trunk of the tree. It seemed he was prepared to stay there satisfied to watch her as she sat in her window. India tilted her head. Perhaps discretion was the better part of valor in this case. Grandmama and Mother were a formidable pair when they set their minds against something or someone and they heartily disliked William Connor, Esquire. Thus far, the reason for their enmity had not been made totally clear other than to say he was a vulgar, social climbing upstart who did not know how to behave in polite society. In all honesty, there was some validity in that accusation. Of course, the fact that he was Irish Catholic and represented workers pro bono against unethical slum lords and overzealous factory owners would definitely weigh as the greater sins in Mother and Grandmama's estimations.

India had learned about Billy in the supper room at the Butler's ball. One of the other girls had been a fount of information. It was clear from the girl's expression she would have been only too glad for him to pay her some attention. India should have been put off by a man who flirted without so much as an introduction, but she was not. In fact, she had tingled a little every time he looked her way that evening. And now, here he was just outside her window. Mother and Grandmama would be shocked, perhaps apoplectic. India's mouth curved into a lopsided grin. She looked at the mantel clock and then back to Billy's tree. Three o'clock was a perfectly good time of day to take the air in the park.

She called for Althea to bring her umbrella, Mackintosh, and her oldest pair of boots. With the requested items in hand, the maid shot India a disgruntled look. "You can't go out. It's raining. Why do you want to do something so foolish?"

"Because I'm dying of boredom and it's not raining that hard." India gestured toward the window. "Look. It's just a gentle mist." Pulling on her rain gear, she continued, "Don't worry. I won't be long. I simply must get out before I go crazy. You won't say anything to the others, will you?"

"Not unless I'm asked. You know I'm not going to lie to your mother. She'd fire me on the spot with no way for me to get home and no reference."

"I know. You're a good friend, but I don't expect you to risk your job." On impulse, India put her arms around her maid and gave her a hug. "I don't know what I'd do if I didn't have you. You're the only one I can really talk to. You're like the older sister I always wanted."

Althea pulled India's arms from her neck. "You just promise me you won't be out long and that you will stay close to the house." She put a hand on India's arm and looked into her eyes. "Hm. On second thought, wait here. I'm getting my coat and hat."

India allowed Althea to precede her down the front steps and kept a pace behind as they turned up the sidewalk toward the park. Watching their approach, Billy broke into a grin and lifted himself off the trunk. He looked ready to start toward them, but India made a stay put gesture. He halted, but the grin did not leave his face. Meeting India's gaze, he jerked his head toward the arch, then walked in that direction.

Althea's back stiffened. She turned on her heel, blocking India's path, a fist on each hip. "So, this is why you were so anxious to walk in the rain. You know as well as I do that Mrs. Ledbetter isn't going to like this one little bit. We need to just turn around and head back to the house."

"You can go back if you want, but I'm going for my walk."

Althea looked at the house and then at Billy's retreating back. "One of these days your stubbornness is going to get you into real trouble."

"That may be, but I'll be twenty-one in two years. I'll be able to make my own decisions about whom I see then."

"Oh really? And on whose dime are you planning to see these folks?"

"Papa has promised. Just because Grandfather Ledbetter thought a girl incapable of managing money, doesn't make it true."

Althea harrumphed. "You were just a baby when your grandfather died. Do you remember him?"

"Not really, but I've heard his thoughts on money matters often enough." Seeing Billy turn under the arch, India stepped around Althea and followed. The maid had no choice but do the same.

India continued, "It really rankles that my grandfather made sure I won't get any of my inheritance until I marry. He barely trusted Papa, so he made sure the blasted trustees have to approve my choice of husband. It's like he thought he was some kind of medieval overlord."

Althea drew up beside India. "It was his money. He earned it, so I guess he got to do what he wanted with it."

"I know, but sometimes I wish I had been born into a normal family that didn't have to deal with trustees and a grandparent who rules our lives from the grave."

"A normal family is what you want, is it?" Irony colored Althea's voice. "So, you're just dying to work in a cotton mill and worry about where your next meal is coming from because you get paid next to nothing for 12-hour days? Or see your daddy work himself to death trying to hold onto the farm with the bank breathing down his neck threatening foreclosure? That's normal for most folks back home. I'd be careful what I wished for if I were you."

Taken aback, India replied, "I'm sorry. You're right. I should be grateful for the abundance we have. I just get so frustrated with never being able to make decisions for myself. I really want to study to be a teacher and open a school on the estate, but Mama forbade it."

"I know you do, and we servants love you for it."

Stricken, India grabbed the maid's arm. "Oh, Althea, I don't think of you as a servant."

Althea nodded. "I know, but it's what I am all the same."

The pair walked on in silence until they drew abreast the arch where a grinning Billy waited. India cast a sidewise glance at Althea. "If he asks, I am going to walk with him. I won't go beyond the park. Please do not follow us."

The maid raised a brow and gave India The Look for which she was so famous among the staff back home. "If you think I'm gonna let you wander 'round unchaperoned with somebody we barely know, you got another think comin'." When she was angry or excited, Aletha's mountain twang emerged full force, replacing the more cultured tones she had worked hard to develop.

India snorted in reply. "Having to be chaperoned is such an old-fashioned idea. Anyone would think we are living in the Dark Ages."

"You can fuss all you want, but if you're goin' to walk with this Billy person, it ain't gonna be without me. And snortin's unladylike."

"Oh, all right, but please stay several paces behind us."

"You mean like a servant?"

"That's not what I meant, and you know it." India fought the urge to stamp her foot and shake a fist. "Why won't anyone let me live my own life?"

"Because with your looks and fortune, you might attract the wrong sort, that's why. Now go on and speak to the young man. He looks like he's about to bust. Just remember I'm watching."

India broke into a smile as she moved further under the arch. "Why Mr. Connor, whatever are you doing out on such a damp day?"

He extended his hand as he gave her a knowing grin. "Well, Miss Ledbetter, I could ask the same of you, but then we both know why we're here, don't we?"

Heat crawled up India's throat onto her cheeks. She silently cursed her lack of sophistication. He must think her a forward female or a fool. "I...I suppose one might think so. Actually, the day has been long and boring. I thought a walk might brighten it a bit."

Billy chuckled and offered her his arm. "May I escort you through the park? My umbrella is quite large enough to shelter two."

India glanced over her shoulder at a scowling Althea. Looking up at Billy, she folded her own umbrella and replied, "Thank you. That is most thoughtful." She put her hand in the crook of his elbow and they passed out of the arch's protection.

Nearing the fountain, India scrambled for something witty or even interesting to say. Nothing presented itself. She settled upon a frequent topic of society small talk. "Grandmama has sent invitations to my debut ball. You should receive yours soon. I hope you will be able to attend. It's on the twentieth of January."

Billy turned to her with a quizzical expression. "I will be delighted to attend, but I must say I am surprised your grandmother has me on her invitation list."

India giggled. "She didn't. Since I helped address the invitations, I added your name. Neither she nor Mother noticed."

He laughed as he led her farther into the park. "How enterprising of you. You have hidden depths, Miss Ledbetter. Will your party be held in Washington Square?"

"Oh, no. Grandmama has invited far too many people to host it at home. She has reserved the ballroom at the Knickerbocker."

Billy paused for several beats before responding, "I see. The list of invitees must be long indeed. I look forward to brushing shoulders with the city's old guard."

"Yes, I believe she has invited everyone she has ever known. Being the center of attention among such a congregation is a rather daunting prospect if truth be told."

The pressure from Billy's arm increased, pulling her closer to his side. He did not comment for several beats and when he did, his voice was not much above a whisper. "Let us hope those invited are worthy of the invitation." The gesture could only be described as protective, but India could see no danger along the path into the park's interior. In fact, they were alone in their perambulation.

India studied his profile from beneath her lashes. What an odd thing to say. Perhaps he did not approve of old New York society. If so, then why did he wish to move among them?

While they walked on in silence, India considered what he might have meant. Finding nothing to which she could attach meaning, she pushed the conversation from her mind, choosing to focus instead on the drifting leaves carpeting their path in reds, golds, and browns. There was a comforting familiarity in the falling leaves and the fragrance of damp earth. It was the same whether she was at home or in Washington Square. In another week, the trees would be completely bare. India loved autumn. It was her favorite time of year. Where others saw only endings and a dismal weather outlook, she saw beginnings, the excitement of the holidays, and the promise of a new year.

The arch came into view again, prompting India to ask, "Do you walk here often?" Although she had intended it as an innocent inquiry, the question sounded gauche and overly eager.

Billy cut his eyes at India. "In Washington Square? Not as a habit, but perhaps you will give me a reason to do so. If say, you were to take the air at the same time each afternoon I predict you will find I frequent this very park."

She had already violated social convention, so one more question could not do greater harm. "Since winter will soon be upon us, perhaps you might call at the house?"

At that, he actually laughed aloud. "I doubt I would be welcome. No, I think the appearance of impromptu meetings would be more acceptable." He stopped under the arch. Lifting her hand to his lips, he bowed. "Until tomorrow at three?"

As India watched him saunter away, it occurred that their plan might not be as easy to implement as it seemed.

CHAPTER 7

India's breath frosted the parlor window as she watched the street for any sign that Billy had braved the frigid temperatures for their arranged afternoon walk. They had managed to meet in the park at least twice per week for the last two months until today when an overnight snowfall left knee high drifts.

Feeling a presence behind her, she whipped around to find Althea glaring. Raising an index finger and shaking it, the maid said, "You aren't going out. Your mother and grandmother aren't fools. They already suspect there's more to these walks than wanting fresh air. Going out in this weather will put them on the scent for sure."

India lifted her hands palms up. "But I can't leave him standing in the cold waiting for me."

"He's not so stupid as to come out on a day like this."

"You don't know that. He may arrive at any moment."

Before Althea could respond, the cook appeared at the door with an envelope in her hand. "A boy brought this to the back door for Miss India. As if I ain't not got enough to do, your young man expects me to be part of his mail delivery service."

India's heart skipped a beat. She didn't think anyone other than Althea knew about her meetings with Billy. "Why I have no idea what you are talking about. There is no young man and you well know it, Mrs. Sears."

The cook's frown indicated she was not impressed. She shoved the note into Althea's hand. "You can say whatever you like, but I'd be more careful if I was you."

When the red-faced Mrs. Sears was out of earshot, India whispered, "Do you think she'll tell?"

"I don't think so. She's not that fond of your mother and grandmother. In fact, I heard it from the butler that Mrs. Sears is looking for another position. Now you have something you can hold over her in trade for her silence."

India hugged Althea. "Thank you. I would be lost without you." Tearing open the envelope, she found a short note.

My Dearest Miss Ledbetter,

It pains me to write that I will not be able to meet with you today or for the foreseeable future. I am called to Boston to my father's bedside. It is feared he will not be with us much longer. Please know that the memory of our walks will be my constant companion while I am away and will sustain me until we meet again.

Your Devoted Friend,
William Connor, Esq.

Tears welled up. It was ridiculous to feel so strongly about such a brief acquaintance but knowing a thing in one's mind was not the same as knowing it in one's heart. She gave the note to Althea.

After handing it back, Althea said, "Well, that's a problem solved for now. If the elder Mr. Connor could linger until after New Year's Day, it would make things considerably easier."

India shot back, "What an awful thing to say. Billy's grief is not something to be manipulated for our convenience."

"You may feel differently when your mother and grandmother figure out what's going on. No, it's better that he's unavailable for as long as possible."

"I can still write to him." India picked up the envelope, inspecting it back and front.

"Didn't give you an address, did he? Did you even know he is from Boston?"

"Yes, he told me about his family. I'm sure I can find an address."

"How? Boston is about as Irish as an American city gets. I bet there are a fair number of Connors there. Do you know his father's name?"

Defeated for the moment, India stuffed the letter into the pocket of her skirt. "Surely he will write to me. He pays court to me as a man with honorable intentions. I know he will write."

But he didn't. December 1 came and went then December 15 and still no letter from Boston. December 24 dawned blustery and frigid, perfectly matching India's mood. She leaned her forehead against the windowpane and looked down from her bedroom at the snow mounded along the park's paths. Jerking back from the glass's sharp cold, she rubbed her fingers together and blew on them. Even the coals blazing away in the fireplace did not give sufficient warmth. Turning away, she crossed the room and backed up to the hearth. She lifted her nightgown until heat toasted the backs of her legs. The coals crackled and settled in the grate sending their scent into the room. The odor was yet another reminder of how different life here in the city was from that at The Falls. At home, Papa insisted good pine or oak was the only acceptable fuel for the fireplaces.

Homesickness settled over her. Taking meals alone with Mother and Grandmama was something she had come to dread. Their constant inspections of her every move and word were almost more than she could bear. If that were not bad enough, they expected her to remain at home with them when she would much rather have gone to the museums, a concert, or shopping. Life at Number 5 was tedious indeed and today would be no different. It would drag until they left for dinner with Lady Clarissa. She must find something to occupy her time or she would surely go mad.

She turned toward the fire to warm her other half and surveyed at the picture over the mantel. It was a lovely watercolor of Washington Square Park in spring. The pastels complimented one another wonderfully, and the balanced composition was pleasing to the eye. She peered at the artist's signature - Peter Van de Berg. She had quite forgotten that Grandfather dabbled in watercolors and oils as a hobby. It was a talent she had inherited, but one she had indulged less and less as she reached adolescence. Mother did not approve of the way the paints stained her fingers and marred her clothing.

India rubbed her upper arms as she went to her wardrobe to find something suitable for the day. She chose a gown of heavy wool. It was old, but it was the warmest thing she owned. Shivering as she dressed, she pulled on a thick cardigan, then looked at her reflection. Yes, that would do nicely for what she had in mind. Her eyes narrowed. Mother got her way with almost everything, but India would soon be of age. When Father made good on his promise of financial support, she would become her own woman. Her lips tightened into a thin line. Perhaps today was the time for her first step toward independence. Later this morning, she would go to Grandfather's studio at the top of the house and see if she could resurrect that which had lain dormant for so long.

India hurried into the breakfast room where Mother and Grandmama were already seated. Mother watched India advance on the table with a speculative expression. "Whatever are you wearing? I thought I told you to discard that rag last winter."

India smiled as she pulled out her chair, determined not to let Mother draw her into a protracted argument. "You did, but I just couldn't part with it. And it's a good thing too because without it I would freeze in this weather. One forgets how much colder New York is. Grandmama, can you pass the jam, please?" With only a moment long enough to draw breath, she rushed on. "I thought I might take a look at Grandfather's studio. The watercolor over my fireplace is quite good. I thought there might be another up there that would suit my bedroom at home."

Grandmama looked at India for several beats before answering, "Wear your heavy coat. The attic is never heated now that no one stays up there longer than absolutely necessary."

"I will. And about anything that I find?"

"You may take whatever you like. My husband's discarded artwork is of no interest to me."

After staying at breakfast long enough to satisfy propriety, India excused herself and made her way to the top of the house. Her breathing increased as the stairs to each floor became narrower and steeper. At the third floor, she went to the back of the house where she approached the door that opened onto the attic staircase. Cold air whooshed down upon her. The thickness of the grime on every surface indicated it had been some time since anyone entered. She clicked on the flashlight borrowed from Mrs. Sears and swept up the stairs. To her surprise electrification had reached the attics, so she flipped the switch. It was the first time she had ventured there. It had been off-limits in her childhood and a lack of interest had kept her away until now. She looked around at the space where Grandfather had spent the last years of his life. It must not have changed at all since his death. Blank canvases lay stacked in one corner and a cabinet with its doors hanging open stood in another.

She went to the cabinet and examined its contents. Brushes, paints, watercolors, and other supplies, all covered in a layer of dust, had been carefully arranged for the time he would return and take up his palate again. It all felt desperately sad for some reason. The knowledge that the objects of a beloved pastime had lain abandoned for so long engendered a sense of longing. The family rarely talked about Grandfather Van de Berg and when they did, very little information was revealed. All India knew was that he died before she was born. It always made her a little sad when other girls talked about their grandfathers with affection because she had no memory of either of hers.

She ran her fingers along the shelf of paints and selected a tube that had its seal intact - ultramarine blue - such a lovely color. Cadmium yellow, red, and cerulean blue lay next to the ultramarine. All seemed untouched. Farther along the shelf lay tubes that had been rolled, squeezed, and pummeled until they might as well have been thrown in the dustbin. These were the dark colors - burnt umber, raw umber, ocher, alizarin crimson, black, burnt sienna. Odd that his paintings displayed in the private areas of the house had those colors only where needed to create the bark of trees, the stems of flowers, or the sheen of a tabletop upon which a bowl of roses sat.

Turning from the cabinet, she strolled to the artist's easel where a canvas sat covered by a dust cloth. Lifting a corner of the cloth, India peeked at the picture underneath and gasped. The half-finished work depicted what could only be described as a soul in torment. An ethereal, naked male body writhed in excruciating pain. Flames licked the subject's feet and thighs as he reached up in supplication toward a sky that was as dark and stormy as any produced by tornadoes. It might have been a depiction of one of Dante's circles of hell, but it did not quite fit what she remembered from reading. The open mouth screamed into the empty canvas, but no human or god had been painted to hear him. His despair seemed to grow as much from his abandonment as from the torment of the flames. A shiver ran through India as she dropped the cloth. Did that painting represent some personal agony Grandfather suffered? What brought the artist who painted the beautiful still life watercolor over her bedroom mantel to paint something so hideous? Catching sight of canvases stacked in the corner behind the easel, she pulled them out one-by-one. She fought back a cry at sight of the first, then shuddered with each successive painting. These were finished. They showed their subjects, all men, in every manner of torture. Unaccountably, the artist's skill seemed to have grown as he developed his theme. The last three were exquisite in their awfulness. She shoved the lot back into the corner from which she had withdrawn them and fled to the safety of the floors below.

***

"Why must we always wait for you, India?" Mother stood tapping her foot, hugging her silver fox stole about her shoulders until the fur reached her chin. "We must not be late for Lady Clarissa's supper party."

"Oh, is it a party? I thought it was just us and her family."
India drew on her coat and checked her reflection in the
mirror over the foyer credenza. "Who else is joining us?"

"One or two other couples, I believe. No one of any
importance. In fact, I am not sure where she meets some of
these people she associates with. At times, Clarissa
demonstrates the oddest taste in friends."

India snorted and giggled. "And what does that make us?
Just peculiar?"

"Don't be absurd. Are you finally ready? Don't forget
your gloves."

India glanced at the stairs. "Is Grandmama not going?"

"She is already in the auto. Come. We must be off."

The trip to Lady Clarissa's took longer than anticipated
due to an unusual amount of traffic around St Patrick's
Cathedral. Christmas Eve Mass apparently drew a crowd.
When they arrived, the butler ushered them into the
drawing room where only Lady Clarissa, her husband, and
her brother awaited them.

Taking a seat opposite Lady Clarissa, Mother accepted a
glass of sherry from their host. "Although cocktails are all
the rage, I still prefer a simple sherry before dinner."
Casting a corrective look at India, she continued, "Sip that
slowly, dear. You are not accustomed to spirits." Turning to
their hostess, she said, "Were your other guests not able to
attend?"

Lady Clarissa smiled. "We did not invite them after all.
We decided a more intimate gathering would suit the
evening."

Mother and Grandmama's exchange of glances did not
escape India's notice. As with their previous visit, there
seemed to be an undercurrent in the room. Her relatives and
friends were plotting something. There was a secret known
to everyone but her. India's teeth clenched.

Forcing herself to appear unperturbed, India sipped her cocktail and gave the assembled company a broad smile. The drink's tangy, bubbly sweetness lifted her mood. Just because everyone else had a secret did not mean she must allow herself to appear at a disadvantage. "This is delicious. What's it called?"

Mr. Rivers replied, "Thank you. It's a gin bump made with gin, of course, lime juice, and ginger ale. I'm glad you like it. I've been honing my barman's skills."

"Well, I would say you are doing quite well." India took a long swig.

Grandmama's intake of breath was audible. "India, my dear, only a sip or two, please. You have not eaten since luncheon."

Coming back with a cutting retort would have felt good, something about the rudeness of keeping secrets in company, but the effects of the gin suddenly made her head swim. Mother was right. She was not accustomed to strong drink. Placing her glass on a nearby table, she dabbed her lips with a napkin.

Lady Clarissa took that moment to signal her butler, who opened the doors and announced, "Dinner is served, Milady."

Their hostess nodded and included everyone in the sweep of her gaze. "Shall we? Charles, will you take Miss Ledbetter in?"

Lord Kilnsey, who heretofore had worn a distracted, bored expression and had made no attempt to join in the conversation, suddenly looked at his sister as though he had just arrived from another planet. After a pause of several beats, he responded, "It would be my pleasure." The blandness of his facial expression belied his words.

He offered his arm and India planted her hand upon it. This was going to be a long evening if she was forced to sit next to him.

To her surprise, Lord Kilnsey roused himself from whatever had earlier occupied his attention and proved a charming dinner companion. The third time India addressed him by his title, he responded, "Might we dispense with the formality? My friends call me Charlie and I hope I may count you among them."

"Of course, you may. Please call me India." She leaned closer and whispered, "Personally, I've never cared for our surname. I much prefer being addressed simply as India."

He winked and whispered in return, "I have always liked the name India." He glanced at his sister before continuing in at a normal volume, "India is a very pleasant name, but I am surprised to find an American bearing it. Does your family have a connection with the subcontinent?"

"Not that I'm aware of. I believe it has more to do with the Southern tradition of giving place names to children. I have an Aunt Tennessee Ann and an Aunt Georgia on my father's side. While not all that common, India is not unheard of as a Christian name for ladies."

"Southern tradition? I thought your family originated in New York."

"My mother's family does. They hail all the way back to New Amsterdam, but the Ledbetters are from North Carolina."

He looked thoughtful before he remarked, "Yes, my sister has mentioned your home there. In the mountains, I believe?"

"It is." India gave a short description of The Falls and the adjacent village of Pisgah, ending with, "I love the Blue Ridge Mountains. They're home."

"I have heard they are beautiful. Your description makes me want to see them all the more. Is the estate an old one?"

"Not by English standards. My grandfather built it after he made his fortune."

Charles, for she still could not think of this English lord as Charlie, raised a brow. "And you grew up there?" His tone indicated more than a polite interest.

"I did and my father, as well. He was only five when Grandpa Ledbetter moved the family south."

"How interesting. What was your grandfather's business?"

"In the beginning he was a stockbroker and real estate investor here in New York. Later on, he became involved in Pennsylvania and Texas oil exploration. Spindletop came in and the rest, as they say, is history. Now, you must tell me about your home. Lady Clarissa says you live in a castle. How exciting." If she allowed him another question, this pleasant interview might start to feel like an interrogation.

A small laugh escaped his slightly parted lips. "I'm afraid my sister exaggerates if she led you to believe Kilnsey Castle is one of the great houses of England. While the earliest parts of the house date to the 13th century, it was never more than a defensive stronghold during the Middle Ages. It was built to guard the Mastiles Drove, a path that dates back to Roman times. Monks from Fountains Abbey once drove their flocks to summer pastures over it. In more modern times, renovations were made and Kilnsey settled into the family home we have today. It's not small, 60 rooms, but neither is it as large as some of the grander estates. For example, Castle Howard to the east has around 150 rooms, I believe. I understand your home is somewhat larger?"

The feeling of being interrogated sparked, but she would not descend into rudeness by an abrupt change of subject. "If you include all the bathrooms, The Falls has about 250 rooms." Enough. That was all the intimate detail about her home she would divulge.

He chuckled softly. "So then, you are the one who actually lives in a castle."

"I guess that's true in a way, but it doesn't have the history of Castle Kilnsey."

Before he could reply, Lady Clarissa rose and pushed back her chair. "Normally, we observe the custom of the ladies leaving the men to their port and cigars after dinner, but as there are only my husband and brother, shall we dispense with the formality for this one evening? Charlie, Jonathan, will you join us in the drawing room for coffee?"

At the drawing room door, Charles touched India's arm and held her back. "I say, would you fancy a stroll in the garden? I'm feeling rather warm. I cannot get accustomed to how Americans overheat their homes."

"But it's freezing out there."

"Let me get your coat. I promise not to keep you outside for very long. I simply must have a breath of fresh air and I wish to speak to you in private."

Once they were in Lady Clarissa's rather small courtyard, Charles reached for India's hand. Gazing into her eyes, he said, "I hope you will forgive me for the precipitous nature of what I am about to say. I know our acquaintance has been a short one, but I feel I must speak now for I may not be able to stay in New York as long as one would wish." Squaring his shoulders, a look of what appeared to be resignation filled his eyes. "India, I am very taken with you. I would like to ask your permission to call upon you as a suitor."

India's free hand went to her throat. She blinked several times. Not only had their acquaintance been very brief, but until tonight, Charles Westmorland, Fifteenth Earl Kilnsey had shown little to no interest in Miss India Ledbetter. For her part, Billy Connor was where her heart lay, but he had not written a single word from Boston. Between Mother's demands, Billy's silence, and now His Lordship's request, life was becoming complicated.

Swallowing hard, she drew a quick breath before replying, "I must say I am surprised by your declaration. I cannot give you an answer tonight. If you will excuse me…" India turned and fled into the house.

CHAPTER 8

"Did you enjoy the evening," Althea asked as she took the pins out of India's hair.

India met her gaze in the dresser mirror. "The meal was excellent, as always. Everything was fine until Lord Kilnsey asked me to walk in the garden."

Before India could say more, Mother entered and sat on the edge of the bed. "I wish a private word with my daughter before she retires. You may go."

Aletha met India's eyes with a raised brow. To Mother, she dropped a curtsey. "Yes, ma'am. May I return later?"

"That will not be necessary. I will assist India should she need it." When the maid was gone, Mother continued, "Lord Kilnsey showed you quite a bit of attention tonight. Did you have a pleasant walk in the garden?"

A tingle of warning shot through India. Mother was showing too much interest in Lord Kilnsey's words and deeds, a definite sign she was plotting where he was concerned. India turned away to prevent her expression betraying her thoughts. Removing her camisole, she said, "It was all right, I suppose."

"What did you talk about? He was quite animated when he conversed with you at dinner." The intensity of Mother's interest was palpable.

"Oh, nothing important." India kept her tone noncommittal. "He just wanted to get some air. He complained we Americans keep our homes too warm."

Mother rose and came to stand beside India. Placing her hand on her daughter's shoulder, she asked, "Are you sure it was just a casual conversation?"

"Yes. We were only out there for a few minutes." India did not meet Mother's gaze. Feigning concern about a thread hanging from her undergarment, she continued, "We talked of nothing memorable. Why would we have anything important to speak of? We hardly know one another."

"I just thought...oh, never mind. I suppose I misconstrued his attention to you."

A small smile played across India's lips. Mother actually seemed lost for words, an unusual state to be sure. India turned to meet Mother's eyes. "Yes, you did. As I said, there is really nothing to tell. I'm tired and want to go to sleep."

As India crawled into bed, the evening at Lady Clarissa's replayed in her mind. A relationship with Charlie Westmorland was something Mother clearly desired. Although she had not stated it outright, her demeanor and questions indicated as much. Pulling the covers up, India closed her eyes and snuggled down beneath the quilts. Regardless of how charming he had been this one evening, Lord Kilnsey was the last person she wished to have as a suitor.

***

Christmas Day and New Year's Day came and went quietly with a few parties interspersed between. In January, the social season began in earnest and India found herself in a whirl of balls, theater outings, and opera performances while awaiting her own ball on the twentieth.

She stood before her bedroom mirror admiring the new gown that had arrived just in time for the opera that night. She had never thought purple a color she wanted to wear, but the panne-velvet, high-waisted dress with the pink beaded and embroidered silk chiffon yoke were lovely. The skirt divided just enough at the knee for the undershirt to show in detail.

Althea patted the last button into place and stepped back. "You look beautiful. The workmanship on that dress is excellent and the color scheme is just right."

India grinned and met her maid's gaze in the mirror. Pinching her cheeks to bring up the color, she said, "I feel like a princess. Of course, this is as close to the real thing as I will ever get, but it's fun to pretend."

Althea reached into her pocket and produced a small pot with a tin lid. "Use a little of this. The color should be just about right."

"Oh, I couldn't. What would Grandmama and Mother say?"

"If they notice at all, say you are feeling a little overheated."

India took the glass container and unscrewed the lid. The contents looked innocent enough. She sniffed the waxy surface. It had no odor, so she smoothed a dab of the contents onto her cheeks and lips. The pink was subtle, but it brought out the contours of her face and mouth to pleasing effect.

Next, Althea dusted India's face with fine powder. Producing a tiny brush and another pot, she said, "Hold still and look toward the ceiling." She then swept a coal black mixture over India's lashes.

India gazed wide-eyed at her reflection. "I feel terribly wicked and daring, but I love how it looks. How did you get these things?"

Althea winked. "I made them. Those magazines your mother gets in the mail tell about more than just high fashion. They have recipes, too."

Twirling before the mirror, India giggled as the fringe on the underskirt danced with her every step. Facing the mirror, she paused for several beats awed by the transformation she saw. "You've worked a miracle. Thank you."

"Miracles are easy when you've got so much to work with."

"You always say just the right thing." India hugged Althea, a catch rising in her throat. "I don't know what I'd do without you. I don't know why, but I feel like everything is changing, and it makes me a little afraid."

Althea returned India's embrace, then pulled back so that their eyes met. "You would be just fine without me and of course things are changing. You'll be a full-fledged adult soon. You can't stay a child forever. It wouldn't be normal."

"I know." The idea that some unnamed trouble lay on the horizon popped into her head without warning. India looked away and then back at Althea in earnest. "Promise me something."

"If I can."

"Promise you will stay with me." India's words tumbled over one another. "Stay with me no matter what happens." Why had such a cloud descended? Maybe she was fey like her old nursemaid claimed to be. If so, she could do without prescience that dampened her spirits.

Althea tilted her head and paused for a couple of beats before replying, "That's a pretty big promise, one I'm not sure I can keep." Disappointment must have shown in

India's face, for Althea added, "If it makes you feel better, I promise to stay as long as I'm wanted. Now, you get yourself downstairs. Go have a good time and stop thinking about things that may never happen."

India gave herself a mental shake. Althea was right, of course. She always was. Wisdom and common sense were all wrapped up in the person of her maid. India pressed her lips together. This should prove to be an exciting evening. Caruso was singing his final performance of Puccini's latest work, *La fanciulla del West.* The opera premiered early in December with a role written specifically for the world's greatest tenor. While she had not had much exposure to the art form in North Carolina, visits to New York had opened that world for her. India pulled on her elbow-length gloves and gave herself a final once-over. The girl reflected in the mirror looked confident and sophisticated. Leaning in, she adjusted the ruched silk headband with its pink rosettes and flicked a crystal pendant earring. Yes, she would do. She glided down the stairs, out the door, and into the waiting auto. As she settled onto the seat, she couldn't help grinning. Tonight, she was ready to see and be seen.

A long line of vehicles squatted at the curbs of 39th and Broadway waiting to disgorge their occupants when Grandmama's limousine pulled up. Some passengers, impatient to get to their seats, stepped from their conveyances and dashed through pelting sleet for the awning covered front entrance of the Metropolitan Opera House.

Grandmama cast a critical eye India's way. "If we do not make it in time for the overture, it will be your fault. Lady Clarissa has been very generous to include us in her box for the season. It is uncommonly rude for guests to be late."

"Yes," Mother chimed in, "We would not want the Rivers or Lord Kilnsey to form a bad impression of us."

While India cared about the Rivers' opinions, what Lord Kilnsey thought was of little concern. He might be a handsome, titled aristocrat, but he had given her no impression other than that he thought too well of himself and that he considered mere Americans so lowly as to be beneath his notice. If he raised the subject of courting her again tonight, she had her answer prepared.

***

Clarissa furled her fan with a snap and slapped it against her palm. Tardiness was not to be borne. She turned to her husband in the chair next to her. "They are late. It would be just like that mother to wish to make a grand entrance. Please go and see if you can hurry things along. Perhaps they are caught stalled traffic." Picking up an umbrella from the corner of their box, she handed it to him. "Take this and try to find them."

Once Jonathan left the box, Clarissa jabbed her brother's shoulder. "Do not lean on the railing." Her tone was sharp, but he deserved it. Sometimes Charlie seemed intent upon trying her patience. "Sit up. Bad posture is indicative of a slovenly nature."

"My word, Sister. No one knows me here." He leaned forward as though to resume his position, forearms on the brass and chin on his fists, but a sharp poke in his spine brought him upright.

Clarissa laid her fan in her lap. "They may not know you, but they know us. I will not be the subject of undue speculation. And do not forget. When the girl arrives, she is to sit next to you. Make sure that neither of the old witches grabs that seat. I want you and the girl front and center for all to see. Sometimes a well-placed rumor can move things along quite nicely."

Charlie chuckled. "I thought you didn't want speculation."

Clarissa's eyes narrowed and her mouth thinned. "You are being intentionally difficult." Popping him with her fan, she hissed, "Stop it. This evening is for you. Since you made such a hash of the dinner party, this may well be your last opportunity to set things right."

A thoughtful expression crossed Charlie's face. "My dear Sister, has it occurred to you that all of this maneuvering may be for naught? If I had to guess, I would say that Miss Ledbetter's heart has already been stolen."

"Then you must see to it that her heart is returned to its owner and her affections transferred to you. It is your duty. The future of Kilnsey depends upon it."

"Ah yes, duty, the highest calling a man can pursue. If I had been low born, I would have worked to become a medical doctor or perhaps a Shakespearian scholar. Curing the ills of mankind or elucidating the bard feel far more noble callings than marrying for money."

"You wish to pursue a noble calling, do you? If you do not find ready cash and plenty of it, you may just get the opportunity to determine if you are cut out for such. Then what will happen to all of those who depend on Kilnsey for their livelihoods? Taking care of one's responsibilities is the best purpose for any man's life."

***

India jumped at a knock on the limousine window. She turned to see Mr. Rivers smiling and beckoning for them to alight and follow him. The chauffeur got out, opened an enormous umbrella, and came to her side of the vehicle.

Mr. Rivers assisted India from the vehicle. Taking her elbow, he said, "Come. We must hurry. My wife does not want you to miss a moment of the performance."

Before she could respond, he whisked her along the sidewalk. She glanced over her shoulder to see Mother and Grandmama huddled under the chauffeur's umbrella, moving crab-like at a much slower pace. Catching Mother's eye, India shot her an inquiring look. Mother smiled and waved India on, apparently not worried about herself for once.

The dash through the sleet, dodging icy patches in their path, left India breathing harder than Grandmama would probably have considered ladylike, but at least she was inside out of the weather. She had lost sight of Mother and Grandmama at the door. Hopefully they weren't too far behind. Grandmama would never admit it, but she had aged a good bit in the last year and seemed to feel the cold more now.

Chimes sounded signaling that patrons should find their seats as Mr. Rivers escorted India into his box. Lady Clarissa greeted her with a kiss on the cheek. "You look a dream, my dear. Please take the chair next to Charlie. The conductor will enter the pit any minute now."

As Charles stood aside so that she could pass to the only other chair at the railing, the box door opened once more. Mother and Grandmama rushed through slightly winded from their hurried climb up the stairs. The house lights went down, and the audience began its applause. For an hour, Minnie, a saloon owner, and Johnson, the stranger from Sacramento, professed their love and promised to guard a keg of gold during the American Gold Rush. When the curtain fell on the first act, India stood to stretch her legs and give her bottom a rest. She peered over the railing at the audience. The house was filled to capacity.

Lord Kilnsey leaned against the wall separating their box from the next. "See anyone you know?"

She scanned the boxes opposite. "No, but the hall is so big, I doubt I would recognize my nearest relatives in this crowd."

India's gaze swept the orchestra seats and mezzanine without interest in the hope her appearing occupied might forestall any further attempts by Lord Kilnsey to engage her in conversation. Her eyes swung right, then snapped back left to survey for a second time the area she had just passed over. Her heart rate kicked up a notch. Was that...? Surely it couldn't be. She peered through her opera glasses. Yes, it was. Billy Connor stood talking with a young woman India had never seen before.

CHAPTER 9

India's heart banged against its boney prison. Had she misinterpreted Billy's intentions? Granted she was less experienced in affairs of the heart than most girls her age, but she was not completely naïve . No, by all that was good, he had paid her court. It was a fact he could not dispute. Blast the man. She bit down on her lower lip. She could not disgrace herself by crying. She simply could not. That would be the final blow to her dignity. All that time spent talking, laughing, sharing secrets and this is how he chose to treat her. Her breath caught as she fought back a sniff. Perhaps Mother and Grandmama had been right. Maybe he was simply the social climbing upstart they described, but it still hurt to see how little he thought of her. A hand on her shoulder stopped her slapping her fan against her thigh and brought her back to the present.

"Has something upset you?" Lord Kilnsey looked at her with concern. "The color has left your face."

The words would not form, so India remained silent. Damn Charlie Westmorland's sympathy. It was the last thing she wanted. Her nails dug into her palms. Finding her voice, she said, "I think I need a bit of fresh air. It's rather close in here and I'm afraid I am feeling a little lightheaded." If anything, the theater was on the chilly side, but she needed a means, any means, to escape prying eyes.

Charlie lifted himself from the wall, took her coat from the rack, and held it out for her. "Please, let me escort you to an outer balcony. We can't have you fainting away." Without waiting for a reply, he urged her to the door.

His unexpected solicitude elicited a strong desire to slap his handsome face. What had come over her? The man may be an arrogant ass, but he was making an effort to be kind.

Within moments, they stood on a balcony overlooking Broadway. Sleet no longer pelted, but the city now had a sheen that portended possible danger on the journey home. India inhaled until her lungs burned. Funny how extreme cold felt like fire. She looked up at the sky to avoid looking at Charlie. The clouds had departed, leaving millions of crystals shimmering in their place. Her breath jerked a little when she exhaled. The same stars shone at home. As she and Charlie stood in silence, one of those far away points suddenly streaked across the sky toward the south. If she willed it, could she grab that shooting star and ride it away from this place and the expectations of those around her? Would it take her away from disappointment and home to the life she knew? A lump rose in her throat.

She felt rather than saw Charlie move beside her. Placing a gloved hand on the balcony rail, she leaned forward pretending to gaze at the traffic still chugging in streams through the night.

"Be careful." His hand cupped her elbow, but he said no more. He simply allowed her to ignore him without complaint, standing so close she could hear the crackle of his starched shirtfront with the rise and fall of his chest. His breath floated toward her in clouds. He edged a step closer. A shiver passed through her, but it had nothing to do with the weather. The totally unexpected reaction left her off balance searching for a logical explanation. Nothing made sense tonight - not Billy's behavior nor Lord Kilnsey's. Neither of them appeared to be the men she thought them to be.

"India, I wish to apologize for my demeanor the other evening. I should not have spoken as I did. It is far too early in our acquaintance. May I be forgiven?"

Her eyes shot up to meet his. He appeared sincere. "I accept your apology. As you said, it is much too early for such declarations."

"Indeed." Chimes sounded signaling the end of the intermission. "My hope is that we may begin again."

India held his gaze for a moment. When she had his measure, she said, "I suppose everyone deserves a second chance."

For the remainder of the performance, the great tenor might as well have been putting on a pantomime for all India heard and saw. Her eyes had a will of their own. Every time she tried to force her attention onto the performance, her gaze shot back to the box where Billy Connor sat with the young woman and an older couple. If he realized she was in the house, he gave no indication.

The performance dragged on. The curtain finally came down. The cast took their final bows. The audience began drifting toward the exits. Still, Billy had not noticed her. A desire to shout swelled while India remained frozen to her chair. A tap on the shoulder made her jump.

Mother leaned forward and hissed, "Get up and stop gawking at Billy Connor. Lord Kilnsey has noticed your attention in that direction and is not pleased."

India rose and followed her party as they moved toward the hall, but at the door, she turned for a final look at Billy's box. The air hissed as she inhaled. Billy stood at the railing, leaning out over the main floor as though he might try to jump the expanse that separated them. She moved back to the railing and watched as he tried to mouth words that she could not understand. Every couple of beats, he looked over his shoulder.

Within moments, the other girl came to his side, laid a hand on his arm, then leaned in and said something. Billy drew back in what appeared to be either irritation or surprise. It was hard to tell which at such a distance. Whatever she said must have had the desired effect because he shot one more glance at India, lifted his hand in salute, and turned away.

India fought back tears as she watched them disappear. It was clear. She must accept that she had misinterpreted his attention. Stupid, stupid, stupid. He had offered only friendship where she had seen the beginning of a romance. Her lack of experience had led her to see something that never existed. She rolled her lower lip between her teeth. She would not cry. She simply would not. It would be too humiliating. Gritting her teeth, she turned to rush after her group and crashed straight into a male chest dressed in evening attire. The gentleman caught her in his arms and steadied them both.

Lord Kilnsey smiled down at her, but his expression contained no derision. Instead, his expression seemed to be one of sympathy. "I think you have had a disappointment. If you will permit, I will take you around the house in the opposite direction from the others. We can say we turned the wrong way coming out of the box. I will take the blame. It will give you time to compose yourself." He offered his arm.

India nodded and slipped her hand under his arm. They walked in silence. From time-to-time, she felt his eyes on her, but she refused to meet his gaze. Crying in the face of his sympathy would complete her humiliation.

When they rounded a corner, the pressure of his arm on her hand increased. He leaned in and whispered, "The others are just ahead. Your mother looks rather agitated. Let me do the talking."

Mother's eye narrowed as she marched toward them with purpose. "India, wherever have you been? You have caused Lord Kilnsey and the Rivers to be late for their reservation at Delmonico's."

Charlie released India's hand and grasped Mother's. Guiding them toward his relatives, he said, "It was entirely my fault. I insisted upon turning right instead of left exiting the box. Miss Ledbetter tried to correct me, but my pride would not allow me to admit my error." India shot him a grateful smile while he continued, "As to the dinner reservation, I believe the maître d' will hold my bother-in-law's table indefinitely. He is a valued customer. Perhaps you would care to join us?"

Having heard the last of her brother's comments, Lady Clarissa smiled. "Oh, indeed. Our table will be available when we arrive. I'm sure the restaurant will be accommodating of additional guests. Do say you will come with us."

Mother's anger faded, replaced by an obsequious excitement. "How kind of you, but Mama and I had a large supper before the opera. India refused to eat a bite. I think she was too excited." India glared at her mother. Nothing could be farther from the truth. If Mother saw India's expression, she ignored it. To Lady Clarissa, she said, "Perhaps you can persuade her to eat something?"

India opened her mouth to protest, but Grandmama gently squeezed India's arm and interjected, "My dear, you have our permission to accompany Lord Kilnsey to the restaurant provided Mr. Rivers and Lady Clarissa ensure your safe return home." She looked meaningfully at Charlie.

He smiled and made a small bow. "Of course. Neither my sister nor I would dream of putting Miss Ledbetter in an unsafe or compromising position."

A self-satisfied smile crossed Mother's face. "It's settled then." To India, she continued, "Since you are in such honorable company, I think we can ignore our usual social requirements."

At this point it would have been conspicuously rude for India to protest, so she smiled and nodded at her dinner hosts, but when they turned toward the exit, she shot her mother and grandmother a blistering look. Mother had always manipulated events to her own liking, but this was beyond the pale. There were no longer any doubts about Mother and Grandmama's intent where Lord Kilnsey was concerned. They could not have been more obvious if they had shouted it for all to hear. India's cheeks flamed. Please, God, do not let him think she was party to her relatives' maneuvering.

During the ride to the restaurant, India did her best to cover her embarrassment and anger by chatting with her hosts about her pleasure in the opera and seeing the great Caruso. After they exited the vehicle, Charlie did not move immediately to follow his relatives. To India he said, "Please, may I have a word?" When India nodded, he continued, "I wish to apologize for your being pushed into accompanying us. I asked on impulse. I did not anticipate your family's…er, eagerness on the issue. I fear you would rather be elsewhere."

India met his gaze prepared to answer him honestly, but saw that he seemed in earnest, so modified her response. "It was a generous gesture. I appreciate your thoughtfulness and I apologize if I appeared ungracious in responding to your kind invitation."

He pushed out a quick breath. "No need to apologize. Your behavior was above reproach, as always. I'm glad you see my invitation was extended in good faith. I was afraid you were angry."

This time, honesty seemed best. "I am angry, but it has nothing to do with you. Sometimes I want to throttle my mother and grandmother. They embarrassed me."

He laughed and drew her arm under his as he guided her toward Delmonico's door. "I know exactly how you feel. My sister, God love her, has at times made her intentions regarding my future a little too obvious. Family. We love them, but they aren't always easy. Let's put our relatives' ambitions aside for the remainder of the evening and simply enjoy a good meal in what I hope is pleasant company."

India grinned. "That is an excellent suggestion. And I like your sister immensely."

He cast her a sidelong glance. "Just my sister?"

"Oh, and perhaps your brother-in-law."

He laid his hand over his heart, a fake grimace on his lips. "You wound me. Tell me what I must do to gain your favor, dear lady." When his gaze met hers, playfulness twinkled in his eyes.

She returned his smile, then replied in all seriousness, "Ignore my mother and grandmother. Pretend they do not exist."

He had not been prepared for such an answer for a crack appeared in the surface of his normally serene persona. After clearing his throat, his bantering tone returned. "But if I do that, I must refuse the invitation to your ball. Surely you would not deny me the pleasure of participating in your introduction to society?"

"Okay then. Come to the ball if you like." India flung her hand aside as if she could sweep away any doubts with a gesture. "Just don't think my relatives speak for me in anything. I intend to be my own woman. This is a new century and I intend to find my way in it under my own steam." She met his eyes with a steady gaze.

Charlie chuckled. "My goodness. I must say you are a thoroughly modern young woman. I am curious, though, as to how you will accomplish your goal."

A warning bell tingled deep within her. It might be an innocent question prompted by the teasing nature of their exchange, but somehow India thought not. "That shall remain my business. Just know that when I set my mind on something, I rarely fail." She lifted her chin and arched one brow. "In that, I am like my mother and grandmother."

"Ah, I see. A family of formidable women. I will make note to remember that should I ever find myself on the wrong side of one of you."

"Yes, that would certainly be in your best interest." India broke eye contact and turned toward the restaurant feigning an interest in Delmonico's entrance, her outward display of bravado at odds with the doubts that plagued her.

CHAPTER 10

It was ridiculous to stand at the window every afternoon at three o'clock, but India couldn't keep herself from wasting time hoping he would come. Each day her disappointment grew along with her anger at herself for caring. January 20, the day of her coming-out ball, the window once again drew her like a siren. Sailors know that to follow the call will only bring grief and tragedy, but they are helpless to resist. India leaned her forehead against the pane where her breath condensed in a halo. The glass against her skin chilled to the point of pain, but at least it provided a brief distraction. The morning's snow lay virtually unmarked - few vehicle tracks, no footprints.

After fifteen minutes of futility, she turned away from the window and slumped into a chair by the fire. This should be the most exciting day of her life, but Billy Connor dominated her thoughts. Had it been love or only friendship? The question tormented her. If she had so misinterpreted Billy's intentions, how could she successfully navigate the world of coming-out balls and society courtship? Her confidence was shaken, but her determination was not. If a mild flirtation, because that was what it must have been, could propel her into such a downward spiral, then she would guard her heart more carefully in future. For now, one word kept pounding through her mind. Fool, fool, fool. The word described her perfectly. She gripped both armrests and pushed herself up from the chair. Brooding accomplished nothing. Perhaps a rest before dressing for the evening would brighten her mood.

***

Sitting at her vanity table, India watched magic being worked. As an unmarried girl, wearing a tiara would have been the height of vulgarity, so Althea wove tiny cream rosebuds and baby's breath into a loose chignon, leaving a few tendrils floating strategically around India's face. While not exactly the latest fashion, the effect of virginal elegance suited her and the evening's purpose.

India turned her head from side-to-side and smiled at her maid in the mirror. "You always know how to make this mop of mine look its best. The flowers are the right touch."

Althea arched a brow. "You have thick hair that is easy to style. It has just the right amount of body. A lot of women would kill for what you have."

"I suppose you're right. I guess I'm just feeling a little anxious about tonight." As Althea fastened a strand of pearls, the fluttering in India's midsection that had plagued her for days reappeared. She crossed her wrists over her abdomen and pressed. "Why do we have to do these things? I couldn't care less if I ever go to another ball again. I just want to go home to The Falls."

Althea planted a hand on each of India's shoulders and gave a light squeeze. "That's nerves talking. You will have a good time once you get there. After all, how many times does an American girl get to be a princess?" Tilting her head and considering the reflection in the mirror, she continued, "You know, that's exactly what you look like. No girl has ever looked more beautiful or regal, not even as a bride. Now promise me you will try to enjoy your ball."

India stood and on impulse threw her arms around Althea's neck, clinging like a child. "I feel like everything is about to change. Nothing will ever be the same again. Not me. Not you. None of us. Not for as long as we live and I'm scared."

India sometimes looked on her maid more as older sister than servant. This was one of those times. Althea patted India's back, then took her shoulders and pushed her away so their eyes met. "Of course life is changing. You are a young woman with certain expectations. You are of marriageable age with a mother and grandmother determined to see you settled in the best possible circumstances. The only real problem you have is finding the right man."

"But that's just it." India's brows knitted together. "I thought I might have found him on the first try. Unfortunately, I was wrong. It seems I'm no judge of men or affairs of the heart. And that's what scares me. If I was wrong about Billy Connor, how can I be sure next time?"

A rueful smile curled Althea's lip. "If I had the answer, I would be a married woman instead of a maid."

India's eyes opened wider. "Really? You never told me you once had a suitor."

Althea's gaze dropped as she sighed. "I did, but my father thought he was too low class." When she looked at India again, irony shone in her eyes. "Why Daddy thought a mill hand was lower down than a dirt farmer is beyond me. Anyway, the boy married the mill owner's daughter and now manages the mill."

"Why didn't you defy your father and run away with him?"

Althea shrugged. "Oh, I suppose I should have, but I was afraid of what people would say and afraid of life without my family. Daddy said he would never allow me in the house again if I didn't obey him."

"Do you regret your decision?" India blurted out before she thought about how rude or hurtful the question might be.

If Althea thought India intrusive, she didn't show it. She pursed her lips and nodded. "Sometimes. My sisters won't let Daddy forget he's the reason I'm still not married. I've forgiven Daddy, but I think he feels bad. He keeps asking me to come home because the man who bought the neighboring farm keeps asking about me."

The thought of Althea leaving created a stab of anxiety. "That sounds promising. Will you go?"

Althea hooted. "I don't think so. Bad teeth, bad breath, and dirty fingernails. Not exactly an attractive prospect. That's enough of my sad story. Get yourself downstairs and go have fun."

The hired driver guided the limousine up Broadway until the lights of Times Square brightened everything around them. They pulled to a stop in front of the Knickerbocker, John Jacob Astor's new palace where the rich went to dine, drink, and stay. They alighted amid a crowd of gawkers.

India paused with one foot on the running board and drew back. "Why are all these people here?"

Mother leaned into the auto and grabbed India's hand. "Come along." Gesturing toward the crowd, she continued, "People sometimes gather in anticipation of seeing the rich and famous. No doubt word of your ball has reached the lower classes."

India cast a sidelong glance at her mother. "Somehow that seems a little far-fetched."

"We are members of one of the oldest and most prominent families in New York. Of course they are here to see us."

India gazed at the crowd but did not detect any interest directed toward her or anyone in their party. Whatever the people were waiting for, it definitely was not the Ledbetters.

Mother tugged India from the auto. "Hurry up. We must be in place to receive our guests. They will begin arriving within the half hour."

India's eyes grew wide as they entered the space in which she was to be presented to society. Mother had spared no expense with the food and decorations. The Knickerbocker's ballroom was festooned with garlands of hothouse roses, carnations, and orchids in white and shades of pink. Large arrangements stood sentinel at every portal and in every alcove. The buffet tables could not possibly have held another dish or platter. At a signal from Mother, the orchestra began a selection of the standards intermingled with new compositions, playing them to perfection. Grandmama supervised India and Mother into a receiving line. And then they waited.

India bent her knees, shifted from one foot to the other, and craned her neck. She had stood thus for an hour after the appointed time for her ball to begin but had greeted only about a quarter of those invited. "Do you think the weather is keeping people away?"

Mother twisted her handkerchief and smiled brightly. "It is the fashion to be late. You just wait and see. All of old New York will arrive within the hour."

At the one hour forty-minute mark with half of the invitees still absent, Grandmama's face was a study in barely controlled fury. "They will not dare snub us. To do so will cost them dearly."

Mother shot her a withering glance. "Always ready with threats of social annihilation as usual, I see. Too bad you did not feel that way twenty years ago. If you had not insisted that I marry Robert, things might be vastly different tonight. You thought everyone would have forgotten my in-laws by now, but apparently memories are long indeed. They did not even show the courtesy of sending their regrets."

Grandmama snorted as her eyes narrowed. "Yes, I can see how you have suffered by your marriage. You have more money than God. You live in a castle and you have a lovely daughter entering society. Yes, your life has indeed been one of tragedy."

If Mother and Grandmama continued like this, there was danger of a scene nobody would live down. A distraction was required. India surveyed the small gathering. "The people who have come seem to be having a good time. Surely, that is all that really matters."

"Of course they are having a good time." Grandmama's eyes flared while she snapped, "These are the ones who barely made the cut. They were honored to receive an invitation."

Unshed tears brightened Mother's eyes. "Well, at least Lady Clarissa did not disappoint us. We can be grateful for that."

Poor Mother. She cared so deeply about what other people thought. India said a silent prayer that they would all survive the evening with their sanities intact, but as she watched dancers swirl around the floor, a question nagged. Why were so many of the socially prominent people Grandmama always claimed were great friends absent? If the family was the paragon of social standing Mother and

Grandmama had always claimed, surely those important people would have come tonight.

A tingle of doubt followed by apprehension slithered through India. Mother and Grandmama seemed to have overestimated their influence to an astounding extinct. Social snubs of this magnitude had to involve more than the weather. Mother had never made a secret that she felt superior to Papa's family, but tonight she made it clear she also resented her marriage. Papa had been very good to Mother and the Van de Bergs. It galled that she belittled him so.

Not for the first time since they left North Carolina homesickness plagued India. She had not wanted this ball or any of the trappings of the New York social scene. This disaster rested with Mother and Grandmama, but India felt the sting of rejection, too. Before this miserable trip was over, there would be a reckoning. Something was not right about her family. Things had been kept secret, but no more. A new determination took root. If she had any hope of success in navigating the world into which Mother and Grandmama were determined to thrust her, she must know the truth. With these two, of course, her timing must be right. India's lips thinned as she pondered just when she might pounce on them with her questions.

***

Clarissa laid a hand on Charlie's arm. "How many dances have you reserved with India?" He could be so infuriating at times.

He shrugged. "One or two, I suppose. I really didn't keep track."

She snapped her fan against her palm. "You are insufferable. If you move too slowly, you may well lose this chance altogether."

Charlie arched a brow as he cast a pointed gaze upon the assembly. "Somehow I think not. There seems so little competition at present." He took a long swig of champagne. "These balls are a colossal bore. There is nothing to hold one's interest for more than a minute or two at most."

"Oh, I know where your mind is, and you would do well to forget you ever met her." Anger tinted her whispers. "Mooning over that girl will do no one any good, least of all you. Her father may be considered a leader among the county's farmers, but she has no lineage and no money. You can't afford her. More importantly, the estate can't afford her."

"And so, like Miss Ledbetter, I am to be sold to the highest bidder." He nodded to a couple who were swaying past on the dance floor. The female partner grinned at him in return. "Or in poor, dear India's case, the greatest title with the longest lineage in Burke's that her family can afford. If she weren't being shoved down my throat, I would no doubt be pursuing her with greater vigor. I like her. A lot, in fact. She's a good-looking girl and excellent company."

Clarissa snapped her fan shut. "Not only insufferable, but perverse, as well." She glared at her brother. "You know, on this side of the water the Van de Bergs were once a social force. In its way, her family is the equal of ours."

"So I have heard. What happened to send them down in the world?"

"One hears different accounts, but it has to do with Petra's marriage to Robert Ledbetter. That apparently is not all, however. A Mrs. Collins has hinted there is a much graver reason."

Charlie stifled a yawn. "Really? And what could that be?"

"While she refused to elaborate, she did say outright that she would never have degraded her family in such a manner even for so large a fortune." Clarissa studied Charlie to see if her words were having the desired effect. One more push might do the trick. While he might feign disinterest, he had displayed a protective streak where India was concerned. "Sadly, I have heard an alarming account from other sources, as well."

Charlie's back stiffened as the expression in his eyes hardened. "Why should this Mrs. Collins tell you what is clearly gossip of the most pernicious kind?"

Was that a hint of gallantry in his manner? Why yes, it was. Clarissa smiled as she unfurled her fan with one sweeping motion. "I suspect she is hoping that by discrediting India's family it will cast her own daughter in a better light."

"Oh, that Miss Collins. Her mother needn't bother. The mere idea is insupportable." Irritation shone in his eyes. "These newly rich Americans hoping to outstrip their old money betters. It fairly sets the head spinning. Though, I do suppose there's nothing like a titled son-in-law to raise one's social standing. Have you met my daughter, Lady so-and-so?" Sarcasm colored his words.

"You may wish to guard your tongue. There is a limit to how much superiority even upstarts will tolerate."

"Why, Sister. You give insufficient credit. I would never be so rude within the hearing of our American friends." Just then, India whirled by in the arms of a handsome, but inconsequential young man. Charlie put his glass on a nearby table as his eyes followed the couple. "You are right. Miss Ledbetter is the best on offer and the estate must be saved no matter the cost to my heart. I'm sure to be happier with her than with any of these other dollar princesses."

***

India watched with interest as Charles Westmorland, Fifteenth Earl of Kilnsey approached with the apparent intent of cutting in. His recent declaration and subsequent apology were puzzling. He was a walking contradiction. One minute he asked to court her and the next he ignored her. He was a conundrum, but an attractive one. To be honest, he was very handsome and rather good company when he made an effort to be charming.

Her dance partner looked rather startled when he felt a tap on his shoulder. "Hey, what's the deal? You can't cut in. It's just not done. That's why the girls have dance cards."

India smiled over her partner's shoulder at Charles as the tune came to an end. She opened her card where only she could see it. "Let me see. Why yes, this is Lord Kilnsey's dance." To her present partner she said, "Thank you for a lovely dance. I had no idea you were...so energetic."

Charles whisked her away before any other partners could present themselves. "So who are you supposed to be dancing with?"

India laughed as the color rose in her cheeks. "Someone that I beg you to help me avoid. During our last dance he nearly crushed the toes on my left foot. I don't think they will survive another encounter with his size twelves."

"Large man is he then?" Humor danced in his eyes.

"Only his feet and belly.'

Feigning shock, he lifted his chin and gazed down his nose at her. "I say, you have a frightfully sharp tongue when you wish. I must remember to stay fit and tread lightly."

"If he had stepped on your toes, you would feel the same, I assure you."

Chuckling, he guided her expertly through the waltz. "I dare say I probably would, but as I am hardly likely to partner him around the dance floor, I will just have to take your word for it." As they neared the buffet room, he leaned in and whispered. "This dance is about to end, but I do not want to let you go. Please say you will stay with me awhile longer and may we drop the formality? I much prefer Charlie to Charles." When she nodded, he continued at a normal volume, "I say, would you take a bite of supper with me? I'm suddenly feeling rather famished."

The music died away as they turned for the buffet room. India took Charlie's arm and listened while he spoke with animation about the selections he intended to take and those they should avoid. He was funny and attentive in helping her make her choices.

All the while they circled the buffet, the back of India's neck tingled as though eyes bored into her very flesh. When she could bear it no longer, she glanced over her shoulder. Her heart leapt in her chest. The very last person she expected to see stood at the threshold watching her, his expression filled with such longing that it appeared he might cry out.

CHAPTER 11

India froze, serving tongs dangling from her hand above a bowl of salad. Of all the nerve. He ignored her for weeks and now he shows up at her ball, insufferably late and dressed far too casually. To think she had stood day-after-day mooning by the window. A fire began to burn. It started in her abdomen and licked its way up through her chest until it seared her throat and heated her cheeks which were now surely the color of flames themselves. She tilted her head back so the swelling tears rolled down her throat.

Dropping the tongs, she whipped around and looked at Lord Kilnsey. She must say something, anything that would take her out of the line of sight. Leaning in, she whispered through a fake smile, "I think I will faint if we do not sit down this minute. I just realized I haven't eaten since breakfast."

If he noticed the sudden change in her demeanor, Charlie had the good manners not to comment. "Of course. I see a vacant table near the door. Please take my arm."

India allowed him to lead the way. Once beside the table, she chose the seat that would put her back to Billy Connor. She'd be damned if she would give him the time of day, much less the pleasure of her attention. Cutting him dead was what he deserved.

Within a few seconds, a presence loomed at her shoulder. His proximity and the sound of his throat clearing made it impossible to ignore him. She tucked her chin, turned her head slightly to the side, and gazed at him from beneath her lashes. When he saw her expression, his cheeks flamed. He nodded and extended his hand to Charlie. After introducing himself, he said, "I apologize for intruding, but I must speak with Miss Ledbetter. I promise not to keep her from the festivities for more than a few minutes. As you can see by my dress, I do not intend to stay."

Charlie raised his brows and looked at India. "Do you wish to speak with Mr. Connor? If so, I will excuse myself." He nodded toward the opposite side of the buffet tables. "I will only be a few steps away should you need me."

Bless him. Charlie seemed to have sensed her distress and hesitation. She looked from him to Billy and back. Would it be better to refuse Billy's request or to hear what he had to say? Maybe there was a logical, maybe even a good explanation for his behavior. If she didn't take this opportunity, she might never know. To be left wondering felt the greater danger to her peace of mind. She nodded to Charlie. "Thank you. Yes, I wish to speak with Mr. Connor, but I would be very grateful if you remained nearby."

Charlie rose from his seat, bowed slightly, and departed. He stopped almost within earshot of where he had left her, sending a surge of gratitude through India. Billy took the vacated chair and pulled himself so close to India their knees nearly touched.

Discomfort marred his handsome face. He met her gaze briefly, then lowered his eyes. After a disturbingly long silence, he reached for her hand. Instead of snatching it away, which was her first inclination, she allowed him to take it in his. He held it palm up atop his right hand and covered both with his left. He sighed before beginning, "I owe you my deepest, sincerest apologies."

When he failed to continue, India withdrew her hand from his. "And for what do you feel the need to apologize, Mr. Connor?" The imperious tone grated against her better nature, but he had acted badly and deserved not to have his way made easier.

"You know why. I paid you court and then abandoned you to wonder why I no longer seemed interested. I have behaved like a dilettante and a cad. My only excuse is that you are so alluring I could not stop myself. I found that the more time I spent with you the more I adored you."

India did not comment immediately. Instead, she allowed the silence filling the space between them to grind on until the tension became palpable. "I see. That is all well and good, but you have failed to explain why you stayed away despite such intense feelings of... adoration? I believe that is the sentiment you expressed, is it not?" Sarcasm dripped from her words. Not a very polite tone, but it was just right for this particular occasion.

He had the courtesy to turn the color of an overripe Winesap apple. "You are right to be angry. As I mentioned in my note before I left for Boston, my father was gravely ill. Unfortunately, he did not recover. I have not felt very sociable since his funeral."

My goodness. Of course he didn't feel like making social calls. Sympathy drove away any vestige of anger. "I'm so sorry to hear of your father's passing. I am the one who should apologize. Please forgive my failure to foresee what you must be going through. I do remember the note mentioned your father's health. It was just when I saw you at the opera, I thought you had forsaken me for another." When he broke eye contact and didn't respond, an alarm sounded in the recesses of India's mind. "Who was the girl I saw you with?"

"I hardly know how to tell you." His reply was barely audible.

"Then you had better just say it. I am beginning to suspect the worst of you."

"You have every right to do so." He finally looked up. His eyes held real pain or perhaps it was shame. It was difficult to determine which. He drew a breath and exhaled slowly. "When you saw me at the opera, I was with my cousin and her parents. They came down from Boston with me. They thought hearing Caruso might cheer me up."

India blinked and jerked back a little. She had expected something very different. "That was very kind of them, but how does that affect my perception of you?"

He laughed softly, but his tone lacked any hint of humor. "Because she is not just my cousin. She is, and has been for these past two years, my fiancée. Our wedding is set for two months hence. All the arrangements have been made. The dress is bought. The church is reserved, the guests invited. I could not back out now even if I wanted to."

"And you clearly do not want to." Instead of anger or hurt, a numbness spread its arms around her heart. "So why pay court to me when all of this was surely in the planning stages when we met?"

"Because I am a callus, self-indulgent fool. I knew it was wrong, but I did it anyway."

India experienced a burst of clarity. His subterfuge and unwillingness to present himself at Grandmama's door now made sense. No doubt he feared her family knew or would find out about his engagement. It was not just that he was apprehensive of being turned away, but knew it was almost a certainty. She had not mentioned him to her family again once they had made their feelings clear, so they had no reason to divulge further knowledge of him. Keeping their meetings secret had been his idea from the start. He was a rogue, and she was a fool not to have seen through him.

Rising from her seat, she did not offer her hand, but cast a glacial expression upon William Connor, Esq. "I think you should go. We have nothing more to say to one another." All she had left was her dignity. It took every ounce of strength she possessed to maintain her composure, turn from him, and walk away. He whispered her name as she stepped away from the table, but she did not look back.

Her emotions must have been written across her face because Lord Kilnsey immediately took her hand and guided her to a darkened corner. "I think it might be wise to return you to your mother and perhaps you should sit out the next dance. You look like you have had a shock."

"Thank you, but please let's stay here while I gather my wits." India's fists clinched at her sides. She had been a stupid girl for sure. Well, no more. A firm grip would be kept on her emotions from now on. Her resolve stiffened but then a cold shower of reality descended. Billy had seemed so right. He was just the kind of man she had always thought she would fall in love with. A little shudder passed through her. The confrontation with Billy tangled her emotions, threatening to swamp what little confidence remained. She needed distraction, something, anything to help her forget him. While she might not be able to trust her heart, maybe she could turn this disastrous evening to some useful purpose.

She forced her body to relax as she looked at Charlie. "My relatives are the last people I want to be with right now. Please take me to your sister. I have questions that need answers and my family will be of little use." Enough of subterfuge and secrecy. Everyone around her seemed to be keeping secrets, and those secrets were affecting her profoundly. The time for reckoning had come sooner than expected, but so be it. There had to be a good reason for people not attending her ball and discovering it seemed more vital now than ever. If she was to survive the battlefield that the New York social season seemed to be, she needed information. Having made the decision, she took Charlie's arm, and they began their circumnavigation of the dance floor.

Thank heavens. Lady Clarissa and Mr. Rivers had found a quiet corner where several chairs were arranged for conversation while still allowing a view of the dancers. India took a seat beside Clarissa and waited for an opening in the conversation. When the opportunity presented itself, India placed her hand on Lady Clarissa's arm. "I hate to intrude with problems, but I am feeling at a great disadvantage and you are the only person I can turn to."

Lady Clarissa's eyes grew wide with surprise that faded to concern. "I am not sure whether to be flattered or frightened. Actually, I think I feel a little of both. How may I help?"

India gestured toward the guests swirling around the dance floor. "I'm sure you've noticed the attendance is rather thin tonight. I've overheard people commenting about it all evening when they didn't know I could hear or maybe they just didn't care. My grandmother is very upset. Perhaps you can tell me why we are being snubbed."

Lady Clarissa's cheeks became quite pink. She looked at her husband, then back at India. "My dear, surely this is something you should discuss with your mother."

"But you see, that's the problem. Mother is the last person I can ask. She has maintained a fiction about our family for so long I doubt she will be honest now. I'm not sure she even remembers the truth. Please help me. I have made the best of all this coming-out business for as long as I can bear."

Lord Kilnsey rose from his chair. "Perhaps it would be best if I excused myself. Sister, if you can ease Miss Ledbetter's anxiety, I beg that you do so. No matter how difficult truth can be, not knowing and guessing can be worse." Before India could object, he gave them a small bow and departed. She watched his retreating form with a surge of gratitude. His consideration and discretion offered new insight into his character.

India looked at Clarissa with her heart thumping in her chest and tears gathering in her eyes. "Please. Tell me what you know. Help to make some good come out of this ghastly evening."

Clarissa's eyes filled with sympathy. "But that is just the point. I would hate to have you feeling worse rather than better."

"Your brother is correct about knowing the truth. The guessing and uncertainty can be far worse."

Again, Lady Clarissa silently sought her husband's counsel. When he nodded, she began. "I doubt I know the entire tale. I am sure there are things various members of your family have managed to keep from even the most inquisitive." She stopped and looked into India's eyes for several beats before continuing. "Nonetheless, I fear you are the victim of guilt by association. Neither you nor your parents are directly responsible for the circumstances in which you find yourselves. As I understand it, the cause of the rift between your Van de Berg grandparents and their social equals has to do with your Ledbetter grandparents. At least that is what I have heard." Lady Clarissa paused, seeming to believe she had said enough.

India twisted her dance card until it was a crumpled mess. "There must be more than that. What else do people say?"

Clarissa looked searchingly at India. "If you insist."

"I do. Please go on."

Clarissa's throat moved as she swallowed a rather large sip of champagne. Placing her glass on the table next to her chair, she continued, "Your grandfather Ledbetter was a rather ruthless businessman. It is said that he lied about his background and family connections in order to secure his first position with a Wall Street brokerage company. Once he had the job, he is believed to have bilked clients out of fortunes. The main charge against him was that he advised his clients to buy Reading Railroad stock in large quantities while the price was still high but not long before it went into receivership. Apparently, he was aware things were not well with the company before others on the street. I have no idea how he knew, but that is the charge. Instead of buying his clients' shares immediately at the higher price, he waited until the price dropped. When it was at its lowest point, he bought the stock in his clients' names and pocketed the difference between what they thought they were paying and what they actually paid. He is said to have finagled the purchase dates on the certificates, claiming there was a significant delay in their availability."

India's eyes grew wide. "That sounds illegal."

"It certainly should be, but the case against him could not be proven. He lost his job, but he left the brokerage company with a fortune that he invested in oil exploration. As I'm sure you know, when the Spindletop oil field came in, his fortune increased tenfold. He built your home in North Carolina and retired to enjoy his ill-gotten gains."

India thought about what Lady Clarissa said. "Yes, I knew about the oil investments, but no one in the family ever talked about how he got his start by manipulating stocks." She stopped speaking while she digested the new information. "I can see he made no friends with his business dealings, but that still does not explain why it affected my Van de Berg grandparents."

"Do you know how and why your Grandfather Van de Berg died?"

India blinked in surprise at the unexpected question. Shrugging, she replied, "All I know is he had an accident while cleaning his pistol."

Clarissa's face became a study in discomfort. "And that may well have been what happened."

India's resolve hardened. "There is more. I can see it in your eyes. What are you not telling me?"

"Are you quite sure you want to hear this?"

"Absolutely. Otherwise, I am at a complete disadvantage when dealing with people here. I will face whatever truth there may be, but I cannot do battle against an unknown foe."

"I would not have put it in military terms, but I suppose I can see how you might view the situation thus."

"Please do not keep me dangling. What else have you heard?"

"If the gossip is to be believed, your Grandfather Van de Berg killed himself because he was one of your Grandfather Ledbetter's clients who lost everything in the Reading Railroad crisis. It is said that he could not face a life of near poverty. Whatever the case, it seems that before your parents' marriage, your widowed Grandmother Van de Berg lived in rather straitened circumstances and was rumored to be on the verge of losing the Washington Square house. After the marriage, her money problems disappeared. There are those who viciously, and perhaps unfairly, accuse your Grandmother Van de Berg of selling her only child into the family of a man who was not only completely unscrupulous but also responsible for your grandfather Van de Berg's suicide."

India's breaths came in rapid succession so that her head began to swim. Losing control of her emotions would not help, so she inhaled deeply and let the air stream out slowly. She had always known about Grandmama's financial distress, but never its underlying cause. The pieces she did know now fell into place within Lady Clarissa's tale and made sense of what had been missing from the family's account. Still, her initial question had not been answered. "Even if what you have heard is accurate, it still does not explain why society has turned against Grandmama. Girls have been given away in arranged marriages for centuries and not always to good men, but my papa is a wonderful man. He couldn't help what his father did."

At that point, Lady Clarissa frowned and looked at her husband. "Jonathan, help me."

Mr. Rivers put his elbows on his knees and leaned forward until he was able to grasp India's hand. "My wife has divulged what we know based on what others have said and from what we have observed. From now on, I suggest you consult your mother regarding your grandmother."

"But she won't tell me anything different from what she always has. Please disclose what you have kept back. I need to know what I am dealing with. After all, this affects my life and possibly my future."

Mr. Rivers remained silent while he searched her face. "All I will say is this. Have you ever met your Grandmother Ledbetter?"

India's brows drew together in a frown. "Of course not. She died before I was born."

Mr. Rivers's expression became grim. "That may not be true. People claim to have seen her over the years here in New York. I do not know whether they saw your grandmother or simply someone who resembles her. You will need to ask your parents about her fate."

India pulled her hand from Mr. Rivers's grasp and leaned against the chair's back to prevent herself falling. She was not given to fainting, but she had eaten too little and drunk too much this evening to deal effectively with Lady Clarissa and Mr. Rivers's revelations. She had not anticipated a particularly pleasant tale, but this was beyond all expectations. Somehow the fact that people thought her Grandmother Ledbetter was still alive had turned society against Grandmama. It did not make sense, but that was what apparently lay beneath tonight's debacle. Mr. Rivers advised consulting her parents, and that was exactly what she would do. Papa may be in North Carolina, but Mother would face interrogation before she slept tonight.

CHAPTER 12

India's ball dragged on until the early hours. Those in attendance, though small in number, seemed reluctant to leave. They were enjoying the abundance of the buffet tables and the excellence of the orchestra. India danced with all the gentlemen who asked so that by the time she crawled into the limousine for the ride back to Washington Square, her feet ached and her mind had long ago become numb from feigning pleasure for hours on end.

She dropped her head onto the seat back, pretending to sleep. Making polite conversation with Mother and Grandmama was out of the question. She needed all of her strength for the showdown that lay ahead.

Once they arrived at the Washington Square house and the front door closed behind them, Mother was uncharacteristically quiet. Grandmama yawned as she approached the stairs. At the bottom step, she paused and cast a speculative gaze over India and Mother. "No good will be gained by discussion tonight. I'm going to bed. I advise you to do the same. We can decide how best to proceed over breakfast."

Mother did not respond but made movement toward the stairs. She looked very tired and completely defeated. Mother had displayed many unhappy attitudes in the past but never one quite like this. A stab of guilt pierced India as she followed because neither of them would sleep just yet.

When they reached Mother's room, she turned at the door. "Is there something you want, India? Surely whatever it is can wait until after we have rested."

"Yes, there is and no it cannot wait, but I don't think you will want to have this discussion out here in the hall."

Mother's face registered surprise but also showed she had no idea what India was about to ask. "If it's that important come inside but make it quick. I'm beyond exhausted."

India closed the door behind her. "There's no need to call your maid. I'll help you undress. Once you are settled in bed, we can talk." India inwardly winced at the delaying tactic. Cowardice was not her favored approach to issues, but now that confrontation was at hand, dread consumed her. Perhaps the truth about Grandmother Ledbetter was better left buried. The woman clearly had no desire to see her son or grandchild if she indeed still lived. Papa never spoke of his mother. In fact, he refused to discuss her on the few occasions when India asked about her "other" grandmother. There was a real possibility he would be hurt or even angry if she delved into that part of his life. On the other hand, if India had any hope of surviving this ghastly social season, knowing the truth about her family seemed imperative. Without that knowledge, she was being sent out into the world naked, unarmed, completely lacking the weapons required for social battle.

As she helped Mother out of her gown, India watched their reflections in the Cheval mirror. Mother was beginning to show her age. The lines around her eyes and mouth were more prominent. The gray at her temples seemed to have become more pronounced overnight. And for the first time, she appeared a little stooped. Wavering between desire for truth and pity for her mother, India weighed her choices while she folded the gown into the wardrobe. In the end, Mother made the decision for her.

Once she was settled beneath the covers, Mother said, "Now what is it that could not wait for morning? Out with it so I can get some sleep."

India squared her shoulders and met Mother's gaze. "I heard some things tonight that I find puzzling."

"And what would those be, dear?" Mother looked up from the pillows with drowsy eyes.

"It has to do with my grandparents."

Mother broke eye contact and gazed into the embers dying in the grate. "Why? You know all there is about your father's parents and mine."

India crossed the room and sat down on the edge of the bed. She picked up a corner of the top blanket and began unconsciously folding and unfolding it. "I believe there is much more than you have ever told me about our family's history. For instance, there is the question of how Grandfather Van de Berg died. You have always said it was an accident, but what if it wasn't?" A touch of fear played across Mother's face confirming India's suspicions. "I no longer believe your version. You see, I think he killed himself because he lost the family fortune through a bad investment. I have learned that Grandfather Ledbetter made his first fortune by swindling his stock brokerage clients, one of whom was Grandfather Van de Berg."

Mother blinked several times as she pulled her bed jacket closer about her. "Wherever did you hear such a tale?"

"From your dear friends Lady Clarissa and her husband."

Mother's hand flew to her throat. "They had no right to say such things. What on earth possessed them?"

"Because I asked." India dropped the blanket corner and extended a hand palm up. "You see, I couldn't understand why we were snubbed tonight after all your plans and everything you and Grandmama have always said about the Van de Berg position in society. Lady Clarissa didn't initiate the conversation, but I think she felt sorry for me, so she answered my questions and tried to help me understand."

Mother's brows drew together to form a deep furrow between her eyes. "I think you might know by now that gossip is the lowest form of communication. I am disturbed that you stooped to listening and appalled that the Riverses would burden you with such. I will speak with them tomorrow and put a stop to their rumor mongering."

"They are not rumor mongering." India's voice hardened as her temper flared. "They were reluctant to speak, but I insisted. They told me things that are apparently common knowledge here in New York."

Mother sighed. "Oh, India, I'm really exhausted. Must we do this now?"

"Yes," India shot back. There was no way Mother was going to wriggle out of this conversation. "Tell me about Papa's mother, Jane. He rarely talks about her. I always thought it was because she died young and he didn't have many memories of her, but I heard something very surprising tonight."

Mother's eyes narrowed. "And that would be?"

"People say they have seen her here in the city, that she is alive. So, tell me the truth. Is Grandmother Jane still living?"

Fear or something very similar darkened Mother's expression. Her eyes widened and her lips moved but she uttered no words. It was as though India had brought forth a ghost with her question, an unwelcome, sinister ghost who snatched the very air from Mother's lungs. The muscles of her throat moved once and a second time. Finally, she managed to speak. "I'm afraid I really have no idea." Notes of insincerity colored Mother's words. She clearly knew more than she had ever shared. "No one is sure what happened to Jane."

"Why on earth not?" India's voice was much louder than she intended. All she needed right now was to rouse Grandmama. Forcing herself to relax, she continued, "Why did you tell me she died when Papa was little?"

"Because it was for the best." Mother now resorted to bristling authority. "Besides, your grandfather said she died not long after the divorce."

India blinked several times. No one had ever mentioned divorce.

The corners of Mother's mouth turned up in an ironic smile. "I see I have shocked you. The divorce created quite a scandal. In those days, people lived together in misery or separately in peace, but they stayed married out of obligation, duty, and to avoid scandal. Divorce simply wasn't done. I must say that once I married into the family, I did not blame Jane. No one could have lived with Thomas Jefferson Ledbetter. He was a bully and a tyrant. I'm sure he made her life miserable, which must be why…" Mother looked like she had stopped herself just before revealing something she might regret. She was quiet for a moment, then with a wave of her hand continued. "It was all so long along. The fact is Robert's parents divorced when he was a very small boy and he never saw his mother again. Ole T.J. forbade the mention of her name and barred her from the house. It was he who insisted she died about a year after they separated. When I became engaged to your father, certain people repeated rumors about Jane, but I discounted them as vicious gossip. At any rate, I believe if she had been alive, she would certainly have contacted Robert after T.J. died, but no one has heard from her during all these years."

"Maybe she can't get in touch." India's pulse beat a little faster. "Maybe she's ill and confined to a hospital. What if she needs care or help? She's Papa's mother, for heaven's sake. It's unbelievable that no one, not even Papa, has tried to find out what happened to her. If I have another living grandmother, I have a right to meet her and I intend to look for her."

Mother sat bolt upright and grabbed India's arm. Her eyes flashed and her lips curled into a snarl. "You will do no such thing. I forbid it. When will you learn to leave well enough alone? If your father wanted to know his mother's whereabouts, he would certainly have looked for her before now." Mother dropped India's arm and pushed it away. "No one, certainly not your father or I, will thank you for raking up old embarrassments. In any event, she's dead."

"But why would people say she is alive?" India hissed.

"I have no idea what the gossips' motivations might be. She's dead or we would have heard from her." Mother dropped back upon the pillows, closed her eyes, and rolled away from India. "Now leave me alone and go to bed."

India stared at her mother's back for a moment, then turned off the bedside lamp. Her jaw clenched while she considered the situation. There was something terribly wrong where Jane was concerned. Given Mother's reaction, it must be a scandal of monumental proportions. Whatever Mother and the family were hiding, it had ruined her debut and made her an object of pity and derision, neither of which she enjoyed. Now that she had little hope of getting any joy out of the remainder of the season, she would pursue answers to her questions regardless of who did or did not like it.

Mother probably would not divulge anything else, so India would begin her search with a more amiable source. She would call upon the Riverses as soon as politely possible. If people had seen Jane, surely Mr. Rivers knew in what part of the city she had been spotted. Determination swelled but there was no more that could be done now and bed beckoned. India made her way to her own room, undressed without waking Aletha, and was asleep as soon as her body stretched out beneath the covers.

Despite falling asleep quickly, she awoke only after about an hour and then tossed and turned until she heard the sounds of the house coming to life. After giving up on sleep, India went downstairs for a late breakfast, nearer luncheon really. Hopefully, the thumping in her head would subside after she had eaten. As she approached the dining room, the sounds of raised voices drifted through the closed door. India paused and listened, gauging the atmosphere before entering. Mother and Grandmama were engaged in spirited debate.

"Petra, you can't simply tuck tail and run back to North Carolina. How would it look?" Grandmama's voice boomed on the other side of the door. "Together, we can control India. I understand your fears in respect to her questions, but you must stay and deal with the greater situation. Show people what you are made of. You're a Van de Berg, after all."

"I will not be humiliated again." Mother's voice was high pitched and quivering. She must be truly enraged. "Staying here will ensure people whisper behind our backs at every event we attend. You forget I am no longer a Van de Berg. You saw to that when you and my dearly departed father-in-law struck your bargain. Mark my words. I will show people exactly who we are. They may snub us at present, but the day will come when they will beg for an invitation to my table."

"And precisely how do you plan to accomplish all of this?" Grandmama's tone would have cut through steel.

"You will find out when I am ready to tell you. I have had enough of your interference. If I had not been maneuvered into marrying Robert, there would be no need to control anyone or staunch vicious rumors. As soon as India has eaten, we are departing for the station."

Oh lord, what was Mother planning now? With her hand on the knob, India leaned against the door's cool mahogany. Every beat of her pulse pounded through her head and bounced off her eardrums. If only she had control over her money, she would not be subject to Mother's and the trustee's demands. She would live her life as she wished and be whoever she wanted to be. She would have no truck with Mrs. Astor's 400, balls, or inveterate gossips. Unfortunately, even when she reached her majority, the trustees would still hold sway in decisions determining her future. Leaving New York today would ensure no chance of looking into Grandmother Jane's fate. The nails of India's left hand dug into her palm. With Mother in full revenge mode, it was clear India needed to know the extent of her family's scandals, especially regarding Jane. Being thrust into society without complete knowledge of the past would only spell additional disaster. So then, perhaps a ruse was in order.

Plastering a smile on her face, she turned the knob and threw the door back. "I couldn't help overhearing your conversation. Mother, I'm surprised you want to go home. You've always complained about being isolated in the wilds of North Carolina. Perhaps Grandmama is right. You know the failure of my ball will be on everyone's lips. I want to stay here and show everybody I'm not afraid of a little gossip."

Grandmama and Mother exchanged surreptitious glances, appearing to reach an unspoken agreement. A tight smile crossed Grandmama's lips before she spoke. "My goodness, you have certainly changed your attitude. Don't look so surprised. I have always known you dislike visiting me." She paused and ran an evaluative gaze over India. "While your desire to face society is admirable, after further consideration, I believe your mother is right, my dear. Returning to North Carolina is the best course."

Taking a seat opposite Mother, a tight smile spread across India's face. Her own attitude was not the only one that had undergone rapid alteration. She must have overplayed her hand for Grandmama clearly suspected India would not let her questions go unanswered as long as she remained in New York. Defeat did not feel good, but it might have one benefit. She would not be forced to attend any more stressful balls, insipid social calls, or boring dinners.

A little wave of satisfaction rolled through India. Perhaps this was all for the best. If she didn't have to enter society, then it would not be so important for her to find Grandmother Jane. She would tell Papa what she had learned and leave him to look into his mother's fate. She would go home to The Falls and life would return to normal. Maybe she could even convince Papa to let her attend Davenport Female College in Lenore.

CHAPTER 13

The trip home from New York was no more eventful than the previous trip north had been, but as they passed between the stone columns supporting the front gate and entered the treelined drive leading up the mountain to The Falls, India clamped her knees and ankles together to keep her feet from dancing. Home, home, home at last. Nothing had changed and yet everything had. The trees, which had been in their fall glory when they left, now stretched bare limbs skyward so that the house on its mountainside could be seen clearly from the valley below. With a frosting of snow glistening in the morning sun, The Falls looked like a fairytale castle. Grandfather TJ may have had some rough edges, but he had built something special. Even Grandmama Van de Berg had admitted it.

India leaned out of the automobile window for a better look. Unable to hold her excitement any longer, she yelled, "Hello home. We're back. I'll never leave you again." A yank on her skirt brought India back down on the seat.

"Really, must you act like a child? Exercise some decorum." Mother scowled from the opposite seat. "It is unseemly and unladylike to shout."

India forced her expression into as neutral an attitude as she was able. A fight with Mother would ruin the day. Seeing Papa after so many months and then getting away after luncheon to see Nanny Gordon would make coming home complete. Of her parents, Papa was the one who understood her best. They had a natural bond which she had never developed with Mother.

Strange how mother and daughter seemed so often at odds, but it had always been thus. Perhaps their differences lay in the fact that Papa and she had grown up in North Carolina away from the social demands of New York, while Mother had absorbed them in her cradle. It was Papa who had insisted on hiring a local woman as nurse to the infant India and the old mountain woman had been a solid rock in India's life ever since. She went to the little cabin near the border of the estate as often as possible. Every time she thought about how some families abandoned loyal servants once they were too old to work, gratitude to Papa swelled. Papa had restored the little cabin and made sure Nanny Gordon had a home for life.

***

Luncheon was laid shortly after their arrival, but India had little appetite. She ate a few quick bites, then pushed her chair back from the table. "I think I'm going to take Zara out this afternoon. I've missed our rides." The sanctuary she found in Nanny Gordon's cabin called, urging her to get away from Mother and her demands.

Mother looked up from the creamer poised above her coffee. "Don't think you are fooling me, young lady. We've been home less than an hour and here you are dashing off to see that old woman. Why you want to spend time with that illiterate creature is a mystery."

India's hands gripped the top of the dining chair until her knuckles were white. Fortunately, Mother did not notice the gesture. India forced calm into her voice. "Nanny Gordon has no family but me. She raised me and I'm returning the care she gave me as a child. It is the right thing to do."

"Perhaps but traipsing off at any excuse is beneath your position. What would Lord Kilnsey think of such behavior? Furthermore, she is not your family. She did not rear you. The very idea is ridiculous."

India's cheeks burned as she lifted a finger. "Personally, I do not care what high and mighty Lord Kilnsey thinks." While not entirely true, she would not let his opinions rule her choices. Lifting another finger to tick off her points, she continued, "Secondly, Nanny Gordon took care of me and made my childhood happy. If that isn't a definition of family, then I'm not sure I know what family is."

Mother threw her napkin beside her plate. "Really, you are a trial. I do not know why I bother. You are determined to be the wild mountain creature New York believes you to be."

"Oh, I think we all know why you bother, but I don't wish to waste time arguing. If you will excuse me…"

"I will not." Mother spoke as though India was still a small child. "Sit down. We have plans to discuss."

Maintaining the peace no longer mattered to India. "Surely your machinations can wait for an hour."

Mother's cup clattered in its saucer. "Do not be disrespectful…"

The sound of Papa's hand striking the table echoed through the cavernous room. "Enough. Both of you." He looked at Mother with a raised brow. "For God's sake, Petra. Let the girl be. If she wants to see her old nurse, what harm is there?" To India's surprise, coughing took control of his breathing. Between gasps, he dismissed her with a wave of his hand. "Go on. You and your mother can talk when you return."

The effort of speaking seemed to tax Papa's strength. India hesitated, torn between her desire to be away from Mother and her concern for Papa.

He looked at her over his handkerchief and again waved her away. "I have a bit of a cold. It's nothing to worry about. Go see Nanny Gordon. It will do both of you good."

Before further argument ensued, India dashed to her bedroom and donned her riding habit. Although Mother would be scandalized if she knew, India wore a pair of boy's breeches under her skirt and rode astride at every opportunity. Once the skirt was removed and her hair was tucked up under a cap, people often mistook her for one of the grooms.

Striding into the stable, she did not bother to wait for assistance from the staff. Instead, she went into the tack room and grabbed Zara's saddle and bridle. At the sight of India, the little bay Arabian whinnied and pawed the floor of her stall. India wrapped fingers around the mare's halter and scratched the star on her forehead, then wrapped an arm around her neck. The mare rested her chin on India's shoulder.

Leaning her head against Zara's, India breathed in the sweet smell of hay and warm horse flesh. "My precious girl, how I've missed you. Let's get out of here." The mare stood quietly as India slipped on the saddle and bridle.

India led Zara to the mounting block and swung up into the saddle. Without encouragement, the mare followed the woodland path leading to the gardener's shed where India would leave her skirt. Once inside the shed, India went to the hook set behind the door and grinned. The cap was just as she had left it.

Transformed from proper lady to stable boy, India nudged the mare with her heels. All the disappointment and stress of the months in New York began to melt away with one niggling exception. She had promised herself she would not think about it further. After all, it was really Papa's decision to look into or not, but the question of Grandmother Jane's fate refused to be quiet. The closer she got to Nanny Gordon's cabin, the louder it shouted.

She jumped down and tethered Zara to the dogwood just outside Nanny Gordon's front door. Turning to look back at the terrain surrounding the estate, India delighted in the sweet breath of Appalachia - damp earth, pine, decaying leaves, and something she could not describe but which was always there. It smelled like green life that only grew in the mountains. That unidentified fragrance signaled she was truly home. India inhaled deeply as she tried to push Jane from her thoughts.

"Come on in." Nanny Gordon's mountain twang sounded through the door before India could even knock. "I knowed you wasn't gonna be long when I seen thay contraptions passin' on the road." When India entered the cabin, the old woman patted the armchair next to hers by the fireplace. "Come sett here by me so's I can git a good look at you. You been gone too long."

The pair sat with heads together for the next thirty minutes while India described all she had experienced in New York. Nanny Gordon had never ventured farther than Pisgah, the village near the estate, but that did not mean she had no knowledge of the wider world. She was especially adept at analyzing human nature.

Nanny Gordon drew on her corncob pipe and blew out a stream of tobacco smoke. "So, you had your heart broke. Glad to see you ain't married to the next feller who asked.

It's best you come home. There's plenty of good menfolk 'bout these parts."

India couldn't hold back a chuckle. Nanny had done her best to make India into a native mountaineer and she had nearly succeeded until the governesses started arriving. The battles that ensued had been epic and were still legend in the servant's hall. Consequently, India held back the question that plagued her until she sensed the time was right. Nanny was not to be rushed or pushed into a confidence, even by India.

Marshaling her courage, she said, "While I was in New York, I heard something I found puzzling." She watched for Nanny's reaction.

The old woman cut narrowed eyes at her. "And what would that be?" Nanny was said to have the sight, to be fey in the parlance of her Scots-Irish ancestors. She clearly suspected India might be about to ask questions she did not want to answer.

"It was about Papa's mother." India stopped again to gage Nanny's reaction.

The old woman took a long draw on her pipe and exhaled. She surveyed India through the haze of smoke. "Well, what is it? Spit it out."

India swallowed and mustered courage. "What do you know about Jane? Papa rarely talks about her."

Nanny Gordon shrugged. "He was just a little 'un when she died, so nothing peculiar in that."

It was clearly going to take probing to get the information India wanted. She took the old woman's hand. "Please tell me what you know. Did you ever meet her?"

Nanny shook her head. "But I saw her one time. She was gettin' off the train in Pisgah. She come down here when the big house was just finished. Heard she told folkses she was here to make sure stuff was done right."

India blinked in surprise. Why had Nanny never shared this story? "Was Papa with her?"

"No, she was by herself."

Nanny Gordon was not making this easy and India's patience snapped. "There's something you're leaving out. I can see it in your face."

Determination hardened the old woman's expression. "Us help was always told not to talk about that time or we'd get fired or worse." Nanny discarded her pipe in favor of snuff. Placing a pinch between her cheek and gum, she seemed reluctant to meet her former charge's gaze.

India pressed on. "There can be no danger now. You can't stop there. I need to know about my family."

Nanny spat into a bucket beside her chair. After several beats, she replied, "Don't suppose no harm can come after all this time. It was your grandpa who didn't want the talk, but he's gone." Nanny leaned back in her chair, squinted, and looked up toward the rafters. "Your grandpa showed up a week after your grandma. They got on the train back up north the very same day. Folkses at the depot said Miz Jane was bawling her eyes out and that ole T.J. held her arm like she was gonna try to run off."

"Did anyone know why she was so upset."

Nanny shrugged. "No idea." Lowering her gaze, she looked at India through narrowed eyes. "What made you ask about her after all this time? You ain't never been interested before."

India spent a few minutes explaining what she had learned from Lady Clarissa, Mr. Rivers, and those engaged in gossip at her ball. Nanny Gordon turned away and stared into the fire. "Miz Jane is maybe alive. You don't say." After several beats, her gaze met India's. "I always figgered T. J. kilt her once they got back up north and that was why we'uns couldn't talk 'bout her." Shaking her head, she continued, "I swanny. He was a mean child and he warn't much different as a man. When we'uns heared she was dead, folkses did wonder. Guess I might owe the ole buzzard a apology."

"In what way was Grandfather T. J. mean?"

"He was a bully. He picked on weaker children when he was a boy, but he was smart and could charm bees out of their honey when it suited him. He liked being noticed, too. My pa said he'd most likely get rich one day if somebody didn't kill him first. Nobody was all that sorry when he moved up north." Nanny Gordon stroked her chin as she looked back up to the rafters. "Do you think them folkses was telling the truth?"

"I think they were telling what they'd heard and believed might be true. If Jane is alive, it seems strange she hasn't tried to contact Papa."

"That it do, but some women ain't very motherly, if you know what I mean."

India nodded. Indeed, she did understand exactly what the old woman meant.

After her final comment, Nanny Gordon refused to be probed further on the subject of Jane Ledbetter.

India glanced at the clock on the mantel. "I have just enough time to get back and changed for tea. May I come to see you tomorrow? I've missed you so much."

"Sweet girl, you know you can come as much as you want. You're my baby girl. Don't you never forget it."

A lump rose in India's throat as she embraced her old nurse in farewell. Spine and ribs pressed against India's arms as though only the thinnest covering of skin held them together. Nanny seemed so much frailer than when they had parted in the fall. The thought of The Falls without Nanny Gordon was unbearable. As India rode away toward the big house, she looked back several times to see the old woman watching and waving. No matter what Mother said, visiting every day would happen. Staying away was not to be borne.

India took the long route around the base of the mountain back to the big house. She needed time to process what Nanny Gordon had told her and to think about how to proceed with Papa regarding his mother. Should she pursue it with him or leave well enough alone? Would it be cruel to tell him his mother might be alive after a lifetime of thinking her dead or did he have a right to the information? It was hard to know what to do. Perhaps if she brought up the subject of Jane in a casual way, his reaction would guide her in understanding which course was best.

By the time India got home and changed, tea was already underway in the solarium. Through the enclosure's glass, she could see Mother and Papa engaged in what appeared to be a heated debate. India crept to the door as quietly as she could. Something in the way her parents were gesturing sent a spark of trepidation racing through her, pushing all thoughts of the Grandmother Jane mystery from her mind.

CHAPTER 14

India stood unobserved at the solarium entry, shielded by the potted palms standing sentinel on either side of the French doors. Of The Falls' many rooms, this was her favorite. With its wicker furniture, floral chintz cushions, dark slate floor, and ranks of potted plants creating the atmosphere of tamed jungle, it was an island of serenity year-round, but today its peace was disturbed by sharp words. Although they could not easily see her, India had a clear view of her parents through the lacy foliage. They sat facing the entrance as though they were both judge and jury awaiting India's arrival so they might decide her fate.

Papa's voice floated through the open doors. The late afternoon sun shone directly upon him, highlighting the peaks and valleys of a face grown noticeably thinner in the months of her absence. His bespoke suit seemed too large and his shirt collar stood away from his throat ever so slightly, yet the gap between his trouser hem and oxford revealed swollen flesh spilling over the edge of the shoe. As India surveyed her father, a lump formed in her throat, and for the first time, she noticed his labored breathing. While she had missed his presence in New York, she had not questioned too closely Mother's explanation of why he did not accompany them. Now she saw how wrong Mother had been. He had not feigned poor health to avoid leaving home. He was ill and must have been for some time, probably before she left for New York. Had he shown signs of illness? She searched her memory of those weeks back in the fall before they boarded the train north, but she couldn't remember seeing anything untoward about Papa. Of course, she had been so intent on her battles with Mother she had paid little attention to anything or anyone else. Shame and guilt washed over her. She had been too self-centered to even notice that Papa was growing ill.

He leaned forward and put his forearms on the tea table. "Petra, what you propose is unreasonable. The girl clearly doesn't care for the life you want to thrust upon her. Furthermore, you care far too much for other people's opinions." Papa paused, seemingly exhausted from the exertion of speech. "What harm is there in letting her stay at home?" Papa, who so often sought the path of least resistance, today humbled India with his defense.

Mother's eyes hardened as the color leached from her face. "What harm? Dear God, can't you see I am trying to ensure her future? If it were left to you, India would hide herself away behind the gates of The Falls never to emerge just as you've done. Had I known this would be my married life, I would have chosen differently."

Papa stared at Mother for several beats, then ran a hand over his eyes. "I suppose you still pine for David Havemeyer, especially now that he has risen so far. That he is one of the trustees of my father's estate never ceases to amaze." Weariness echoed in his voice. "Had I realized it would come to this, I might have chosen differently, as well, my dear. Nonetheless, I don't see the urgency where India is concerned."

"Mama and I, and by extension your daughter, have just been snubbed by the people who matter most, by the people who courted my family's favor only a generation ago. It is a situation that cannot go unchallenged."

Papa added milk and sugar to his cup and watched the liquid swirl as he moved the spoon. "I think I begin to see your true motives. If she can't take her place among the people who matter, as you put it, you are cut off as well." He stopped stirring and looked at Mother with tired eyes. "There's something I would like to know. Why did you not anticipate the situation?"

Mother's cheeks took on a rosy glow. "Mama thought her name and Lady Clarissa's support would be enough. We're eleven years into a new century, after all. Things are not as prescribed as they once were."

"You and your mother seem to put a lot of store in this Lady Clarissa. Exactly who is she?"

"Oh, Robert. Do you never listen?" Mother's voice took on a whining quality. "I've told you multiple times. She's the daughter of the Fourteenth Earl Kilnsey married to Jonathan Rivers, the investment banker. With her title and social connections and his wealth, they have established themselves among those who matter."

An ironic smile lifted the corners of Papa's mouth. "But apparently not enough to save India's ball. And now you want to drag the girl across the Atlantic. What if the same thing happens in London?"

"Lady Clarissa assures me it will not, but we must act now. She and her brother are…"

India had heard enough. She did not wait for Mother to finish. "Are what? I didn't want that wretched ball and I don't want to go to London. And as for Lord Kilnsey, he may seek a purse elsewhere." India smirked at Mother's wide-eyed expression. "Oh, you thought me so unworldly I did not understand his true motivation in asking to court me? Charlie Westmorland is a nice enough fellow when he chooses to be, but he's not for me." Actually, Charlie was nice and India had enjoyed the attention he paid her, but she certainly would not admit it in present company.

Mother's lips thinned before she snorted. "Let me remind you, dear girl, of the terms of your grandfather's will. If you ever wish to see a dime of your own, the trustees must approve your choice of husband. Oh, you would have an income sufficient to live modestly, but the bulk will go to turn The Falls into a shrine to T.J. Ledbetter."

"I don't care about money or the ridiculous, outdated ideas of an old man whom no one liked."

"Oh you will, my dear, you will when you find out what life without money is. Money governs most of life's decisions as surely as the sun rules the day. Being without it can lead one to make decisions one regrets. Mark my words." Mother took a sandwich from the tray and dropped it on her plate. "Are you going to join us or continue to lurk in the doorway?"

Any hunger India might have felt fled under Mother's barrage of invective. "I'm going to my room until dinner. I want to read and rest. It's been a long day." She turned and headed toward the grand staircase with Mother's retort to suit herself dogging her steps.

Once in her bedroom, India reclined on her chaise trying to make sense of the latest best-selling novel, *The Window at the White Cat*, but she found herself rereading the same paragraph several times before its details registered. The novel, a purchase made on the sly in New York, contained all the elements of intrigue one could want - a murder, a disappearance, stolen valuables, and somewhat salacious settings - but it couldn't hold her attention. Papa's pallid face haunted her. That image pushed her to a decision.

Telling Papa the rumors of Grandmother Jane's existence at present seemed unwise. He clearly needed all of his energy to deal with the condition that was stealing his vitality. Besides, what purpose would it serve? If the woman was alive, she would have contacted them long ago if she had wanted to. Alive or dead, a search for the truth might end in one very real possibility, that Papa would feel the loss of his mother all over again. Best to let it go and leave well enough alone. Closing the book, India left her room and went to the balcony railing overlooking the foyer. No sounds floated up nor was there any movement below. Confident tea had ended, she made her way to the library where Papa spent most of his time.

She found him staring into the embers of a dying fire. Settling herself in the wing chair opposite his, she asked, "Would you like for me to put some logs on the fire? The room seems chilly."

He smiled and nodded. "I've missed our little chats. This house is hollow without you." He took a sip of amber liquid from a tumbler while he watched India over its edge. "And it will be again when you leave for England."

India's head snapped around, a log still in hand. "I thought you were on my side. Why have you changed?"

After placing the tumbler on a side table, he leaned forward and rested both forearms on his knees. "I am on your side, darling Child, but as much as I hate to admit it, your mother is right. I've given her arguments consideration and have concluded she's correct. We must prepare for your future in the best way possible. When I'm gone, you'll inherit a sizable fortune and I would like to know you have the right sort of man to protect you and your estate."

India dropped down onto the floor at Papa's feet. "And what makes you think the titled fortune hunters of Great Britain are such men?"

"Whatever you may think of your mother, she actually has your best interest at heart. Granted, she has her own motives, but your happiness is also a priority." He reached out and lifted her chin with a finger. "Go to England. Visit the museums. Go to musicals and the opera. Stroll in Hyde Park. Visit Regent's Park Zoo. It'll be a chance for a pleasant sojourn. London in spring is beautiful and it should help you forget those insufferable snobs in New York. If you find a young man who suits your fancy, all the better."

"Will you go with us?" India's voice held a small tremor.

"I'm afraid not. There are too many business concerns for me to be away for months on end."

"That's not true. You and I both know it." Her words were sharper than she intended. "What are you hiding from me? You seem unwell. What's the matter?"

He smiled and patted her shoulder. "Nothing in particular. I'm just getting old. Complaints come with age, I'm afraid."

"You're not telling me the truth. I can feel it. I won't leave when you're ill."

Papa sat back, rested his elbows on the chair's arms, and made a steeple of his fingertips. He tapped his lips a couple of times before replying, "If you want to make me feel better, go find a man who will take care of you. I'll rest better knowing you're settled. In fact, it is my wish that you go to London and let this Lady Clarissa introduce you to the right sort. Your mother, being the particular woman she is, will not allow anything less."

"But Papa, I can't bear the thought of leaving you like this."

He leaned forward, placed a hand on each of her shoulders, and searched her face, communicating through touch rather than words. After several beats, he kissed her forehead. "You have nothing to worry about. I'll be here when you return, with or without a husband in tow."

CHAPTER 15

Alighting from the train at Pennsylvania Station for the second time in less than four months had an otherworldly quality about it, one that pierced the calm veneer India presented as camouflage for her inner turmoil. Resentment had stirred the minute she boarded the train north and had not abated. She stepped down onto the platform, came to rest beside her trunks, and took in the sights, smells, and sounds of the cavernous arrivals hall. Steam and acrid coal smoke drifted to the iron rafters where the six-months-old glass ceiling was already showing signs of grime. The hall rang with the sounds of locomotive brakes, the chuffing of idling engines, luggage being loaded onto trolleys, passengers shouting to gain the attention of redcaps and chauffeurs, and the general bustle of a busy terminal. Nothing was unusual or out of place, but even so, India's fingers tapped against her handbag in anxious anticipation.

Once she and Mother were settled in the hired limousine, India's head swiveled from side to side taking in the buildings as they traveled south on Fifth Avenue. The drive to Washington Square should by now feel as familiar as the drive from the Pisgah depot to The Falls, yet nothing felt as it should. The buildings themselves looked no different, but India sensed something within the beating heart of the city had altered since her departure only three weeks ago. She peered at the mansions of people that Grandmama once counted among her fast friends. Not a stone had been added or taken away from the stately structures. In truth, nothing was different. It was not the city that had changed.

Maybe her feelings of disorientation arose because she no longer understood the girl who inhabited her body. As a younger version of herself, allowing Mother to dictate her comings and goings had not felt unusual or out of the ordinary, but now she chaffed at the heavy bit forced upon her as though she were an unruly filly. Being led first to New York, then kicked into running back to The Falls, now jumping hurdles back to the city for one night so they could board an ocean liner the following morning had taken on the feel of a steeplechase. This race was not of her choosing, but she had submitted to it because Papa had asked her to. She dropped her head against the top of the seat. Gazing at the ceiling's fabric covering, she allowed tears of frustration to roll down her throat.

There was disquiet growing within India, an unwillingness to be pushed and prodded by other people's expectations and desires. This trip and all the trappings associated with a London season were beginning to feel like a colossal mistake. She wasn't ready to get married. She didn't want to live anywhere but The Falls where she could ensure Papa got the best of care. Why had she allowed her parents to manipulate her into this looming disaster? It was time she made her own decisions and lived life on her own terms. The trustees could control the damned money and have joy of it. She would always have a home wherever Papa was. She would convince him to give her the tuition for

Davenport in Lenoir. She would study art and develop the talent her governesses had always praised. In addition, she would get a teaching degree. She would pursue her dual passions, art for herself and a school for the children of the poor. Mother would simply have to make peace with India's decisions as best she could.

India would abide by her promise to complete a London season, but that would be the end of Mother's tyranny. Her hands drew into fists and her nails dug into her palms as she visualized the future. A reckoning was coming. As the vehicle turned left onto Washington Square, a small smile played at the corners of India's mouth. She settled into the seat and felt tension lift. In the morning they would sail. The sooner she got the blasted season over with, the sooner she could get home to The Falls and begin her real life.

***

India pushed scrambled eggs around her plate, eying her breakfast without enthusiasm. Despite the self-made promise of last evening that all would be well, she had slept fitfully and awoke with a headache. Yesterday's confidence had melted and slipped away on the currents of an angst swollen river. It was all well and good to plan independence, but last night's dreams had been filled with an undefined foreboding that left her jumpy and cranky.

Picking up the sugar bowl, she dumped four overflowing shells into her coffee followed by enough cream to bring the liquid to the cup's rim. Coffee usually helped a headache and maybe the sugar would sweeten her temper. She lifted the cup carefully to her lips, sipped down half the contents, and returned it to the saucer all without spilling. There. That was better. It was a small task, but she had accomplished it with the right amount of finesse. It might be silly to take pleasure in something so trite, but India's confidence began to shyly show its face again. And what of last night's disturbances?

As she slathered butter and strawberry jam on a slice of toast, she reviewed her dreams and reached a conclusion. They had just been the creation of an overstimulated, tired mind, just vague night terrors that had no foundation in daytime reality. There was no reason to allow them to dictate her mood or intrude upon her thoughts. Furthermore, as long as she had to board the blasted boat later today, she might as well make up her mind to enjoy life abroad ship and all the delights that London had to offer. Taking up her cup again, she hid a grin behind it. Indeed, Mother might well come to rue the day she planned this little jaunt.

Movement at the door caught her attention. The butler glided over the parquet flooring with a self-important air and a silver salver in his hand.

"Thank you, Spenser." Grandmama turned over the envelope he offered. "It's from Lady Clarissa." Placing pince-nez on the bridge of her nose, she tore it open and read the enclosed note. "Yes, that will do nicely." Looking at Mother, she smiled. "Please pass the salt."

India's eyes narrowed. "Well?"

"Well what, my dear?"

"Aren't you going to share the contents?"

"Oh, it's nothing to be concerned about. In fact, she says all is well in hand." A look of satisfaction passed between Grandmama and Mother.

They were plotting again. India could see it. "What is it she has in hand?"

Grandmama's smile appeared somewhat disingenuous. "Why, the details of your debut, of course. What else would Lady Clarissa have to communicate? London should be especially exciting because of the coronation in June. I almost envy you the experience." Placing the note beside Mother's plate, Grandmama continued, "I do hope you enjoy sailing on the Lusitania. It's such a shame the Mauritania is still disabled as a result of last month's crash. As the faster vessel, Mauritania would have arrived earlier, giving you time to rest before the first engagement. Ah well, that cannot be helped. At least you were able to book a suite at the Savoy on short notice." She looked pointedly at the mantel clock. "Goodness, is that the time? You must hurry, my dears, if you are going to get to the dock before the onslaught of the usual riffraff."

India watched Mother jump to her feet and dash for the morning room door. Within seconds, the tap-tapping of footsteps flying up the stairs echoed from the hall. India looked at her grandmother in disgruntled admiration. Nice job of deflecting and redirecting. It was a skill at which Grandmama excelled. Fortunately, she would not be going with them, so challenging her would be a waste of energy. India pushed back her chair and followed Mother to prepare herself for travel.

***

India leaned on the ship's railing and watched other passengers waving to people on the dock below. There were probably happy families down there sending off loved ones with sadness and maybe a little trepidation. Yes, two women were tabbing at their cheeks with handkerchiefs while waving vigorously. Lucky people to be so loved. She tried to follow the line of their gazes, but the objects of the women's devotion became lost in the crush along the railings.

So many people leaving home. Did any of them feel as she did? A smile played across her lips. Despite her initial reluctance to take this voyage, there might be an unexpected benefit. Five days at sea with no one they knew aboard, no one who would gossip about circumstances over which India had no control. No one who may have heard of T.J. Ledbetter, Grandmother Jane, or the Van de Bergs. It was a sort of freedom, one to be cherished before the onslaught of a London season.

India leaned out a little farther. Grandmama would be appalled by her posture, but then Grandmama was not here and Mother was nowhere in sight. She quelled the laughter that bubbled up. No need for her fellow passengers to think her demented even if they did not know one another and might never see each other again once they disembarked. Unable to contain herself, she stretched her arms wide, closed her eyes, and spun around until her head swam. As she teetered on wobbly legs, strong hands clasped her shoulders.

"Best be careful, Miss. We can't have passengers falling overboard before we even set sail." The voice was British and decidedly masculine.

Opening her eyes, she blinked until her head settled, then looked up. Her breath caught in her throat. She gazed into a pair of limpid blue eyes set in a dazzlingly handsome face. A tremor started in her toes and raced upward bringing warmth to her cheeks. The gold braid and buttons of his navy topcoat shone in the morning sun. His well-formed frame cast a long shadow. Greek gods came to mind.

Raising one brow, she asked, "And do you have passengers falling overboard mid-ocean, Captain?"

She couldn't tell whether her attempt at being coy had the desired effect. She had had too little practice in the art.

The gentleman smiled and released her shoulders. "Not once and it's First Mate. If you promise to stay away from the railing, I should return to my duties, Miss..." When India failed to answer, he raised his brows and tilted his head.

"Uh, Ledbetter. India. Miss." Well, that put paid to any hope she had of impressing. "Thank you for your help. I'm afraid my mother is probably looking for me." Ugh. Why had she mentioned Mother? He would think her not only unsophisticated, but callow as well. She extended her hand. "Nice to have met you. I'm sure we'll meet again."

He chuckled in reply. "I'm sure we will. Lusitania is a large ship, but even so, it's really a rather small world when one thinks about it." He bowed as he clasped her hand. "I hope you will enjoy your time with us."

"Yes, I'm sure we will. Well, goodbye." He nodded and turned away. He hadn't even told her his name.

She should have turned away also, but she remained glued in place watching his retreating back. The wool of his topcoat draped his shoulders as though the garment had been custom made. No doubt it had been. When he had gone about three yards, he stopped and looked at her over his shoulder. Was that an overly confident smile she detected? Did it matter? Giving herself a mental shake, a small plan sparked. Perhaps potential for a little fun lay in that retreating form. Delicious visions of Mother's shocked face danced before her mind's eye. Feeling rather wicked, India stifled a chuckle.

As crew members passed along the decks calling the all-ashore-going-ashore and the ship's horns rumbled, she sought a deck chair. Watching the ship glide past the Statue of Liberty was an experience she was determined to have. As she settled herself with a cushion and a lap rug, she caught sight of Mother trudging toward her with Lady Clarissa and Lord Kilnsey in tow. A crease formed between

India's eyes. So that was what Lady Clarissa had communicated to Grandmama. Very clever to have kept it quiet until the last possible second. A wicked smile played across India's lips. Well, she could play games, too.

CHAPTER 16

Clarissa dropped onto the sofa in their Regal Suite parlor, removed her shoes, and massaged her feet. "Why I allowed Mrs. Ledbetter to drag me the length and breadth of this wretched vessel until we found the girl is beyond me."

Jonathan turned in his chair at the desk, laid his pen on the blotter, and shot his wife a knowing look. "I believe we both know the reason. How did you find Miss Ledbetter? Was she pleased to see you and Charlie?"

Clarissa pursed her lips and shrugged. "In truth, she was not as overjoyed as one might have hoped. She wasn't cool per se, just not terribly enthusiastic. If I didn't know better, I would say Charlie's shine has dimmed somewhat."

Hearing his name, Charlie stuck his head around the door of his stateroom. "Sister mine, if you and India's dear mama weren't so obvious in your intentions to force an alliance, you might find that she is more interested than she lets on. India was simply being discrete and more power to her. No one likes being manipulated and I'm rather certain she's on to you."

Clarissa cast a cool gaze on her younger brother. "Perhaps her lack of enthusiasm should be laid at your door.

You could hardly be described as effusive upon greeting her."

A chuckle rippled across the room. Charlie waggled his brows. "Unlike her mama, I'm not given to overplaying my hand. You should consider doing the same. I'm beginning to realize there is more to Miss India Ledbetter than meets the eye."

"Perhaps. While she's less sophisticated than one might expect, she does seem to possess a certain innate intelligence." Clarissa pushed a cigarette into her carved ivory holder, lit it, and drew smoke deep into her lungs. Flicking ash into a crystal bowl, she fixed Charlie with a corrective gaze. "You have five days advantage over the competition. I advise you to use it wisely."

His eyes narrowed. "And I advise you to stop this secret vice of yours. What other woman of your position do you know who smokes cigarettes?"

"None, but there are more than a fair few who take laudanum in copious quantities. Now I ask you. Which is the greater vice?" When Charlie failed to reply, she continued, "Yes. That's what I thought. Take care of business, Little Brother. Too many people depend on your making a successful marriage."

Apparently chastened or perhaps irritated, Charlie stepped back into his bedroom and closed the door. Clarissa exhaled a stream of gray cloud, then ground out the tip of her half-finished cigarette with far more force than necessary. Was she doing the right thing by pushing Charlie toward a marriage that would ensure the estate's continuation for another generation? In exchange, he faced the very real possibility of a lifetime's unhappiness. The Ledbetter girl was sweet enough and certainly pretty enough, but these marriages of convenience too often produced, if not outright antipathy, at the very least a vague mutual tolerance, sometimes misery, all in the name of preserving patrimony.

Her gaze settled on her husband's back as he bent over some last-minute business correspondence. Papa had done his best in promoting her marriage to a wealthy American. She'd had a title, but no dowry. Titled Englishmen of her generation had found her wildly attractive, but not marriage material. How fortunate she was in Jonathan, a decent man who loved her. She could not have asked for a more devoted husband, but still, it might have been nice to experience marrying for love rather than necessity.

***

India glared at her mother from the depths of the armchair in her stateroom. "I was perfectly civil to Lord Kilnsey. Why must you always be so critical?"

"I am not always critical and you could have been more welcoming." Mother jabbed her index finger in the direction of India's frowning visage. "Anyone would think you were uninterested by the coolness of your greeting."

"And what makes you think I'm interested in Charlie Westmorland? Sometimes he can be an insufferable bore."

"Now see here, young lady. The trustees~"

"Yes, yes, yes. I know." India folded her arms over the space just beneath her breasts. "The trustees must approve my future husband. Perhaps that little issue can be circumvented. I may never marry. There is no reason why I must." Her tone sounded petulant, like that of a child asserting a confidence it might not feel.

"Good God, girl. Have you any idea what the life of a spinster is? Never invited to the dinners and balls that truly matter. Entertained only when absolutely necessary and only by those who are feeling charitable. As a woman, you will have very limited choices in this world. Better to learn that now. You are no more and no less than the man you marry."

"Oh, for heaven's sake." India's jaw clenched. She lost any hesitation she might have felt. "You speak as though we're still living in the Dark Ages. This is the twentieth century. Women hold jobs and go about unaccompanied. There is even great hope we will soon have the vote."

A smirk lifted one corner of Mother's mouth. "What would you know about women who have jobs? The majority are servants or work in conditions not to be envied. As to going about unaccompanied, only those of the lower classes do so. The vote? We will never have the vote, nor should we. Ladies are above sullying our hands with something so sordid as politics and the lower classes haven't the time or understanding. We must continue to work in cooperation with our husbands rather than compete with them."

India's face flushed. "I see. In your world, we never left and never will leave the Dark Ages. How disappointing and depressing. Please excuse me. I think I need to rest. I'm afraid I may not be a very good sailor. I'm feeling a little queasy."

"But we've not even left the harbor." All sudden concern, Mother rested the back of her hand against India's forehead. "Are you ill? Thank goodness you haven't a fever."

"Perhaps I'm just tired from all the rushing around we've done. Please, I just want to lie down for an hour or so." Anything to get rid of Mother. Her presence was suddenly intolerable.

India removed her shoes, stretched out on the bed, and closed her eyes. Presently, the door to her stateroom clicked shut. Opening one eye, she found herself finally alone. Her ruse had worked. She picked up her shoes and tiptoed to the door that opened from her bedroom directly into a passageway. When they were first shown to their suite, India had insisted she wanted the bedroom with the two twin beds because she wanted Althea available at all times rather than consigned to the servants' berths in third class. Mother had fumed and objected to this most unusual arrangement, but India had threatened to find a berth in third class unless she got her way.

Althea and Mother's maid had been dispatched to direct the storing of trunks they would not need during the voyage. The time was right. Easing the door open, she peeked into the hall. Deserted. Excellent. Delicious freedom lay just around the corner.

***

India once again leaned against the ship's railing. This time, she watched the Manhattan skyline glide past as Lusitania set her course east toward the northern Atlantic. The air coming off the water sent a chill through her. She pulled her coat closer and drew its fox collar up around her chin as a shiver traced its course down her spine. Despite the chill, returning to the lounge just on the other side of the glass felt too confining. Besides, what was a little discomfort compared to blessed solitude?

Within minutes, the sight she had been awaiting came into view. She gazed up into the enormous face and smiled. It could not be described as pretty, but it was certainly what an earlier generation would have declared handsome. The words inscribed on her base came back to India from childhood civics lessons.

Give me your tired, your poor,
Your huddled masses yearning to breathe free,
The wretched refuse of your teaming shore,

Send them, the homeless tempest tossed to me,
I lift my lamp beside the golden door.

"She's an inspiring sight, is she not?" India jumped and spun around to find Charlie smiling down at her. "I see we had the same notion. I wanted to come on deck at this point. I'm drawn to her like so many others. I feel she speaks directly to me."

India raised a brow. "I would hardly think of you as homeless or tempest tossed."

Surprisingly, what could only be described as a cloud passed over his face. "Perhaps not, but I am, after all, just a humble immigrant. And like all immigrants, I find her promise alluring."

She cocked her head. "You aren't exactly an immigrant either." Surely, he had no need of Lady Liberty's solace.

"Ah well, you have me there. I should have said traveler, I suppose. Still, no matter my condition, I find her magnificent."

No suitable rejoinder presented itself, so India turned back to the railing and craned for a final glimpse. If she ignored him, maybe he would go away.

He didn't take the hint. Loosening a button on his topcoat, he continued, "I'm finding the interiors of the ship somewhat overheated for my taste. Do you like your suite?"

She did not look at him, but simply replied, "Yes." She winced inwardly. How unmistakably rude.

He stood beside the railing for a few moments. "I believe I have intruded. Earlier, when you mentioned your desire to be on deck as we passed the statue, I did not realize you wished to be alone. Please forgive me." An edge colored his tone.

India glanced over her shoulder and nodded.

"Perhaps we will meet at dinner." Charlie bowed stiffly and left.

India watched his retreat from beneath her lashes. Pray she would not come to regret her behavior. Surveying the deserted deck chairs, she selected one and dropped onto it. Soon, a steward rushed out of the lounge with several lap rugs. The temperature would only become more frigid as they moved farther out to sea. Well, the cold be damned. This was a taste of freedom and she would relish it for as long as possible.

***

When the door to their suite slammed shut, Clarissa looked up from her novel. "I take it your promenade was not a resounding success."

Charlie glared at his sister and plopped down on the sofa beside her. "The little chit needs teaching some manners. She was insufferably rude."

Clarissa turned so she could assess her brother's mood. With a tight smile, she said, "I suspect India is stretching her wings a bit, trying on what is most likely her first ever taste of freedom. Be patient and work harder. Women have always fallen at your feet. This is a new experience for you. Let us hope it is also an edifying one."

Charlie broke eye contact and slumped deeper into the cushions. "India's not the only one who wishes freedom. Sometimes I think about just chucking it all and emigrating to Australia or New Zealand. I hear both have a great deal to offer."

A tingle of alarm sounded deep within Clarissa. It would be so like Charlie to do just that. "And what of the estate and the village?"

"I would say to hell with both, given the opportunity."

Clarissa sat forward, put her hand against her brother's chin, and forced him to meet her gaze. "You have a duty to the land and to its people. You cannot, you must not shirk your responsibilities."

Charlie jerked his chin free. "They're burdens I never asked for."

Warmth filled Clarissa's face. "No one ever asks to be born with the expectation of a title and entailed estate, but you owe it to previous and future generations to take up the task left to you." Her voice was hard and commanding. "You are Fifteenth Lord Kilnsey and as such, your position in the Dales is vast. Pick up the mantle that is yours by birth and be glad of it. I certainly would, had I been the first-born male."

Charlie's gaze hardened. "Perhaps it would have been better if you were."

"Wishful thinking is not helpful. India is in a position to solve all of your financial woes. Do your duty and see that she does."

Sometimes being born female drove her to distraction. Things would have been so much easier had she been the heir. It was tiring and frustrating to continually be called upon to remind her younger brother of his duty. Damn entails and damn tradition.

CHAPTER 17

India shivered despite the layers of lap rugs that passing stewards dropped upon her outstretched legs. The solitude was wonderful and much needed after this morning's encounters, but not at the price of frostbite. Her feet were becoming numb and icy needles tingled in her cheeks and nose. When she tried to rise from the deckchair, she stumbled on uncooperative feet until strong arms came to her rescue. She took in the navy sleeves of a ship's uniform. Gazing up into the eyes of the handsome First Mate, a blush crept across her cheeks. She prayed he mistook the cause of her high color.

A slight frown creased his brow as he withdrew his arm from around her shoulders. "I apologize for the familiarity, but it looked as though you were about to slip."

"Oh, no. Thank you. You saved me. It's perfectly all right. I would have certainly fallen without your help. Please do not apologize. Thank you." Babbling. Perfect. No doubt her performance now cemented his opinion of her as a naïve, unsophisticated girl. If this was how she was going to react to every handsome face, disaster loomed in London without doubt.

Humor lifted the corners of his mouth and danced in his eyes. "I admire your fortitude, but I really must insist that you come indoors. Your cheeks are quite red with the cold. We wouldn't want you ill from exposure. The temperature in the northern Atlantic can dip below freezing very quickly this time of year."

"Of course. Thank you for the warning Mr...." India paused and looked into his eyes.

"First Mate Samuel Goldman at your service." He completed her sentence and offered his arm. Together, they passed from the deck into the main companionway.

When they reached the grand staircase, he stopped and asked. "May I escort you to your suite or would you prefer a seat in the lounge?"

"There is no need. I'm sure you have more important things to do but thank you all the same." For no reason she could define, a sudden need to be by herself swept through India. Taking her hand from Mr. Goldman's arm, India smiled. "I think I will walk around inside. I feel the need for movement now that my feet are thawing."

He bowed slightly. "As you wish. Should you ever wish a guided tour of the ship, I would be happy to conduct it."

Surprised, India stammered, "That would be lovely. Thank you. Perhaps later in the week." As she watched him walk away, the thought of a guided tour in the company of such a charming, handsome man became an alluring prospect. It would provide a welcome diversion from the pressure of Mother's demands. For the present, she would do a little exploring on her own.

India stepped to the lounge entrance. Her eyes widened as her gaze swept over the enormous room. No New York hotel or mansion could boast a more finely appointed space. Gold brocade wing chairs were gathered around mahogany tables in groups of threes and fours. They sat atop a jade green carpet with a yellow flower pattern. All were surrounded by mahogany paneled walls and columns supporting a barrel-vaulted skylight that contained four stained glass panels, each representing a season of the year. Marble fireplaces anchored either end of the space and elaborate plasterwork unified the overall theme. Fashionably dressed ladies and gentlemen gathered in small groups, some reading companionably, others appearing to be conducting animated conversations. Despite the size and elegance of the room, it felt claustrophobic after the wide-open vistas of the decks. The fact that Lord Kilnsey and his brother-in-law sat at the far end of the room may have contributed as well to her need for escape. Facing him again for the third time in the space of a morning would be tedious, especially considering her coolness to him on the two previous occasions.

She backed away but not soon enough. Charlie had spied her and gave a curt nod before quickly returning his attention to a book. Oh dear. Perhaps she had overplayed her hand earlier. When she had seen that he and his relatives were taking the same ship, the feeling of being tricked and manipulated had made her edgy, suspicious, and more than a little angry. Then her behavior toward him as they passed Lady Liberty had been downright rude, but she truly had wanted to be alone. She needed time to prepare herself for what lay ahead and having Charlie thrust upon her at every turn was tiresome at best.

India sucked her lower lip between her teeth. She liked him. She really did. If only their respective families would simply leave them alone and allow their friendship to develop on its own terms, she would not feel the need to push him away but promoting Charlie Westmorland had become Mother's raison d'être. On the other hand, alienating him and his family was not something India really wanted to do. Lady Clarissa had promised to make her London season an easy success. While India didn't care about the success factor, read marriage proposal, she definitely liked the idea of something being made easy, especially after the stressful misadventure in New York. Should she approach Charlie and try to make amends? Probably not. Trying to make amends in full view of so many strangers was something she was not prepared to do. The muscles at the base of her skull tightened into a knot. The feigned headache had become reality, making returning to their suite a necessity. She would lie down and try to sort through her conflicted emotions.

She was across the grand entrance and nearing the passageway to the staterooms when she heard her name called.

"Are you avoiding me, Miss Ledbetter?" It was impossible to tell whether Charlie was serious or making a joke at her expense.

India squared her shoulders and plastered a smile on her face. "Whatever gave you that idea?"

"Perhaps seeing you turn away when you caught sight of me in the lounge?"

India's cheeks burned. She did not try to keep her irritation from showing. "I did nothing of the sort. I suddenly felt the need for rest before luncheon."

"I hope you are not becoming ill. Your mother said you had a headache and were resting in your stateroom."

"I am perfectly fine. Thank you for your concern. Is there something I may do for you?" My goodness, rude again, but she could not seem to control herself.

"I thought perhaps you might need an escort to your suite." His smile seemed tinged with condescension.

Never one to accept being patronized with good grace, India gave him a brittle smile. "That is most gallant of you, but I believe I can find my own way. Now if you will excuse me?"

"But I will not."

"Will not what?" Surely he could feel the heat of her displeasure and would leave her alone.

"Excuse you. You act as though I have offended you in some way. I will apologize if you will tell me what I have done. It will be a very long voyage if we're at odds with one another. Our families are determined to throw us together."

India studied his face for several beats. Perhaps it was not insufferable superiority she saw there, but something else entirely. Insecurity? Surely not, but it seemed a real possibility. The thought that Charles Westmorland, Fifteenth Earl Kilnsey would feel any form of intimidation in her presence surprised her beyond measure. Her irritation melted away replaced by a stab of guilt.

She stared at the floor before meeting Charlie's gaze again. "I believe it is I who should apologize. You have been a perfect gentleman while I have acted like a petulant child. I fear I have let Mother's rather blatant maneuvering bring out the worst in me. I find it all terribly embarrassing." She arched a brow and extended her hand. "Forgive me?"

He took the proffered hand and held it longer than necessary. "Of course. If I had to guess, I would say that you are not as thrilled to be on your way to London as your mother is."

"Oh my, does it show?" A hint of sarcasm clung to her words.

Charlie waggled his brows and grinned. "Only if one looks closely. I have observed in you what I believe to be a kindred spirit." He extended his arm. "Will you take a turn with me before you return to your suite? I wish to have a sincere conversation with you, if you will permit it."

India accepted his arm, and he guided them toward the doors leading to the promenade. Although she still felt the effects of having been in the cold too long, she was intrigued by what he might say. Once they were on the deck, she asked, "Kindred spirit? How so?"

"I, too, do not wish to be flung into the London social season."

India arched a brow. "And what would you rather do?"

"In truth, I would return to Kilnsey and marry a local farmer's daughter."

India blinked as she stopped and snapped around to face Charlie. "I hardly know what to say. Why do you not marry the girl and live happily ever after? Does your family object to her being from a lower class?"

"Perhaps not as much as to her lack of dowry."

India gulped. "Your honesty overwhelms me." Her eyes narrowed. "As long as we are being frank, I must say that your request to call on me is now cast in a rather unflattering light."

"And for that, you have my abject apologies. My sister, our mother, the estate workers, and the villagers all have expectations of me that I find a burden, but I have come to the realization I can no more abandon the people who depend on me than I can turn tin into gold. I see my duty and accept it, no matter the personal cost."

"And what of the girl you love? Does she return your affection?"

"Most assuredly, but her father objects to our relationship, as well. To thwart us, he has put her into service in an Anglo-Irish house outside Belfast." A wistful expression played across his face. "No one wants us to be together but ourselves. I will probably never see her again."

India watched unhappiness cloud his eyes. These disclosures clearly pained him. "I'm humbled by such devotion to duty and saddened for your loss. The woman who eventually becomes your bride will be a lucky woman. If you feel so strongly for people who are not your kin, how much greater will be your devotion to your wife and children."

"Perhaps. Only time will tell but having accepted my obligation and the conditions it entails, I felt I should be completely honest with you regarding my situation. Our respective families have expectations where we two are concerned. You are too nice a person to be led on and duped."

India took her hand from his arm. "While I appreciate your honesty, I'm stunned by it as well. You've made clear what I've suspected since we first met in New York. I hardly know how to respond." She searched for any plausible excuse to end this humiliating and embarrassing conversation. "I really must go. Please excuse me. Mother has ordered a late luncheon which will be served shortly."

"Certainly. The suites' private dining rooms are a convenience, are they not?"

"Indeed."

"Will you be taking dinner in the main dining room this evening?"

"I believe so."

"I have a request before you go."

India peeked at him from beneath her lashes. "Pray, what might that be?"

"That we be friends and allies. It will make our situations much more tolerable if we face our relatives as a united front. In that way, we will be able to forestall their attempts at manipulation." He extended his hand. "Will you make a pact with me?"

Hardly knowing what to say, India looked toward a spot above their heads and stared as though the crown molding running the length of the walls was of the greatest interest. The swirls, curlicues, and figures created an intricate pattern that seemed to move with a life of their own. The more she studied the details, the more they mesmerized her. Or maybe her mind was simply finding escape from her conflicted emotions as best it could. She blinked once then twice. It had to be her imagination run amuck, but she could have sworn a tiny angel in the detailing winked at her. The prospect of Charlie Westmorland as ally and co-conspirator suddenly became very appealing.

She nodded and extended her hand. "I think that's a good idea. We'll circle the wagons and face the enemy as one. You've got a deal."

Charlie's eyes widened as he took her hand. "You really are a remarkable young lady, you know." Tucking her hand under his arm, he continued, "For the present, I think we should return to the warmth before frostbite sets in."

Once inside, he raised her hand and brushed it with his lips. A small twinkle lit his eyes. "Until this evening, then."

He bowed and left her to find her own way down the grand staircase to the B deck where the first-class staterooms and suites were located. As she crept into her bedroom, India's head spun with all he had revealed. One might suppose she should feel gratitude for his being so forthright, but the emotion that swam through her muddled brain felt more like anger. It was not directed at Charlie, however. He was as much a victim of others' machinations as she. In reality, who was to be more pitied - Charlie for being in the position of having to place himself and his title on the auction block or she for being forced into a life she did not want? Perhaps the answer would be revealed once the London season had been completed.

CHAPTER 18

On the fourth afternoon at sea, India sat alone in the library with a book that did nothing to hold her attention. Resting her elbow on the arm of the chair, she put her chin on the upturned palm and stared through the window at the rolling Atlantic. Shades of gray colored the world outside Lusitania - gun metal gray water, lead gray horizon, battleship gray sky. A shiver ran over her. She snuggled into her wrap and scooted her chair closer to the fireplace. Despite the weather, India smiled. She cherished these infrequent moments of solitude.

Mother, thank goodness, had felt the need of a nap, not having been content the evening before to leave India with Lady Clarissa' party in the ballroom where the first-class passengers gathered after dinner for music and dancing. This voyage was proving more diverting than anticipated for there were several young men aboard who sought India's company each evening. The memory of Mother's face when First Mate Goldman asked for a waltz filled India with malicious glee. And bless Charlie, for he had handed her off to Mr. Goldman before anyone could object, winking at her when no one else could see.

They were becoming friends, a condition that worked well for both of them. The stress of other people's expectations no longer overshadowed every minute of their time together. Without it, Charlie was proving a kind, considerate companion who was also good fun. She, in turn, listened to his heartbreak over his lost love and offered sympathy and compassion. They championed one another's causes when their relatives tried to interfere. Their three-day-old pact was working out well and India prayed it would last beyond the voyage as he had promised. She needed a friend like Charlie for what lay ahead. He was warm, true, and above all, steady and calm. With the clouds of emotional turmoil that hovered around Mother, the famous British stiff upper lip and calm restraint were a most welcome change.

Stiff from sitting in one position, India shifted in her chair, sending her book clattering to the floor. As she bent to retrieve it, a shadow fell across her lap and she looked up into Mr. Goldman's blue eyes. Her heart rate kicked up a notch. There went her uncontrolled reaction to male beauty again. With any luck, by the end of this voyage exposure to Mr. Goldman would help her gain some immunity to handsome faces. Of course, at the rate she was going it seemed a distant goal. She couldn't stop the broad smile that parted her lips and crinkled the corners of her eyes.

He smiled in return and bent slightly at the waist. "You look rather forlorn all by yourself on this gloomy day. I wondered if a tour of the ship would brighten things a bit."

While she hated that he thought her an object of pity, his invitation presented an opportunity for diversion. She mustered what she hoped was a confident, sophisticated attitude. "Why yes, that would be lovely. It's rather cozy here by the fire, but a little exercise might be welcome, as well."

Mr. Goldman offered his arm. "What would you like to see first?"

India cocked her head and narrowed her eyes. "I'm not sure...oh, wait. I know. Can I see the bridge? I would love to know how this big ship is steered. I've watched ocean liners glide up to the New York docks. The tugboats make it look so easy, but I'm sure it must take a lot of skill."

"Well then, the bridge it is."

India spent a pleasant hour with Samuel, as he requested she address him, learning about navigation and steering an ocean liner. It was all rather daunting when one considered the number of lives the captain and his crew had in their hands. As they walked toward her suite, Samuel pulled the hand enveloping India's elbow against the fine gabardine of his uniform jacket and laid his other hand atop hers.

Smiling down at her, he said, "You would make a good sailor. Have you ever considered a sailboat of your own?"

"I'm not sure why you think that but thank you. And no, we live in the mountains where the lakes and rivers are not suited to sailboats. It is an attractive thought, though. I've lived pretty much as my family dictated for my entire life. I'm ready for a little adventure." When Samuel directed humor filled eyes toward her, India's cheeks grew warm. "Perhaps I should not have said those things to someone I have known for such a short time. Please accept my apology." It seemed she found herself apologizing to every handsome man within shouting distance these days - first Charlie and now Samuel. Irritation with Papa for asking her to make this voyage and with herself for agreeing bubbled beneath the surface of what she hoped was a calm exterior.

He patted her hand and smiled. "You have nothing for which to apologize. You were simply stating facts. And don't worry that I will share your desires with others. Part of my job is to maintain absolute discretion where passengers are concerned."

As they walked down the main passageway to her suite, India stopped at the entrance to the small hallway leading to her bedroom door. "Thank you for a lovely tour. I hope to take your suggestion about sailing someday. I'm not sure when I will get the opportunity, but perhaps one will present itself. I would like to use my private entrance to our suite. It's just down this passageway."

"Of course. Whatever you wish."

At the door to her room, she took her key from her skirt pocket. Before she could insert it, Samuel held out his hand and said, "Please allow me." She gave him the key, but he did not put it in the lock. Instead, he spoke almost in a whisper, "I understand that your party and that of Mr. Rivers will be seated with the captain this evening. I have been invited to join the table. May I instruct the wait staff to seat you beside me?"

India did not answer for a couple of beats as though thinking it over, then smiled. "That would be lovely." As he slipped the key in the lock and opened the door, she stopped on the threshold just long enough to collect her key and then batted her lashes. "Until this evening." With a swish of skirts, she stepped into the room and closed the door.

Althea stood beside a trunk shaking out the dress India would wear to dinner. "So the lovely First Mate saw you to your door."

"He did. Is Mother still resting?"

"She is, but her maid says she is determined not to miss dinner with the captain, so you best be careful where Mr. Goldman is concerned. Your mother is none too pleased by the attention he's showing you. I overheard her tell her maid that she has a mind to complain to the captain."

"Just let her and she will regret it because I will speak on his behalf and get Charlie to do the same."

Althea's head snapped around and she gave India an appraising look. "Please tell me you haven't formed an attachment in so short a time."

India's eyes narrowed as an impish grin split her lips. "Not really, but Mother needs a lesson and I am going to give her one. She thinks she is going to rule my life as she always has, but Charlie has convinced me there are ways to deal with tyrants other than acquiescence."

"Hmmm. And what form will this defiance take?"

"I will be seated next to Mr. Goldman at dinner this evening and I intend to dance with him at every opportunity."

"And what of Lord Kilnsey?"

"Charlie will support me in this. In fact, we have made a pact to help one another survive the London season. He doesn't want to be involved in it any more than I do. We'll look out for one another and come to the rescue when needed. It will be most convenient. Then, when this gruesome season is over, I can go home to The Falls and Papa. I'll have done what he asked, but I cannot force a young man to ask for my hand, now can I?"

Althea raised a brow and pursed her lips. "You mean you plan to discourage any young man who shows the least interest."

India shot her maid a wicked grin. "Indeed. And there will be nothing Mother can do about it. The last thing she will want is a scene, but she will get one if she tries any manipulations in public."

"And when she explodes with you in private?"

"I'll simply refuse to be intimidated or cowed by her temper. Charlie says that I have the upper hand and I agree. He's a nice man who possesses great common sense and a firm grasp of social situations. He is exactly the kind of friend I need right now."

"So, he's a friend, is he?"

"Yes. He may prove to be a very good friend, indeed." India eyed her maid. "I need all of my friends to be on my side."

"You know I have always been and will always be on your side."

"Yes, you have and I'm grateful for all that you do." Plopping down on her bed, she scooted back against the pillows and opened her book. "I think I'd like to read until it's time to dress for dinner. I only have a couple of chapters left. Why don't you take the afternoon for yourself?"

Althea smiled and moved toward the hallway door. "That would be lovely. I'll be in the third-class lounge if you need me. Otherwise, I'll see you when it's time to dress for dinner."

***

India paused in the doorway to the first-class dining room and scanned the assembled crowd. The captain's table was where one might expect, in the center of the room under the stained-glass dome. Ah, good. Charlie and company were already seated, leaving only two seats unoccupied. Wishing to make a grand entrance as usual, Mother was still dressing when India left the suite. A flicker of guilt sparked at the memory of sending Althea to announce her departure. It had been cowardly, but India was determined to take her seat beside Mr. Goldman. As she approached the table, the gentlemen rose and Mr. Goldman pulled back a chair for her. It sat strategically between his own and Charlie's, who winked at her when she glanced his way.

When she was seated, Charlie tapped her arm and leaned in. "Mr. Goldman was most obliging when I requested the seat beside you. He seemed less pleased to seat your mother on his other side, but that, I am afraid, is the burden of leadership. It actually gives your mother one of the seats of honor beside the captain, as well, thus she cannot complain." He stopped and allowed his gaze to make a circuit of the table and grinned. "Yes, I believe this will prove a most entertaining evening. Are you ready to be swept off your feet?"

India smiled and nodded at the others around the table while she responded through clamped teeth, "Thank you for helping with the seating. Whatever do you mean about being swept off my feet?"

He chuckled before replying, "I fear I may have led the captain and Mr. Goldman to believe it is Mrs. Ledbetter's wish that her daughter not be left without dance partners during this final evening of the voyage. Mr. Goldman, good man, offered himself as tribute and the captain gave his blessing." Leaning just a smidgeon closer, he waggled his brows at her. "Personally, I think the first mate has taken quite a fancy to you, Miss Ledbetter."

Stifling a giggle, India raised a brow in reply. "Stop. You will make me blush."

"But surely there is no harm in that. You blush so charmingly. By-the-by, I see my encouragement has borne fruit. You came to the dining room unescorted this evening. Bold, my dear, very bold indeed."

"It is not a performance that will be repeated, I assure you. I'm certain there will be no opportunities for such once we have disembarked."

"Well, be that as it may, it is enchanting to watch this evening." A buzz rippled through the room and everyone's attention shifted to the entrance. Charlie whistled softly.

Out of the corner of his mouth he whispered, "You know, your mother is still a remarkably beautiful woman. I can see what you will look like in the future. You favor her so much. Your future husband will be a lucky man."

India drew back and eyed him coolly. "And what makes you think I will have a husband? I may choose to be a spinster." A crease formed between her eyebrows. "Given my parents' example, remaining unmarried has certain attractions. Mother is beautiful, but she is also difficult."

Charlie shot her a quizzical smile. "I sincerely doubt you would ever be difficult. You are much too nice. And as for becoming a spinster, that is the last future I see for you. No, you are going to make some lucky man very happy."

Before India could think of a response, Mother descended upon them and the gentlemen rose as a body. Giving Charlie a quick nod, India turned to engage Mr. Goldman. With amusement, she watched the conflicting emotions reflected in Mother's eyes - delighted to have the place of honor beside the captain and furious that India flirted with the first mate.

***

Clarissa put a hand on her brother's arm to prevent his leaving the sitting room of their suite. "During dinner, I noticed the girl spent far more time in conversation with Mr. Goldman than with you. I found that concerning for I am sure she has been taught the importance of dividing one's time equally among one's dinner companions. And then she danced almost exclusively with him. Take care, Brother mine, for you appear on the verge of losing this opportunity. There will not be another this attractive."

Charlie frowned at her. "I thought you liked India, but you speak of her as though she is a commodity to be traded, bought, and sold. I find that beneath you. In fact, it is rather disgusting."

"Find it disgusting if you like, but it is the way of the world. The sooner you accept that, the better for all."

Charlie's face flamed. "It is not the way of the entire world. There are millions of people who marry for love. Some do not marry at all. They go about their ordinary lives as the masters of their own fates, freely choosing with whom they spend their time."

Clarissa nodded and tapped his arm. "You have inadvertently put your finger squarely upon the issue. Your life is anything but ordinary. You were born to position and title. There are plenty of ordinary people who would gladly trade places with you. So, what do you plan to do about India?"

Charlie's mouth became a thin line. "I plan to be her friend. She's a jolly nice girl. I like her. She's been a good friend to me this week and I hope that will continue once we're in London." Shaking off Clarissa's hand, he continued, his voice harsher with each word. "Furthermore, I will not be party to her being hurt or humiliated - not by her mother or by you. Excuse me. We all have an early day tomorrow."

As she watched Charlie storm off, a smile lifted the corners of her mouth. He might think it was friendship, but to Clarissa it had the hallmarks of a budding romance. His need to defend the girl and to protect her from undue influence were very telling. Even more so was the anger that rang in his words. Yes, her little brother might not realize it, but he sounded more like a lover than a friend.

***

From the comfort of her bed India watched Mother pacing her stateroom. The woman had worked up a head of steam and was on the verge of blowing. India allowed herself a small smile when Mother's back was turned. Before they set sail, she would have been at least a little in awe of Mother's temper, but something had shifted this week and she had Charlie to thank. He had asked a simple question that had made all the difference. It caught her off guard while opening her eyes. He had asked what was the worst that could happen if India did what she wanted instead of what Mother dictated. After a time of reflection, the answer had been a revelation. Nothing. Absolutely nothing, if she discounted the tantrums to which she would learn to close her ears.

Mother rounded on India. "And just what did you think you were doing dancing all night with the hired help? Have you no consideration for our position? There were people marking your behavior who we will see again in London. And believe this, my girl, they will be only too happy to spread the tales until no respectable man will be interested."

India arched a brow and tilted her head. "That might have been true when you were young, but this is a new century. Men appreciate a woman with spirit, one capable of making her own choices. Lord Kilnsey says today's men appreciate a modern girl." Having delivered the coup de grâce of invoking Charlie's name, India waited with interest for the rejoinder.

Mother's eyes actually bulged while her cheeks turned a bright shade of puce. Shaking her index finger, she said, "I simply do not know what has gotten into you, but whatever it is, you better have it under control by the time we disembark tomorrow. And as for Lord Kilnsey, I assure you he was simply saying what he thought you wanted to hear." Mother paused and huffed before continuing, "You may as well know I am beginning to think we might do better than an earl of lesser standing. After several enlightening conversations with English passengers, I think we are in a better position than I first thought. This being the coronation year, all of English society will be gathered in

London and you very well may be the last heiress to cross the Atlantic for some time. The other passengers talked about you like you are an American princess. Play your cards right and you could be a duchess one day."

India blinked. Charlie was losing some of his shine with Mother. Apparently, she was setting her sights much higher. Well, there was only one way to deal with this. "I am not a princess and I do not want to be a duchess. I will keep my promise to Papa to endure this season, but I do not intend to marry unless I want to."

The door rattled in its frame with the force of Mother's departure. A trickle of satisfaction drifted through India as she snuggled down beneath the duvet. She could get accustomed to the independent life.

CHAPTER 19

After the freedom of the ocean voyage, India found the trip aboard the express train from the Cunard docks on the Wales coast rather confining. She had expressed disappointment to Mr. Goldman that they would not be docking at Southampton. He had explained that disembarking Lusitania's and Mauritania's passengers at Fishguard and then putting them on a special train via the Great Western Railway afforded the quickest and most direct route between New York and London. So, here she was speeding through the English countryside.

The views flashing past her window were lovely but did not hold her interest for her mind was filled with dread at what lay ahead. India rolled her head from side-to-side while she considered the choices she had made and those that had been thrust upon her. If it weren't for Charlie's promise of support, she might have refused to get off the boat. There was really nothing keeping her from booking passage home other than her promise to Papa to give the London social season a chance. Oh, and also the fact that she would have to wire Papa for the money. And then there was Charlie's plea that she not desert him in his time of need. He claimed to have grown dependent upon her counsel and sympathetic ear where his lost love was concerned. In fact, Lady Clarissa had hinted that until his friendship with India restored his equilibrium, she had once despaired, fearing her brother was falling into melancholia. It was not a responsibility India exactly welcomed, but it was one she accepted. Charlie was a good fellow, and she liked him.

A feeling of lethargy produced by the stuffy atmosphere of the carriage settled over her. She drew a deep breath, but still felt as though she was suffocating. Apparently, her Cunard hosts believed all Americans wanted the heating set to boil. Rising from the horsehair upholstered seat, she stepped to the window and lowered the sash. A blast of winter air stung her cheeks and eyes and elicited a gasp as it filled her lungs, reawakening her mind and restoring her spirit. That was much better. She caught the eye of a passing cow. Feeling impish, she winked at it. It winked back. The sound of her laughter whipped away on the wind. If she was to live the next months dancing to other people's tunes and putting their wishes before her own, then by God she was going to do whatever necessary to enjoy it. Since she was forced to endure this temporary exile from home and hearth, she would make the best of it.

The sound of the compartment door sent her wheeling around, fearing that Mother was descending. Instead, she found Althea with a conspiratorial smile parting her lips. "Lady Clarissa sent me to ask if you will join her in her compartment. She wants to talk about London. Mrs. Ledbetter is with her."

India grimaced. "Oh bother and I was just beginning to enjoy this train trip." Rolling her eyes, she continued, "I suppose now is as good a time as any to learn their battle plans."

Althea chuckled and nodded. "Yes, better to know what the enemy has in store."

India made her way through the carriage passageway by squeezing between passengers attempting to pass in the opposite direction. With windows lining the passage's entire outside wall, it seemed demented that someone had not opened at least one of them. Taking a handkerchief from her skirt pocket, she dabbed her forehead and upper lip. The train seemed uncommonly crowded, but then her experience of train travel was her father's private car so perhaps her perception was somewhat altered. Thank goodness the compartment she sought was only a few doors from hers. Pausing just out of view of its occupants, she spied her mother and Lady Clarissa deep in conversation. Lady Clarissa appeared calm and in control as was her norm. Mother's face glowed red and her eyes flashed with temper. India breathed deeply before stepping into full view of the others. As soon as they perceived her presence, they beckoned her enter.

Mother grabbed India's arm and pulled her onto the seat. Tears shining in her eyes, she fairly shouted, "Lady Clarissa has just shared the most appalling news. I hardly know how to tell you."

India braced herself. So, it was going to be one of those days. "Tell me what has you so upset. I'm sure it can't be as bad as you think." In truth, it never was.

Mother sniffed and looked aggrieved. "You will not be presented at court. King George's coronation is planned for June and Lady Clarissa says it is just too complicated to get an unknown American presented this year. This is a disaster. All of our efforts will be for naught."

India couldn't help it. She laughed without thinking. Covering her grin with a hand, she said, "Is that all? It's not as though someone died. I'm sure there will be plenty of parties to attend even without the royal seal of approval."

"You really don't understand, do you? This means you will be cut off from the most important members of English society. Only the lesser nobility will make our acquaintance." Wringing her hands, she hiccoughed. "Oh, what are we to do?" She must have realized the insult to Charlie for she cast an apologetic glance at Lady Clarissa. "Your brother is, of course, not included among the lesser peers."

India glanced at Lady Clarissa. She wore a completely bland expression. Sensing neither encouragement nor discouragement, India rolled her lower lip between her teeth before she spoke. "We will do whatever Lady Clarissa deems important. She has promised to shepherd me through this dreadful season. I do not mind in the least not going to court."

"You are so ungrateful. I have tried to create the best path into society for you since the day you were born. But for your father's request that you come to London, you would have thrown all my efforts in my face."

Before India could reply, Lady Clarissa leaned forward and covered Mother's hand with her own. "Now my dear Mrs. Ledbetter, do not despair. Your daughter is correct. There will be many opportunities to meet eligible young noblemen even without a court presentation. Please leave the details to me. I assure you all will be well."

***

Clarissa watched her brother enter her compartment and stroll to the windows. Dropping down onto the seat opposite her, he raised a brow and nodded. "Well played, Sister dear, well played. I must say your ability to manage people and situations is beyond any I have observed. Your handling of India's mother was positively masterful."

A small smile lifted the corners of Clarissa's mouth. "I know not of what you speak."

He chuckled and nodded again. "Oh, yes you do. I had a chance meeting with India in the passage. She told me about the little contretemps that has just transpired in this very compartment. So, there is to be no court presentation?"

Clarissa wilted a little with a spark of shame. It had been underhanded of her to trick India's mother into believing a court presentation was not possible. It was out of character for her to be so devious, but the stakes were simply too high to allow error. "No. We cannot risk it. I am beginning to sense that India's mother may be cooling to you in hopes of an even grander title. Is the girl terribly upset about the presentation? She didn't seem so at the time. In fact, she laughed about it."

Charlie chuckled. "Far from it. She is greatly relieved. It is her greatest wish to get this season over with and return posthaste to the wilds of North Carolina."

Clarissa was quiet for several beats. "Then you had better work fast to change her mind. Your future and that of Kilnsey depend upon it."

***

After four hours aboard the train, Wales to Paddington, the twenty-minute taxi ride from the station to the hotel was even worse. The smoke of industry and coal fires mixed with the fog coming off the Thames created a choking gloom. It was only 4:30 in the afternoon, but the streetlamps were already shining. Unfortunately, their efforts were mostly for naught. Their beams created circles of illumination around their bases but could not breach the dark beyond two or so feet.

From the Strand, the taxi turned into a short lane leading to the hotel's entrance. Walls of windows overlooked Savoy Court on three sides with the hotel entrance in the central position. On the gable end of the porte-cochère, the hotel's name blazed in a simple, modern script backlit by electric lighting. Mother chose the Savoy over Claridge's and Grosvenor House for its electric lighting, dependable hot and cold running water, electric elevators, and en-suite bathrooms. Just because they were staying in London did not mean that they must endure the inconveniences the English appeared to accept without complaint. The Savoy was the newest and most luxurious of the great hotels, specially built to appeal to an American clientele and Mother would have nothing less.

They alit from the taxi and made their way into the hotel lobby followed by bellmen pushing and pulling numerous carts transporting their luggage. While Mother dealt with the details of their stay, India looked about the space. Potted palms and torchieres were scattered about the lobby as were strategically arranged chairs and tables whose occupants could not only carry on conversations but could also keep an eye on who might be checking in or out.

India saw no one they knew. She had lost sight of Charlie and his party after they said goodbye at Paddington, agreeing to meet again once they were all installed and settled in their suites at the Savoy. Charlie had been embarrassed when he explained he and his relatives would be staying at the hotel, as well. Their London townhouse had been sold upon his father's death to pay debts and death duties, so a hotel was the only option.

Her gaze swept over the area once more and then jerked to a stop. At the far end of the lobby near a service door, she saw a most curious sight. Charlie stood speaking in great animation with a uniformed maid. He towered over her and had one hand on her upper arm. With the other, he gestured emphatically. The girl had her body turned partially away as though she were trying to flee.

Now what business could the Fifteenth Earl of Kilnsey possibly have with a chambermaid?

CHAPTER 20

Charlie must have felt India's eyes on him for he turned, meeting her gaze with sad, haunted eyes. Taking advantage of the distraction, the maid jerked her arm from his grasp and slipped away through the service door. The expression on his face dissolved into one of neutrality without the usual good humor India had come to appreciate. If ever a man looked like he was trying to hide being gut punched, it was Charlie. Whatever the maid had said to him clearly left him shaken. Should she go to him or leave him be? He did not move, but merely continued to stare. After hesitating for a couple of beats, India made a decision.

Holding his gaze, she crossed the lobby with as much haste as possible, but not so hurried as to draw attention. When she reached Charlie's side, he seemed to wilt and to be on the verge of fainting.

Alarmed, she took his hand and led him to an alcove where two chairs were strategically placed, partially concealed behind potted palms. "Whatever has happened. You look positively ill."

He leaned his elbows on his knees and looked up at India through the forelock that had dropped down over his eyes.

"I'm sure you saw the girl I was talking with." India nodded. "She is sister to Annie, the farmer's daughter whom I love. Apparently, Annie was not sent to work in an Irish house after all. Oh, she went to Ireland all right, but it was to marry a distant cousin. It seems she is with child - my child. I'm sure of it." His voice quivered with emotion.

India blinked several times before looking away. What does one say in such shocking circumstances? She could not stop a blush creeping across her cheeks. No gentleman should speak of such an intimate subject with an unmarried lady. It must be a testament to his trust in their friendship that he felt he could do so. At any rate, the depth of his distress was clear and that may have pushed all propriety from his mind.

Her cheeks burned with thoughts of his revelation. Expressions of deep emotion always caused discomfort, probably because she had such little experience with it. Mother always frowned upon expressing anything other than what was socially acceptable and polite. She had not been allowed to cry even as a small child. It took a moment to reach a decision, but it seemed that speaking truthfully would be most helpful. "Did the sister say when the baby is due?" His eyes grew wider as he shook his head. "You've been away from England for months now. How can you be so sure the child is yours?"

Surprise filled his eyes followed by resignation. "I suppose my feelings are based in hope, but I can't really know with any assurance. I thought perhaps her husband would reject her if he thought the child was not his and she would come home to me. I would certainly do the honorable thing. I will always love her."

"Always is a very long time. Wouldn't it be best to try to forget her and the child? Maybe if you participate in the season with that intent, you will find the distraction you need."

"Easy for you to say. You've never had your heart shattered."

The irony made her want to laugh or cry or maybe both. Although she did not want to admit it, Billy had broken her heart. She had thought he might be the one. Her pain was certainly not the depth of Charlie's, but she had been hurt, nonetheless. She gathered herself and took a firm grip on her emotions. "I can understand why you might think that, but I have had my share of disappointment. Of course, my pain in no way eliminates yours. What can I do to help?"

A smile tinged with sadness drifted across his features. "Be my friend. You're so easy to talk to, not like the girls I'm expected to mingle with. In fact, you are unlike anyone I've ever known. Our society debs would never consider sitting unchaperoned in a hotel lobby with a man pouring out his heart. You don't seem to care what other people think."

India wasn't sure whether he had just complimented or insulted her. She studied him for a few seconds. Seeing his pain was still so fresh, she reached out and put her hand over his. He grasped it as though it was a lifeline and he a drowning man. Perhaps he was drowning, adrift and sinking in a sea of longing for what he could now never have. An emotion that felt a lot like protectiveness swelled within India. Although Charlie was a good five years older, at the moment it felt like she possessed the greater age. Giving his hand a squeeze, she said, "Of course I will be your friend. I *am* your friend and have been for some time now. From now on it will be you and me against the world."

His smile was warmer this time. "Yes, that is what we will be. India and Charlie *contra mundum.*" He sat up and shook himself like a dog ridding itself of water after a thorough soaking. "I've kept you here long enough. Please forgive my wallowing in self-pity. I promise to buck up and not embarrass you further with unseemly displays. All the same, thank you for letting me cry on your shoulder."

"You did not embarrass me." She ran her hand over each shoulder and grinned. "And my shoulders are quite dry, but if you ever need one, it will be available."

He stood and extended his hand. "Let me see you to your room. You must be tired after rising early. I believe your first social engagement is less than four hours away."

Feeling suddenly less confident, India asked, "Will you be there?"

Charlie drew her hand into the crook of his arm. "Of course. Remember, it's India and Charlie *contra mundum*."

***

Clarissa drummed her fingers on the armchair in her suite. Where could that feckless boy be? The last she had seen of him, he was crossing the Savoy lobby going God only knew where. He had a demented look just before he dashed away. Something or someone must have caught his attention in the most alarming way. Charlie was going to be the death of her. She seemed to care more about the estate than he did. Perhaps she should just let it all go, but Kilnsey was her childhood home and she couldn't abide the thought of it going under the hammer. She couldn't bear an inch of its land being sold. If only she had been born a boy, none of this worry and maneuvering would be necessary. If only their father had been a better manager. If only, if only. It was enough to make a person lose her sanity, or at the very least, her patience.

The knob twisted on the door connecting the suite to the hallway. Thank goodness. "Where have you been? What sent you scurrying into that mob in the lobby?"

Charlie looked at her with a grim expression. "I saw Annie's sister. I had no idea she had been sent to work here. I had to speak to her." With that, his mouth snapped shut, and he slumped into the chair opposite hers.

"And what has that to do with your present mood?"

After Charlie's recitation of his lost love and the baby on the way, Clarissa cast an appraising gaze over her brother. "You, my boy, have had a lucky escape. Fortunately, Mrs. Ledbetter and her daughter will not hear this story until it is too late. Thank goodness your paramour's father had the good sense to send her out of the country."

Charlie shot her a scathing glance. "I have already told India."

Fury shot through Clarissa. "You fool. That girl will never consider you now."

"You completely underestimate India. She is kind and considerate. She shows compassion for those who need it. In fact, you are doing her a considerable disservice. I refuse to discuss her with you from now on. I am going to my room until it is time to leave for whatever occasion is on offer tonight. Where is it we're going?"

"To Lady Brisbane's dinner and musical soiree. I believe she has engaged a soprano whose star in on the rise at Covent Garden. The Ledbetter's are to accompany us." Attempting a soothing tone, she continued, "Jonathan has hired a limousine, so there will be room for all of us. I hope you will take this opportunity to establish your position as India's primary suitor. Lady Brisbane is an inveterate gossip. Word will spread before the last notes of the evening have faded. It will really be for the best and will forestall any further erosion of your standing with India's mother. I have only your future in mind."

Charlie cast a cool gaze upon his sister. "As I said, I will not discuss India or our relationship. Rest assured, however, I will keep her best interest at heart as she has promised to do for me. We will face this wretched season together and find what happiness there may be. She is a good person and even better friend. I will not have her manipulated and prodded into situations that will lead to her unhappiness."

Clarissa watched Charlie's retreating back. That was quite a speech for a man who feigned disinterest and no romantic designs.

***

India stopped in the doorway to Lady Brisbane's Mayfair drawing room and took a deep breath, then exhaled slowly. The butler held their cards at a distance greater than probably needed for reading, cleared his throat, and announced their arrival with great solemnity. It was as though he sensed this evening held importance beyond a mere dinner and evening of song, but then how could he know what lay ahead for India? She was nothing to him. It was doubtful he would even remember her name after this evening. Her imagination was in rare form reading far too much into the situation.

She plastered a smile on her face and stepped into the room. The dreaded moment had arrived. Tonight, she would be launched upon London society despite the lack of a court presentation. Lady Clarissa was opening doors that would otherwise have remained shut. India could not claim to be exactly excited, but at least she had Charlie to guide and defend her. Mother could plot all she wanted, but India would do as she liked, even if it meant being dependent on Papa forever, even if it meant she would be a spinster. For the first time in her life, she would stand against all wishes save her own because it was her life. To do anything less was to be a passive participant in creating her own doom.

CHAPTER 21

February melted into March and then blossomed into April with India and Mother attending various dinners, the opera, and theater outings all under the aegis of Lady Clarissa, but only where she deigned to introduce them. Easter was late, not until April 16, so the season had a late start as well. Mother awaited it in some agitation, for she had yet to finagle a court presentation. India suspected the events to which they were invited were what Grandmama would call second, maybe even third tier. The hosts and hostesses were certainly cordial and entertained in a lovely style, but Mother had come to expect no less than dukes and marquesses. Instead, the highest up the peerage ladder they had climbed was the dining room of an earl formerly of the Marlborough House Set.

How he had fallen from favor was somewhat murky, but he was no longer included in King George's circle. The earl's wife, the countess, had been delighted to introduce her eldest son to India. The young man had been charming, outgoing, and possessed of excellent manners. India had been charmed but not in the least interested in his continued attention, especially after Lady Clarissa confided that the family faced financial ruin due to the earl's untoward interest in a certain type of woman and the gaming tables of Monte Carlo and Biarritz. Lady Clarissa also hinted that the tainted earl's inability to entertain his monarch in the lavish style expected had caused his banishment from the king's inner circle. As to Mother's ambitions, India so far had not met a single gentleman she even considered particularly interesting, much less potential husband material.

This evening had proven no different from the previous ones. India sat on the bed in their Savoy suite and watched Mother pace. When her face had attained a shade of puce rivaling her dressing gown, Mother stopped and pointed at India. "You seem determined to be a failure before the season even starts. I watched you after dinner as you ignored those perfectly nice young men's attempts at conversation. You made no effort to be cordial or entertaining. You spent the bulk of the evening in a corner laughing with Lord Kilnsey. The other gentlemen will think you are spoken for and will spread it around that no one need bother paying court to Miss India Ledbetter."

India shot Mother a disdainful look. "My, my. Only a couple of months ago you were throwing Charlie at me as the catch of the century. How times have changed. Is he no longer acceptable?"

Mother jabbed a finger in India's direction. "Are you forming an alliance with him? Are you?"

"No, but would it be so bad if I did?"

Mother's lip curled. "If he is your only choice, then he would do well enough, but there are better out there. Won't you at least try?"

It was late and India's patience was growing thin. "Why is this so important to you?" Her tone was harsher than intended.

Mother looked away. When she turned back to face India, tears brightened her eyes. "I want the best for you."

"And by best, you mean a titled husband?"

Mother moved to the bed, dropped down beside India, and took her hand. "Would it be so bad? Just think. When you returned to New York for visits, I would be introducing my daughter, the marchioness or even duchess. No one would dare snub us then."

"I see." India withdrew her hand from Mother's grasp and turned so that their eyes met. "This is really about making an impression among Grandmama's former circle. You want me to marry a duke so you can lord it over old New York. That hardly speaks of maternal devotion. And you seem to forget that without a court presentation, I am unlikely to meet any dukes or marquesses."

Mother scowled as she swiped at a tear. "When you have been rejected by the people who count, you will better understand my position."

"I think you forget." India could not keep the sarcasm from her voice. "I have already been snubbed by your people who count. It was a little embarrassing, but otherwise I couldn't have cared less. The world no longer turns according to Mrs. Astor's wishes." That was not quite the truth, but Mother would never know the extent of her heartache over Billy Connor's confessions at her debut ball in New York. In any event, the pain of Billy's betrayal had begun to fade. If first love was only a prelude, she was not sure she was ready for the real thing.

Mother rose from the bed with a look of defeat furrowing her brow. "I despair of you. If you are determined to fail, I suppose there is nothing I can really do to prevent it. You are correct in one thing, however. The world has changed and not for the better for people like us of the old New York families. You very well could be the last heiress to marry a title. People of our standing and means are the closest America comes to having royalty. If only you would take advantage of your position."

"Being the last of the dollar princesses to purchase a title might make you and Grandmama happy, but I cannot envision myself stuck in England for the rest of my life away from everything and everyone I love."

"By everyone, I suppose you mean your father and that old woman. Mark my words. Neither of them will live forever and then who will you have? After we are all gone, you may very well find yourself a lonely spinster with no one who cares a hoot for you. Oh, I know you will be living in ole TJ's castle, but The Falls can be very empty and lonely despite the numerous servants. I know from personal experience. I will leave you now before we say things we will both regret."

A mixture of emotions raced through India. Anger with Mother's demands and manipulations warred with guilt. Did Mother really think she did not love her? India called, "Mother, I..." The bedroom door slammed, cutting off what India wanted to say.

***

Holy Week and Easter finally came and went with all the solemnity and piety one would expect of the high church Anglican services they attended with Lady Clarissa, Mr. Rivers, and Charlie. With Easter behind them, the season could now get into full swing. Mother spent all of May searching the Tatler and the society pages of The Times for tidbits about upcoming luncheons, dinners, and balls. Once an event had been selected, Mother then harangued Lady Clarissa about securing an invitation for India and herself. Surprisingly, this method met with some success. India had gone to dinners, luncheons, a couple of balls, and an opera party in which she otherwise would not have been included.

Over breakfast in their suite on a Saturday in June, Mother sat with the latest Tatler spread beside her plate, pencil in hand. After making several check marks, she looked up as India took the chair opposite. "The society pages are so thoughtful in giving the dates of upcoming events so that hostesses have some way of avoiding disastrous conflicts. I have marked several dinners and balls that I am going to speak to Lady Clarissa about. Oh, and did I tell you? She has managed an invitation for us to the Shakespeare Memorial Ball on the twentieth. I couldn't believe it after all the times she has said things are more difficult than she expected. Isn't it exciting? The invitation cost a fortune. God only knows how she got it, but it will be well worth the price. It is only two days before the coronation, so Albert Hall will be filled with the type of people you should be meeting. Rumor has it there may even be a royal appearance, so you might actually meet King George and Queen Mary after all. Of course, this means we must have Elizabethan costumes. Getting something appropriate at this late date may be difficult, but we will manage. I have the maids making rounds of the costume shops and dressmakers."

India selected a piece of toast from the silver rack and spread strawberry jam on it. She watched Mother return to marking the magazine. Perhaps she was distracted enough for India to make her announcement. "This afternoon, I would like to take tea at Claridge's and then walk in Kensington Gardens. The flowers are said to be beautiful in June and the weather is so glorious right now."

Mother massaged her temples and rolled her head. "I'm rather tired after last night's dinner. Who knew it would go on until the wee hours? I have a headache and really do not feel like going out."

"I'm sorry you're not feeling well. You've been doing too much." India poured milk into her tea and swirled the liquid with her spoon. Mustering what she hoped was a casual tone, she continued, "I forgot to mention Lady Clarissa is going with me, so you needn't worry about my going out unchaperoned." India glanced at Mother from beneath her lashes to see if her subterfuge had worked.

"All right then. Go enjoy the flowers."

At three o'clock, India stepped from the elevator into the Savoy's lobby. She scanned those milling about the cavernous space. He had promised to arrive before she did, but there was no sign of him. Drat. If he didn't come soon, she would have to go back upstairs. She couldn't risk news of her going out unaccompanied reaching Mother's ears. One must pick one's battles where Mother was concerned. Just when she was about to give up, she spotted him standing near the front entrance scanning the crowd. Waving to catch his attention, she crossed the lobby.

He greeted her with a warm smile and a slight bow. Offering his arm, Charlie said, "Shall we? The day is too beautiful to spend another minute inside."

"Won't I be thought rather fast going out in public with a lone gentleman?" India smiled and waggled her eyebrows.

"Perhaps, but if I recall what you told me about walking out with Mr. Connor, propriety has never stopped you doing what you really want."

India giggled, put her hand on Charlie's arm, and they strolled outside.

As they approached, the doorman asked, "Taxi, sir?"

Charlie looked at India. "I know we said we would walk, but it's really rather a distance. Shall we take a taxi?"

After the doorman gave their destination and specific route directions to the driver, he turned to Charlie. "I apologize for giving the longer route, but it is wise to avoid The Mall this afternoon. It's those women, you know."

"Will it be a large crowd, do you think?"

"Oh yes. I should think so if the newspapers are correct." The doorman shook his head. "What this world is coming to is beyond me, if I may say so."

"You may and I quite agree."

Once they were settled in the taxi, India looked at Charlie. "Were you talking about the suffragists' march?"

"We were."

India cocked her head and raised her brows. "I'm surprised that you're opposed to votes for women. You've always seemed so modern in your thinking."

"I don't suppose I actually oppose the vote for women, but don't let that be known among the people of my class." Charlie grinned before continuing, "The nobility always support the Conservatives on pain of expulsion from all good society for doing otherwise. But you must see the way these Pankhurst women go about it is beyond the pale. I ask you. What lady would chain herself to a fence, break windows, or go on a hunger strike?" He ended with a small chuckle.

India's eyes narrowed and her lips thinned. "Perhaps one who believes we will not get the vote any other way. How many times has a suffrage bill been defeated here in England? Women in the US have been asking for the vote since the 1840s. We haven't gotten it so far. I guess no taxation without representation only counts if you're a man."

A condescending grin lifted the corners of Charlie's mouth. "Yes, I seem to recall something about that notion in regard to you colonials."

"You can laugh all you want, but it isn't fair or right that we must pay like men, but do not have a voice in choosing those who pass the tax laws or set the rate."

Charlie had the good grace to look chastened. "Point taken."

"After tea, I want to watch the march. We'll be in Kensington Gardens and they are walking to Albert Hall. Let's see how many people actually show up."

"I'm not sure that would be wise. There have been incidences of violence at these suffragette demonstrations."

"All the more reason to see for ourselves who is in the wrong. I strongly suspect it's not the women."

Looking exasperated, Charlie hissed, "Young women of quality simply do not attend such events."

It was India's turn to laugh. "How stodgy you sound. I believe it is you who has encouraged me to be bolder and from now on, I am taking your advice. Like you said, when have I ever let propriety stop me from doing something I want to do. If you won't go with me, I'll go alone."

Charlie sighed. "I will not let you go into danger unescorted. If you insist, we'll observe the march, but only from a safe distance."

"I do insist."

CHAPTER 22

India stood on the top parapet of the Albert Memorial steps with a hand on Charlie's shoulder for support. Shielding her eyes with her free hand, she scanned Kensington Gore back toward Knightsbridge. There were women five abreast as far as the eye could see, rank upon rank of them hailing from every part of the Empire. Some groups wore the traditional costumes of their countries. Others wore simple summer dresses of white cotton lawn. At the head, two Englishwomen on horseback led the procession. There were flags and banners of all types, but the unified theme was one of universal suffrage for women. India's heart beat a little faster as a contingent from her namesake subcontinent came into view.

Bouncing on her toes, she squeezed Charlie's shoulder. "Oh look! Aren't those saris beautiful? I've always thought I should have one. How can someone named India not?" Charlie's weight shifted beneath her grasp. He hopped on one foot, then righted himself.

A crease formed between his eyes and his lips thinned. "Be careful. You nearly sent us toppling. A little more decorum would be appreciated. Remember you are a debutant, not a scullery maid."

India laughed loudly enough to draw stares from those nearby. "There you go again. You are beginning to be a real ole fuddy-duddy. Aren't you the one who has been encouraging me to spreads my wings?"

"Yes, but not at risk to life and limb. There seems to be a commotion in the crowd along the curb. Perhaps you'd better step down beside me."

"No, I want to see it all. This is so thrilling. Just look at all of those women coming together in common cause. There must be tens of thousands. Who knew there could be so many? It gives me hope that one day I shall cast my ballot for the candidate of my very own choosing. I'm glad I grabbed one of the leaflets before the crowd got so big. I may visit the suffragists' office and volunteer to help. Theirs is such a worthy cause."

Charlie cut his eyes up at India and smirked. "I'm sure your mother will be ecstatic to learn of your interest."

One minute, there was cheering and polite applause, the next the crowd surged toward the marchers and swayed back into place. India froze on her perch. Something was amiss. Yelling and cursing emanated from somewhere near the road followed by men and woman scattering, pushing those around India into a tightly packed huddle. She dared not step down at this point. Without warning, something hit the front of her dress with enough force to send her reeling. She stumbled backward trying to regain her balance only to find she had stepped into thin air. The last thing she saw before she fell were policemen on horseback wading into the pandemonium. The air whooshed from her lungs as she landed in outstretched arms.

"Open your eyes. You're safe." Charlie's voice held a small quiver. "You aren't injured, are you?" When she shook her head, he continued, "It seems a fist fight broke out among supporters and opponents of the march.

Fortunately, the police broke it up quickly. It's all over now." He made no move to set her upon her feet.

India could feel the hammering of his heart and the rise and fall of his chest. She gasped quietly when she realized their hearts and breathing were in tempo. His arms tightened around her until it seemed he had no intention of putting her down. "Thank you for saving me. I think I can stand now."

It was Charlie's turn to blush. Putting her upright, he said, "You may be all right, but I'm afraid your dress is ruined."

India looked down. Where the object had hit, a gash in the fabric now stood open. "Oh, no. Mother will be furious. Maybe Althea can think of something."

"Let's hail a taxi and get you back to the Savoy as quickly as possible. I wouldn't want anyone to think I am responsible for the damage."

Before India could answer, a bright light flashed nearby. Looking in the direction of the flash, India's worst nightmare was realized. A man with a camera tipped his hat and began gathering his paraphernalia. "Do you think he took our picture?"

Charlie called over his shoulder as he headed for the photographer, "I am quite sure of it. Stay there." The authority in his voice kept her in place.

It was impossible to hear what Charlie said to the man, but within a minute, the photographer took the glass plate from his camera and handed it to Charlie. Slipping his hand into his coat, Charlie withdrew a rectangle of leather and handed over several bills. With one final comment, Charlie marched back to where India waited.

"Whatever did you say to him?"

"I thought I recognized him. He took a photo of a friend caught in a compromising situation. He sold the picture to a salacious rag and my friend's life has been much more difficult ever since. I threatened him with legal action and made it worth his while to give me the plate. We will shatter it and dispose of the pieces where they will never be found."

"You are my hero."

"Sarcasm is uncalled for, don't you think?"

"No. You misunderstand. I'm serious. You *are* my hero. I don't know how to thank you."

Charlie grinned. "That will do for now." He was silent for a few seconds, then tilted his head. "You know, my dear, there may come a day when I ask you to show your gratitude in a more permanent way."

India gasped. Surely, he had not just made a proposition of the most compromising kind. "Lord Kilnsey, I find your impertinence shocking. How dare you?" Frost clung to her words.

Charlie's eyes grew large, then he laughed. "You are the one who has misunderstood. After defending your honor only moments ago, how can you think I would make a highly improper suggestion?" All humor disappeared from his face. "I was talking about marriage, Miss Ledbetter. Don't look so annoyed. I will not press my suit until I sense you are amenable, but I hope the day is not too distant."

India blinked several times as a blaze started in her chest. "I hardly know what to say. I thought we were to be friends... allies against the pressures and expectations of our families. You have just complicated our friendship, possibly ruined it." She turned to march away, but he grabbed her upper arm.

"Don't be an idiot. You can't go alone in this crowd. It's unsafe." By his tone, he seemed as angry as she. "I apologize for making a suggestion that you clearly find so repugnant. We will dispose of this plate and return to the hotel with our relatives hopefully none the wiser for this afternoon's misadventure."

He led her away from the marchers and the crowd to the other side of the park where he hailed a taxi. If the driver noticed the state of India's dress, he did not comment upon it or even bat an eye. London cabbies must be accustomed to all types of human conditions. Charlie gave instructions for a less frequented area of the Thames Embankment near the Chelsea Bridge.

Alighting from the vehicle, he said to the driver, "The lady will remain here with you. I will return shortly. You will be rewarded for your time. Agreed?"

The driver tugged the brim of his peaked cap. "Whatever you say, Gov."

When Charlie returned and settled himself beside India, he gave the order to drive to the Savoy.

Conflicting emotions stormed through India as they chugged toward the hotel. It was possible she had overreacted to his awkward mention of marriage, but then it caught her completely off guard. They had agreed to be friends and now he had changed the plan without consulting her. He just dropped his bomb without warning. Furthermore, he hadn't mentioned love or anything like it. Should she be delighted, insulted, or angry? She leaned toward anger and insult.

After ignoring him by watching the passing traffic, she turned to him as the hotel came into view. "Were you able to dispose of the plate?"

He expression radiated irritation before he replyed, "I did. I broke it into pieces, ground the shards to splinters with my heel, and pushed everything into the river."

"Thank you. I appreciate your concern for my safety and reputation." Her tone belied the sincerity of her words. She was still angry with him, but she did owe him gratitude. He had not wanted to go to the march, but she had insisted.

"You are welcome. When you are safely in your suite, I will send the maid you saw speaking with me the day we arrived and have her collect your dress. I'm sure she can take it to the dressmaker located in the hotel block. Perhaps she can add lace or something to hide the repair."

"But my maid…"

"And what if your mother's maid talks or your mother sees your girl working on the repair?" He fixed her with the kind of look governesses gave wayward pupils. His tone was ironic and condescending. "No, I really think the dressmaker is a better option. Get it out of sight and repaired before Mrs. Ledbetter is the wiser."

There he went again. Saving her and making her angry at the same time. Rather than make matters between them more tense, she simply said, "Thank you." They parted in the lobby, she to try to get into her room without Mother knowing and he in search of the maid.

India opened the door to their suite just enough for her to peek around it before she entered. The sight that greeted her sent a chill down her spine. Mother sat in an armchair facing the door. Her arms were crossed beneath her bosom and a scowl darkened her face. "Come in, Daughter, have a seat, and give an accounting of yourself. Where did you go this afternoon and with whom? And do not try to lie. I already know the answers."

India squared her shoulders and stepped into the parlor. The door clicked shut behind her. Moving closer to Mother, India did not sit. Instead, she stood and looked down on her parent. Anger boiled. She refused to be interrogated like she was still a child. "If you already know where I've been and with whom, why ask?"

Shock registered in Mother's face as her gaze ran over India. "What has happened to your dress? And what is that paper in your hand? For God's sake, are you trying to ruin yourself?"

"Yes, thank you for inquiring about my health." Sarcasm dripped from every word. "I am unharmed, but I'm afraid the dress is the worst for wear. Please explain how you know where I've been."

"You were seen, you stupid girl. Of all the nerve. How dare you go out amongst that rabble? Those women are a disgrace and you should not be associated with them even by whisper. Were it to become known you are in sympathy with them, it could ruin your chances for a favorable match. I shall speak to Lord Kilnsey about his part in this. I blame him for encouraging your waywardness." Mother's eyes narrowed. "I have reconsidered your association with him. Now that we have the invitation to the Shakespeare Memorial Ball, we may no longer need Lady Clarissa's assistance. I am beginning to believe we should sever those ties."

India's temper erupted. "Charlie is not to blame. He didn't want to go. I made him. As for severing ties, if you treat Lady Clarissa so shabbily, I will wire Papa for passage home. I refuse to be party to such underhanded treatment of someone who has been kind and gracious to us." Her words bounced off the fourteen-foot ceiling and echoed down the bedroom hall.

Mother gripped the arms of her chair until her knuckles turned white. "You stubborn, intractable child. You have inherited the worst traits of the Ledbetter's."

India cocked a hip and planted her fist on it. "Would that be Papa, TJ, or Jane?"

"All of them." Mother's words came in a strangled hiss. "TJ and Jane passed on bad blood to you and your father. He has never amounted to anything. If it weren't for his father's money, Robert would be a failure just like his mother is. As for you, my dear, you have all the deviousness of the old goat."

The shock of Mother's unintended revelation silenced India momentarily. When she found her voice, she said, "You speak of Jane in the present tense. What do you know? I demand you tell me."

A snide smile crossed mother's face. "You can demand all you wish, but you have proven yourself untrustworthy. What you don't know, you can't tell. Give me what you are holding."

India threw the leaflet at Mother. "Take it. Maybe you will learn something." Shocked by her own rudeness, India modulated her tone. "Charlie is sending a hotel maid to fetch my dress. A dressmaker will mend it. I should change before the girl arrives. Now, if you will excuse me?"

"Go. And keep to your room. I don't want to look at you for the remainder of today. I will have dinner sent up. We will dine separately."

"That's an excellent idea." India turned on her heel and marched to her bedroom. When she was inside her room, she slammed the door. Althea jumped and dropped the dress she had been laying out. India's shoulders drooped. "I'm sorry. I didn't mean to startle you."

Althea picked up the dress and smoothed the wrinkles. "No harm done. I'm just glad that door is still on its hinges." Glancing at India, her eyes widened. "My goodness. What happened? You okay?"

Without warning, tears welled up and rolled down India's cheeks. "Not really. I'll tell you about the dress later. I've just acted abominably toward Mother, but she made me so mad. I don't know what's wrong with me these days. I used to be able to let Mother just roll off my back, but I can't seem to manage it anymore."

Althea glanced at India with a sympathetic smile. "Maybe you are finally becoming your own woman. Forgive me, but Mrs. Ledbetter has ruled you with an iron hand all of your life. I'd say it's past time for some showdowns like what just happened in the parlor."

"You heard?"

Althea laughed. "Are you kidding? I suspect everyone on this floor heard. I wouldn't worry about it, though. Most mothers and grown-up daughters have arguments."

"But most mothers and daughters do not lie to one another all the time."

"Really? I'd say it happens more than anyone suspects. I heard you mention your grandmother Jane. Do you really think Mrs. Ledbetter knows something that she hasn't told you?"

"I'm sure of it. When this blasted season is over, I'm going to find out exactly what happened to Papa's mother. Her story has haunted me long enough."

"And I hope you will get the answers, but we are still in London for a while longer." Holding up the dress she was fiddling with, Althea continued, "This came by courier this afternoon. What do you think? Will it do for the Shakespeare Memorial Ball?"

India pushed her guilt and anger aside and picked up the dress's skirt. The fabric felt heavy, rich, and expensive. Dropping the skirt, she stepped back and inspected the dress. It was lovely. The royal blue velvet with an under skirt of cream embroidered silk would complement her coloring. The sleeves had those cutouts that one saw in so many portraits of the period. "I love it. I'm surprised you could find something so nice this close to the ball."

Althea put the dress on a hanger and hung it on the outside of the closet door. "I didn't. Lady Clarissa asked a favor of one of her friends who apparently has a whole room devoted to gowns and costumes for fancy dress balls. With a few nips and tucks, it should fit you nicely."

"Lady Clarissa has been a very good friend to us. I must remember to thank her for once again coming to the rescue."

"Yes, she has." Althea, who knew India's measurements by heart, began pinning the costume at the waist. "Have you considered her true reasons?"

"Oh, not you, too," India huffed. "Mother has cooled toward her and Lord Kilnsey, which I find detestable. Mother may try to see less of them, but I will choose my friends when and where I like."

"U-huh." Althea stopped pinning and glanced over her shoulder. "And I will dance with the king at his coronation ball. I'd be careful, if I were you. Your mother has a method for always getting her way."

"True." India sucked on her lower lip. "We'll have to see our way around her."

"We? Our way?"

India flashed Althea a knowing grin. "You have always been my sister-in-arms."

CHAPTER 23

India grinned as she read the article in the Monday morning paper. The headline of "50,000 Suffragettes in London Parade - All Social Barriers Down - Titled Women Walk Along Side Girls from the Slums" was followed by a lengthy description of which ladies of the nobility supported the cause. When Mother looked up from her perusal of the Tatler, India folded the paper to the article and laid it beside Mother's plate.

"Take a look at who supports votes for women and then tell me only the lower classes participate." A touch of spiteful glee tinted her words. "I think I'll visit their office while we are here in London. I bet I could learn something to take back home."

"You are clearly trying to provoke me with teasing, but I doubt you will have time for such shenanigans. Lady Clarissa has arranged a luncheon, tea, and the theater for today and the same followed by the opera for later in the week. That brings us to the ball tomorrow night. You will want to rest tomorrow to be at your best."

The question of "who says I'm teasing" hovered on the tip of India's tongue, but instead she said, "I thought you were going to sever ties with Lady Clarissa."

"We will after the ball. Not a complete cut, mind you. I don't want to cause speculation. Just a casual drifting apart as sometimes happens. At this point, I have made enough connections through my own efforts. By the time we host your ball in July, people will be vying for an invitation. We have made quite a splash, my dear."

India pushed her chair back and tossed her napkin on the table. She would love to refuse to attend the events Mother had just outlined, but she refused to embarrass Lady Clarissa. "I may take some exercise until it is time to get ready for the luncheon."

"Don't you want to know who our hosts will be?"

"No. I'm sure they will be charming as all of Lady Clarissa's friends are." She did not add as Mother's friends were not, but the implication was there for anyone who listened. Irony was often lost on Mother.

Mother's gaze swept over India. "I suppose a brief walk will not bring you to harm. Where do you intend going?"

"There's a lovely church designed by Christopher Wren about a ten-minute walk from here. St Clements. The interiors are supposed to be wonderful."

"Very well. Make sure your maid goes with you. Young ladies do not go out unaccompanied in London as they do at home."

Without excusing herself, India nodded and turned toward the bedroom hall. Mother's constant reminders regarding propriety were long past tiresome.

India found Althea in the bedroom attending to clothes for the day's outings. "Are these okay for today and tonight? I thought you might save your newest for the events later in the week. Mrs. Ledbetter said those invitations are more important."

"How like Mother to pay attention to such details." Seeing the surprise in her maid's expression, India continued, "Please forgive my sharp tongue. It was not directed at you. Of course, these will do beautifully." As Althea began hanging the dresses in the closet, an idea took hold. "Do you have anything to do this morning that can't wait?"

Althea eyed India with suspicion. "Not particularly."

India adjusted her features to the blandest expression she could muster. "I thought we might walk out and see something of the city."

Althea raised a brow. "I know that look. You're up to something."

India grinned, picked up her parasol, and twirled in a circle. "I thought we might take the air for about an hour. There's a church I want to see."

"Why do I think that isn't your real purpose?"

India stopped twirling and grinned. "Because you know me too well." Lowering her voice, she continued, "I've discovered that the main office of the Women's Social and Political Union is only a fifteen-minute walk. It's on St. Clements Lane just off the Strand. I wish you could have seen the march yesterday. It was so exciting. There were 50,000 women from all over the Empire demanding justice and equality. I want to be part of that."

Althea smiled and nodded. "I understand your enthusiasm. And actually, I did see the march. I slipped away between luncheon and teatime. It was pretty thrilling."

"Then you understand why I want to get a closer look. I'm going to take what I learn here and put it to work back home. American women will one day have the vote. I just know it."

Passing through the parlor, India called over her shoulder as she swished by Mother, "We're off to St. Clements. We'll be about an hour or so." She didn't wait for a reply.

Fifteen minutes' walk along the Victoria Embankment, left through Temple Gardens, past St Clements, and on to Numbers 3 and 4 St Clements Inn brought them to the offices of the W.S.P.U. India and Althea stepped through the door into a whirl of chatter, clattering typewriters, and women dashing about with arms loaded down by stacks of newspapers.

The girl at the reception desk did not even look up until India cleared her throat rather loudly. "May I help you?"

India smiled, glanced at Althea, then introduced herself. "I'm hoping to speak to someone about your work. I was at the march yesterday. It was very inspiring."

The girl looked harried and distracted. "Yes, it was a success. Did you walk with us? I don't remember a Miss Ledbetter among the Canadian contingent."

"Oh, I not Canadian. I'm American. Would it be possible to speak with one of the organizers?"

"Afraid not. We're snowed under getting our newspaper out."

"Perhaps Mrs. Despard or Miss Drummond is available?"

The girl stopped typing and looked up in exasperation. "Look, I don't mean to be rude, but no one has time to see you. You can make an appointment." She searched through an appointment book. "The first opening in anyone's calendar will be next week and not before Thursday."

After accepting a day and time, India said, "I apologize for keeping you from your work, but might I at least have some printed material?"

The girl reached behind her to the floor, grabbed a newspaper from a stack, and shoved it at India. "Take this and some of those brochures from the table by the door."

India opened her handbag and withdrew several bills, but the girl held up her palm. "No, these are free this time."

India held out the money. "I want to make a donation. When I return, I hope to learn pointers for organizing a group at home in North Carolina. If anyone needs help, it's the women in my home state."

At last the receptionist's lips parted in a smile. "Thank you and I wish you the best of luck. We women must stand together no matter where we live."

As they walked back to the Savoy, India looked at Althea. "Well, that didn't go as well as I hoped, but at least I have an appointment with Mrs. Drummond. I understand she has quite the reputation for getting things done."

"So the newspapers say." Hearing Big Ben strike the hour, Althea continued, "We'd better hurry if you are going to be ready in time for that luncheon."

The remainder of the day and the following one passed as Mother predicted. Gripping a bedpost, India sucked in her mid-section while Althea fastened hooks and tugged on her corset's lacing. "Ouch. Can you loosen that just a little?"

The maid pursed her lips. "Mrs. Ledbetter wants your waist to look as small as possible. She said this may be the most important night of your life."

"I doubt that. Of course, if I die of suffocation, I guess that would count as being important."

Althea smiled and loosened the laces. "There. Better?"

India nodded. "Some." She shifted the stays to a more comfortable position. "I guess this will have to do. Let's get that monstrous costume on."

India ran her hands over the exaggerated hips supported by a wire cage undergarment. "Imagine having to wear this stuff every day. I wonder if we will be able to sit down or even fit in the taxi." She cocked her head and smirked. "I can just imagine Mother's reaction if we must walk to the ball."

"I believe your mother anticipated that possibility. She's ordered two cabs. One for each of you."

India rolled her eyes. "Of course. Mother would think of everything with the success of the season at stake."

After a ten-minute ride, the taxis pulled in behind the private autos and limousines lined up along Kensington Gore waiting to disgorge their occupants in front of Royal Albert Hall. Ordinarily, the round red brick building's glass dome would be illuminated, but tonight it was surprisingly dark. When their turn to alight finally came, India stepped onto the sidewalk and looked up at the frieze running just under the dome. Would those scientists and inventors depicted approve of tonight's use of their hall? Probably not, but then being made of stone, they had no voice to complain. India stifled a giggle and winked at one of the doctors-of-science whose downward gaze was particularly severe.

Once inside the hall proper, an usher conducted them to their box where Lady Clarissa, Charlie, and Mr. Rivers awaited them. Surprisingly, they were in formal attire instead of Tudor costumes. On second thought, perhaps it was not so surprising considering what decent costumes must cost. She glanced down at hers. It must have cost Clarissa's friend a small fortune. With Charlie unable to afford a costume, Clarissa and Jonathan would never embarrass him by wearing such. Family solidarity won out.

The men stood and Mr. Rivers assisted Mother to a chair at the railing. Charlie stepped forward and guided India to the chair beside his. She had been somewhat surprised by his absence from the previous day's luncheon, dinner, and theater outing. It was good to be in his company again even if she was still miffed with him for mentioning marriage just when she was hoping for independence.

When seated again, Charlie leaned in. "I hear you visited St. Clements Inn yesterday. Learn anything?"

"How did you hear about that?" India hissed.

"Our friend the maid saw the materials you carried when you returned to the hotel and I surmised the rest."

India's breathing became more rapid. "Are you having that girl spy on me?"

Charlie shrugged and tilted his head as though considering the notion. "I hadn't thought of doing that, but it's not a bad idea since you seem determined to get yourself into trouble with these suffragettes."

India's eyes narrowed. "Have I mentioned that you just may be becoming insufferable? How dare you judge my interests?"

"Well, someone with common sense must. Furthermore, it is in my best interest to do so. My bride must be above reproach."

The palm of India's hand itched with the desire to smack his smug face. "Why must you continue to talk of marriage when just yesterday you promised you wouldn't?"

With a self-satisfied smile, he replied, "Once again, someone with common sense must take the lead. Your costume is wonderful by the way. Royal blue suits you, as does the cut of the gown."

India's face burned. Rudeness was unbecoming, but she was too angry to continue speaking to him. Instead, she turned her attention to the transformation that had been wrought by Sir Edwin Lutyens. As she gazed out over the hall, a small gasp escaped. Light had not shone from the glass dome for good reason. The architect had suspended blue fabric near the ceiling. He then illuminated the hall beneath to create the effect of a glorious summer day. Below the artificial sky, an Italian-style Tudor garden spread from one end of the hall's ground level to the other. Above the stalls, Lutyens had erected a dance floor that would accommodate the swaying forms of hundreds of couples. He had converted the Circle into a slopping green lawn. The tiers featured stone columns and draping vines while the Gallery's pillars were hidden by groves of cypress trees. The overall effect was breathtaking. How could anyone view such a spectacle and remain in a foul mood? She was about to lean over to Charlie and say as much when the sound of a throat clearing near her shoulder made her turn around.

A gentleman dressed as what appeared to be one of Shakespeare's kings loomed above Charlie's chair. "Kilnsey, my good man, you must introduce me to your charming companion."

A disgruntled expression clouded Charlie's face. "Miss India Ledbetter, may I introduce His Grace, Lord Hawik, better known as Bumpy to his friends and enemies."

Hawik grimaced. "Enemies? Oh surely all that silly schoolboy nonsense is long forgotten." He then bowed slightly and extended his hand to India. When India gave him her hand in reply, he brushed her kid glove with his lips. "Charmed, my dear. May I tear you away from your party for the next dance?"

Before India could reply, Mother jumped to her feet. "I am Mrs. Ledbetter, India's mother. She would be delighted."

After being led down the flights of stairs from their box to the floor of the hall, India found herself awaiting the opening strains of a waltz in the arms of a man of above average height, slight frame, and unimpressive visage. When the music began, he guided her among the other couples with skill and grace while she searched for something to say.

Since he seemed content to remain silent, she finally said, "Your costume is interesting. Is it from one of the plays?"

"Why yes, it is. I am portraying Macbeth, he of the historical play and my ancestor, as it so happens."

"I thought Macbeth was a made-up character."

"Oh, no. He was quite real, according to family lore." He peered down his pointed nose and continued, "Of course, as an American you may not completely appreciate such a heritage considering how limited yours must be."

India's head jerked back. She studied Lord Hawik's weak-chinned visage. The man had the effrontery to smile pleasantly at her as though he had no idea of the insult he had just delivered. A change of subject was in order. "So, you knew Charlie at school?"

"I did." He nodded while offering another bland smile.

"I have never asked Charlie about school. Was that Eton?"

"No, Durham. My family seat is in the south of Scotland, so my father thought Durham was old enough and far enough to send his sons. I suppose Kilnsey's father thought the same. Whatever his reason, Charles's father did not see fit to send him on to university. Heard it was due to failing finances. The Fourteenth Earl Kilnsey was a drunkard and a gambler by all accounts."

Shocked by Hawik's level of indiscretion, India did not pursue further conversation.

When the dance ended, Hawik returned India to her box. Bowing again, he said, "Thank you for a delightful dance. May I ask for another?"

India looked at Charlie and signaled pleading with widened eyes. Charlie nodded ever so slightly. Turning back to Lord Hawik, she answered, "I believe the next few belong to Lord Kilnsey. Perhaps later in the evening?"

After Hawik exited, Charlie said, "Well, what did you two find to talk about?"

"Oh, he bragged about Macbeth being his ancestor. Imagine, as if Macbeth was a real historical figure. I guess he thought a mere American would believe anything he said." India frowned. "That man is not a gentleman. Furthermore, he is an arrogant, insufferable bore. If he comes to ask for another dance, please help me. Mother has her heart set on a duke." She wrinkled her face in a grimace. "Any duke, no matter how repulsive, will do."

"Of course. He shall bother you no more." Charlie drew a long breath and let it out with a sigh. "I suspect he spoke of my father, as well?"

India did not answer. There was no need to hurt Charlie by repeating vicious gossip.

He shot her a sidewise glance. "I'm sure it's nothing that hasn't been said before. Tell me what he said. It's the price of my protecting you from pursuit."

India looked away before answering. She did not want to see the pain her answer might cause. "He did speak of your father, but I refuse to believe what he said."

"Don't be embarrassed. Everyone at school knew how Father lost the family fortune." A faraway look entered Charlie's eyes. "The older boys were pretty rough on the younger ones, but Hawik was the worst. He was cruel to the point of torture until one of the prefects reported him for causing injuries that sent a boy to hospital. After that, he limited his cruelty to verbal assaults and insults. I was a particular target for his malice. The irony is, he is also my heir unless I marry and produce a son."

Surprise filled India. "Your heir? But he must be at least ten years older than you."

Charlie laughed. "He is, but he is my heir, nonetheless. It has to do with an unfortunate marriage a few generations back. He is my cousin several times removed. We are the last of the direct line. He will inherit the estate and my title if I do not produce an heir. He may be a duke, but Kilnsey is a much older title than Hawik. And no, I do not claim descent from Macbeth."

CHAPTER 24

India fanned herself with a souvenir booklet of the evening that was quickly drawing to a close. The Shakespeare Memorial Ball had gone according to the program. There were tableaux vivants from an assortment of the Bard's plays, some presented by actual descendants of characters in them. Among those portraying their ancestors were the Howards, Talbots, Cecils, Burghleys, Fortescues, Lytteltons, Hamiltons, and Comptons. The arrivals of Prime Minister Anthony Asquith and Home Secretary Winston Churchill caused something of a stir, but the most attention and speculation was reserved for the foreign dignitaries and European royalty who were in London to attend King George's coronation.

Mother's dearest desire was realized when several young men from prominent, noble families had begged introductions and dances with India. By her facial expressions, it became clear Lady Clarissa was less than pleased, but she complied with the requests because not doing so would have been the height of rudeness. As India prepared to leave their box for the last time, she paused to survey the emptying hall. In spite of her initial misgivings and resistance, it had truly been a glorious evening, one to remember for the rest of her life.

Charlie shifted beside her. "It's been fun, hasn't it?"

India smiled up at him. Her mood was lighter than it had been for weeks. "Yes, it has. I haven't enjoyed anything so much in a long time. I hope they raised all the funds they need. Remind me exactly what they were raising money for."

"It's to fund a Shakespeare Memorial National Theater. It's long overdue, in my opinion. Can you believe it took the British people until 1908 to form a committee to organize the project? Glaciers move faster, but at least we should be well on our way after tonight."

"I didn't know you are a devotee of the Bard."

"Had my father not lost the family fortune, I would have read history and literature at Oxford. I had dreams of becoming a Shakespeare scholar or perhaps a doctor. Alas, Father's extravagances and my duty to the estate crushed all hopes in that quarter." He laughed softly. "Of course, a gentleman is expected to study wine, women, and rowing at university, not academics." He had tried to hide his pain behind laughter. It had not worked. India saw that as clearly as she saw the white rose in his lapel.

Without thinking, she stood on her tiptoes and kissed Charlie's cheek, then brushed her fingers against the warm flesh of his temple. Gazing upward, she whispered, "Our ancestors have a way of reaching out from the grave to control our lives, don't they? I'm sorry you didn't get to fulfill your dreams. I think you would have made a wonderful Shakespeare scholar or gifted physician. And I'm sorry that you're saddled with so many responsibilities and so little to help you fulfill those obligations. You deserve better."

Charlie's expression lifted in pleased surprise. After India dropped back to her feet, he grasped her hand, but did not move toward the door. "You really are a wonderfully kind person. No one has ever spoken to me quite like that or with such sympathy, compassion, or understanding. You have made my burdens lighter simply by being yourself. Thank you."

India swallowed hard. What had she just done? Leading him to believe she felt more than she did was not what she intended. Kissing him had been her instinctual response to someone working hard to hide his pain. Surely it was a maternal reaction. Confused and irritated with herself, she tugged against his grip. "I think we should go now. The others will be wondering where we are. It's late and I'm sure everyone wants to get to bed."

***

India awoke with a start and looked at the bedside clock. Eight a.m. When they parted at four, everyone agreed they would not meet again until a late luncheon, but she distinctly heard voices coming from the parlor. A wail followed by sobs carried through the closed door. It was Mother's voice. Something was terribly wrong.

India scrambled from the bed and grabbed her wrapper as Althea opened the door and stuck her head around the jamb. "Good. You're already up. Mrs. Ledbetter wants you in the parlor immediately. She has called Lady Clarissa and Mr. Rivers to come for support. There's news from home."

India searched her maid's face and her heart jumped in her chest. "What's happened? You look like the world has ended."

Althea swiped at a tear. "I think it would be best if you read the telegram for yourself."

Entering the parlor, she found their entire party from the previous evening seated in a tight circle. Everyone looked as though they had just gotten out of bed and dressed in whatever lay at hand. The men rose, but it was Lady Clarissa who came to her, put an arm around her shoulders, and drew her to a seat on the sofa beside Mother. Mr. Rivers went to the drinks cart and poured a generous amount of amber liquid into two tumblers, which he placed on the table before the sofa. Mother shoved a piece of paper into India's hand before grabbing a glass and downing the drink in one gulp.

With shaking hands, India read the telegram. The message was simple.

Pisgah, North Carolina
Advise come home Stop Mr. Ledbetter's condition grave Stop Galloway M.D.

India became dizzy as the blood left her head. She leaned back against the cushions and tried to regulate her breathing. The sensation of fainting eased, leaving her wilted and anxious. "Dr. Galloway makes it sound like Papa is dying." Rounding on Mother, she continued, "Did you know he was this ill when we left for London? Did you?" Her voice bounced off the ceiling and echoed into the bedroom hall.

The color left Mother's face. She dropped her gaze before looking at India. "He said it was nothing to worry about. He wanted you to have a London season. You remember that, don't you?"

India's heart pounded. Between rapid breaths, she spat, "This trip was your idea. You insisted we come. If he dies before we get home, I will never forgive you."

Mother gasped and covered her mouth with a hand before hissing, "You cruel, ungrateful girl. It is my life that will change if he dies. I will be a widow stuck in a mountain wilderness populated by ignorant, uncouth hillbillies. The Falls must be maintained to the specifications of your grandfather's will before any annuities are dispersed. The old man insisted on a memorial to himself that will last in perpetuity." Her bitter laughter filled the room. "Your father has been happy to entomb himself in the back of beyond, but I have been buried there with him. If he dies, I will never again be able to leave for any extended periods. Any chance at a normal social life will end. You, at least, have the chance to escape this tyranny from the grave by making a suitable marriage."

India felt as though someone had just slapped her hard. Her anger drained away, replaced by sympathy at the knowledge of how miserably unhappy Mother had been.

Before India could speak, Mr. Rivers cleared his throat and moved to stand beside the sofa. "This is very difficult for you both. Perhaps you would allow me to make your travel arrangements?"

Mother's mouth twisted as though she might burst into tears. Lady Clarissa reached over and took her hand. "Dear Petra, please allow us to do whatever we are able to make this sad time less stressful. Jonathan has excellent connections and can make all of your travel arrangements with ease, if you will permit."

Mother did not speak but nodded her agreement. A fog descended over India, making thought and comprehension difficult. She knew she was in the room, but she felt as though she was observing the others from somewhere outside of it, maybe even outside the hotel. It was weird and frightening. A hand gently shaking her shoulder and a voice calling her name brought her back to reality.

Charlie knelt before her, a look of concern clouding his eyes. "I will not countenance you and Mrs. Ledbetter facing this journey alone and unprotected. Please allow me to conduct you to your home in North Carolina. Once you are there, I will not stay if you do not wish it."

India processed the sounds until his words made sense. Struggling to hold back tears, she answered, "Thank you. We would be grateful for your help, but are you sure? It's such a long way with ship and train."

Charlie placed his hand over hers and grasped them gently. "I have never been surer of anything. I will not have you traveling alone at such a time." Only after this did she realize she had been twisting her hands in her lap until the skirt of her wrapper was a tangled mess.

***

Clarissa watched as Charlie placed his belongings in his luggage. "You should have had your man come up to Town or asked Jonathan's valet to pack for you."

He frowned and cast a disgruntled look upon his sister. "First, I can no longer afford a body servant and second, I do not like your husband's valet. I am quite capable of packing for myself."

She crossed to the bed, picked up a shirt, and began folding it. "I must say you handled arranging exclusive time with India beautifully. Do not waste this opportunity to secure your place in her future. She was far too popular at the ball last night. If she returns to London, you will have several rivals whose titles and estates are far grander than yours."

His mouth twisted in an ironic grimace. "That was the gamble you took in arranging a London season for her." He took the shirt from her, refolded it, and threw it into his valise. "And for your information, I'm going with them because they need my protection. I do not want India and her mother negotiating such a lengthy journey on their own, certainly not at a time like this."

Clarissa sat on the bed and considered her brother. He was handsome, titled, smart, master of an ancient estate, and possessed of wit and charm when he chose. In the negative, he was stubborn, begrudged his inherited responsibilities, was not always practical in his choices, and believed himself in love with the farmer's daughter whom he could not have. Only time would tell if he had the good sense to follow her advice where India was concerned.

CHAPTER 25

For India, the voyage to New York and the train trip to North Carolina passed in a blur. The days melted into one another with little to distinguish them other than the soup de jour on the ship's menu cards and the changing scenery flashing past the train's windows. It wasn't a conscience decision to ignore her surroundings or the people she saw or the food she ate. Rather, it was self-defense - plain and simple.

Mother had not functioned with her usual authority, either. Despite the way she had talked about her marriage and Papa, she clearly feared losing her husband more than anyone could have anticipated. Thank goodness Charlie had come with them. He was a godsend. Mother listened to his advice and followed his directions. It was so surprising, but after a lifetime of control, Mother had finally revealed a chink in her armor.

When India stepped down from their private car at the Pisgah Depot, the sun was painting the western mountaintops in shades of pink and gold. She was numb in mind and body. She could not have related a single detail of the past twenty-four hours no matter how hard she tried. It was as though one minute they were boarding the train in

New York and the next they were climbing into the estate automobile headed for home.

The one thing that did make an impression on her was the look that passed between Charlie and the chauffeur. The unspoken communication contained therein sent a spasm through India. Something must be wrong or maybe her mind had lost its grip on her imagination. Racing across oceans and continents took a toll, and she was no exception. Best not to speculate. She would know soon enough whether her intuition or her imagination was in control.

Once seated beside Charlie, she instinctively slipped her hand under his arm. He glanced down in surprise while he covered her hand with his own. Dropping her head onto his shoulder would have felt so good, but Mother would make a scene. India didn't possess the energy for dealing with one of Mother's outbursts, so she leaned her head against the seat back and closed her eyes. Perhaps shutting out the world would calm her nerves.

It didn't work. The tension building with every foot they traveled toward The Falls threatened to consume her. Although the scene outside the auto whipped past, they seemed to move at a crawl. It took all of her strength to not leap from the vehicle and run the rest of the way to the house. After an eternity, the chauffeur applied the brake, and the auto rolled to a halt beneath the front portico. Charlie helped India to step down onto the stone pavers.

Hobbs, the butler, opened the door and stood back for them to enter. When India focused on him fully, her hand flew to her mouth, covering a gasp. His black armband told her all she needed to know.

Clutching Charlie's arm for support, a wail tore from her. "Oh God, we didn't get here in time."

Centered under the dome of the rotunda, Papa's casket stood on its bier, the lid open. India wrenched free of

Charlie's grasp and ran. The sound of his footsteps followed her to the center of the grand hall. She came to rest beside what remained of Papa. Subdued light from wall sconces cast a golden hue over his snowy hair and created a natural glow in his skin. He looked like he was merely sleeping. After staring for several beats, she laid the backs of her fingers against his cheek. He looked so alive. His flesh should have been warm, but it was as cold as the metal handles on the box that held him. He was really, truly dead. He would never kiss her cheek or offer fatherly advice again. His quiet, stabilizing influence was gone from the house and her life forever. Tears rolled down her cheeks while she stifled a sob.

Looking at Papa again, her thoughts raced. If Mother hadn't insisted on a damned debut season, India would have spent Papa's final days with him, comforting him, being by his side to the last. She would have been able to say goodbye, to tell him how much she loved him. Did Mother know how ill Papa was before they left? India might never know for sure, but one thing was certain. Mother had never loved Papa. She had admitted as much.

Somewhere deep within India, a lock clicked open and her breathing became more rapid. She withdrew her hand from Papa's face and dropped balled fists to her sides. Her pulse pounded against her eardrums and her nails dug into her palms. When Mother recovered from the shock of finding herself a relatively young widow, she would resume control unchecked unless India had the will to forestall it. There could be no doubt. Mother may be moving through life in a disengaged state at present, but it would not last. India stared at the back of the rotunda into the darkened solarium. Mother's continued domination was beyond endurance. She must be thwarted no matter the cost.

Movement nearby interrupted her musings. The butler looked apologetic and uncertain. "We, I…, the undertaker and I were unsure, but thought these arrangements might be suitable. If you will forgive the liberty, I have spoken with Pastor Johnson of Pisgah Methodist about conducting the service. He suggested Friday at noon. The undertaker is prepared to come from Asheville then or at a later date, should you wish it. I hope this meets with your approval." Not trusting herself to speak, India nodded.

Charlie stirred beside her. "Mrs. Ledbetter is still in the auto. I should bring her in."

Gratitude filled India as she watched Charlie walk away. His kindness and concern touched her more than she would ever have thought possible. She inhaled slowly to control the sobs that threatened. She must not give in to overwhelming grief. She could not afford it. If a new order was ever to be established, now was the time to begin the process. She rolled her head and straightened her back.

"Thank you, Hobbs. You have done well. It is what Papa would have wished." She stopped and crossed her arms over her abdomen before continuing, "Tell me, please. When did he pass? Did he suffer?"

India watched the butler's Adam's apple jerk up and down as though the words he needed were stuck in his throat. After a discrete cough, he replied, "During the night on Monday. We sent a telegram but feared you would not get it before the train left New York. I can assure you he died peacefully in his sleep. When his valet went to Mr. Ledbetter's room at dawn, he found him already beyond aid. Dr. Galloway was called. He will confirm these details." Hobbs's words trailed off to a near whisper. Ordinarily, having delivered himself of such a speech, he would have asked permission to retreat to his pantry until called upon for further service. Instead, he remained stiffly in place.

India watched him for a few seconds. "Is there something else you wish to say?"

Mother chose that moment to make her grand entrance complete with threats of fainting. The butler rushed to bring a chair while Charlie guided her to it. "That's better. Thank you, Charles." Her gaze lit upon Hobbs. "I must have something to calm my nerves. A sherry at once." In familiar surroundings, the tyrant seemed to be making a recovery.

The butler disappeared without answering India's question, but her heart thumped a little harder all the same. The answer had been in his eyes. Whatever additional calamity lay in store India would learn its details before the evening ended. For the time being, she would deal with present needs.

A rush of anger shot through her, generating new depths of energy, concentrating her attention. Maybe it was simply her mind's way of dealing with a grief that would otherwise drive her to despair. Perhaps it was the shock of finding Papa dead. Whatever the cause, her perception was now clearer than ever before. In the space of a few hours, she had grown from a girl who bent her will to that of others in order to keep peace into a woman determined to make her own decisions and live life on her own terms. In reality, this shift probably began the day of the suffragists' march. That day had opened her eyes and planted seeds that promised to flower. Mother must no longer be allowed to dominate her life. Taking charge of their homecoming was the first step toward emancipation.

She turned to Mother with a calm determination. "We should retire to our bedrooms and rest." Mother opened her mouth, but India cut her off. "Hobbs, please have someone show Lord Kilnsey to the blue room and send Papa's valet to unpack for him." She looked at Althea and Mother's maid standing in the shadows, waiting patiently for instructions.

"Please unpack only the essentials for now and then you may rest in your rooms until it is time to dress for dinner. Lay out black for Mrs. Ledbetter and myself. Hobbs, inform the staff that black armbands will be sufficient until the funeral service and send a message to the preacher asking him to come tomorrow morning to discuss the service. That will be all." India caught Charlie's quizzical expression. Perhaps she was overdoing it. If so, everyone would just have to smooth their own ruffled feathers. For the time being, all she wanted to do was go to her room, throw herself across her bed, and scream into her pillow until she had no voice left.

India remained upright and stiff backed while the others departed. The maids scurried toward the service stairs. Mother leaned on Charlie's arm after another wilting spell. Hobbs hesitated, then bowed and turned toward the service hall. Alone at last, she went to Papa once more and kissed his cheek. The coolness of his skin against her lips confirmed finality and loss. There was nothing she could do for him nor he for her. Life as they had lived it was truly, devastatingly over. She bolted to the grand staircase and fled to the seclusion of her bedroom. After slamming the door, she leaned against it. She closed her eyes and stuffed her fist in her mouth while tears streamed down her cheeks.

India sensed rather than saw that she was not alone. Opening her eyes, she found Althea holding a black garment and peering at her with concern. India swiped her fingers across each cheek and crossed the room. "I need for you to find out something."

Althea's eyes widened no doubt surprised by the abrupt nature of the request. "Of course, if I am able."

"Go to Hobbs and find out what he has not told us. There is more. I could see it in his expression. Whatever else has happened, it cannot be good." India turned away in dismissal. Dropping down into her favorite wing chair beside the fireplace, she rested her head against its back.

Within a few minutes, Althea returned with the butler at her heels. When they entered, Hobbs stepped ahead of Althea and came to rest before India. "I thought it best to deliver the information myself. I fear there has been another tragedy." He stopped speaking as if seeking the courage to continue.

India's heart plummeted. "Go on."

He glanced at Althea, who nodded. "I am deeply saddened to report another death on the estate. Mrs. Gordon, your former nanny, passed away not long after you set sail for England."

From the depths of her being, India's heart raced back with force until it pounded against her breastbone. "Why did no one wire us? The Lusitania has ship-to-shore capabilities."

Fear shone in the butler's eyes. "But we did. Mr. Ledbetter was most adamant that you be informed immediately. I sent the wire myself that very evening and checked the following morning. I was assured the message had been delivered directly to Mrs. Ledbetter."

A dam broke open deep within India. Mother had proven manipulative and controlling throughout her life, but this underhandedness was beyond endurance. India swallowed hard. "I see. Where is she buried?"

"In the family plot. Your father insisted."

India turned to Althea. "Please organize flowers. There should be something blooming in the hothouse. I will go to her grave before breakfast. I shall wish time alone."

Instead of more tears, a sense of resolve settled over India. Her heart should have been pounding out of her chest. Instead, its beats slowed into a pattern of rage fueled calm. Mother's deceptions would be dealt with when the time was right. At present, India would rest, take dinner, and go to bed early. Tomorrow she would have to face the reality of planning Papa's funeral and laying flowers on Nanny Gordon's grave. A shudder passed through her as she stretched out across her bed and closed her eyes.

CHAPTER 26

India remained seated by Papa's open grave long after her mother, the servants, and the mourners from the village departed. Her interlaced fingers formed a temple in her lap. Her hands clasped one another with such ferocity that streaks of tension shot up her arms, but she did not ease the grip. The discomfort was all that stood between her and a complete numbing of mind, body, and spirit. Off to the side of the small family cemetery, a group of men in work clothes stood leaning on shovels and speaking to one another in hushed tones. India could not hear what they said. In any event, their words would have had no effect upon her. All she could focus on was the wooden box that had been lowered into the pit a few feet from where she sat.

The sound of footsteps crushing grass penetrated her grief. The undertaker came to rest beside her and removed his tall hat. From the corner of her eye, she watched the black plume in the band flutter as the hat came to rest against his thigh. He bowed slightly. "Miss Ledbetter, would it be acceptable for my men to begin their final work?" India looked at him as if through a fog. She recognized the sounds of vowels and consonants, but her mind refused to form meaning. The undertaker moved a step closer. "You see, it is long past our time. The train to Asheville leaves in an hour and we were hoping to avoid an overnight stay."

India forced herself to focus on his question. "Of course. Please forgive me. I did not intend to keep you. I guess I lost track of time."

A look of sympathy crossed the man's face. "It is to be expected in present circumstances. You have suffered a great loss." He nodded to his gravediggers and moved away to supervise the shifting of dirt.

A great loss. The words echoed through India's mind and settled in her heart. Yes, Papa was the greatest loss of her life. She grieved for Nanny Gordon, but with Papa gone, life would never be the same.

She jumped when a hand pressed her shoulder. Looking up, she saw Charlie gazing at her, deep creases furrowing his brow. "You have eaten nothing today. Perhaps you can force something down now?"

His compassion and concern touched her more than she could have imagined. The tears rising in her eyes threatened to become rivers flowing over her cheeks. Speech was beyond her, so she simply shook her head.

"May I sit with you then?"

Again, she did not speak but merely nodded. If she opened her mouth, there was a real possibility only guttural cries like those of an injured animal would emerge.

They sat in silence for some time before he said, "I am most heartily sorry. The loss of a parent is always difficult, but especially so when we lose them unexpectedly and before their time." He did not add that he understood how she felt having lost his own father in much the same way as Papa. For that, India was grateful.

They remained by the grave until the sun dipped behind the mountain peaks. A shudder passed through her as the damp of evening settled over them.

Charlie slipped his hand over hers where they still sat clenched in her lap. "I think we should go in now. Catching a chill will do you no good."

She allowed him to assist her to her feet, which tingled as the blood returned to them. Taking a tentative step, she swayed a little. Charlie pulled her hand firmly under his arm. As they walked down the hill toward the house, she noticed they moved in rhythm like they were accustomed to walking together for many years, like a long-married couple. Funny the things that made an impression when your mind seemed beyond sensible thought.

***

The days following the funeral left India depleted. Everywhere she went in the house or on the property reminded her of her dual losses. At the one-week mark, she could stand the house and gardens no longer. Hobbs mentioned during breakfast that the staff would soon need to clear Nanny Gordon's little cottage of her possessions and as she had no family, what could not be used by members of the community would be put on the burn pile. India might not be functioning at full force, but by God, what little remained of the woman who raised her would not be discarded like so much trash.

The groom had Zara saddled and ready by the time India arrived in the stables. She stepped from the mounting block into the saddle and kicked the little mare's flanks. They were off at a gallop. Earlier in the week, she had collected her boy clothes from the shed and now wore them openly while riding astride. She no longer cared that Mother might see and be outraged. She reached up, whipped the cap from her head, and removed the pins holding her hair in place. Her dark blonde strands flowed behind her. The Arabian might be small, only 14 hands, but she was surefooted and swift. She knew the estate paths as surely as she understood every inch of her stall.

Nanny Gordon's cabin came into view after only a few minutes. India pulled on the reins, sending Zara into a sliding stop. After tying the mare to a tree near the front door, she stepped into the cottage. At first glance, nothing had changed. The sun poured through the east-facing windows giving the room a cheerful glow. The rocker by the fireplace sat empty as though Nanny had only just then stepped out the back door to gather vegetables from the garden. Going to it, India dropped down in Nanny's chair and leaned her head against its high back. She pushed with her feet, setting the rocker in motion - back and forth, back and forth. The movement soothed - simple, calming, homey. She couldn't bring herself to rise and do what she had come for. It could wait. She hadn't slept well in days. She closed her eyes and drifted away.

When she awoke, the room was darker and the logs were glowing embers. She must have slept for several hours because the sun now came through the back windows filtered by forest. Something else was different as well. She felt it before she saw she was not alone. Charlie stood before the kitchen window gazing at the mountain rising behind the cottage. He turned when she squirmed in the rocker, which squealed under her shifting weight.

He smiled and nodded. "Ah, you have returned to the world."

"How long have you been here? Why didn't you wake me?"

He held up a finger. "One, for about a half of an hour." He lifted a second finger. "Two, because you haven't slept well this week and you needed the rest. Feeling better?"

"Some. I'm afraid I have a crick." She rolled her head and massaged the back of her neck. "How did you find me?"

"When you didn't come back for luncheon, I was deputized as official searcher. Your maid told me where I would most likely find you and, as you can see, she was correct." He extended his hand with a gesture that encompassed the whole room. "It's a lovely cottage. It reminds me of the ones in the village at Kilnsey. I've made coffee. Care for some?"

The brew's fragrance filled the room. Why she had not noticed until he mentioned it was odd. She must have been so exhausted that even her senses had been unconscious. "My goodness, I didn't know you could cook."

"I wouldn't call what I do cooking, but I can measure coffee and water. I also know how to light a stove." The rattle of a spoon clinking against pottery sounded. "Milk and sugar. Just as I have seen you prepare it for yourself. I checked the milk, by the way. Surprisingly, it's fresh."

"The dairy must still be delivering it every morning. I wonder why."

"Perhaps they anticipated your visit to the cottage?"

India shrugged. "I don't see why, but I'm glad they brought it."

He sat in the chair opposite, the one she had always thought of as hers, and held out a mug of coffee pale tan with milk. She accepted the mug and sipped. The sweet liquid slipped down her throat, warming her and making her more alert. "You make a good cup of coffee. Perhaps you have missed your calling."

His eyes grew wide, and he laughed. "As what? A street vendor of beverages? No, thank you." He put his mug on the hearth, then his face lost all humor. "No, I have accepted my fate. I will return to Kilnsey and do what I can to preserve my heritage." He became quiet and studied her before asking, "Have you thought of what you will do once the estate is settled? Will you return to London, or perhaps New York?"

Cold washed over India as though she had been doused with water straight from a deep well. Uncertainty over what the future held had been one of the reasons for her week of insomnia.

Her voice caught in her throat. She swallowed hard, then answered in a near whisper. "The idea of staying here at The Falls is unbearable. I guess I never realized how fully Papa was its heart. Now the house and estate feel dull and lifeless. But worse than staying here is the prospect of returning to New York. You must remember my last foray there. It was far from successful. As for London, I can hardly bear the thought of parties and being put back into the marriage market while still in mourning." Her voice broke, and she dissolved in tears.

Charlie rose from his chair and dropped to his knees beside her. Taking one hand, he slipped his free arm about her shoulders. "My darling girl, it pains me to see you so sad and hopeless. If you will forgive the impertinence, I believe I have a solution to your dilemma." When she looked up at him, he continued, "I know you have forbidden the subject, but that was before…before your losses and the present situation in which you find yourself." He stopped and appeared to fear continuing.

India gasped softly, "Go on."

He leaned closer. She could feel his breath on her throat when he spoke. "I have a castle that needs a young mistress, one who can take up where my mother must leave off due to her age and declining health. You have two homes, neither of which you wish to inhabit. I can offer you a life unlike any you have known here. You will have position and standing. You will never again be snubbed by society. You will have a title and a heritage of which you can be proud. Ours is an ancient and noble family. You will have a community who will hold you in the highest regard. As my countess, you will have the protection of my title and my connections. More importantly, you will be beyond your mother's control. As your husband, I will not prevent you pursuing your own interests, as long as they do not conflict with mine or damage the family." He paused and moved around to face her. Placing one knee on the floor, he lifted her fingers and brushed them with his lips. "My dearest India, will you do me the great honor of becoming the next Lady Kilnsey?"

India should have felt surprise or even anger, but she didn't. She felt nothing. The whole afternoon lost any sense of reality. She shook her head.

"Does this mean you are refusing me without so much as a civil word?" He sounded more hurt than angry.

She gazed at him through weary eyes. "No, that is not what I meant. I'm sorry. I was just trying to clear my mind."

"Are you saying you will consider my proposal?"

"I'm saying that I haven't said no. That is as far as I am willing to commit. I simply cannot make such an important decision right now. Can't you understand that?" Her voice was shrill with emotion.

She put her head in her hands. Her shoulders convulsed with sobs until Charlie drew her to his chest. She stiffened and started to pull away, but he held firm until she melted into his embrace. After several minutes, the tears were spent.

Wiping her face with the handkerchief he offered, she smiled weakly. "I will not give you an answer now, but I thank you for your kindness. I will think about what you have said."

As they walked Zara back to the stables, it occurred to her that while his tone had been one of concern and compassion, he had said nothing of love.

CHAPTER 27

During the days following Papa's funeral, Charlie had the good grace to leave India to consider his proposal without pressure. Though he didn't mention the subject again, he showed no desire to leave The Falls without an answer. Despite her promise to give it consideration, she simply could not bring herself to do so. To think about becoming someone's wife, much less Charlie's countess, required more mental and physical energy than she possessed. She was a small boat adrift, pushed one way then another, but never brought to shore. The little boat had no rudder to steer its course nor did it have the desire to do so. It simply went where the currents took it, floating through the minutes and hours on a sea of inertia. Even choosing between poached and scrambled eggs at breakfast seemed beyond her ability. All the energy she had felt when they first arrived home dissolved as the full weight of grief settled upon her.

Two weeks after they buried Papa, Mother breezed into the breakfast room. After spending the period since the funeral ensconced on the chase in her room, she emerged appearing refreshed and more herself. After Hobbs served coffee, she blessed all present with a smile communicating her return to full force.

Warning bells clanged within India as Mother opened her mouth. "I believe we will have had a sufficient period of mourning and may return to New York at the end of the month. We will stay with Grandmama for a suitable length of time and then return to London. If we time it well, we will still be able to participate in the last of the season."

India's head snapped back. "I thought you said you are required to stay here and see to the estate." Her voice filled the room.

Mother's cup clinked against its bone china saucer. She skewered India with a look. "I was in an unsettled state when we last spoke of the matter. I may have exaggerated the conditions under which I receive maintenance from the trust. I have consulted an attorney and communicated with the trustees. They all assure me that as Robert's widow, my mother and I will continue to receive sufficient financial support to live wherever we wish and I wish to live in New York once I have you properly settled. They have agreed a curator can be hired to manage The Falls. Grandmama is expecting us on the first. We will stay at Washington Square long enough to oversee the arrival of my possessions, then it's off to London."

A tremor raced through India sending her coffee sloshing onto the snowy tablecloth. Never had a decision been made as quickly nor had her path ever been so clear. Drawing a deep breath, she exhaled with force. "I am happy for you if that is what you want, but I will not be returning to New York or London. I am going to remain here in North Carolina and pursue a degree as I have always wanted."

Mother's eyes narrowed. "You will not. A girl of nineteen cannot live alone with no one but the servants. It is unthinkable. I'm appalled you would even suggest it. As to college, what lady of any standing needs a college degree when she can have position and a title? No, we will leave The Falls in competent hands and you will return to New York with me."

"And if I refuse?"

"You are a minor child and a dependent. You have no say in the matter."

"But I'm Papa's heir."

"Being an heiress is what makes you so attractive as a potential bride, but the amount and distribution of any money you receive remains under the control of the trustees and I assure you they will listen to me, not a mere chit of a girl. You will be cut off from all funds for your own good if necessary. You have no skills, so finding suitable employment is unlikely. How do you propose to live without money? Perhaps as Jane did?"

"What do you mean? How did Jane live? You said she died not long after she and Grandfather TJ separated, or are the rumors true after all?"

"That is quite enough. Charles does not wish to be regaled with the tragedy that is your paternal history. I have instructed our maids to begin packing. We leave within the week. Accept that you must do as you are told."

"I'll be twenty-one in a year and a half. Things will be different then."

"If you were a man, perhaps, but as a young woman it is highly unlikely."

"But the trustees seem to listen to you."

"I am a mature widow and I have a longstanding friendship with one of the principal trustees."

"I see. I suppose your former beau, David Havemeyer, is eager to do your bidding after all these years?"

Mother did not reply, but a smug grin spread across her lips.

India threw her napkin on the table and shoved her chair back. "I'm no longer hungry. Excuse me." She did not wait for Mother's response. As she fled the room, she heard another chair scraping back.

She ran through the entrance hall and out onto the gravel drive. Without really thinking about her destination, she started down the mountain. When she reached the turn off to the waterfall from which the house took its name, she dashed between the trees under an overhanging canopy. The narrow trail had been left as natural as possible. The verges were covered in overgrown blades of the soft grass one finds in the mountains. The sound of cascading water grew ever louder the farther she went. When she reached the wooden bridge that gave access to the other side of the small river, she crossed at a run.

A three-sided hut erected in her grandfather's time stood sentinel on the banks of the river that coursed through the entire estate. Benches provided a place to sit before the ascent to the top of the falls, the estate's highest point. The little building was unpainted. The wood had been allowed to weather to a silvery gray. Cutouts at the tops of the walls were of a Nordic design. On snowy winter days, one might imagine oneself in Scandinavia while sheltered there.

India entered and dropped down on the bench at the back of the enclosure. Forest surrounded the hut creating deep shadows within. She leaned against the rough-sawn wood wall and stared outward. The thunder created as water poured into the pool at the base of the falls soothed her jangling nerves. This had been her refuge since childhood when she needed time alone to sort out a problem. She inhaled the woodsy, evergreen scent that one found only in alpine areas. Her mind began to clear, and with that, her strength of will flowed once more.

Mother's plans must be thwarted no matter the cost. There had to be a way out. She would not tolerate such tyranny any longer. The more she pondered, the firmer her resolve. Whatever it took, she would win this battle.

The sound of footfall on the bridge broke the water's spell. Charlie marched through the trees and up the path toward the shelter. India shrank back and scooted deeper into shadow. He was a complication she had not yet sorted out. Seeing him now would only confuse things further because she instinctively knew what he would say. He could be the solution to her problem and she to his, but was it the right one for either of them?

He passed the shelter and took the path leading up the mountain. After a few minutes, she could hear him calling her from the top. Conversation was the last thing she wanted, but the path beyond the falls broke into branches that led in multiple directions. Some led back to the house. Others led one into wilderness. Someone unfamiliar with the estate and mountains beyond could easily become lost.

Emerging from the hut, she answered his call. "Stay where you are. I'm coming up to you."

She found him on the bench beside the water, his elbows on his knees and his head in his hands. She stopped at the edge of the clearing and watched him. He looked forlorn and dejected. Something bubbled up within her. She could brush it off simply as sympathy for a friend, but it was more than that. The thought that he was troubled or possibly in pain made her want to put her arms around him, to comfort him as he had comforted her since they left London. He had protected and supported her in a time of great need. He had put her desires first, had held her hand when she cried, had listened to her worries, and had left her alone when she wanted solitude. He could be arrogant and stubborn, but he also showed compassion and consideration when they were most needed.

Maybe she had confused what she had previously thought of as maternal or sisterly feelings for something quite different. Maybe somewhere along the way she had fallen in love with him. If wanting only the best for someone and wanting to protect him from hurt counted, then maybe she was looking at something real and permanent. As she pondered, other questions vied for attention. At her age shouldn't she be feeling swept off her feet? Shouldn't Charlie be affecting her emotions more akin to how Billy Connor had? Instead of giddy, she felt calm.

She breathed deeply and exhaled slowly. Within the next few days, she would have to sort out exactly how she felt about a lot of things, including Charlie.

CHAPTER 28

Charlie must have sensed her presence for his head snapped up and he cast wide eyes her way. He seemed flustered to have been caught in an attitude of despair. He flushed in the way English schoolboys do - bright red streaks across the apples of his cheeks - giving him an innocent, youthful appearance.

"I'm sorry. I didn't mean to startle you." Still puffing from the steep climb, India continued, "Did you not hear me answering your call?"

"No, I guess I was too deep in thought. I'm struggling with a rather serious conundrum."

A sliver of tension pierced India. "What's wrong? Has something new happened?"

He shot her a rueful smile. "No, nothing new."

She dropped down beside him on the bench. Placing a hand on his arm, she searched his face. His gaze met hers and darted away. A tremor passed through her as a door within her heart clicked softly open. He really was a gorgeous man. Why had she not noticed how beautiful he is until now? A tingle traveled down her spine.

Without thinking, she brushed the forelock out of his eyes. "Do you want to talk about it? We promised to help one another whenever we are able. Sometimes just getting trouble out in the open makes things clearer. It's something about hearing the words as well as thinking about the issue that is supposed to help, I think. At least that is what I have read."

He sat up and took her hand. "Actually, that's part of the problem. We've already talked about it."

"What do you mean?" India smiled in confusion. "We've hardly said a word to one another today."

"That's true, but we have spoken of the issue twice before."

India searched her memory, but she could think of nothing that should create such a state in him. "What?" India's voice bounced off the cliff face on the opposite side of the falls. "What is it?"

He did not answer but pointed to elderly mountain laurels whose top branches leaned in on one another forming a tunnel. "Is that a walkable path or just an animal trail?"

"It's a path down to the village. Would you like to try it?"

He nodded. "I think we both need a change of scene. That also helps clear the mind. Is there a tea shop, perhaps?"

India wrinkled her nose. "No, at least not the type of tea you are accustomed to. The pharmacy has added a few tables and serves light lunches. You can get a glass of sweet iced tea there. Interested?"

"You know, in all the time I've visited your home, no one has offered an iced tea. I thought you Southerners with your warm climate preferred your tea iced rather than hot."

India laughed and cast him a sidewise glance. "You're correct, but Mother will not countenance iced tea at The Falls. Much too southern and far too plebeian for her. No, tea is only to be served hot at four o'clock and at breakfast. Mother is a New York Knickerbocker through and through." She kicked at a pinecone near her feet and nodded. "I think you are right about needing a change of scenery." Waving toward the path, she continued, "It's a two-mile walk to the village and four miles back. Up for some exercise?"

He stood, locked his fingers behind him, and stretched his arms and back. "I think I'd better get some. I've been far too sedentary since leaving Kilnsey. At home, I work on the farms every day. I need to use my muscles again. An added benefit will be shaking the cobwebs from my brain."

At the trail head, Charlie lifted an overhanging branch for India to pass. "What do you mean two miles down and four up? Is there a different path leading back to the house?"

India grinned and waggled her brows. "No. Same path. It just feels twice as long going uphill because the climb is rather steep."

They started toward the village in companionable silence, but half-way down the mountain, India stumbled on rolling stones. Charlie grabbed her hand to steady her. Instead of letting it go, he tucked it into the crook of his elbow without looking at her or asking permission. With another man, she might have felt managed or been angered by the impertinence. With Charlie, it felt right and comfortable. In fact, it felt as though her hand belonged on his arm, as though it had always been there and always would be.

He must have sensed her mood for after several yards, he looked down at her with a gentle smile and pulled her arm under his, drawing her to his side.

They reached the village and found the pharmacy's little cafe deserted. Charlie guided India to a table next to the front window and pulled out a chair for her. When she was seated, he took the chair opposite and picked up the menu card. "Neither of us ate much at breakfast. It's a little early for luncheon, but could I persuade you to have something to eat as well as a beverage? I'm feeling a bit peckish myself."

"You know, I think I could eat something." Until the mention of food, she had not realized she was hungry. Charlie was having a remarkable influence on her. She felt better about life than she had in weeks. "By the way, there is no wait staff. You will have to order at the counter."

After receiving her order for an egg salad sandwich, he strolled to the marble-topped counter. No one appeared. India watched him rocking back on his heels. He looked relaxed and calm, not at all the dispirited man she found by the falls. The walk down the mountain had done them both good. After a few moments, she remembered the bell on the counter. "I forgot. You will have to ring for service."

The druggist emerged from the back wiping his hands on a towel. "May I help you?" Charlie gave their order, but the man interrupted him. "I'm sorry, but the woman who fixes the food doesn't come in until 11:00. I can get you some lemonade, maybe."

Charlie accepted the drinks, paid with a generous tip, and carried them back to the table. "I guess we will have to prevail upon Cook to give us something if we want to eat before luncheon." He took a sip. "My goodness. This is very sweet."

India giggled. "Yep. Just the way we like down here. We find sufficient sugar makes everything sweeter, including our problems." She cocked her head and raised her brows trying to communicate her question through her facial expression. When he failed to take the hint, she said, "You had an issue to discuss with me?"

Placing his arms on the table, he leaned forward and studied her as though looking for some clues in her face. After several beats, he seemed to reach a decision. "My dearest India, we have spoken of the subject twice in the past and both times I believe you thought I was in jest or at least insincere. At any rate, you did not take me seriously."

The subject to which he might be referring suddenly dawned on her. While her heart had definitely softened where he was concerned, she was not ready for that particular conversation. These past weeks had been hard, at times clouding her thinking and playing tricks with her memory. "I think that subject is best left for another time. Neither of us is in a position to deal with something so serious and this is certainly not the place for such a discussion."

"So, you know what I am thinking?"

"While I am not a mind reader, I am fairly confident of my conclusions." She pushed her chair back and stood. "I think we should return to the house. Will you accompany me or must I walk unescorted?"

"I see there is a park with benches across the street. Would you at least do me the courtesy of hearing what I have to say?"

India allowed him to lead her to a bench deep within the park bordering the French Broad River which ran through the little town. When they were seated, Charlie did not speak, but took her hand, stroking it with his thumb. He sighed and looked into her eyes as though asking permission to break the silence.

When India did not look away, he began. "We are good friends, I think." It was a statement, not a question, yet he waited for her reply. She nodded once to get him to the point. "As friends, we understand and support one another. We have stood back-to-back against gossips, interlopers, and cads who would cause us harm." He raised his brow in question.

India avoided being completely rude with a brief answer. "Yes, and I am grateful."

"If so, I offer the following. You have said you will be miserable in either of the homes available to you. The Falls holds too many memories of loved ones lost and New York promises a life controlled by others." He stopped, waiting for her response.

She nodded. "What you say is true. I cannot bear the thought of either location." She raised her gaze so that her line of sight was over his shoulder to the west. The mountains' namesake blue haze still hung low even though it was late into the morning. It matched the mood Charlie's words stirred up.

He lifted a finger and drew her face so that their eyes met. "Kilnsey holds painful memories for me, too, but ones that I will deal with because I have no choice. Too many people there depend on me. My conscience will not allow me to abandon them nor allow my ancestral home to go under the hammer. It will be very hard, but you have it within your power to ease my burden." He paused once more and pressed her hand.

She could utter no more than two simple words. "Go on."

"I offer this for your consideration. Would making Kilnsey your home and helping me to restore it to its former glory be such a terrible alternative to what you face here? I must book passage to England soon. My hope is that I will be booking for my bride-to-be, as well. Will you at least think about it?" He dropped down onto one knee and lifted her hand to his lips. "Will you become my countess?" Her face must have reflected the turmoil coursing through her. He sighed and stood, maintaining a firm grip on her hand. "I will not press you for an answer, however, I will not ask again. I believe we can make a good life together that will benefit us both. We can be contented if only you will say yes."

It was not the kind of proposal young girls dreamed of. There was no mention of undying love, just practicalities, but he looked so earnest, so vulnerable that her heart skipped a beat anyway. Was this the solution she needed to end her troubles?

CHAPTER 29

Althea had just finished helping India dress for bed when a knock on the door sounded. Without invitation, Mother stepped into the room. "Althea, I am glad you are still here. You will begin packing all of Miss India's belongings in the morning. We return to New York within the week. Say your farewells to your family. We will not be returning to The Falls. Our home will be in Washington Square with Mrs. Van de Berg."

As the door clicked shut on Mother's pronouncement, waves of turmoil flooded India. She had delayed giving Charlie an answer and now she must decide. For his part, he had been a gentleman. He had not mentioned his proposal again and India had procrastinated, drifting along in a dreamlike state that bore little relation to reality. She had buried herself in her grief, leaving the future to fend for itself.

Althea shot her a questioning look. "So, it is to be life in New York. Are you ready to deal with that or will you fight to stay here?"

India frowned. "There is something I have not told you. There is another option, but I am unsure whether I should pursue it."

A smile spread across the maid's face. "Might it have to do with Lord Kilnsey?"

"It does, but I'm confused by him and by my own reactions. I always thought being in love would feel different, like the way I felt about Billy Connor. My heart skipped every time he came in sight, but that is not what I feel for Charlie."

"But you do feel something for him?"

India nodded. "I can't bear the thought of his being hurt or losing his home. Instead of feeling all fluttery and excited, I feel comfortable and calm with him. I feel like I can tell him my deepest thoughts and he will not criticize or find them foolish. I think he feels the same."

"And you are holding back for some reason?" Althea's tone communicated disbelief rather than lack of understanding.

India tilted her head and frowned. "He has not used the word love. He has said all the right things about what our life together can be, but he has never said he loves me."

"Could it be that English lords do not express their emotions? Could it be that stiff upper lip we hear about?"

Oh that it were so, but India feared a different explanation. "Possibly. More likely, he still pines for the farmer's daughter, the one who was sent to Ireland to marry her cousin. He believes the child she carries is his."

"That is certainly a complication, but he cannot have her."

India plopped down on the bed. "Yes, but that makes me second best. I don't know if that will be good enough."

"You say you can tell him anything. Have you told him what you just told me?"

"No, I am afraid it will make me sound weak and needy."

Althea placed her fists on her hips and locked eyes with India. "When it comes to making a decision about the rest of your life, maybe honesty is more important than appearances. Anyway, Lord Kilnsey is not the only one who has failed to use the word love. Do you love him?"

"I think so. If wanting the best for him and wanting him to be happy is love, then yes, I guess I love him."

A crease formed between the maid's brows. "If I may be so bold, I would say it is a mature love that can be the foundation of a good marriage. What you felt for Mr. Connor was a young girl's infatuation, but would you really have married him if he had asked?"

India pressed her lips together in thought. "You know, now that you ask, I don't believe I would have. I think it was the excitement of meeting on the sly and the attention that I enjoyed. I think, at least I hope, that I would have come to see him for the scoundrel he really is."

"Maybe it is time for a serious conversation with his lordship."

India threw her arms around Althea's neck and hugged her close. "You really are the older sister I always wanted. No matter where I end up, please say you will go with me."

Taking India's wrists and holding her at arm's length, Althea replied with an ironic chuckle. "There will never be any reason for concern about that. I have nothing to hold me here. Moving away would put paid to my daddy's plans to marry me off to his neighbor." Althea searched India's face, then released her wrists. "I should leave you now. You have a big decision to make."

"Talking with you always clears my mind. I have made my decision. I am going to him now."

"Your mother will be scandalized if she catches you."

India paused at the door. "She can hardly criticize a woman who is accepting a proposal of marriage."

Slipping out of her room and across the balcony above the grand staircase, India entered the guest wing. She soon found Charlie's door and knocked timidly. When she got no answer, she knocked louder. Footsteps sounded on the hardwood flooring and the door swung back. Charlie's eyes grew large when he saw India standing there in her robe and slippers.

Glancing to one end of the passage and then the other, he said, "I think you had better come inside." As the door closed behind them concern darkened his eyes. "Has something happened? Is someone ill?"

"No, all is well I think and I hope you will find it so too." India's voice suddenly failed her. The realization that she was on the verge of changing her life forever hit full force and she faltered. She exhaled slowly before forcing the words. "I have come to say I accept your proposal of marriage."

His look of surprise melted into one of pleasure. He took her hands, and turning them palms up, placed a kiss in the center of each. "I had almost given up hope. This is wonderful news. We must tell your mother first thing in the morning. Thank you, my darling. You have made me the happiest of men."

In the end, her courage failed when it came to discussing love and other emotions. It was enough that he seemed so pleased. Even without protestations of love, this felt right. After four days of inner turmoil, the conclusion had been rather anticlimactic. It did not create the over-the-moon excitement girls are taught to expect, but it brought a welcome calm.

Over breakfast the next morning while Mother chattered away about life in New York, India met Charlie's gaze and raised her brows. Taking the hint, he patted his lips with his napkin, then cleared his throat. Mother paused and cast a speculative glance his way. When he did not open his mouth for several beats, India's lips thinned and she nodded. Finally, his voice filled the silence. "Mrs. Ledbetter, India and I have something we wish to tell you. We hope you will be pleased."

The application of cream and sugar to her coffee suddenly captured Mother's attention. Between clinking swirls of tan liquid, she asked, "Am I to understand this is an announcement as opposed to seeking permission?"

A flush crawled up Charlie's cheeks. "Forgive me. I am going about this clumsily. What I should have said is India and I have reached an understanding and wish to speak with you about it. I hope this is not completely unexpected but please allow me to review my position. I can offer the life you have always wanted for India. I have an estate of no mean size, an historic manor, and a pedigree of which anyone would be proud. As my countess, she will have a position among the most ancient peerages in the land." He stood and bowed slightly. "I humbly ask that you grant me your daughter's hand in marriage."

Mother eyed him for a moment, then her lips curved into a tight smile. "A very nice speech, Charles. And while I'm sure everything you say is true, I fear I cannot grant your request."

The stain on Charlie's cheeks grew deeper. He blinked a couple of times and dropped back onto his chair. "May I ask why you reject my suit so out-of-hand? If I have done something to offend you, please let me know what it is so I may make amends. I assure you I am in earnest in my desire to marry." Flummoxed best described his expression.

"Oh, I have no doubt about your desires and why you have chosen this particular bride, but I believe India has the chance of a much greater match than a mere earl no matter how ancient the title. She will make an excellent duchess or marchioness, don't you think?"

At the boiling point, India shoved her chair back and jumped to her feet, her pulse pounding against her eardrums. Resting her fists on the table, she leaned toward Mother. "How dare you insult Charlie? He has crossed an ocean and half the continent to see us safely home. He has been nothing but kind and thoughtful, especially where you are concerned. His sister did her best to help us, as well. You will see that this marriage is approved by the trustees or you will live to regret it."

If Mother was shocked or disturbed by India's outburst, her facade showed no cracks. Instead, her eyes simply narrowed. "I sincerely doubt that, my girl. We leave for New York tomorrow." Turning to Charlie, she continued, "You may accompany us in our private car, but once we arrive in the city, I expect you will wish to depart for London. If you act quickly, you may still be able to solve your problem. I understand an Astor relation remains unattached. At any rate, we do not expect to see you. Have I made myself clear?"

Charlie stood and gave a stiff nod. "Abundantly so. If you will excuse me, I must see to my own preparations for departure." He stormed from the room without a backward glance.

India watched Charlie's retreat in some disappointment. He might be willing to give up easily, but she was far from finished. The tyrant would be thwarted no matter the costs. If she had to be the stronger of them, then so be it. Despite all of Mother's attempts to crush it, the lesson of independence learned from Nanny Gordon endured. India might have bowed to Mother's demands while Papa was alive because he wished peace above all else, but he was no longer with them. It was time she claimed her true self.

Due to Nanny Gordon's influence and Papa's stories, India was at heart first, last, and always, a mountaineer. While Mother scoffed, Papa had always been quietly proud of his descent from what he called the most stubborn, independent-minded breed the world had ever known - the Scots-Irish. His stories about how his ancestors settled in the Appalachians because the mountains reminded them of their ancestral home still rang clear and strong. She knew the history of her people, as Nanny Gordon phrased it. Thinking about Papa brought Nanny Gordon's words back. "You was borned and bred in these here mountains..."

Mother's great mistake had been in leaving the time-consuming, tiresome aspects of child-rearing to the hired help. Charlie might possess some Yorkshire stubbornness, but like Papa said, she was descended from tartan-wearing clansmen who had been forced from their ancestral Highlands, transplanted to Ireland, and finally driven to escape English tyranny in the New World. Her ancestors had been survivors. There was no comparison.

Deep within her, a bird caged for far too long pecked at the bars that enclosed it until one-by-one they fell away. Once the bird took flight, there was no calling it back. Charlie could lead or he could follow. It really did not matter, but India suspected she would have the greatest influence on their future. In all fairness, she knew what he did not. She had intimate knowledge of where Mother was most vulnerable, where her deepest insecurities lay. With knowledge, comes power.

CHAPTER 30

India steeled herself for their arrival at Pennsylvania Station. She had already forewarned Charlie that stepping off the train would put into motion a series of events from which there would be no return and that he must trust her. Furthermore, he should follow her lead no matter what was said when they were joined by Mother. He had reluctantly agreed.

Brakes shrieked, couplings clanked, and the train rolled to a halt under the steel girders of the terminus. India inhaled deeply before opening the carriage door to the smoke-filled arrivals hall. After stepping down onto the platform, she glanced left then right. No sign of Mother. India clasped her hands at her waist in hopes of presenting a calm attitude.

She jerked around when a luggage cart creaked behind her. A redcap puffing under the strain of his burden stopped and tugged on the brim of his cap as Althea came to rest behind him. India surveyed the pile of luggage. Thank goodness she had ensured their bags and trunks were separated from Mother's things. Drumming her nails against her palm, she looked at the far entrance to their private carriage. How like Mother to draw out her descent onto the platform to ensure the grand entrance. Did she somehow sense a showdown was eminent?

Charlie came to India's side and took her hand. He leaned in and whispered, "No need to worry. You have my support and that of my entire family."

India shot him a nervous smile. "I couldn't do this without you."

He raised her hand and brushed it with his lips. "My bride shall have nothing less." His head swiveled searching the platform. "Ah, here she comes. Courage, my dear. It will be over in an instant."

India followed Charlie's gaze. Mother steamed toward them with another redcap in tow. She came to rest before them and ran her gaze over India. "You look like you have something on your mind."

Butterflies flitted around India's mid-section. Swallowing hard, she replied, "Charlie and I will be staying with Lady Clarissa and Mr. Rivers until we sail for England. Within the fortnight, we will make an appointment with the trustees to draw up the marriage contracts. You may attend our wedding, if you wish."

Mother's eyes bulged, then blinked. "Have you taken leave of your senses? I will not countenance such disrespect. You will come to Washington Square. There will be no discussion." Casting her gaze onto Charlie, she continued, "Thank you for your assistance. We will detain you no longer." Her curt tone belied the civility of her words.

The pressure of Charlie's arm on India's hand increased. She saw his nod from the corner of her eye. To Mother, she said, "I am going with Charlie. There is no way you can prevent it. Unless you want one heck of a scene right here on the platform, you will stand aside."

"Well, I never. You are demented. Come home with me now and we will call a doctor." Mother reached out in an attempt to grab India's arm.

India stepped aside, leaving Mother snatching at empty space. "No. And if you try to make trouble, you will find out just what trouble is." Clutching Charlie's arm with her free hand, she said, "I believe I see Mr. Rivers's chauffeur. We should not keep him waiting."

Leaving Mother mouth agape and puce faced, Charlie led their party straight to the waiting limousine. To the redcap, he said, "Miss Ledbetter's maid has been instructed to bring our luggage in a cab. See she is not delayed."

Once they were speeding up Fifth Avenue, Charlie relaxed into the seat and draped his arm around India. "I say, my dear, you were fierce. I have made note of that scene with Mrs. Ledbetter for future reference."

India leaned into his side and rested her head on his shoulder. "Is your sister going to be completely appalled by my arrival on her doorstep uninvited, demanding room and board?"

He chuckled and kissed her temple. "Far from it. She will be delighted, especially when we share our news."

India jerked forward. Her head snapped around and her eyes locked onto Charlie's. "Do you mean you have not told your sister about our engagement?"

"No, I thought we would surprise Clarissa. Had I sent a telegram before we left North Carolina, my dear sister would already have our nuptials planned down to the food for the wedding breakfast and who would serve as your bridesmaids. I thought you might have your own ideas on the subject." He ran the backs of his fingers along her jaw. "My sweet, I am curious, however, about your threat. It seems to me that your mother holds all the cards save for possession of your actual person."

"Appearances can be deceiving. There is a way to gain the upper hand, but I'm afraid I will need your brother-in-law's help to make good on my threat."

"I'm sure Jonathan will help, if he can. All you need do is ask. What have you in mind?"

"I think he has access to information I will need in order to contain Mother. Once he shares what he knows, I will need your help in pursuing the evidence."

"Evidence?" Incredulity filled his voice. "Evidence of what? Surely not illegal activity. I can hardly see either your mother or grandmother involved with the criminal underworld."

"Just as you chose to delay making our announcement, I would rather wait until we are with your family to discuss my plan." Why was she reluctant to tell Charlie? Perhaps it would make her seem audacious or unladylike in his eyes. Maybe he would not understand and try to stop her.

India pressed her lips together and choked back a sigh. It seemed she did not trust her fiancé as much as she initially believed. But why? He had been nothing but wonderful these last weeks. Perhaps the memory of Billy Connor's betrayal lingered, making her less trusting than she once had been. It was hardly fair to Charlie, but it was an acceptable explanation. Then another reason presented itself and it was most unwelcome. The idea crept into her consciousness like a predator stalking its prey, attacking her peace-of-mind. Perhaps she was trading one tyrant for another by marrying. Women had so few rights. They were their fathers' property as girls and that of their husbands as wives.

The automobile swayed as the chauffeur guided it to the curb in front of Lady Clarissa's house. India glanced down at the skirt of her costume and saw a wrinkled mess. Lost in thought, she had unconsciously bunched it with nervous fingers. She also had no memory of quite a few blocks of Fifth Avenue. She must get a grip on herself. She had made her choice. There was no turning back now.

If Lady Clarissa and Jonathan were surprised at India's arrival on their doorstep with luggage in tow, generations of training forbade they show it. Within minutes, she and Charlie sat in Clarissa's solarium being served afternoon tea. The Earl Grey and finger sandwiches provided a welcome distraction as India worked out exactly how to approach the topic uppermost in her mind.

After a few minutes of polite conversation regarding their stay in North Carolina, India felt Charlie move forward on the sofa. His inhaled breath whispered beside her and she peeked at him from beneath her lashes. Cutting his eyes at her and smiling, he took her hand and gave it a squeeze. "We have an announcement. I hope you will be pleased for us. I have asked India to become the next Lady Kilnsey, and she has accepted." He lifted India's hand and kissed it.

After exchanging a satisfied smile with his wife, Jonathan stood and extended his hand to Charlie. "My hardiest congratulations, my dear fellow." To India, he said, "We couldn't be more pleased. Welcome to the family. We wish you both great joy."

A further fifteen minutes discussion regarding potential wedding plans allowed India additional time to consider her next move. When she had marshalled her courage, she put a cucumber sandwich on her plate and took a sip of sweet, milk-laced tea. She might as well explain the full situation now. Jonathan would either help or he wouldn't. Nothing would be gained by delaying her request and valuable time would be lost. Returning her cup to its saucer, she dabbed her mouth with a napkin. "As happy as we are, there is an impediment with which we need your assistance."

Clarissa frowned. "What on earth could possibly stand in the way of your marriage?"

India cleared her throat. When she spoke, it was in a near whisper. "It pains me to share this, but my mother is not in favor of our marriage."

"Why ever not? She has always seemed enthusiastic in the past."

"I'm afraid our time in London...how shall I put this?" India's heart rate kicked up a notch. She had no desire to insult her fiancé and his family, but they must be told the truth if they were to help. "I fear her expectations have become somewhat grandiose, far beyond reason, I assure you. It is as though her experience there played havoc with her faculties. This brings me to a subject that I find...embarrassing."

A sudden failure of confidence stilled India's tongue.

Jonathan broke the silence. "Do not stop there. Nothing you have said makes us think less of you, my dear. Far from it. We admire your honesty. Please tell us whatever is on your mind."

"There is a way to bring my mother to heel and ensure her supportive influence with the trustees who control my fortune and my future."

Clarissa leaned forward, full attention on India. "Go on."

"Do you recall the conversation about my Grandmother Ledbetter the night of my ball here in New York?"

Both Clarissa and Jonathan looked uncomfortable. After a pregnant silence, Jonathan finally replied, "That was unfortunate, but you did ask. In fact, you were quite persistent. I hope you do not now regret the information we imparted or hold us responsible for any unhappiness that may have resulted."

"Hardly. It may hold the key to my freedom from Mother."

"How so?" Jonathan watched India with piqued interest.

"I intend to find out what happened to Jane, my Grandmother Ledbetter. Whatever it was, Mother will not want it broadcast here in New York. She will do anything to avoid a new scandal. With the trouble between my grandfathers, one's suicide, the divorce, and my parents' subsequent marriage, our family has already had its fair share of those. Another one and Mother will never be granted entrance to any home regardless how low its position on the social ladder. Jane is Mother's Achilles Heel. Come to think of it, she is Grandmama's as well. The thing that matters most to them is admission to the drawing rooms of Mrs. Astor's 400. That's why Mother decided a more exalted title is needed." India's breath caught in her throat as she searched Charlie's face. She put her hand on his arm. "Please forgive me. And please do not believe that I in any way think as my relatives do. Becoming Lady Kilnsey will be the greatest honor of my life."

Charlie did not speak but smiled with a gentleness that reassured. The silence surrounding her became deafening. She watched in interest tinged with trepidation as a look passed between Jonathan and Clarissa.

Jonathan shifted in his chair and crossed his legs before asking, "How do you propose going about locating your grandmother, provided she still lives?"

"If you will loan me the money, I want to hire a Pinkerton. They can find anyone."

This time, Charlie, Clarissa, and Jonathan exchanged glances. Jonathan pursed his lips before replying. "I suppose we can do as you ask, but please let me make the arrangements. It would never do for word to get about that a young lady was involved in such an investigation."

***

From her chair beside the parlor fireplace, Clarissa watched the two most important men in her life argue about how best to proceed with the India situation. Thank goodness the girl had gone to bed not long after dinner. It gave them time to sort her outlandish plan.

Charlie pounded the sofa arm with his fist. "I will not see her hurt. You must not pursue this line of inquiry. It can only lead to heartache. There must be another way to convince India's mother to sway the trustees in my favor."

Jonathan stroked his chin and did not answer immediately. Finally, he said, "I don't see how. Clarissa, my dear, have you a thought?"

While men always believed themselves in charge of every situation, she knew these two would eventually turn to her. Of the three of them, she had far more imagination and far greater skill in societal machinations. "I believe there may be no need to actually consult the Pinkertons. After a suitable passage of time, let's say two weeks, we will tell India the agent had no success in locating Jane. We can suggest that she is either dead as Petra Ledbetter says or that she simply does not want to be found. Whatever will best suit India's mood."

Charlie jumped to his feet and strode to the fireplace. Placing both hands on the mantel, he leaned against it and looked over his shoulder at Clarissa. "But how will that help with Mrs. Ledbetter and the trustees?"

"Once India has accepted the futility of a continued search, I will call upon Petra and old Mrs. Van de Berg. I will make it clear that certain journalists will receive information regarding the state of relations between our families. Society columnists thrive on such tittle-tattle.

Charlie, you and India will be portrayed as Romeo and Juliet. Petra and her mother will be seen as cruel, social pariahs attempting a comeback by selling their only daughter to the highest bidder, as long as he has a great title. It will be made clear to them that they can either agree to the marriage or I will ensure no desirable doors will ever open to them again. The choice will be theirs. And if they choose to stop interfering and accept my terms, they must remain silent. If they do not keep the agreement, the story will go out as though we had never spoken."

Jonathan laughed and patted his wife's knee. "Sometimes you amaze me, my dear. Beneath that lovely facade beats the heart of a true Machiavellian prince."

Jonathan's words shot an arrow of guilt through Clarissa. She liked the girl very much. In any circumstances, she would do whatever she could to help India's situation, but Charlie and Kilnsey must be her first consideration. The estate's very survival depended upon it. As it was, her mind would rest much easier knowing that marriage to Charlie was also India's desire.

CHAPTER 31

Clarissa stepped from her limousine onto the sidewalk in front of Number 5 Washington Square North and surveyed the house she was about to enter. It was lovely. Great care had been taken to preserve it over the generations. Only a little paint peeled here and there. Flowers bloomed in the small front garden. The beds could use some weeding, but they were not completely out of hand. Unless one compared Number 5 with its neighbors, one would not notice the small signs of decay setting in. Old Mrs. Van de Berg clearly needed the regular injections of cash from the Ledbetter estate. That observation might prove useful in the confrontation about to take place. The thought of Petra trying to cast Charlie aside in favor of a more exalted title made Clarissa's pulse race. She and Jonathan had been more than gracious to the two old biddies and this is how they chose to repay the kindness? So be it. Within the next few minutes, Petra Ledbetter would receive the comeuppance she richly deserved.

The butler opened the door and made noises about seeing if the ladies were at home. Clarissa ignored him and breezed past straight to the morning room where she knew her quarry were generally found at this time of day. Flinging the door ajar, she marched into the room and came to rest in front of her startled hostesses.

Petra spluttered and choked on her beverage before setting the cup in its saucer. "Lady Clarissa, what a pleasant surprise. Will you take tea with us? I will ring for another setting."

She started to rise from the sofa, but Clarissa stopped her with a raised hand. "This is not a social call. I have come to issue a warning. My brother and your daughter intend to marry. You will not stand in their way."

A crimson glow flooded Petra's face. "Whatever do you mean?"

While Petra silently feigned incomprehension, her mother filled the void. "How dare you come uninvited into my house and issue edicts?"

Clarissa clasped each of her forearms and rested them against her midsection. "Yes, I do dare. And if you do not agree to my terms, this is exactly what you can expect."

For the next fifteen minutes, Clarissa outlined the extent to which she was willing to go to cast Petra and her mother into the bowels of societal hell. With each new scenario, Petra's color paled a little more.

At one point, the woman looked as if she might faint. Her eyes rolled from left to right while she clutched the lace at her throat as though the fabric had come to life and strangled her. Petra leaned against the sofa back. Her mother patted her hand, then dabbed her brow with a handkerchief moistened with water from the samovar. Why the old woman thought hot water would help the faint was not explained.

Clarissa watched the antics playing out on the sofa in some amusement. Either Petra Ledbetter was an excellent actress or she intended to keel over within the minute.

Petra closed her eyes and slumped a little lower, but old Mrs. Van de Berg was made of sterner stuff. When ministering to her daughter failed to yield the desired result, she barked, "Sit up and stop this melodramatic nonsense. We do not give in to fits of the vapors even when being blackmailed by a former friend." She then fixed Clarissa with a glare.

Clarissa stepped closer to the sofa, the crease between her eyes deepening into a glare of her own. "You may call my demands by any foul name you wish, but it will not change them. I will ensure you are social pariahs unless you agree to the marriage. You will not only agree to it, you will let the world know how delighted you are that your dollar princess will soon be the new Countess Kilnsey. What say you?"

Petra and her mother exchanged a long look. They seemed to wilt in unison. Finally, Mrs. Van de Berg replied, "We agree."

Satisfied the two women had been thoroughly defeated, Clarissa said, "You will make clear to your trustees that Charlie has your full and unconditional support as India's future husband. It is your choice whether you attend the wedding. It will take place in our family church. We will notify you of the date by cable in time for you to book passage, if you choose to do so." She tossed a business card onto the table beside the sofa. "This is the firm that attends to our legal affairs. Your trustees can expect to hear from them shortly. Negotiations of the marriage contracts will begin immediately." After several beats, Petra and Mrs. Van de Berg nodded in unison. Clarissa turned and left without a backward glance.

***

When the search for Jane yielded no results at the end of two weeks, India had to accept what Jonathan reported, that all traces of Jane had disappeared about a year after she and T.J. divorced. She had either indeed died in some location outside of New York or had gone to ground so completely that Jane Ledbetter effectively no longer existed. If she still lived, in the words of the investigator, she simply did not want to be found. Jonathan had made all the arrangements and had met with the Pinkerton agent. He was adamant no connection should ever be made with India or Charlie. Thank goodness such a man would soon be her brother-in-law. She and Charlie needed family they could depend on.

India selected a book from Jonathan's library and settled herself in the solarium. Sitting among the potted palms and flowering plants lifted her spirits. Without many social calls to make, life in the city was rather boring. Most of the Rivers's friends had departed for their summer retreats in Newport or Long island. There were only so many walks one could take in Central Park. She had too much time with nothing to do but wait for her plan, actually Clarissa's plan, to be accomplished.

Before Clarissa left for Grandmama's, she had described exactly how she envisioned the visit would unfold. India suppressed a giggle. It was rather pleasant to think of Mother and Grandmama's reactions to Clarissa's proposals and threats. They would no doubt be apoplectic while being impotent to anything but agreement. Apoplectic and impotent. What a lovely combination of emotions. She really ought to feel ashamed for such thoughts, but she didn't. Living under Mother's thumb her entire life had only increased her determination to make a decision solely on her own. Charlie was her future and she would have him and her fortune, too, if all went as Clarissa believed it would.

The front door clicking shut echoed through the house. Voices came next. Although she could not understand his words, Charlie's rising tone indicated he was asking a question. A soft feminine reply floated to the solarium followed by a shout of glee. Clarissa's visit with Mother and Grandmama must have been successful.

Placing the book aside, India rushed to the foyer. Skidding to a halt beside Charlie, she cast an expectant look on Clarissa. "Well?"

Clarissa graced them with an enigmatic smile. "Well what?"

Charlie's exasperated sigh filled the space. "Stop it, Sister dear. Being coy at your age is unbecoming."

Clarissa laughed and stroked her brother's cheek. "Oh, Darling, being coy at any age is a woman's prerogative as you well know, but I will keep India in suspense no longer. Your Mother has agreed to the marriage. The contracts should be signed within a fortnight."

Warmth bubbled up in India. "How is that possible? Won't your solicitors in London have a say in this?"

"Of course they will. Thank goodness for transatlantic cables and fast ships. Jonathan's attorney is drawing up a draft as we speak. It will go into the mail tomorrow or the next day at the latest. A telegram to our London solicitors should already be on its way alerting them to the happy news."

***

And just like that, the contracts were negotiated and finalized. Neither India nor Mother had attended the signing at David Havemeyer's offices in the interestingly shaped Flat Iron Building. As the beneficiary of the deal, Charlie signed on his own behalf while each of the three trustees signed for India. Jonathan's attorney attended as well to ensure the final version protected Charlie's rights and estate in the fullest. Charlie was to get full use of a large share of the Ledbetter fortune save for the portions reserved for Mother and Grandmama's upkeep, that of The Falls, and a trust to guarantee the futures of any issue from the marriage. For her part, India gained a husband, a title, and a new life independent of Mother and the trustees.

As Althea gathered toiletries into a small carry case, India hugged herself and spun around the room. Her mood was lighter than it had been in months. Decisions made and arguments behind her, she was actually beginning to feel like a bride. "Just think. In a few weeks, I shall be married. Everything has worked out." She waltzed over to her maid and flung her arms wide. "I am happier than I ever thought I would be, but I'm sort of scared, too. Thank goodness you are going with us. Who knows? You may find an Englishman of your own to marry." India stopped and put an index finger on her cheek. "But promise me you will never move farther than Kilnsey Village. You're more than my maid. You're my best friend." With that, India slid her arms around Althea's neck and hugged her close.

The gesture hid tears that unexpectedly hovered in the wells of her eyes. Her happy mood had dissipated as the realities of her wedding dawned. Papa would not be there to walk her down the aisle or answer the time-honored question all fathers dreaded. Jonathan had offered to fill in so she would not walk alone, but it would not be the same. India's chest heaved with a shudder. She would never forgive Mother for taking her away when Papa was so ill.

Althea tugged India's arms away and searched her face. "All will be well. Lord Kilnsey is a good man and he will give you a good life. Are you going to see your mother before we board the ship in the morning? You haven't spoken to her since Lady Clarissa returned from that last visit."

A sliver of guilt pierced India, but she shoved it away. "Yes, this afternoon. There are a few things at Washington Square that I want to take to England. I will not tell her which ship we are taking, so please don't mention it. Once we are aboard ship, I will send Mother a telegram."

"Do you think she and your grandmother will come to the wedding? Considering how their cooperation was achieved, I've wondered."

"Are you kidding? Mother would never miss being mother-of-the-bride, especially when the bride is marrying into the English nobility. How would she ever explain her absence to the people that matter?" Sarcasm dripped from every word. "Oh, she'll be there no matter what she may have said. As for Grandmama, I have no idea what she will do."

Althea returned to the case and closed its buckles. Without looking at India, she asked, "Are you sure allowing Mrs. Ledbetter to come to the wedding is wise?"

India ran her fingers over the bed's counterpane to straighten an imaginary wrinkle while she thought about how to answer. "No one understands my relationship with Mother better than you. She has done and said so many things that have broken my heart. On the other hand, she is the only mother I will ever have. Seeing a daughter get married is a mother's special day, too. I guess I feel like I owe her that much. If it were not for her and Grandmama, I would not have met Charlie. In any event, Lady Clarissa assures me she will intervene with Mother, if the need arises."

After luncheon when India and Althea arrived at Washington Square, Spencer informed them that both Grandmama and Mother were out. They had gone to call upon an old friend who was recently bereaved. India suppressed a wayward smile. She had not let Mother know she was coming. She had dreaded seeing them, but that did not keep guilt at bay. They were her only living relatives, after all. All the same, pity the poor friend. If there was one thing Grandmama and Mother were ill suited to, it was comforting the grieving.

Once they were alone in her bedroom, India pointed out the things she wanted and helped Althea stow them into a suitcase. After a final inspection of the room, she went to the wardrobe to close the doors, but stopped at the sight within. A couple of tangled hangers rattled, otherwise, nothing but empty space greeted her. The void brought home something she had so far refused to acknowledge. She brushed away tears that rolled uncontrolled down her cheeks.

This wardrobe was a near twin to the one in her bedroom in North Carolina. Her entire life had been spent at The Falls. Every dream she had dreamt had been dreamed in her bedroom there. Every garment she had ever worn had hung behind those matching doors. Now that house, that room, and that piece of furniture were cleared of all signs of the girl she had once been, just like her room here in Washington Square would soon be.

As an idea dawned, India raced to the fireplace and removed Grandfather Van de Berg's watercolor from above the mantel. The lovely pastels depicting Washington Square Park in spring lifted her spirits whenever she looked at it. Grandfather Van de Berg may have created those horrors of tortured souls stored in the attic, but India believed this work represented his true nature, the one he possessed before he killed himself, before his fortune was destroyed by Grandfather Ledbetter. Perhaps when she got to England, she could take the art lessons she had always wanted. In the novels she read, ladies of the nobility were always learning to paint or producing simple art. Even without lessons, she might try her hand. Her governesses always said she had talent.

She put the picture on the bed and said to Aletha, "Please see that this is packed for transport. I'm taking it with us."

"Of course, but won't your grandmother be angry when she finds it's gone?"

"I doubt it. She always resented Grandfather's hobby. Have you noticed there is not a single one of his paintings displayed in the public rooms? No, I am the only person who cares what happens to this picture. It will be a connection to my American roots, to my history."

Of course, her family history elicited mixed emotions. It had played a part in ruining her coming-out ball. It had kept Papa detached from the wider world. It had turned Mother into a scheming, unhappy woman. India, however, would not trade her childhood at The Falls for any other. India traced the scroll work on the gilt frame. The watercolor would be a lovely keepsake, one much happier than what it represented.

Tomorrow she would leave her haunted family history behind and sail away to a new life among strangers. She would acquire a new home, a title, and a new country. Soon, she would be an English citizen. No, that was wrong. She would be a British subject and a peeress of the realm.

Was she up to the challenge? In reality, she had no idea what it meant to be a countess responsible for the running of a grand house or to be the leader of local society in an English village. Charlie and Clarissa assured her of their mother's help, but India had not received so much as a postcard from the good lady. Maybe Charlie's mother would not like her new daughter-in-law. Maybe the present Lady Kilnsey would resent an American taking her place as principal countess and would hate being assigned to the Dower House. That was a potential problem, but other more immediate things plagued India.

Worrisome questions tormented her in the quiet times when she was alone. Often as she was drifting to sleep, thoughts of what Charlie's life with the other girl might have been crept in to mar her peace. How much of his heart still belonged to that girl and did he long to know her child? Was the baby truly his or did he merely hope it was and what effect would that have on any children they might have together? These were issues they would have to face together because there was no other choice.

In some ways, the final fear was the greatest concern because it got to the heart of who they were as people. In marrying Charlie, was she simply trading one form of tyranny for another? He had promised to let her follow her own desires, which had sent a thrill through her. Then he had added a caveat - only if her pursuits did not reflect poorly on the estate and his family. Were English earls with ancient titles really capable of maintaining a modern outlook or tolerating a woman who craved independence?

CHAPTER 32

For the third time in less than a year, India stood at a ship's railing as the vessel steamed into the Atlantic. Looking back to the west, she watched the Statue of Liberty fade into the distance with a wistfulness greater than she expected. All that she had known was receding and becoming her past. She and Charlie had not discussed when they might return to the States for a visit. Her heart hammered as she contemplated the future. Soon, America would cease to be her home. Glancing down at her summer frock fluttering in the breeze, it occurred to her that her past was as ephemeral as the silk used to weave the fabric of her costume. The threads were strong in the beginning, but they were being stretched and thinned until one day they might break completely. A shudder passed through her as she considered what she was leaving behind.

Charlie, a possessive arm around her shoulders, leaned in and whispered, "You're cold. Let's go to the lounge and order tea."

"No, I want to watch as long as America is visible. It may be a long time before I come home."

"Are you really so sad to leave?" His voice actually held a note of surprise.

India let her gaze drift to the now distance Manhattan skyline. "Not New York, but this is as close as I can get to The Falls. It's the only home I've ever known."

"I guess I had not thought of it like that. What will you miss most?" His tone was kind and genuine.

India did not look at him for fear tears would fall. He must not think she regretted her decision. "Now that Papa and Nanny Gordon are no longer living, I guess next on the list is Zara."

"Who is Zara?"

A crease formed between her brows. Surely he had a better memory than that. "My mare. You met her. The little bay in the first stall."

"Oh, yes. She is quite the beauty, and she clearly adores you."

Now tears threatened in earnest. "Stop or you are going to make me cry."

They stood in silence until Lady Liberty was only a speck on the western horizon, then Charlie moved off the railing. "Let's go inside. I want to explore the ship."

Once in the main rotunda, Charlie turned toward the staircase leading to the ship's bowels. "I've not seen the cargo holds. There is a case that should have gone to my stateroom but is missing. I am hoping it is with my trunks."

Feeling a little grumpy, India tried to keep her tone light. "Why not send your brother-in-law's valet? Didn't he see to your luggage, as well?"

"I really do not want to impose. Besides, I want some exercise. Come with me, please." He grabbed her hand and pulled her toward the staircase. His manner was oddly jovial. "I don't trust my beautiful girl around so many unattached men. I well remember the attention you received from that first mate on the Lusitania."

Although she had no interest in seeing where the luggage and cargo were stowed, Charlie looked so anxious that she accompany him, in the end India acquiesced. They descended four floors and entered the cargo hold where Charlie flipped on the lights. He was either clairvoyant or he had visited before because he knew exactly where to find the light switch. India passed through the hatch door and leaned a hand against the wall to catch her breath. Charlie had practically run down the steps. Whatever was in that bag better be important, or she was engaged to a madman with obsessive tendencies.

A soft thrumming and thumping echoed through the metal floor from the engine rooms below. India looked about in surprise. For a place that was used for storage, it was remarkably clean. The metal walls gleamed with white enamel paint that showed little wear. The black paint on the floor showed similar care. Oddly, a faint barn-like odor mingled with the expected one of burning coal that drifted up from the engine deck. It was as though hay and sweet feed lurked among the crates, pallets, and baggage. From the depths of the hold, a whinny called to them.

India's eyes grew large. "That sounds like an Arab. I wonder who brought a horse aboard."

Charlie grinned and took her hand. "Why don't we see. I'm sure the horse would welcome some company stowed away down here as she is."

India moved toward the sound, then broke into a run. She skidded to a halt beside a wooden fence. A little bay mare stood secured by ropes tied to iron rings in the hold's walls. A head bumper covered her pole and was tied under her chin. Leg wraps and shipping boots protected her legs and hooves.

India wrapped her arms around the mare's neck and nuzzled her cheek. "Oh, Zara, I thought I would never see you again." She turned to Charlie who looked very proud of himself. "You did this, didn't you? I don't know how to thank you."

"I can think of an excellent way, but that will have to wait until after we are married." He reached out and scratched the mare's forehead. "I had some help from The Falls' head groom and Jonathan, but yes, it was my idea. I couldn't think of a better wedding gift than this. When we dock at Fishguard, Zara will be transported straight to the stables at Kilnsey."

She let go of Zara and threw her arms around Charlie. "It is the most thoughtful present you could have given me." She placed a hand on the back of his neck and stood on tiptoe as he bent toward her.

When their lips met, the kiss was sweet at first, then blossomed into something much fierier. A burning started in India's depths. It grew into a yearning to draw Charlie to herself so that there was nothing between them. The throbbing in the deepest part of her begged to be satisfied. She could not stop her hips as they pressed against him and began a rhythm all their own.

Charlie broke away and held India at arm's length, his eyes wide in surprise. "If we go on, I won't able to stop. I had no idea you are such a passionate creature."

India's face burned. "I...I'm sorry. You must think me very forward." She looked down because she could not meet his eyes. "I've never been kissed in a romantic way. I didn't expect it to be so.... Please forgive me."

"My darling girl, no man could be more delighted. I believe you are going to make me a very satisfied husband."

India gave him a grateful smile. "I think we should go back up to the lounge." Giving Zara a final hug and pat, she turned away without waiting for Charlie to agree.

It was surprising and humiliating to find there was a part of herself over which she seemed to have so little control. On the other hand, her responsiveness had thrilled her future husband. One thing worried her, though. Neither of them had yet to mention love. The specter of the farmer's daughter hung over her future happiness. Could the physical side of marriage lead to love? If their kiss was any indicator, they appeared to be a good match in that area.

Though she might be naïve about some things, she had a rudimentary understanding of how babies came into the world thanks to the breeding programs on the farms at The Falls. She had even helped deliver a couple of foals. If she remained responsive to Charlie, maybe she would drive the other girl and her child from his mind and heart.

***

The remainder of the transatlantic crossing sped by for India. Between daily visits to Zara, she and Charlie stole time alone so they could continue to explore the physical side of their relationship. While they never went farther than passionate kisses, India's confidence grew with each encounter. If they did not yet fully love one another, they certainly felt something more than friendship, at least she hoped that is what their ardor meant.

On the final day of the voyage, they stood together at the railing watching the Welsh coast draw ever closer. A flutter roamed India's midsection. Once they docked, life as she had known it was truly over. In a little more than a month, she would be India Westmorland, Countess of Kilnsey. She and Althea would have to adjust to life in an English manor.

Sometimes she felt guilty about making Althea agree to come with her. Although she promised it was her preference, India feared the other servants would not accept an American lady's maid. They might find her mountain accent strangely foreign and deem her low class. They might even shun her company. Shame washed through India as she realized the extent of her own selfishness.

India felt Charlie stir beside her. He slipped his arm around her shoulders and pulled her close. "You look so pensive. You are a million miles away. Having regrets already?"

India leaned into the embrace. "Yes, but not ones you might fear. I'm worried Althea will regret coming with us. Maybe I put too much pressure on her. What if your servants resent her?"

Charlie chuckled and kissed her temple. "I assure you she should have no fears on that count. The only servant likely to have her nose out of joint is my mother's maid. Her chief complaint will likely be that she has come down in the world since she is no longer maid to the principal countess, but she knew that day would come, so she will simply have to accept it. As for the others, the housekeeper and cook run a tight ship. The lower servants tremble in fear of displeasing them. I will see that everyone understands the importance of making Althea welcome."

India noted with surprise that he failed to speak of a butler. It seemed a valet might not be the only position left wanting for lack of funds. "How many servants are there?"

"Sadly, not as many as are needed to run a house of Kilnsey's size."

India tapped her jaw in thought. "Perhaps that should be my first task as mistress. Do you think Lady Kilnsey or the housekeeper would help me recruit new members of staff?"

"I think Mrs. Wilson, the housekeeper, would be a better choice. My mother is rarely pleased with any applicants no matter how good their references. She hates the job of hiring staff."

India blinked at the implication embedded in Charlie's final sentence. Pray her future mother-in-law would not be so hard on new additions to the family.

India looked up with what she hoped was a confident smile. "Perhaps we can send word to Mrs. Wilson to start advertising and have a full staff in place before we arrive for the wedding."

"That is an excellent notion." He kissed her temple again and gave her a squeeze. "You are going to make a wonderful chatelaine. I will also ask my solicitor to start the search for a butler. Mrs. Wilson will be greatly relieved to have that particular position filled. She has felt very put upon since the last one retired and was not replaced."

A little shocked to have it confirmed that Kilnsey indeed lacked a butler, India let the subject of new staff drop. Whatever additional deficiencies she might find in her new home, at least they had her inheritance to solve the estate's financial woes.

She looked toward the horizon and put her hand over her eyes to shield them from the sun's glare. The Cunard docks were in sight, bringing a surge of emotions. She was delighted Charlie had confidence in her abilities but was none too sure she deserved it. In reality, she knew very little about running a large house. Mother had always employed excellent staff and had left many of the decisions to the housekeeper.

Sighing inwardly, she added disappointing her husband by making a mess of house management to her growing list of worries regarding the life upon which she was about to embark.

CHAPTER 33

For India, the trip from the Cunard docks at Fishguard to London via the Great Western Railway passed very differently from the previous one. She spent many miles chatting with Clarissa about which shops they would visit during their London stay and where she might find the perfect wedding gown. When that topic was exhausted, a comfortable silence descended. Clarissa flipped through the latest edition of Tatler, while Jonathan and Charlie perused the Times. India enjoyed watching the verdant hills of southern England roll past her window, but the gentle rocking of the carriage made her drowsy. Soon, her head dropped onto Charlie's shoulder and she drifted off.

She found herself in bridal gown and veil with Charlie beside her in morning dress. His pinstriped trousers, black tailcoat, and dove gray weskit were impeccable. Her gown was not of the latest fashion but of an earlier time with a gloriously long train. They stood before the altar in an old stone church with an Anglican bishop in full ecclesiastical regalia, a Book of Common Prayer open on his palms. Sunlight pouring through a rose window above the chancel scattered colorful patterns at their feet. A feeling of warmth and joy enveloped her until the bishop came to the portion of the service where he asked if there were any impediments to the marriage. Mother stood up and pointed at Charlie. She shouted that he was of lesser standing than India's fortune deserved. The inheritance was worthy of no less than a marquess and Charlie was only an earl. India's heart pounded as though it was clawing its way out of her chest.

Just as Charlie's mother and his present heir, Lord "Bumpy" Hawik, were adding their objections in chorus with Mother, gentle shaking brought her out of the depths. "You were crying out in your sleep. Bad dream?"

India rolled her head to clear away grogginess. "Unfortunately, yes, and I'm glad it was just a dream. It couldn't possibly happen."

Charlie leaned forward and looked directly into her eyes. His brow wrinkled with concern. "Perhaps, but bad dreams have basis in our fears. What is haunting you, my dear?"

When India described the scene in the church, Charlie laughed and stroked her cheek. "Oh, my darling girl. Fret not." He raised a hand and began ticking off reasons on his fingers. "First, your mother cares too much about what other people think. She would never cause such a scene. The scandal would be devastating. Second, my mother has no reason to object. She is greatly relieved that you are coming to the estate's rescue. Third, and finally, we don't have to invite the odious Bumpy if you do not wish it. He probably won't come anyway. I hear he is livid at the prospect of being pushed down the line of succession and inheritance, but on the off chance he might show, we can strike him from the invitation list." He tilted his head before grinning broadly. "Actually, the thought of ole Bumpy's face when he realizes he has been snubbed is most tantalizing. What do you think? Should we strike him?"

India giggled as she joined him in the visualization. "While that picture is most entertaining, keeping peace in the family is probably the better option. I think we must invite him despite his manifest deficiencies as a guest and as a human being."

Kissing the tip of her nose, he sighed. "Oh well, I suppose needs must." He withdrew his watch from his waistcoat and opened the cover. "We will be in the station in little over an hour. Clarissa and Jonathan are in the dining car taking luncheon. Perhaps we should join them."

Their arrival at Paddington was uneventful and Charlie found taxis with ease. The luggage was to be delivered by separate transport under the supervision of Althea and Jonathan's valet. When the two couples were settled in the first taxi, Charlie eyed India, Clarissa, and Jonathan in turn, but did not say anything. India watched in fascination as a curiously self-satisfied smile crept across his face.

She shot him a sidewise glance. "You are up to something. What have you done? Nothing impulsive, I hope."

"I? Why I am as innocent as a babe. Furthermore, I never act without a well thought out plan."

India poked him with her index finger. "And that plan would be....?"

"Well, since you insist. We are not going to a hotel tonight or any other night."

When he didn't continue, Clarissa's eyes narrowed. "You pulled it off, didn't you?"

"I did indeed, Sister dear. The house is ours once more."

"How ever did you accomplish it?"

Charlie's chest seemed to puff out before India's eyes. "The recent occupants found themselves in somewhat reduced circumstances, so they were rather relieved to receive an offer before they even advertised. The promissory note against my expectations was finalized via cable from the ship and our solicitors arranged a small down payment with the balance due after our marriage. They have already moved out and the staff are preparing for our arrival as we speak."

India, whose head had been moving like a tennis ball at Wimbledon, put up a hand palm out. "Stop. What house? Where?"

"Kilnsey House. Grosvenor Street, Mayfair." Charlie and Clarissa declared in unison.

Clarissa grabbed Charlie's hand and drew it to her cheek. "Well done, Little Brother. Well done, you!"

Promissory note against his expectations. The phrase was chilling. India blinked a couple of times. "Oh, my goodness. I had no idea that was in the works. I can see how...uh, thrilled you are to have the house back in your possession."

Charlie put his arm around India and hugged her close. "Thrilled for us, darling. It will be your home, too."

She in no way wanted to snuff out the flame of Charlie and Clarissa's joy, but it was disturbing that he had already committed what must be a considerable sum from her fortune without so much as mentioning it and before they were even married. Papa had not been much for life lessons taught at his knee, but one thing he had pounded into her head. Never under any circumstances touch the principal of one's fortune. Invest, let it grow, and spend only the income.

Though she had not been taught the particulars of financial management, maybe it was something best studied. Math had been one of her favorite subjects, one in which she had excelled, but then a cold wave of reality washed over her. Though she would soon be Countess

Kilnsey, she would have very little control over how the majority of her money was spent. Once they were wed, a large portion of her fortune would pass out of the trustees' hands and into those of her husband. Her money would become part of the Kilnsey estate as specified in the marriage contracts and by the terms of Grandfather T.J.'s will. While she retained a small income for her personal use, the bulk of her inheritance would go to supporting Charlie's ancestral holdings.

India sighed and tried to focus on the city through which they traveled. There was nothing she could do at the moment about money that had already been as good as spent.

Noting her focus on the passing scenes, Charlie described various points of interest, giving her a lesson in the history and architecture of central London.

The taxi turned left, joining the traffic on the Bayswater Road as it edged along Hyde Park. At Marble Arch, they turned again, this time onto Park Lane, which they followed until they turned onto Grosvenor Street.

Charlie shifted beside her, straining to share her view through the taxi window. Pointing to a large green space, he commented, "That is the heart of Mayfair, Grosvenor Square. We're almost home."

India admired the lovely Georgian houses lining the square. "This must be the most exclusive area in London."

"Certainly one of the most. After all, the King and Queen are near neighbors. And Kilnsey House is one of its oldest addresses. My five times great grandfather was one of the first to get permission to build on the estate. He and the Grosvenor of that time belonged to the same club, otherwise, I doubt my ancestor would have been able to acquire the land lease. The house dates from 1728."

Within minutes, their taxi pulled to the curb in front of a three-story townhouse. India's breath caught as she gazed up at the cream color stucco facade. Unusually tall windows and a roofline only about a foot below that of its four-story neighbor indicated spacious, high-ceilinged interiors. This was more than she could have imagined based on what Charlie had told her about his family's history and finances. Clearly, his ancestors had once had plenty of money and had put it to good use. The house was the loveliest example of Georgian architecture on the entire street.

When the driver opened the vehicle's door, Charlie assisted India in alighting and led her to the mahogany double front doors. They stepped through the enclosed portico into a two-story entrance hall. India could not stop herself spinning around gaping in awe. The Falls' foyer was in many ways far grander, but this one had historical significance embedded in every inch. Diagonally laid black and white marble squares covered the floor. Though they were worn in places and one in a corner was cracked, India could imagine great figures of the past treading upon them. Perhaps no less than a prime minister had once entered here.

She ran her fingers over the nearest oak paneled wall and held them to her nose. The scents lingering there spoke of a couple centuries' application of lemon oil and beeswax. The walls glowed softly in the subtle light of brass sconces and a center-hung chandelier. But by far the grandest feature was the double story wall-hung stone staircase. It wound around three sides up to the floor above. A delicate lyre pattern decorated its wrought-iron balustrade which complemented the molded handrail on the wall opposite. The space was topped off by plaster cornices of acanthus-leaf scrolls and rosettes.

India stepped to the center of the foyer and gazed upward. The plaster pattern continued onto the ceiling and even decorated the underside of the staircase. While she worried about the expenditure required to retake possession, it was clear why Charlie and Clarissa so longed to have it in the family once again. India had fallen in love with it, too.

The sound of feet treading on the oak floored hallway drew India's attention to an elderly, somewhat bent figure in a black tailcoat shuffling toward them. Stopping before Charlie, the gentleman bowed slightly. "Begging your pardon Master Charles…I mean, My Lord. Please forgive me for not being present to receive you, but we were not expecting you until much later this afternoon. If I may be permitted to say…" The old man paused and cast an inquiring look upon Charlie.

"Of course. Say what is on your mind, Robbins."

"Thank you, My Lord. The staff is most pleased with your return to Kilnsey House. Most pleased, indeed. You will remember many of them from your younger days. And…my goodness, is that Lady Clarissa come home from America? Oh, this is a happy day." Having delivered himself of the welcome, Robbins fell silent, but his gaze wandered to India.

She did not wait for Charlie to remember his manners. She extended her hand and introduced herself. A look of surprise passed over the old man's face while he left her hand dangling in the air. A ripple of irritation passed through India. The old gentleman clearly found her effort at being friendly improper.

Robbins coughed and said, "Thank you, Miss Ledbetter." He turned to Charlie. "Will the Dowager Countess be joining you here in London?"

"No, my mother detests travel. She goes no farther than the village these days. Says the jarring from the railway makes her bones hurt." Charlie looked at Clarissa. "The pink room for Miss Ledbetter, do you think?"

Taking her cue, Clarissa nodded. "Robbins, tell the footmen to assist with the luggage when it arrives. Our American staff know which cases and trunks are to be delivered to the bedrooms and which can be stored in the box room. And please ensure that the staff make the Americans feel welcome. Have beds been made ready for them in the servants' quarters?"

"Indeed they have, My Lady. Mrs. Thorne and I have the staff well in hand."

A knowing smile lifted the corners of Clarissa's mouth. "Of course. I should expect nothing less. The two of you have been running Kilnsey House impeccably for as long as I can remember. I was so relieved when we learned the previous tenants saw your worth and retained you. You are a treasure."

Robbins, basking in the warmth of such praise, bowed and left.

Charlie took India's hand. "I hear bustling at the back of the house. No doubt the luggage has arrived."

Clarissa must have sensed India's confusion, for she said, "The houses on our side of the street are served by a mews area, Three Kings Yard. No tradesman or delivery is ever admitted by the front door." Glancing at the tall case clock in the corner of the hall, she continued. "I'm feeling rather grubby. Perhaps we should retire to our rooms for an hour or so and freshen up before tea."

When India was conducted to the pink room, she found it empty. Althea had already hung an afternoon dress on the wardrobe door, so she must be seeing to the storage of trunks in the box room. India sank into a wing chair beside the fireplace and took in her surroundings. The room, papered in a pattern of pink roses, daisies, and pale green ferns, looked as though springtime had exploded on the walls. Not completely displeasing, but rather juvenile and overly feminine to India's taste. Perhaps this room belonged to Clarissa when she was a girl.

She leaned against the high back and rolled her head from side-to-side. Maybe she was tired from the journey or perhaps the pace of change in her life was impacting her emotions, but India suddenly felt very let down. The confidence of the past weeks melted away and doubt crept into its place. She closed her eyes and recounted all that had transpired. Not yet out of mourning, she found herself in a foreign country among virtual strangers planning a wedding to a man who was probably still in love with another woman. That said, Charlie's behavior toward her was in fact beyond reproach. He excelled in the role of fiancé, but she had made the decision to marry him almost on a whim. Had it been the grief of Papa's unexpected death, her desire to thwart Mother, or her fear of the future that had prompted her accepting his proposal? Dear God, was she making the mistake of a lifetime? She stuffed her fist in her mouth as her shoulders heaved and tears flowed.

India's sobs were interrupted by a tap on the door. Clarissa came into the room all smiles until she saw India's face. Rushing to her side, she knelt and put an arm around India's shoulders. "Oh, my dear. Whatever is the matter?"

India did not trust herself to speak.

Clarissa drew back and put a finger under India's chin, lifting until their eyes met. Taking a handkerchief from her pocket, she dabbed India's cheeks. "Are you having second thoughts?" When India did not answer, Clarissa continued, "Yes, I think you are. A lot has happened to you in such a short time. You are hardly recovered from your father's sad passing and here you are about to plan a wedding in a village that you have never even visited." Clarissa rose and pulled a hassock away from its place before the hearth. As she dropped down on it, she covered both of India's hands in hers. "Many brides have doubts. Believe me. I certainly did in the days before I married. May I ask an impertinent question?"

India blinked back more tears. "At this point, there are no questions I won't answer if it will help me sort through this confusion."

Clarissa took India's hand and gave it a gentle squeeze. "Do you love my brother?"

India's head jerked back. This was not a question she had anticipated. "In all honesty, I'm not sure and I don't know how he feels about me."

"I see. Your circumstances are similar to mine before I married in one important way. These may seem vulgar comments, but I believe honesty is more important than propriety. Money is a driving force in the marriage. It complicates everything, but this is what I have learned. Happiness is a choice. One can choose to make the best of one's situation or one can choose to be miserable. I chose happiness. I did not love my husband when we married, but I learned to love him. I chose to focus on his good qualities and the fact that he loved me. This has made all the difference."

"I know you are trying to help, but there is one big problem. Jonathan loved you from the start. I think Charlie is still in love with that farmer's daughter. I'm afraid we are both making a huge mistake."

"Yes, I admit he has lingering feelings for the girl. One does not easily forget a love of such intensity. So, you have a job ahead of you, but you have all the tools to make a success. Charlie may not be ready to say the words, but I know my brother. He is on the verge of falling deeply in love with you. It is your job to see that he does."

Great. If Clarissa thought she was making India feel better, she was sadly mistaken. Not only was India responsible for transforming herself into an English countess who could run an ancient noble house, she also had to make sure her husband fell in love with her. So exactly what were Charlie's responsibilities? Was anyone talking to him about what he should do to create a happy marriage? The suffragists were right. Women must attain equal rights with the men in their lives.

CHAPTER 34

Clarissa waited a full three minutes after knocking on Charlie's door. He finally answered with a frown. "What is it? I thought the idea was to rest before teatime."

She pushed into the room. "You have work to do. Your bride may be having second thoughts."

Charlie extended his palms. "And you would know this because...?"

"I have just come from comforting a sobbing girl who is afraid she is about to make the mistake of a lifetime because her bridegroom is still in love with another woman. So, how do you plan to deal with this?"

Charlie smirked. "Why do I think you already have a plan?"

"Because, as usual, I do." Clarissa tapped Charlie's chest with her index finger. "If you cannot use the word love, you must at least make India feel cherished. Marriage contracts can always be broken at the last-minute. India's mother would be only too delighted to put her back on the market in hope of catching a more elevated rank. So, exactly how do you feel about India and the other girl?"

"That's a rather intrusive question, even for you."

Drumming her nails against her thigh, Clarissa countered, "I would not intrude if you were more effective in taking care of business. Out with it. What are your feelings? If I know what we are dealing with then things can be managed."

Charlie leaned against the door and looked over Clarissa's head, presumably at the ancestral portrait of questionable quality hanging over the mantel. After several beats, his eyes met hers. "In all honesty, I don't know. I'm rather muddled when it comes to India and Annie. If I could see Annie one final time, it might help me let go. On the other hand, I will also gladly kill anyone who attempts to hurt India, including you."

"There will be no need for such drastic measures. If your feelings for India run as deeply as you say, then you should be able to convince the girl of your devotion. Let her rest for now but find time before we retire for the night to reassure India marrying is the right choice. After the wedding, you have it in your power to make your wife happy or miserable. Make sure the marriage is a happy one. India deserves no less."

Charlie shot his sister an ironic smile. "For all your practicality, I see I am not the only one who cares for India. And for your information, I intend to do my utmost by her. You can rest assured on that point."

"Good. We have an appointment at ten in the morning with a wonderful dressmaker in Oxford Street. She will make the wedding gown since we do not have time to travel to Worth's in Paris. Have you contacted the Reverend Howard about the banns? They must be posted this Sunday if we are to keep the date we've chosen."

"I sent a telegram before we left New York. All is on schedule."

As Clarissa returned to the room she shared with Jonathan, she said a silent prayer that Charlie would be able to keep his word. She knew him so well. His intentions were always the best. His execution, on the other hand, was less sure. As long as Annie stayed in Ireland for the next few weeks, Charlie and India could be married without complications.

***

For India, the days after their arrival in London flew by. Clarissa helped her complete her trousseau and choose the design for her wedding dress. The dressmaker suggested a beautiful pattern with fitted lace sleeves ending in a bell at the elbow, a flowing lace adorned train and veil, and a simple skirt that dropped from the waist in clouds of cotton lawn. The dress was not as regal as Mother had always declared a wedding dress should be, but it suited India. She loved the design and Clarissa said it possessed just the right esthetic for a country wedding in a village church.

Interestingly, Charlie seemed to be making every effort to reassure her they were doing the right thing. He was most solicitous of her needs and concerns. Perhaps Clarissa had said something to him. Whatever prompted his attentiveness, India now looked toward their wedding and saw a brighter future than the one she had envisioned at her lowest point.

She dropped the magazine she had been flipping through onto the hassock in front of the fireplace. Her days were beginning to all feel the same with non-ending wedding planning. It was becoming tedious. She needed a diversion. Glancing at Althea, she pursed her lips, an action that for some unexplained reason helped her think. "You know, I never got to have my meeting with Mrs. Drummond."

Althea turned toward India with raised brows. "You mean that suffragette woman?"

India nodded. "I think now would be a good time to see her. In a couple of days, we are going to be whisked away to the wilds of deepest Yorkshire. I'm going to make a telephone call and see if they can give us an appointment."

"Us?"

"Yes, us. Every woman should be interested in gaining the vote."

A dry expression thinned Althea's mouth. "I suppose you're right, but you have to admit it's a lot easier for some women. Some women do not have to work for a living. Some women do not have to worry about losing their jobs." Irritation colored Althea's words.

India's head snapped back at the sting of Althea's words. She blinked a couple of times while she sought a soothing response. "I'm sorry. You're right. Although I hope you know your situation with me is safe, I will not put you in a compromising position. I'm going to make a telephone call and make the appointment, but you don't need to go with me. Whatever you do, though, don't tell anyone. Charlie thinks I've forgotten all about the movement."

Althea snickered as she laid out an evening dress for the dinner India would be attending. "Not on your life. Lord Kilnsey would have me skinned alive for allowing his future countess to go into such a dodgy place by herself. You might not fire me, but he certainly would. He's made it clear he expects me to keep you out of trouble. Looks like he just might understand you better than you think."

At luncheon, India watched the others and waited until she thought the time was right. "I think I would like to visit a charming little church just off The Strand. St. Clement

Danes. Do you know it?" Charlie and Clarissa nodded. "I meant to see it when we were here before, but, well, you know what happened."

Clarissa glanced at Charlie. "Oh, no. I wish I had known. I'm afraid I have an engagement with the dressmaker this afternoon. I've decided I need to take advantage of her skills while I can, but I could put it off."

"I don't blame you for wanting to engage her and I certainly don't expect you to change your plans. Besides, Althea is going with me." India looked at Charlie with an apologetic smile. "I know churches and museums aren't really your favorite pastime."

Charlie dabbed his lips with his napkin. "I will be happy to go, if you wish it. I'm not entirely sure I want my bride wandering around unaccompanied."

"No, that's quite all right. Althea and I will manage just fine on our own."

At two o'clock, the pair set off for the offices of the Women's Social and Political Union in St. Clements Inn and the formidable Mrs. Drummond. Their taxi turned off The Strand onto the lane and chugged toward their destination. For some reason, a touch of anxiety trickled through India. She had nothing to fear from the suffragists, yet she couldn't shake the feeling that she was embarking upon an unexpected journey. The premonition had begun at luncheon with her deception about seeing the church. It wasn't as if she had never been less than forthcoming in the past. She had certainly deceived Mother often enough. Perhaps it was how easily she had lied to her future husband and family. Shouldn't one be able to tell the man one was about to marry the truth about anything? An image of her parents' conversations floated through her mind. If they were any example, the answer to her question was decidedly no.

The taxi pulled up to the curb, and the driver turned to them expectantly. After paying the fare, India alighted onto the narrow, cobbled sidewalk and marched toward the door with Althea in her wake. She paused long enough to draw a deep breath for confidence before grabbing the knob and entering.

The same harried young woman who was at the reception desk on India's previous visit barely glanced up from her typewriter. "How may I help you?"

India adopted what she hoped was a friendly smile. "I have an appointment with Mrs. Drummond at two thirty. I'm afraid we're a little early."

"Yes, you are." The girl waved at a couple of lumpy armchairs shoved into a corner on the opposite wall. "Have a seat over there. I'll see if she's free."

At precisely two thirty, India and Althea were shown into an office at the back of the building. Books and periodicals sat stacked on tables and floor. Dust motes floated in a beam of sunlight admitted by a window behind an enormous desk. The form behind the desk filled her chair nearly to overflowing while her ample bosom rested against the desk's edge. The lady was bent over what appeared to be correspondence.

Mrs. Drummond dropped her pen on the blotter and ran her gaze over her guests. "Please have a seat and tell me how I may be of service."

Now that the time had come, India didn't quite know how to begin. "We...I should say I...want to know how one becomes involved in the movement." A sharp pain spread through her foot where Althea kicked it while feigning a fit of coughing. Ignoring the warning, India charged on. "I am about to be married to Lord Kilnsey. When I made the other appointment, I thought I would be returning to America permanently. The women of my home state are in great need of education about gaining their rights. But as it is, well, you can see I will be living in England. Is there a branch of your organization near Kilnsey?"

A somewhat confused expression crossed Mrs. Drummond's face. India realized she must have had no idea that there had been a previous appointment. "I must say we are always delighted and grateful when a member of the gentry steps forward offering support. Lord Kilnsey's seat is in Yorkshire, I believe?" When India replied in the affirmative, Mrs. Drummond searched among the stacks on her desk. "Ah, here it is." She handed India a brochure. "This will tell you who to contact in our York branch. The ladies there are quite active, you know."

India had no idea what the ladies of York did, but she took the pamphlet and tucked it into her handbag. "I'm not sure how I might help, but perhaps the ladies can find something for me."

Mrs. Drummond chuckled. "Oh, I should not worry about that. I assure you there is plenty of work to go round, especially when a peeress is offering her services." She reached out to a little holder on her desk and withdrew a card. "Take my card. Present it to the York branch president with my compliments."

At the sign of dismissal, India and Althea bid Mrs. Drummond good day and went in search of a taxi. They had to walk down to The Strand in order to hail one.

Once they were seated, Althea glared at India. "Surely you are not going to get yourself involved with the suffragettes. What on earth will Lord Kilnsey think?"

India lifted her chin. "He and I agreed that he would not interfere with my personal interests. It was one of the reasons I agreed to marry him."

"You may find that once he is your husband, he has changed his mind."

Althea had spoken India's secret fear aloud. Charlie was a wonderful man. She felt he would try to be a good husband. Nonetheless, he was still a man and most men thought they should be in charge of everything and everyone. India conveniently pushed aside his admonition that her activities should not reflect poorly on the family.

CHAPTER 35

The train carrying India north to her future home pulled out of Paddington exactly on time. After the whirlwind of London, what with the shopping, dressmaking, dinners, concerts, museums, the prospect of several hours enforced idleness was alluring. The morning promised a beautiful day with sunshine, cloudless skies, and England's verdant hills beckoning from outside her compartment window. She leaned back against the seat and allowed her head to loll just enough so that she had a good view of the passing scenery.

Charlie folded the newspaper he had been reading and picked up her hand. Kissing its back, he asked, "Happy?"

India rolled her head so that their eyes met. "Mmm. Very much so. You?"

"More than I have been in a very long time."

India felt the smile fade from her lips. It was hardly an expression of unbridled joy, but he was an Englishman and the English were hardly known for their exuberant expressions of emotion. She looked back to the window while shoving the trickle of doubt into the darkest corner of her mind. All would be well. It had to be. There was no turning back now.

If Charlie noticed her disquiet, he made no mention of it. Instead, he took a folded piece of paper from his pocket and handed it to her. "In the rush to get to the station, I forgot to give you this. It came just as we were leaving. Good thing we were running late or we would have missed the glad tidings."

India read the telegram, then crumpled the scrap of yellow into a tight ball. "Well, it was inevitable. I see we will arrive approximately twenty-four hours before Mother. You and Clarissa will have to prepare your mother and the staff. I don't think I can face meeting my future mother-in-law while at the same time trying to explain my mother to her."

Charlie slipped an arm around India's shoulders and kissed her temple. "I will speak with Clarissa. She has the most sway with Mama. As to your mother, the drive up to the house from the valley is beautiful. As the lane emerges from a copse, one has a rather stunning view of the house sitting atop a rock ledge. The views of Kilnsey Moor are rather spectacular from almost every window. I am hoping she will be so impressed by its grandeur and antiquity that its deficiencies will be overlooked."

"What possible deficiencies could there be?"

India watched Charlie's Adam's apple move as he swallowed, discomfort written in the creases between his eyes and across his forehead. "Well, I may have neglected to mention the lack of plumbing and gaslighting. Papa often said he would get around to them one day, but his extracurricular activities always had the greatest part of his attention. By the time he awoke to the need for repairs and renovations, the money was gone."

"What exactly needs repair?"

"In a house of Kilnsey's age, dry rot and roof leaks are a constant worry. I'm afraid the roof over the east wing is so damaged that we have closed off that part of the house. But don't worry. There are plenty of bedrooms in the west wing ready for use. They are dry and have beautiful views out over the dales. And now that we are fully staffed, carrying bath water, tubs, and chamber pots to and from the bedrooms will no longer present difficulties."

India held back a gasp. Visions of Althea lugging pails of hot water up and down long staircases created a sick feeling in her midsection. It had never occurred to her that Kilnsey would be so far behind the times. This simply would not do. Having lived at The Falls all of her life, she took modern conveniences for granted, but then she remembered Nanny Gordon's exclamations over the plumbing and carbide lights Papa installed in her cottage. He had apologized for not connecting the cottage to the generator that made electricity possible for the main house. Nanny Gordon responded that she thought she would be dead and buried before common folk had such.

A realization struck her as though someone had jabbed her with a penknife. Nanny Gordon had always said India knew she would be buried at The Falls because she was mountain born and bred. Mother had always disparaged such sayings, but since she left most of the child rearing to Nanny Gordon, her complaints had been ignored. India had always believed she would never live anywhere other than North Carolina, much less be buried somewhere beyond its borders. In all likelihood, her final resting place would be beside Charlie in the Kilnsey cemetery along with generations of Westmorlands. With every mile, her connection with the life she imagined she would live slipped away. She rested her head against the seat back and lifted her chin toward the ceiling, sending tears rolling down her throat instead of her cheeks.

Charlie glanced at her in concern. Patting her hand, he said, "I hope that is not the sign of a headache coming on. Mama always rests her head like that when she is conjuring up a pain. Of course, the ones who usually suffer are those around her."

India did not look at him for fear her tears would flow in earnest. "No headache. I'm just feeling a little overwhelmed. There is so much to do before the wedding and not a lot of time to do it. Mother will want to be in charge, but she absolutely must not be allowed. I'm not really sure what will be expected of me once I am Lady Kilnsey. It's a lot to take in all at once."

"There is no need to worry. Clarissa has the wedding details well in hand. She will make your mother feel included. My sister has a talent for managing difficult people. Mama will help you learn your role as my countess. You will also have my support. All will be well and you, my dear, will be a smashing success." He placed a finger against her cheek and turned her face to his. He smiled, then kissed her gently. Both the kiss and Charlie's reassurance warmed India, even if they didn't completely set her mind at rest. Wedding preparations and the thought of facing Mother after their estrangement consumed her.

The hissing of brakes broke India's revery. She leaned forward and watched the Skipton Station settled into view. It was larger than India had imagined with several platforms serving multiple tracks.

Charlie consulted his pocket watch and grabbed her hand. "We must hurry if we are to get the Dales train. If we miss it, we will have either a fifteen-mile cart ride over rural lanes in approaching dark or be forced to stay the night here in Skipton. I want to get home. I've been away for what seems an eternity." Longing echoed in his voice. India well understood his desire for home, but rising anxiety must have been reflected in her face, for he continued, "It's really only a few more miles, I promise. We will be home by late afternoon." And that was the problem. India had hoped to meet her future mother-in-law well-rested and refreshed after a night in a hotel.

The trip aboard the Yorkshire Dales Railway was indeed as brief as he had promised. They pulled into the Grassington Station as the sun was beginning its western traverse. India's heels crunched on the gravel platform separating the track from the station proper. Beside the mock-Tudor building, a couple of horse-drawn carts and a barouche pulled by a matching pair of bays stood waiting. A man in livery of forest green and gold braid paced beside the carriage while puffing on a cigarette. When he saw their group approaching, the driver threw away his smoke and straightened himself into a formal attitude. He greeted Charlie with a stiff nod and slight bow.

Charlie smiled. "You must be Barton."

"I am, My Lord."

"Thank you for agreeing to act as coachman. Most convenient that you are capable with the reins, but no need to worry. We will be purchasing an automobile in the near future, so your skill will not be put to waste for too long. How have you found things? Can the stables be converted to a garage or will we need to build new?"

"I believe Mr. Reed, the contractor from Skipton, has decided a conversion is possible. Mr. James allowed me to be present when they discussed the project."

"Very good. Delighted to hear it." To India, Charlie said, "James is the estate manager. He's been with us since my father's time. Started as a gillie under his own father who was game manager and worked his way up." Charlie assisted India into the carriage and climbed in after her. "James is a fine fellow, near family. He will like you." A small nod followed the pronouncement. It was reassuring to hear that at least one resident of Kilnsey would like her on sight.

India waited until Clarissa and Jonathan were seated before placing a hand on Charlie's arm. "I've been wondering if perhaps we should go more slowly with these expenditures. Papa always advised to never touch the principal, to spend only the income. You aren't dipping into the principal, are you?"

Charlie's face turned a bright shade of pink. He looked away while he sucked in a long breath. India looked from him to Clarissa and Jonathan. Clarissa in turn looked at her husband with an imploring gaze.

Jonathan cleared his throat, cut his eyes at Charlie, and sighed. "India, my dear, since I have a financial background, Charlie asked that I look over the marriage contracts and advise as to the management of the funds. I assure you there will be more than enough income to cover any expenditures you wish to make."

"But Charlie told me Kilnsey needs a lot of repairs and renovation. Is there enough for all of that without spending principal?"

Jonathan shifted in his seat. He appeared to be searching for the right way to answer. After glancing at Charlie a couple of times and getting no reaction, Jonathan said, "With proper management, the funds needed to fully restore Kilnsey and secure the future of the estate will be available."

Heat rose in India's cheeks. "I guess I have never paid much attention to the extent of Grandfather T.J.'S estate or the amount that comes to me. Still, you have not answered my question. Has the principal been touched?"

Jonathan frowned and pursed his lips, which made a slight tutting sound when they parted. "Not as such. Not at this time. When the promissory note on Kilnsey House comes due, the amount will not be so great that you need worry. The purchase price exceeds expected income which is based on the remaining months of the year only. That income and a small amount from the principal will be required to discharge the note, renovate the stable block, and purchase an automobile, but I assure you if further expenditures are delayed for a reasonable period, renovations on the castle proper can be accomplished without further incursions."

India felt rather than saw Charlie's body stiffen. Clearly her questions had upset him. Well, too bad. He was the one with a family history of financial ruin caused by irresponsible behavior. He had made plans and decisions regarding her money without so much as mentioning his intentions. This was an issue that would be discussed before, not after the wedding. The men in her life may control her money, but she would have her say. If she had learned anything over the last year, it was that being complacent and silent for the sake of peace could create a prison of lies. She refused to begin her married life wound in a web of deceit.

CHAPTER 36

The carriage bumped over a river on a narrow stone bridge and followed a single track out into a landscape of green pastures enclosed by low, drystone walls. After about three miles, they passed through a small village nestled at the base of a ridge. As it turned toward an upland path, India craned over her shoulder for a better look at the topography. In the near distance, a massive rock face topped by an overhanging ledge rose from the valley floor. It reminded her of a monster with raised arms hovering over an unsuspecting victim. A shiver ran through her and she swiveled back so that she faced forward once more.

The track left the village behind and meandered past a farm cottage, barn, and a patchwork pattern of drystone walls separating one shade of green from another. In the distance, a great expanse of open land spread out in all directions. The carriage emerged from a stand of oaks and India's breath caught in her throat. It was just as Charlie described.

Atop a low ridge sat an edifice that might have been unaltered since the thirteenth century. Four square towers with crenellated parapets rose four or five stories from the rocky ledge and were connected by three storied walls. Although the sun painted the castle's stones a warm, golden hue, it did nothing to soften the fierce exterior. India squinted for a better look at the vertical slits where archers once stood. They would be hard pressed to shoot at an enemy now for there was glazing over each opening.

Charlie had not exaggerated. It really was an ancient defensive stronghold situated to guard the way into the surrounding dales. A sinking sensation settled around India's heart. It was hard to imagine such a structure being an inviting family home.

As the carriage rounded a curve, a lane left the main track and rose toward the top of the promontory. A small group of cottages huddled opposite the castle, a steeple towering from their midst. It occurred to India that she did not know the names of the two communities closest to her future home.

She pointed to the castle dependencies. "Is that village called Kilnsey like the castle?"

Charlie tore his gaze from his home and smiled. "No, we passed through Kilnsey a little over a mile back. What you see here can hardly be called a village. There are only a few cottages for the estate workers and the family church. It's called Cragfast Mastiles, after the old Roman road we are presently on. That large rock ledge you observed earlier is Kilnsey Crag." He pointed to the treeless landscape that rose and fell ahead of the carriage. "That is Kilnsey Moor."

To India, it all looked very *Wuthering Heights* and *Jane Eyre*. While she loved the Bronte novels, how she would like living on the moors was another matter. At the height of summer, everything was green and the breeze ruffling the tendrils around her face was quite pleasant. Come winter, things would look and feel very different. Her heart rate kicked up a notch.

The carriage left Mastiles Lane and began its ascent. Beyond the cluster of cottages, the path curved, revealing a driveway lined with oaks leading directly into the castle itself where solid, bolt-studded wooden gates stood open. As they rolled into a cobbled courtyard at the castle's center, India gazed up at a set of bay windows directly ahead. A shadow moved behind one of them. India squared her shoulders and sat up straighter. Someone watched their arrival without joining the line of uniformed servants flanking the path to the entrance. It could only be Charlie's mother. No one else would dare fail in greeting the return of the master.

Charlie and Jonathan assisted India and Clarissa from the carriage and led the way toward the servants all standing at attention.

A gentleman in a tailcoat stepped forward and bowed. Charlie took India's elbow, halting their progress. "Ainsworth, I believe?"

"Yes, My Lord. Welcome home."

"Thank you." Charlie brought India forward. "This is Miss Ledbetter, soon to be your mistress." Nodding toward Clarissa and Jonathan, he continued, "My sister, Lady Clarissa and her husband, Mr. Rivers." His gaze swept those assembled behind the new butler. "I see we have a full complement."

"Indeed. I hope the arrangements will meet with your approval." Ainsworth turned toward the other members of staff. "Mrs. Wilson and Mrs. Bertrand, you know, of course." He then introduced the other household staff, but none of the names registered with India. There was simply too much to take in all at once.

The sound of boots scuffling over stone drew her attention to a figure exiting what must be the castle's front door. A gentleman with dark hair brushing the collar of his

THE LAST DOLLAR PRINCESS

tweed jacket paused at the bottom. The gray at his temples indicated he was some years older than Charlie and his handsome face was weatherworn in the way of middle-aged gentleman farmers. When he grinned, deep creases formed at the corners of his eyes. He might have been anywhere from forty to sixty years of age. He saluted, then strode toward them.

The newcomer grabbed Charlie's outstretched hand and pumped it. "Charles, so glad you came straight home. You've been missed. And most hearty congratulations on your wonderful news." The speaker eyed India. "This must be Miss Ledbetter." He bowed slightly. "Robert James, Estate Manager, at your service. Welcome to Kilnsey. Everyone in the county is most anxious to make the acquaintance of our new countess."

India blinked, unsure exactly how to respond. She wasn't Lady Kilnsey yet. To cover her confusion, she extended her hand and fell back on the lessons drilled into her by governesses. "Thank you, Mr. James. I'm looking forward to meeting our neighbors." Her voice sounded stiff.

"And they you. And please call me Robbie." To Charlie, he continued, "We should go in now. Your mother is impatient to see you and meet her future daughter-in-law."

At the sound of the luggage carts clattering into the yard, India looked over her shoulder. Althea sat beside the driver on the first cart. India hesitated to desert the only American member of staff and a stranger to all. Althea smiled, nodded, and made a shooing gesture. With one last look, India turned and followed the others into the house.

They entered through a vestibule designed to allow callers refuge from the weather while awaiting admittance to the house proper. Once beyond the great oak front doors, India stopped to allow her eyes to adjust to the darker interior. Before her lay a huge expanse of stone floor leading to a fireplace large enough for two or three grown men to stand upright and abreast. Other than rugs on the floor, a few straight-backed chairs set beneath the windows, and weaponry mounted on the walls, the space was rather bare.

Charlie raised his arm in a sweeping gesture. "This is the Great Hall and the oldest part of the castle. It will make a nice ballroom, don't you think?"

It was all India could do to keep her mouth from falling agape. If the rest of the castle was like this, life would be much harder than she had imagined. For all of its grandeur and antiquity, the hall felt cold and lifeless.

Instead of replying, she simply nodded as a touch of sickness churned her midsection. To tamp it down, she made herself focus on her present reality. This place was her fate, and she had best get a handle on it and on herself. Better to see the possibilities than conjure up potential horrors. To that end, she imagined couples in fancy dress waltzing in the glow of hundreds of candles beneath ancient beams festooned with garlands of flowers. Quite a large number of dancers would fit comfortably into the space. It could be magical if done well. Though she had not appreciated them at the time, she now saw a purpose to the lessons Mother had pounded into her. Mother had deficiencies as a parent, but she had ensured India knew how to put on a fine party. She stifled a giggle as she envisioned herself hostess in this place. If she stopped worrying and let herself dream, this countessing thing might prove fun.

Charlie led her to the back of the hall and through another heavy door. Instead of the bleakness of medieval stone and armaments, polished wainscoting with beautiful green damask above drew the eye upward to the coffered ceiling. An enormous crystal chandelier hung over the mahogany dining table that would seat at least twenty. India turned a full circle trying to take it all in. There may not be flush toilets or gaslighting, but at some point, the family had possessed a considerable fortune. Had they sold off the china, crystal, and silver to pay the taxes or the mortgage? If so, perhaps she would ask that any missing pieces be sent from the collections at The Falls. Heaven knows there was enough of it there. Dining on familiar china would give her a touchstone with home and this room deserved an elegant table service.

Charlie put his arm around her with a chuckle. "It is rather awe inspiring, is it not? You will have plenty of time to explore in future. Let's not keep Mama waiting any longer."

They passed through a chamber that housed a grand staircase of carved stone and dashed on into another huge room even more elaborate in its decor than the dining room. A carved marble mantel and surround anchored the space. Before it sat two sofas and several chairs. A woman dressed in a mauve summer silk styled from an earlier era perched stiff-backed on the sofa facing the door. Sunlight streaming through a tall window made a halo of her white upswept hair. Though the vestiges of youthful beauty were fading to a regal handsomeness, her complexion still retained an English rose quality unmarked by the deep lines of old age. India swallowed hard and summoned what she hoped was a winning smile.

Charlie took her hand and led her across the expanse of oriental carpets and parquet oak flooring. They came to rest before his mother where he bent and kissed her cheek but did not speak.

Lady Kilnsey remained silent while she ran her gaze over India. An insect under a microscope would not have been so scrutinized. After several uncomfortable beats, the great lady said, "So, you are to be the new Lady Kilnsey.

Welcome, my dear. You may call me Mama. Come. Give me a kiss." After India did as bid, Charlie's mother continued, "Clarissa, Jonathan, do not lurk. Have you no kiss for your Mama?" India watched in fascination as the pair stepped forward like a couple of children whose behavior had been found wanting.

Formidable. It was the only word to describe India's future mother-in-law. The woman had clearly been in charge for a long time. Would she be willing to pass the reins to a twenty-year-old American who had no training in the ways of the English peerage? She said a silent prayer, then without warning, a giggle bubbled up. India coughed, hoping no one had noticed the mirth threatening to escape. She must be more tired than she realized because she was on the verge of hysterics. A vision of Mother and Lady Kilnsey sparring for control of the wedding invaded just when she most wished to be calm, but the thought of those two at loggerheads was really quite funny. India smiled as another idea presented itself. Clarissa's presence might prove more of a godsend than originally anticipated. *She* could act as buffer between Boudica and Betsy Ross.

CHAPTER 37

Clarissa gauged her mother's reaction to India and did not like what she saw. Mama could hide her thoughts from most but never from her daughter, and at present, those thoughts were not as positive as the girl deserved. It would be a shame if Mama queered the marriage at the last minute due to her overweening snobbery. Best step in before anyone else noticed the coolness of the reception.

Clarissa sat on the sofa opposite Mama and patted the seat beside her. "Come, India. Sit by me. It has been a long day." She cast her gaze on Charlie. "Ring for tea and tell Ainsworth to include sherry. We need fortification." To her mother, she said, "I assume dinner will be at the usual hour? If so, we will not have time to dress. You agree, do you not, Mama?"

Mama's brows rose a fraction, but true to form, she could be counted on to not create a scene so early in her acquaintance with India. "Of course. We will put aside formalities for this evening. I have asked Cook to prepare a light meal. I thought you might want an early night after your journey."

Not long after the bell rang in the servant's hall, the butler entered and received his instructions. India settled into the sofa beside Clarissa and became less animated than one would have hoped. The girl let the conversation float around her, answering questions when asked, but not putting much effort into being entertaining. India must be feeling overwhelmed. Who would blame her after all she had recently experienced? Clarissa cast a critical eye over her mother. Unless distracted, Mama would soon go into grand inquisitor mode, something India did not appear up to at the moment. Tea arrived, and Clarissa guided the conversation to people and things of which the girl knew nothing, so would not be expected to comment upon.

***

India gave herself a mental shake. That second glass of sherry during tea had been a mistake. She gazed across the dinner table at Clarissa as though awakened from a dream. A question had been asked, but for the life of her, India could not discern its contents.

"I'm sorry. I think I drifted away for a second. What did you say?"

Sympathy filled Clarissa's eyes. "My question is of no importance. Charlie, the twilight over the moors is particularly lovely this evening. Perhaps India would like a breath of air."

India shot a grateful smile at her soon-to-be sister-in-law. "I would very much like that. I always find a stroll after dinner refreshing."

Lady Kilnsey frowned as she pushed her chair back. "Take a wrap. Our evenings can be chilly even in August." If India had to guess, her future mother-in-law did not approve of dinner guests abandoning the table without first asking permission. She made a mental note that at present the table belonged to Charlie's mother.

With a borrowed woolen shawl about her shoulders, India joined Charlie in the Great Hall. He led her out into the courtyard and on through a smaller gate built into the wall on the opposite side of the castle. Once they passed the postern gate, as he called it, they entered a garden in the formal French style. Gravel paths passed between rows of low boxwood hedges which crisscrossed in an orderly geometrical pattern much like a Chinese Chippendale chair back. At the end of the garden, a small stone structure offered a tranquil spot to rest upon wooden benches whose backs mirrored the pattern of the garden. Though the folly's design and materials were vastly different, it had an ambience similar to the hut overlooking the falls back home - a place of respite where one might refresh one's spirit or while away a summer afternoon with a good book.

India placed a hand over her eyes and looked beyond the folly to where the sun rested on the crest of a distant hill. Its waning light bathed everything with the burnished quality one only sees on a summer evening where the air is pure, unmarred by the smoke of factories and overcrowded cities. To her left and right, stands of junipers provided protective borders, but did not obscure the view over the moors. Their fragrance floated on the breeze, reminding her of the forests surrounding The Falls.

Peace stroked India's fretful soul. Perhaps this place on its lonely moor would come to feel like home after all. As long as she could get out on her own astride Zara several times a week, she would be okay. She would take up painting again, which she so longed to do. As a child, she had enjoyed her art lessons until Mother put a stop to them, saying they were a waste of time. She would speak to Charlie about a room to use as a studio. There must be at least one suitable space in all this great castle that was not used for other purposes. As for her sweet little mare, an ache had been building in India since they left the train at Grassington, but there had not been an appropriate time to ask until now.

Lady Kilnsey had been right about evenings on the moors. The breeze had cooled since their arrival. India pulled the shawl closer and slipped her hand into Charlie's. "Could we go to the stables? I want to see how Zara is doing."

Charlie turned them back toward the postern gate. "We will need to go to the courtyard. The original stables, soon to be garage, are right inside the main gate."

Mention of the garage conversion rankled now just as much as it had earlier in the day. Perhaps this was the time to talk about the large sums Charlie was spending.

India waited until Zara's head rested on her shoulder to broach the subject. Nuzzling the mare's cheek, India looked down the long row of stalls of which her mare was the only occupant. "I think we need to talk about this conversion you have planned. How much of the stable do you plan to take?"

A look of surprise drew Charlie's brows together. "Well, all of it really. We will have to make a space suitable for Barton to manage upkeep and do repairs. And I doubt one auto will be sufficient, so we will need room for at least two or three." He waved toward the end of the row. "That will pretty much take all the space you see. Automobiles are the future. Horses are the past."

India's eyes felt like they might pop from her head. "Do you mean you intend to stop keeping horses? Where will I stable Zara? She absolutely must have an enclosed stall. I will not allow her to be thrown out onto a moorland pasture to fend for herself." Her unguarded tone sounded harsh.

Charlie's head snapped back. "Now wait just a minute. There is no need to take that attitude. I do know how to take care of my animals. We have a stable block in Cragfast

Mastiles where my hunters and the carriage horses are kept. They are seen to by a village lad. I had Zara brought to the stables here because I knew you would want to see her as soon as possible."

He was clearly affronted, but India would not stop. The more important subjects had yet to be explored. "I'm sorry to be abrupt, but you have made plans without telling me anything about them. The least you could have done is show me the courtesy of discussing them with me. It is my money, after all."

Charlie's face turned the color of the setting sun. "I say, that is completely unfair. It was agreed when we signed the contracts that the money would transfer to the estate as soon as we are wed. Your money, as you so crassly put it, will be used to restore Kilnsey Castle and to retake Kilnsey House, the homes where you now live and our children will grow up. It will support the estate, the source of my income. I would have thought you would be glad of a fine London townhouse in the best neighborhood and improvements to the castle to bring it to the standards to which you are accustomed. I thought you would want an automobile as opposed to being carted about in a carriage from last century." His breath came in hard gusts when he finally stopped speaking.

India's heart beats matched the rate at which Charlie huffed. "Of course, I expected you to make improvements, but not all at once. Do you have any idea what happens when a family starts spending from their fortune's principal? And don't say you haven't already promised a portion of it to buy back Kilnsey House and now you want to immediately tear into the castle stables and buy an automobile. Where do you intend to stop? When my fortune is completely depleted and you are back where you started before you met me? Furthermore, I would think indoor plumbing, electric lights, and central heating might have taken priority over a London house which we will see once or twice a year and an automobile that is far less suited to country lanes than a horse and cart."

Charlie stiffened and his mouth became a thin line. "I see. Well, there is something you should know before you complain so bitterly about the London house. I am being encouraged to pursue a seat in the House of Lords. Our part of Yorkshire is lacking representation. If I agree, we will be using Kilnsey House whenever Parliament sits." His eyes narrowed and his gaze hardened. "If you believe me such a fool, it is a wonder you agreed to marry. Do you wish to break our engagement? Do you? If so, be forewarned the marriage contracts are very clear regarding the settlement that would still come to me."

India's pulse pounded in her ears. "I have not said any such thing. But since you mention it, do you? This is a marriage of convenience for both of us. Have I become so inconvenient that you no longer wish to marry me?"

A look of shock replaced the anger in his eyes. He did not answer but held her gaze as though searching her very soul. India stopped breathing while she waited for his reply, jolted by her own words. The notion of breaking their engagement upset her more than she could have anticipated, forcing her to take a hard look at herself. What she found brought confusion and disquiet followed by cold realization. Somewhere in the past weeks, she had fallen in love. Exactly when or how it happened was not clear. Perhaps it was when he insisted that he see her safely home for Papa's funeral or when he saved her reputation at the suffragist rally by destroying the photographer's plate, damning evidence of her obstinance.

For her entire life she had bent her will to that of others. She had stilled her tongue to keep peace. Now when she had finally found her voice, it may have ruined her future and lost her the man who held her heart. Fear, confusion, but mostly anger washed through her. With whom she was most angry was hard to say. The mixture of emotions within her warred until they overflowed. Unashamed, she allowed the tears to roll unchecked until they dripped from her chin.

Charlie's expression remained grim as he stepped forward and grabbed her shoulders. When his mouth met hers, it was not the gentle kiss of a faint ardor, but deep and passionate. Heat welled up from the depths, setting India's breathing to near gasps. When she most wanted him to take her where they stood, he broke the spell.

Pushing her back at arm's length, he said, "Let that be your answer." His tone was rough, perhaps passionate. It was difficult to tell which.

They stood frozen in place, their eyes locked in a silent battle of wills, the tension so palpable India could have held it in her hand like a living thing. They might have remained thus for a long time, had Zara not taken that moment to paw the floor of her stall, then kick its walls. Satisfied that she now had their attention, she nudged and poked her water bucket until it slipped its hook, sending the contents flying. Eying the mess she had made, she curled her lip as though she smelled something foul, tossed her head, and snorted at Charlie.

The anger glittering in his eyes dissolved into surprise followed by amusement. His chuckles turned to laughter. The harder he laughed, the more difficult it was for India to hold on to her own anger. With each of Charlie's guffaws, the flame flickered until it smoldered and died, doused by her own giggles.

Wiping his eyes, Charlie said, "I think Zara's telling me to have a care. You have a fierce champion in this little Arab." He scratched the mare's poll and gave her a pat. "But you are also wise, little mare. You are right. We argue foolishly when we should most be happy. I hope your mistress will forgive my ungentlemanly outburst." Taking India's hands, he raised them to his lips. "And you, my dear, are as wise as you are beautiful. You are correct, of course. I have allowed my desire to restore the estate to take such hold that I have steamed ahead without proper planning. You are also correct that I should have discussed expenditures with you. It was disrespectful of me not to have done so. When Kilnsey House came available, I could not bear to let it go to someone else. I have acted rashly. I apologize. I have lived without funds for so long that I have let the considerable size of your fortune go to my head. I promise to do better in future. Forgive me?"

India nodded, but her heart was not in the gesture for it had plummeted to her feet. He had failed to say the one word she most needed to hear. Now that she had acknowledged her own vulnerability, she needed reassurance that she was not alone in what she felt. The balance of power in their relationship had shifted in these few minutes, leaving her enlightened, but deeply troubled.

***

Clarissa watched the pair marching across the courtyard from the stables. Unless her powers of observation had diminished, something was amiss. Perhaps they had argued. If she had to guess, she would say the large sums Charlie was planning on spending with such haste could be the source of contention. The boy had to be made to see reason before he ruined his chances and lost the girl through his own carelessness or stupidity. Oh, he would get a handsome settlement if the engagement was broken, but it would be nothing like the fortune that was to come after the wedding. The estate needed that fortune to survive.

She went to the Great Hall and waited for the sound of the front door clicking shut. Charlie looked annoyed when he spied her there in the center of the hall, no doubt anticipating the inquisition to which he was about to be subjected.

Clarissa summoned her warmest smile. "India, darling, you look positively exhausted. I have alerted your maid to prepare a hot bath and then bed, I think. What do you say?"

The girl nodded gratefully. "That sounds heavenly, but I have no idea where my room is."

"Mrs. Wilson awaits you by the Grand Staircase. She will conduct you to your room and ensure you are able to find your way downstairs in the morning." Clarissa slipped her arms around India and gave her a quick hug. "Off to bath and bed for you, young lady. We can't have our lovely bride looking haggard and overwrought." To Charlie, she said, "When you have released India into Mrs. Wilson's charge, I would like a word, please."

Returning from his mission, Charlie marched toward Clarissa looking for all the world like a runaway locomotive. Steam fairly poured from him. He would have to be managed with care.

When Charlie came to rest beside Clarissa, she ran a critical eye over him. "Is anything wrong? I thought India looked a little upset." When he did not reply, but simply glared, she continued, "You know you can call on me to assist in any way. I feel toward India as I might have toward a younger sister and I think she will listen to my counsel. She is a dear girl. I hope you have not said or done something untoward."

His expression stiffened. "If there is anything that needs your attention, I will let you know."

Exasperation filled Clarissa and set her tongue in motion with more force than common sense dictated. "If it's that farmer's daughter standing between you, you have to put her aside. Surely you see that. Your affection must be solely with India. Have you been able to do that?" He did not reply and let his gaze wander. "Look at me, Charlie. In the past, you have evinced at least some affection for the girl. You have jumped to her defense on more than one occasion. Please tell me this return home has not undermined your feelings for her. I am fairly sure she is in love with you." In her agitation, Clarissa grabbed his arm. "What do you feel for her? Tell me."

Charlie yanked his arm from her grasp. His eyes blazed as he turned for the door, shouting over his shoulder, "What we feel for one another is between India and me. Do not presume to meddle or question me again. For once in your life you will mind your own damned business."

The sound of the front door slamming behind him echoed through the hall.

CHAPTER 38

The clatter of carriage wheels summoned India to the drawing room windows. She stood in the spot where yesterday Charlie's mother had looked down upon the arrival of her future daughter-in-law. Surely Lady Kilnsey's nerves had not jangled as India's did now. Movement behind her made her jump.

Charlie settled beside her and put an arm around her shoulders. He leaned in and whispered, "Courage, my darling. All will be well." To the group assembled beside the fireplace, he continued, "Mrs. Ledbetter has arrived. We should go to the courtyard to greet her."

India inhaled, held the breath, then let it slip out in a long stream. Not only was Charlie taking charge of what may be a difficult situation, he had called her "my darling." He had not yet used the word love, but surely it was the next best thing. Fortified by these thoughts, she slipped her hand under his arm and together they sallied forth.

Mother, assisted from the carriage by Barton, paused to take in her surroundings. Fixing Charlie with an inscrutable gaze, she opened her mouth, but appeared to be trying to find the right words. India quaked at the thought of what might come out.

With a tight smile, Mother said, "Charles, dear, you have made me feel quite regal. I haven't ridden in a barouche in…why I'm not sure how long it's been. India, come give your mama a kiss."

After she did as bidden, India shot Clarissa an imploring look. Bless her. She got the message.

Clarissa stepped forward and took Mother's hands, placing a kiss upon each cheek. "Mrs. Ledbetter, dear Petra. You have arrived at last. I trust your night at the Skipton Arms was pleasant. Mama is most anxious to make your acquaintance." Clarissa guided Mother toward Lady Kilnsey.

To India, the scene took on the atmosphere of naval actions described in her old history books. Mother sailed across the cobbles with her gaze locked straight ahead, her antagonist clearly in her sights. Lady Kilnsey, posture erect and stiff, could have served as a ship's mast with sails furled against a gale. Mother came to rest about a yard away from Lady Kilnsey and the two great dreadnoughts sized up one another while deciding who would fire the first shot.

Mother tilted her head in the way she did just before she was about to issue a veiled insult, but Lady Kilnsey outmaneuvered her. "How delightful you are able to come after all. A bride wants her own family represented, however slight the number."

Unruffled, Mother squared her shoulders. "I was unaware my presence was ever in doubt. One simply does not miss the wedding of one's only daughter, but I must admit I was rather rushed given the date is only two days hence. I am surprised it was allowed to move forward with such haste knowing we are still in mourning. I fear there will be gossip."

Lady Kilnsey's nostrils flared. "That might be the case in New York, but I assure you no one here would dare. We took your sad situation into account, of course, when planning. Kilnsey brides have traditionally married from Kilnsey House, but given the circumstances, such a display would have been unseemly. Instead of a large London wedding, it will be a simple, dignified family affair here in our village church."

"I see. Very well." Mother's eyes glittered with unexpressed anger. Skirmish to Lady Kilnsey.

Accepting she had been momentarily bested, Mother cast her gaze upon India, but Clarissa stepped in, deflecting potential assaults. "We must not keep poor Mrs. Ledbetter standing out here any longer. Please forgive us. I have taken the liberty of leaving instructions that you are to be shown to your room immediately upon arrival as I knew you would want to change after your journey. We can discuss wedding plans in depth at luncheon."

Within a half hour, they were seated at one end of the long mahogany dining table sipping chicken consommé with snipped summer herbs.

Mother laid her spoon on the rim of her soup plate and cleared her throat. When all eyes were on her, she proceeded. "Lady Clarissa, I understand you have made most of the arrangements for the wedding. That would normally have fallen to me, as mother-of-the-bride, but of course that will not be possible given the circumstances. However, the music is of particular concern. Perhaps I might be left that small task? Does the church have an organ or will we be hiring musicians?"

Lady Kilnsey did not give her daughter time to respond. "I assure you the village church has an excellent organ and an accomplished organist. He comes from Skipton and is glad of the work and the instrument we provide. My husband's grandfather was a keen enthusiast and would allow only the best installed. Kilnsey weddings have always featured the same pieces. The organist is prepared."

Mother eyed Lady Kilnsey. "I see. I am sure he will be just as capable of playing the pieces I have selected. I wish the processional for family to be *Jesus Joy of Man's Desiring* and that India enter to Handel's *Bridal March*."

Lady Kilnsey was not deterred. "Kilnsey weddings have followed the same musical program for over one hundred years. I see no reason to change that simply because the bride is an American. The family will process to Clarke's *Trumpet Voluntary* followed by Purcell's *Brides Entrance* for your daughter. After the ceremony is concluded, all will recess to Handel's *Arrival of the Queen of Sheba*. It is too late to change the program nor should I wish to."

India watched her mother inhale and exhale slowly and felt a little shock of gratitude. She was actually trying to keep her temper in check. Mother looked at Clarissa, then back at Lady Kilnsey. "You have not mentioned attendants. May I at least know who will accompany my daughter down the aisle?"

Lady Kilnsey deferred to Clarissa with a glance. "Jonathan has agreed to escort her. With such a small affair, are attendants really needed?"

Mother's face crumpled like an overbaked soufflé. "Not even one? If we were in New York, she would have at least half a dozen bridesmaids."

A smirk lifted one corner of Lady Kilnsey's mouth. "One supposes that could be. However, I have it on good authority that the opposite would be the case given your colorful family history."

Mother threw her napkin onto the table and rose from her chair so quickly that it rocked in danger of toppling over. "And I have it on good authority that insulting a guest is a sure indicator of low breeding. Our family tree is populated with as many persons of high standing as yours, probably more given the late earl's... colorful history, as you put it. India, conduct me to my room. This is not to be borne a moment longer. I will take a tray in my room for the remainder of this meal." She lifted her hand with a wave that included the group. "I will not stand in the way of this marriage if it is truly what my daughter wishes but understand this. India is an exceptional young woman of good breeding, considerable fortune, beauty, and intelligence. You are fortunate she has chosen to marry Charles and in so doing, will save your estate for you."

Mother did not wait for anyone to respond. She crooked her finger at India, turned on her heel, and marched from the room.

India bent and hissed at Charlie and Clarissa, "I am going to see what I can do to placate her. I will be down when I am satisfied there will be no further outbursts. I would appreciate it if you two would take your mother in hand, as well. Our wedding day should be a joyous one, not one filled with bickering and acrimony."

As angry as she was, India also glowed in the warmth of Mother's praise. It was quite a change from her usual criticism and castigations.

As they left the dining room and headed toward the stairs, Ainsworth rushed from behind them and skidded to a halt beside the newel. "His Lordship asks that I guide you to your room. It is a large house and the passages can be confusing. Trays will be delivered to your room, if that meets with your approval, Madame, Miss."

India straightened her spine and glided across the hall. "That would be most helpful. Thank His Lordship when you return to the dining room and inform him that I will speak with him presently."

Once they had navigated the labyrinth of hallways and passages, they entered the guest wing and a guest bedroom with west-facing windows overlooking the moors.

Mother flung herself into a chair by the fireplace and waved India into the one opposite. "I do not envy you your future mother-in-law. Are you sure you want to go through with this wedding? We can get out of the contract, you know. It will cost a small fortune, but it would be worth it if you do not truly want to marry Charles." Her tone was unexpectedly solicitous.

India looked at Mother with suspicion. Why the sudden concern? Mother always had ulterior motives. "I know I can break the contract, but I don't want to because I have fallen in love with him. I want to be his wife and have his children."

Mother's eyes widened. She rose, went to the windows, and stood gazing over the moors. "This is such a desolate, isolated place. You know no one here and after Clarissa, Jonathan, and I return to America, you will be alone with these people. Can you really see yourself being happy here for the rest of your life?"

India tilted her head and ran her gaze over Mother. Something was definitely afoot. Mother seemed like a totally new person. Gone was the woman who had been more critical than loving for as long as India could remember. In her place was a stranger.

"I can no longer bear The Falls and I have never liked New York. I am confident this beautiful, wild place will grow to feel like home."

When Mother turned away from the window, surprise filled India. Tears rolled down Mother's cheeks. "You are my only child and all I have ever wanted is to see you married to the right man. I see now how poorly I have shown my love. I have been selfish in many ways, but your happiness was never out of my mind. I do love you, Darling. If you are sure this is the right course, I will be happy for you and will not make trouble."

India could contain herself no longer. "What's happened? Why are you so changed?"

Mother's chin dropped until it came near to resting on her chest. She dabbed at her tears with a linen handkerchief. "You are correct. Something has happened, but I dare not tell you. I am afraid you will never forgive me. You loved your father so."

India went to stand before Mother. "Go on. For once let us speak frankly."

"Let's return to the chairs. What I have to tell you may come as a shock." When they were seated, Mother continued, "While you were staying with Clarissa and the marriage contracts were being negotiated, I reconnected with someone from my past. He is the man I should have married. Had it not been for my parents' financial crisis, I would have married him. I am ashamed that I did not make a better effort for your father's sake. It has become a great regret as has the way I have treated you. I simply could not see beyond my own unhappiness, but one cannot change the past."

India suspected she knew what was coming next, but she wanted to hear Mother admit it. "It is sad that you and Papa were so unhappy. Marriages of convenience often are. Now tell me. What are your plans for the future with this renewed connection?"

Mother twisted the handkerchief until it was a tight wad. "When I return to New York and after a suitable period of mourning, I will remarry."

"And the lucky groom's name?"

"I think you may have guessed. It is David Havemeyer." When India did not respond, Mother left her chair and knelt beside India's. "Dearest, please do not be angry. I now have a chance at happiness for the first time in my adult life. Can't you see that? Please be happy for me. As your mother, you owe me that much, at least."

India quelled the urge to comment upon the return of Mother's true self, but she could not keep a touch of sarcasm from her voice. "If this is what you want, I wish you joy of one another. You have waited long enough. Are you breaking up a marriage to attain this happiness?"

Mother looked as though India had slapped her. Tears welled up once more. "No. David never married. He never got over losing me nor I him."

India could bear the conversation no longer. A range of emotions raged through her, none of which were helpful. Her relationship with Mother had always been complicated and even strained at times. On the surface, she wanted Mother to finally be happy, but deeper down in her true heart, India was seething that Mother had never tried to be happy with Papa. She now knew that Mother had made Papa's last years miserable, that no effort had been made to see to his needs. Mother had even belittled Papa's poor health and made light of it.

India rose from her chair and went to the door. She turned back toward Mother. "I do hope you will be happy. I really mean it. I am sincere. I'm going to do my best to make Charlie happy and I think he'll do the same for me." She opened the door and stepped into the hall, calling over her shoulder, "I'm going to take Zara out on the moors. I need some fresh air to clear my mind."

India fled straight to the stables. The startled groom followed her orders to saddle Zara but hesitated when he saw India intended to ride out alone. "Begging pardon, Miss, but it's easy ta git lost out on they moors. Maybe I otta go with you or maybe wait for His Lordship."

India fixed the young man with a glare. "Thank you for your concern, but on such open terrain, I'll be fine. I rode in dense forests at home and never got lost. Please inform His Lordship that I have gone for a ride and may not return until teatime."

Once in the saddle, she tapped Zara's flanks. The pair trotted through the main gate, across the green swath beside the garden, and out onto the open moors. Wind tossed Zara's mane and loosened the pins in India's hair. She urged the mare into a canter. A sense of freedom settled over her with every yard of moorland. Soon, the castle dipped behind the brow of a hill and was lost to sight. India clicked to the mare, who jumped into a full-on gallop.

CHAPTER 39

Exhilarated by the freedom of the open moors, India failed to notice a rider approaching from behind until he grabbed Zara's reins, jerking both horses to a stop. India flashed angry eyes in Charlie's direction. Was she never to have a minute's solitude? Was she simply trading one tyrant for another? Well, he could try, but she would be damned if she would succumb to tyranny ever again.

Charlie jumped from the saddle, his eyes blazing, his face grim. "Have you taken complete leave of your senses? The moors are dangerous even to people who have lived here all their lives." He stretched his arm toward a low-lying area of waving grasses. "That may look like a pleasant field, but it is actually a bog. Step into it and you stand to lose not only your horse, but your life. We're going back to the house. Make sure Zara follows my horse exactly. Do you understand?"

He did not wait for a reply. Still holding Zara's reins, he leapt into the saddle and turned his mount back toward the castle. Chastened by how close she had come to real danger, India followed in silence. Her hands trembled as they gripped the pommel. She must not let her desire for independence overcome her common sense. Her stubbornness could have gotten Zara injured or even killed.

When they arrived in the courtyard, Charlie helped her to dismount. India glanced up at him unsure what she should say to make amends. His gaze swept over her before he pulled her into a fierce embrace. "You little fool. I could have lost you before our life together even began. Promise me you will never put yourself in such danger again. Promise me." His tone was as fierce as his embrace.

India's heart swelled and a calming warmth spread to the tips of her fingers and toes. Charlie may not have used the word love, but he clearly cared for her. It wasn't just the money. He really seemed to care for her as his future wife. She smiled up at him. "I promise and I'm sorry I gave you a fright. I didn't know about the moors. I was foolish, as you said. Forgive me?"

He kissed her forehead and released her. Nodding, he said, "Clarissa wishes you to join her in the drawing room. Reverend Howard is with her. He wants to review wedding procedures. He's a distant cousin who has been the vicar here since I was a boy. He's rather dry and humorless in the pulpit, but a good sort all the same."

***

Two days later, India stood in the church door, her hand on Jonathan's arm. Seed pearl encrusted lace trailed along her dress, train, and veil which was supported by a crown of orange blossoms matching the bouquet she carried. All little girls dreamed of being princesses. She had been no different and today her dream had become reality, at least that was how she felt when she had looked at herself in her bedroom mirror.

The small sanctuary was filled to capacity. Charlie waited with Robbie, his best man, at the altar where Reverend Howard signaled for the congregation to stand. Feeling a tug at her back, India looked over her shoulder to where Althea lifted and arranged the gown's train for the umpteenth time. She gave the veil a final fluff and looked up with a wink like she always did when she wanted India to know everything would be all right. The trumpets of the Purcell piece faded into the march and India was off down the aisle.

Within the next hour, she would be Lady Kilnsey. She glanced at the congregation as they passed the rows of pews. She didn't know a single soul save for family and the upper servants allowed to attend. As a tremor passed through her, Jonathan looked down, smiled, and gave her hand a squeeze.

From the corner of his mouth, he whispered encouragement. "You are a beautiful bride and will make Charlie very happy. He's a lucky man." India prayed his words would prove true.

As they passed, India peeked around Jonathan at the pew reserved for the bride's family. Mother sat poker straight and dabbed at her eyes with a snowy linen handkerchief. Seeing India's eyes on her, Mother smiled wistfully. Was it real or for show? India decided she really didn't care. She had lived under Mother's thumb long enough. Cutting her eyes to the groom's side, she saw Lady Kilnsey equally straight-backed wearing an expression that could only be described as stoic, sending a tremor down India's spine. Clarissa peered around her mother to nod and smile encouragingly. Bless her soon-to-be sister-in-law. Clarissa's emotions seemed to be the most genuine of all.

India arrived at the altar and Charlie took her hands in his. His firm grip eased the trembling in hers. If he was equally nervous, he did not show it. He stood tall and at ease. When he looked down into her eyes, her heart soared. He seemed to be saying that this was right and that all would be well.

The ceremony passed in a blur with the plighting and giving of troths and promises to keep only to one another as long as they both should live. A little tingle passed through her as Charlie repeated the unfamiliar words of the Anglican service, "...and with my body I thee worship." India glowed from within. Indeed, it was a good thing the congregation could not read her inner most thoughts just then.

India and Charlie exited the church, hands tightly clasped, to a shower of rose petals thrown by villagers for whom there had been no space in the sanctuary. The wedding party and guests promenaded through the village and up the lane toward the castle amid cheers and shouts of long life and good health.

The castle's main rooms were awash in flowers and candles. Extra footmen had been hired to assist with the number of guests to be served and fed. Mrs. Bertrand and the kitchen staff had outdone themselves with the wedding breakfast laid in the dining room. India smiled at the stranger in Kilnsey green, black, and gold livery who pulled out her chair. The man was well trained for he looked straight ahead and kept his face stonily neutral. Once seated, she looked down the long table to where Mother, Lady Kilnsey, Clarissa, and Jonathan sat. They appeared to be engaged in congenial, if not exactly animated, conversation. India caught Clarissa's eye and gave her a grateful smile.

The wedding party was tucking into a full English breakfast when an unwelcome figure appeared at Charlie's shoulder. Bumpy, Lord Hawik, Charlie's heir for the present, sniffed and leaned in closer than was polite.

"I say, Charles, good show. You are to be congratulated. I see you have managed to snare yourself beauty, money, and good birthing hips all in one convenient package. Pity. I would have liked to add Kilnsey to my titles, but then the future is uncertain for all of us, even the young."

Charlie smiled and said through gritted teeth, "And I see you are still the same boorish misanthrope you have always been. If I didn't know you to be a coward, I could interpret that as a threat to my wife. But bullies are usually cowards and you have always been both. Now do please have the courtesy to take your seat."

"Cousin, I wish you all happiness, even a gaggle of children, though it will profit me nothing." Hawik half turned and smiled. "Of course, the bloodline is said to be tainted, but then bad blood often produces robust offspring."

Fists balled, Charlie tried to jump up from his chair, but India grabbed his arm. "Don't. Just let it go. Please. After today, we never have to see him again except for weddings and funerals. Don't let him ruin this beautiful day." Charlie's muscles rippled under the pressure of her fingers. He peered down at her with fury still shining in his eyes. For a moment, she feared he might strike her instead, but his eyes cleared. The anger melted, replaced by an expression filled with both kindness and protectiveness. India's heart swelled. Charlie cared for her. It was there in the eyes that never left hers as he leaned in and kissed her.

After the toasts, the well wishes, after Charlie and India had gone to each guest to thank them for sharing in their day, only after all the social niceties had been observed, only then did Charlie and India retire to their bedrooms to prepare for their wedding trip. It would only be three days in Ripon because Charlie was so impatient to begin repairing all that had been neglected during his father's incompetent custody of the estate. He had taken a suite in a small country hotel that guaranteed privacy in the evenings.

India descended the grand staircase to where the family had gathered to see them off. Mother dabbed at her eyes with a handkerchief for the second time that day. India watched to ascertain if the emotion was genuine or simply for show. A small spasm of sorrow swept through her. Mother really appeared to be sad at their parting. The years of domination had ended. The woman who had brought her into this world would be traveling back to America by the time she and Charlie returned from Ripon. It was uncertain when they would next meet. Tears welled in India's eyes for what they had missed and for what might have been, but not for having Mother an ocean away. She and Charlie would need space to establish their life together. Whether the dowager countess would interfere or be a hindrance was a worry for another day.

Seated in the barouche with Barton at the reins, they retraced the path they had taken from Grassington Railway Station to the castle. It had only been four days since that journey, but India's whole world had changed. The first time Ainsworth addressed her as My Lady, she had looked around for Charlie's mother. The man kindly busied himself with a chaffing dish to cover her confusion, then asked his question again. She now felt she had another ally among the staff at Kilnsey Castle. With Althea, who was staying behind, that made two.

A hired automobile awaited them when they stepped onto the station platform at Ripon. After a short drive out of town, they arrived at The Old Orchard Inn, a lovely 18th century manor house that had been converted. Standing in the south-facing window in their bedroom, Charlie slipped an arm around India's waist and pulled her close so that his lips nuzzled her ear.

With his free hand, he gestured toward a wooded area in the near distance. "Just beyond those trees lies one of the loveliest gardens you will ever see. The estate also owns the ruins of a Cistercian monastery, Fountains Abbey. The views are quite spectacular. The owner is a family friend and has agreed to give us a tour. Would you like that?"

India nodded. In that moment, she would have agreed to most any suggestion he made. They had rarely been alone before their wedding and now that she had him all to herself for three whole days, doubts crept in. What if she was a failure at what Mother had described as her wifely duty? What if he found her body unappealing? What if she found the act as repulsive as Mother had hinted it was? She really had very little knowledge of anything beyond the mechanics. All she knew was that when he kissed her, she lost the ability to think clearly, that a burning desire took hold deep within her body. Surely that was a good sign. They were married. Why let this torment continue?

She turned to face him and rested her hand on the back of his neck, letting her fingers caress the nape. His eyes grew wider as they locked onto hers. He bent and drew her into a kiss that was gentle at first, then filled with unbridled passion. India wanted, no needed, to be out of her constricting clothes. She needed to feel skin against skin. The spark ignited by his kiss quickly became a flame. Though Charlie fumbled with laces, buttons, and ties, India soon found herself naked atop the featherbed. Naked as well, he hovered above her, his gaze traveling over her body, his lust clearly visible.

"My God, you are beautiful. Had I known what all those layers were hiding, your virtue would have been in far greater danger."

He did not give her time to respond for his mouth covered hers with a hunger held in check for far too long. Her desire blazed with his until they were both consumed.

Settling beside her, Charlie let his fingers trail over her breasts and down her belly. "Rather than going down for dinner, what would you say if I asked for it to be served here in the room?"

India gazed into the eyes of the man who had given her such pleasure, a wicked smile lifting her lips. "Yes, please."

***

At the end of three days, they had left their suite only long enough to take tea in the hotel's garden, take solitary walks along the River Skell, and make a call upon the owner of Fountains Abbey who gave them a brief tour of the ruins. India had no idea married life could be so wonderful, so fulfilling. It was the happiest she had ever been. She knew they could not live in a constant state of euphoria, but she prayed they could take just a little of it with them when they returned to Kilnsey Castle. Not wanting to break the honeymoon spell they had waited until after luncheon to catch the train home.

India stepped down from the train onto the Grassington platform and waited for Charlie while he tugged on her bag. Its clasp was caught in the netting barrier on the luggage rack. A light breeze fluttered the ruffles on her summer frock and curled the smoke from the locomotive's stack. The clear afternoon sky promised an evening filled with stars. A stroll in the garden after dinner would be lovely before they retired to their suite for the night. The thought of what would follow warmed her in the most intimate parts of her body. It would be a perfect ending to their perfect, albeit brief honeymoon.

A slamming carriage door accompanied by an infant's wail broke the spell and drew her attention to a red-faced young mother with a baby in her arms. Despite her disheveled state, India could see she was a lovely English rose. The sun's rays caught in her hair, making it look like spun gold. From her attire, it was clear the girl was perhaps a servant or farmer's wife. Nonetheless, she would turn the heads of most men.

Boots scuffed on the platform behind India. She turned with a smile expecting Charlie to slip an arm around her and lead them to Barton and the waiting barouche. Instead, he nearly stumbled into her banging her legs with the bag in the process. His gaze was fixed on a point farther down the platform. His mouth was slightly agape, and his face wore an expression somewhere between surprise and anguish. India looked toward what had so transfixed him. It was the young mother and her child. India's heart plummeted to her boots. She suddenly felt as though she would be sick. There was only one woman who could have such an effect on her husband.

India managed to find her voice. They might as well get this over with. "By any chance is that young woman Annie?"

She had to ask a second time and give his arm a shake before he answered. "Yes." His tone was curt. With one final glance, he turned his back on the scene of mother and child hugging an older couple. "That is Annie and those are her parents. I had no idea she was coming home. We mustn't keep Barton waiting any longer."

On the ride to the castle India opened her mouth to ask a question, but Charlie turned his head away, staring out over the fields. It was as though he had forgotten she existed.

With each mile, the situation became more unbearable, but India was at a loss for how to break the dark spell Annie had cast over her joy. Her perfect three days were ending in the most disastrous way possible. Dear God. What if the girl had left her husband and was returning to Cragfast Mastiles permanently? By the time they reached the castle courtyard, India was fighting to keep tears at bay. She didn't wait for Barton or Charlie to help her from the carriage. Instead, she jumped down, stumbled on her skirt, and rushed to the entrance.

Ainsworth opened the door, a puzzled expression darkening his features. "Welcome home, My Lady. The dowager countess awaits you in the drawing room."

India forced herself to slow down. "Thank you. Please give her my apologies. I have a terrible headache and will rest in my room until tea." Instead of leaving, she froze. It dawned on her that she had no idea where she would be sleeping. She had not been housed in the family area before the wedding and did not know exactly where the master suite was. In confusion, she turned back to the butler. "Please show me to my rooms."

He conducted her through a labyrinth of corridors until they came to a dead end. There, Ainsworth opened the door on a sitting room that had double sets of windows in two walls on either side of a corner fireplace.

"This is the private parlor. You will find your rooms through the door on your left. Your windows face west. His Lordship's rooms are to the right facing north. Will you be needing anything else, My Lady?"

"No. Thank you. I am going to lie down now."

India stepped into the room and Ainsworth closed the door. With both north and west- facing windows, the parlor must be in a tower. The room was lovely. Damask the color of new spring foliage covered the walls. Settees sat on either side of the fireplace. Instead of portraits, floral still-life paintings and landscapes hung from the picture rails.

Under normal circumstances, she would have been delighted to find herself in possession of such a space. Finally alone, she allowed the tears to stream. She fled across the Aubusson carpet to the door Ainsworth had indicated and fumbled with the knob, her fingers clumsy and shaking.

Once inside her bedroom, she did not stop to look at its decor, but went to the bed and flung herself across the counterpane. Stuffing a fist her mouth, she muffled her sobs. Her whole body heaved with the force of her anguish.

Presently, a knock at the suite's entrance made her jerk upright. Her pride would not allow Charlie to see her so broken. Dashing away her tears, she rose and went to the dresser mirror. Her eyes were puffy and her hair disheveled. She did what she could to shove the hairpins back in place. There was nothing to be done about her eyes.

The knock sounded a second time. Satisfied she had done the best she could, India went into the parlor, settled herself on a settee, and straightened her spine. "Come in."

Her heart lurched when she saw who opened the door. Her mother-in-law's unsmiling countenance stared at her from the entryway. Without invitation, the older woman sailed across the room and seated herself on the opposite settee.

Holding up a hand to indicate she wished India's silence, the dowager began. "I can see you are distraught. I told my son he should see to you first, but he would not listen."

India's chest tightened and her breathing became jerky. "Where's Charlie?"

Lady Kilnsey shifted on the settee and pursed her lips, her eyes never leaving India's face. "I realize we did not begin on the best of footings, but I am sincere when I say that

I wish for you and my son to make a successful marriage." The old woman arched a brow. "In our family, marriages are for life which can be a very long time. If you are to achieve anything as my son's countess, you must learn to manage him. That begins by keeping your emotions in check. No man likes a woman who is constantly in tears. You must buck up and accept that he may not always be as attentive as you might wish. You must learn to read his moods. His desires must be paramount in your mind and heart. It is what is expected."

India wasn't sure what response her mother-in-law expected, but those archaic views on marriage and a woman's place in it shot through India like a fiery arrow.

Since she did not want to fight with Charlie's mother, redirection seemed the best course. "Thank you for your advice. I am glad we have your support. Now tell me. Exactly where is my husband?" The hint of sarcasm in India's tone failed to register with Charlie's mother.

A wistful expression entered old Lady Kilnsey's eyes, which drifted toward the western windows. Her chest rose and fell with heavily drawn breaths. "He has gone to a tenant farm where I hope he will bury his ghosts."

CHAPTER 40

Charlie's mother rose from the settee. "I will leave you now. You need time to yourself. Think about what I have said."

India's eyes narrowed as the older woman sailed across the room and through the parlor door. Oh, she would definitely think about what her mother-in-law had said. In fact, the words acted as a slap across the face bringing clarity where there had only been raw emotion before. Thoughts flew through India's mind as though blown by a gale.

So husbands had to be managed, did they? Charlie had promised to not interfere with her chosen activities, but nowhere had she agreed to his continuing to moon over the farmer's daughter. India's fists balled until her nails dug into the palms of her hands. This issue must be settled now and for all time. She would not live her life caught in an unhappy marriage as her parents had done.

She jumped up from the settee. Surely there was a washstand with a basin of cold water somewhere in this blasted apartment. Once inside the bedroom, she jerked open and slammed doors until she found an old-fashioned hip bath standing before a fireplace. A washstand with basin and pitcher rested against the outside wall between windows. India marched to it, finding the water in the pitcher pleasantly cool. She splashed her face until satisfied the evidence of her tears had disappeared as much as it was going to.

She pulled the bell cord to summon Aletha, then searched through her wardrobe for her riding costume. She had removed her shoes and was struggling with the buttons on her blouse when the maid arrived.

"Here. Let me help you with that." Althea stepped behind India and started unfastening. "I apologize for not coming up to greet you, but I was unsure whether you wanted it."

India glared at Aletha via the wardrobe mirror. "You saw, then?"

A red glow crept across the maid's face. "I'm not sure what you mean."

"Oh, yes you do. You saw us when we arrived, didn't you?" Aletha nodded but did not meet India's gaze. "You know where he's gone, don't you?" Another nod. "And the whole staff probably knows, too. Tell me. What are they saying below stairs?"

"I haven't paid any attention to their conversations. I've been too busy."

India arched a brow. "Why do I think that is less than the truth?"

Aletha's eyes darted away toward the windows. "I don't want to be the bearer of petty gossip."

"Out with it. What are they saying?"

Aletha finished the unfastening and lifted the blouse from India's shoulders. She sighed heavily before looking at India once more. "I've done what I can to dispel it, but they are saying Lord Kilnsey has never gotten over the farmer's daughter and that he is her child's father. They are taking wagers on how long it will be before he sets her up somewhere nearby so they can continue as they were before he sailed for America." Althea unfastened hooks and helped India step out of her skirt. She appeared to struggle with some unspoken concern.

India relaxed a little. She turned so she could look at Aletha fully. "I can tell you want to say something else. I won't hold it against you no matter what it is. We Americans have to stick together."

Aletha frowned while she folded the skirt. Laying the garment aside, she looked back and searched India's face. After several seconds, she finally said, "Please don't tell His Lordship. The English servants don't trust me, and they will know where he got the information."

There was real distress in Aletha's eyes. India pressed her lips together before speaking. "I will do what I can to ensure the other servants treat you well, but I can't promise not to tell Charlie. This gossip and speculation must be stopped now before it spreads throughout the county." India's jaw tightened with every word. Without thinking, she slammed a fist against her palm. "I will not have it. Furthermore, I will fire anyone spreading rumors and they can kiss any hope of a reference goodbye. You can tell the others my views the next time you hear them stirring up gossip. Please help me into my riding costume."

The remaining traveling clothes were discarded and riding attire donned in silence. After a quick glance in the mirror, India strode from the room and through the house to the stables where she saddled Zara before the groom even knew she was present. She jumped into the saddle, kicked the mare's sides, and was off down the driveway, the groom's anguished pleas to wait for him floating behind her. Her first stop was the vicarage.

She tapped her foot while pounding on the Reverend Howard's door. He opened it, his eyes bulging, a large linen napkin tucked into his ecclesiastical collar. "I say, India, I mean, My Lady. What is the emergency? Is someone ill?"

"Not in the least. Everyone is in excellent health. My husband, however, may not be after I finish with him." Her voice echoed off the church wall next door.

"Oh, dear." Rev. Howard's gaze darted around the village square and he opened the door wider. "You best come in, my dear, and tell me what has happened."

"Thank you, but that will not be necessary. Just tell me where I can find Annie's home."

"Annie?" He had the good grace to look embarrassed. "There are several girls and women by that name in the community."

"Do not be evasive. You know perfectly well to which particular Annie I refer. How do I find the farm?"

The sound of pounding hooves and a sliding stop drew their attention. The distraught groom tugged his forelock and leapt from the saddle. "Begging pardon, Milady, Reverend, but I got my orders. Lady Kilnsey ain't supposed to ride out over they moors by herself. It's too dangerous what with her not knowing the lay of the land."

India wheeled around on the groom. "Excellent. No doubt you are well acquainted with the area?"

"I was born here. Never lived anywhere else."

"Good. You will conduct me to the home of my husband's former lover."

Reverend Howard cleared his throat. "Do you think it wise? Surely Charles will not be pleased that you have gone there. What possible purpose could it serve?"

India cast a cool gaze over Charlie's cousin. "Good day. I will keep you from your tea no longer." She put her foot in the stirrup and launched herself into the saddle in one smooth motion. She glanced at the groom. "You must lead the way. Let's go." He opened his mouth as though to protest but wilted under her glare.

After directing a silent appeal to the parson, who ignored it and closed his door, the groom turned toward the lane and urged his horse out of the village. They rode in silence for about a mile, then turned down a single track guarded on either side by drystone walls. Sheep grazed in pastures that looked well-tended and weed free. Farther down, a line of oaks led to a neat stone cottage whose slate roof glowed softly in the late afternoon sun. Pink climbing roses covered the low walls separating the cottage's front garden from the lane. The whole effect would have been quite charming had Charlie's hunter not stood hipshot beneath the nearest oak. The groom stopped and India came alongside.

She dismounted and threw Zara's reins to him. "Wait here. I don't know how long I'll be."

In truth, she had no idea what she would say once inside the cottage or if she might be returning to the castle alone save for the groom. She would just have to see how things played out. Everything would hinge on Charlie's reaction to her presence. He had behaved very poorly on the ride home from the station. Well, one thing was certain. He was badly mistaken if he believed she was going to live her life in the shadow of another woman.

As she passed through the gate and entered the garden proper, a hound well past his prime lifted one lid, eyed India, and emitted a couple of tentative woofs. Apparently deciding she presented no danger, the dog yawned, then settled back into his dreams. A curtain flicked in the cottage's front window where a startled face briefly appeared before the cottage door swung open.

A woman of about fifty watched India's approach while glancing over her shoulder every couple of seconds. "Lady

Kilnsey. What an honor. Please come in." The woman's voice was abnormally loud.

"Thank you, Mrs.... I'm sorry, but I am afraid I do not know your name." India offered her hand which was taken in a limp grasp.

The woman blinked, confusion or fear darkening her eyes. "Mrs. Holden, Milady."

"Would you be Annie's mother?"

"That I am. She's home for a visit. Brought the bairn to see his Grandmam and Pap. Looks just like his pa, he does."

India's heart lurched at the mention of the baby's father. Was there a hidden message in Mrs. Holden's words? Charlie believed or perhaps feared the child was his. "I believe my husband is visiting also?"

A fleeting smile crossed the older woman's face. "His Lordship come not long ago."

"Perhaps I might join him?"

"Of course. Forgive me forgetting my manners. Please come in." Although Mrs. Holden's hand had not been damp when they clasped hands, she ran them down her apron, nonetheless. It seemed India was not the only one whose nerves were frayed.

Annie's mother guided India into a sitting room made cozy by an inglenook fireplace with settles on either side. Charlie stood with one arm resting on the mantel, a look of irritation marring his handsome face. On the settle nearest him, the girl Annie sat cradling a baby in her arms. India's breath caught in her throat. The child must be very young for it was still in swaddling clothes.

Charlie lifted himself off the mantel and came to India's side. Taking her hand, he drew her to the inglenook. "Let me present my wife, Lady Kilnsey. Mrs. Annie Kennedy and her son Patrick."

India didn't have the courage to look at Charlie. Instead she smiled and peeked into the swaddling clothes. "What a sweet baby. How old is he?"

"Six weeks tomorrow."

"He has beautiful red curls. Do you think his eyes will be blue or green?"

"Oh, his eyes will for sure be green. He gets his coloring from my husband. Won't you sit? Ma, can we have tea, please?"

India did a quick calculation. The baby could have been born no earlier than mid-July. Nine months before would have been October. Charlie was already in New York by then. A wave of relief washed through India. Weak from the release of pent up anxiety, she lowered herself onto the settle nearest Charlie. There was no way that baby was his. He was a fool if he believed otherwise.

Tea was consumed quickly along with stilted small talk, the weather and approach of fall being of particular interest. Placing her empty cup on its saucer, India glanced at Charlie. He must have felt it for his eyes darted her way and he gave a subtle nod.

She smiled at their hostesses. "This has been most pleasant, but I fear we must take our leave. I am very glad to have made your acquaintance." After shaking Mrs. Holden's hand, she turned to Annie. "Mrs. Kennedy, will you be staying long in the village? Perhaps we shall meet again."

Annie gave the baby to her mother and rose from the settle. "I'm afraid not. My husband only agreed to let me come when I promised not to stay more than a week." She cut her eyes at Charlie before continuing, "He misses us, you see. I'm a lucky woman."

Something subtle passed between Charlie and Annie. It was not the anguish of forever parted lovers as India feared. In fact, it seemed to be something akin to anger or even spite.

From beneath her lashes, she sneaked a peek at both. Yes, there it was. Annie wore a crooked smile with a spiteful gleam in her eye while Charlie seemed to seethe. India tore her gaze from the pair and her heart plummeted. Charlie was angry. That much was clear, but with whom was less so. If it was with her, she could muster a rage to match his own, if needed.

Stiff pleasantries completed, Charlie guided India through the door and into the garden. They stepped through the gate and the groom assisted her into the saddle. Charlie took Zara's reins and nodded to the young man. "Lady Kilnsey has no further need of your assistance. I will see she gets back to the castle. Please let my mother know we have had tea, so she need not wait for us."

The groom looked to India. When she nodded, he turned and rode away. Odd that he would look to his mistress for confirmation after receiving orders from his master. Perhaps he had more knowledge of the situation than anyone might suspect.

India made a mental note to show the young man her gratitude when the opportunity presented itself. Taking Zara's reins from Charlie, she straightened in the saddle. Her heart beat a little faster with the knowledge of what she was about to say. She dropped her hands onto the saddle's pommel to hide their shaking. "I think we need to talk, don't you?"

He launched himself onto the gelding and urged it forward. "Yes, I believe we do." He held his mount to a walk as he glared at India. "Whatever were you thinking in following me here? This was none of your affair."

Of all the nerve. Her pulse pounded against her eardrums and set her head throbbing to the point of near explosion. If it was a fight he wanted, then by God he was going to get one.

"Excuse me? None of my affair? You can't be that stupid. My husband of three days rides off without a word to see his former lover and it is none of my business?" India's breaths came in rapid puffs. The pent-up emotions from a lifetime of bending to other people's wills took control. She raised a fist and shook it at Charlie. "Let me tell you something, buster. If you think I'm going to put up with you mooning over another woman and a child that clearly belongs to another man, you've got another thing coming. There is no way that child is yours. Furthermore, if we are going to have any chance at happiness together, I have to come first in your heart. If you can't give me that, then I'm contacting David Havemeyer. It will be expensive, but not as expensive as staying married to a man who will never love me." The words were out of her mouth almost before the thought had been formed. Dear God, what if he wanted out of the marriage? Visions of life with Mother and Grandmama darkened the future and sent her pulse soaring.

Charlie looked startled then raised a brow and chuckled. The chuckle grew into a chortle and finally into outright laughter.

Of all the effrontery. Heat started in India's chest and crawled up to her hairline. "What the hell is so damned funny?" Her voice echoed from the surrounding hills.

His laughter died, but the humor did not leave his eyes. "You should see your face."

"And exactly what is wrong with my face?"

"Nothing. It's beautiful, even more so when you are enraged." His expression turned thoughtful. "You have every right to be angry. There is no excuse for my behavior this afternoon, but there is an explanation. Will you allow it?"

India glared. "Go on."

"When I saw Annie at the station, I became angry. Her sister, the maid at the Savoy, had led me to believe the child was mine. Naturally, that would have been an encumbrance, but one I was willing to shoulder. I will not shirk my duty to family like my father did. When I saw how young the child is, I suspected the truth, but I did not wish to speak about it until I knew for certain. You can at least understand that, can't you?"

India was certain of no such thing, but she wanted to hear the rest of the story. "Maybe. So, what really happened?"

"It seems that Annie was pledged to Cousin Kennedy before she and I began. When it became clear I could not marry her, she set their wedding date. I'm not sure whether her sister really believed Infant Patrick was mine or if she told me that as punishment for deserting Annie. I suppose I deserved it. I allowed us to fall in love when I knew there was no hope of marriage. Annie and her family have every right to be angry. Although I believe she is happy enough with her husband, there is still some bitterness there. I only hope her father will see past it and stay on the farm. He is an excellent tenant. We need men like him." He ground to a halt, seemingly incapable of continued speech.

Too bad. His explanation was not nearly enough. Not by a long shot. India folded her arms across her bosom. "Is that all you have to say? If so, you are far from the man I thought you to be. You are not someone I wish to be shackled to for the remainder of my life."

She clicked to Zara to urge her forward, but Charlie grabbed the reins. "Wait. There's more. I want to get it right, so I needed time to think."

India snatched the reins from his grasp. "You've had all the time I'm willing to give."

Charlie wheeled his gelding around in front of Zara, blocking the path. "Please. Let me finish. To have caused you pain was not my intention, but it is what I have done. I see how much my actions have wounded you. I am deeply ashamed. I have been so caught up in my own fears that I failed to think about how all of this affects you. I could say that having lived with only my own concerns for twenty-five years is my excuse, but that would be hollow indeed. I am a husband now and must consider your welfare above all others, including my own. I have been a self-absorbed, utterly foolish halfwit, but please believe that today has taught me a valuable lesson."

When he stopped so abruptly, India watched him for several beats. He seemed to be waiting for encouragement. "And that lesson is?"

"That it must truly be India and Charlie *contra mundum.* I can't imagine anyone more suited to the task of helping me rebuild Kilnsey." He shifted his gaze toward the castle. "Kilnsey needs you. I need you." When he turned to face her once more, there was real pleading in his eyes. "Please say you will forgive me."

CHAPTER 41

India watched Charlie through narrowed eyes. She was a bride who had just asked her new husband if he wanted to end their three-day-old marriage. His behavior had been atrocious and deeply hurtful. Anyone with good sense would end this now and return to America, albeit with her tail between her legs. The prospect of returning to New York or North Carolina held no appeal, yet the thought of living with a man who could be so thoughtless and selfish was little better. India needed time to think. She leaned forward over the pommel pretending to adjust Zara's bridle and cheek strap.

Charlie's mother had said husbands needed to be managed, but how did one go about managing a grown man, especially an English peer? An idea began to form. Perhaps there was a way. A marriage was not something to be discarded lightly, yet there was no way she was going to repeat the example set by her own parents. Living a life dominated by unhappiness and disappointment would not be endured, not in the twentieth century. Underneath his male arrogance and stupidity, Charlie was at heart a good man. But even so, he was still a man with the ideas of previous generations dominating his thinking and attitude. Could she sway him enough to establish a better foundation for their marriage? There was only one way to find out.

Giving Zara's shoulder a tap with her crop, she guided the mare around Charlie's gelding. Over her shoulder she called, "If we are going to continue Charlie and India *contra mundum*, then there are going to be some ground rules."

She kicked Zara's sides, and the mare leapt into a canter. They were passing the village when Charlie caught up with them. Catching a glimpse of him from the corner of her eye, India gripped the saddle with her knees, gave Zara her head, and kicked her into a gallop. They raced away from Charlie and his gangling hunter. The little Arabian might stand a full two hands shorter than the gelding, but she was more agile and showed her desert racing heritage in every stride. India arrived in the courtyard at a sliding stop, threw the reins to the groom, and marched into the house.

Charlie's mother, breathing hard, entered the Great Hall. Drawing herself upright as far as possible while still leaning on her gold handled cane, the old woman waylaid India with a raised brow and unsmiling countenance. "I see you ride astride. When you join the local hunt, you will find that all our ladies ride side saddle. I assume you have attained that skill. Riding astride simply will not do."

India returned her mother-in-law's glare. "I can ride either way, but I prefer astride. Perhaps the ladies of the hunt will learn something new. I am going to my room. I do not wish to be disturbed."

"Well, I never. You are proving yourself to be an impudent, low class upstart, just as Lord Hawik predicated. In my day…"

India did not wait for Lady Kilnsey to complete her invective. She strode to the grand staircase and began her ascent. When she was sure she could not be observed, she ran, her pounding footsteps muffled by a thick hall runner. Raised voices from below followed her to the suite's parlor where she yanked the door open and slammed it behind her. Instead of sitting, she paced from door to window to fireplace and back, making a circuit that did nothing to calm her.

When Charlie finished arguing with his mother, he would no doubt seek out India for her share of his anger. So be it. They might as well get it over with. He might be angry, but she could match him stroke for stroke. Footsteps sounded just outside the parlor door. She stopped in the middle of the room, ready to face whatever came. The door opened without a knock and Charlie advanced on her from the hallway.

India squared her shoulders prepared for the fight of her life. Where the will to do battle came from was not clear but came it did. She welcomed it like a freezing person wrapping herself in a bearskin coat. The analogy seemed odd given that anger was usually aligned with heat, but hers had grown into an icy berg waiting to crush anything in its path.

Placing a fist on each hip, she stared down her husband. "If you want to talk, fine, but I will not be shouted at. I heard you and your mother. I suspect people in the next county heard you."

Charlie drew up short. A hurt expression flitted across his face. "If you heard us, then you know I was defending you and your insistence on riding astride. I will not have Mama dictating to either of us."

A feeling of the unreal swam through India. How could he be so self-centered one minute and so protective of her the next? It took several beats for her to form a reply. Her body relaxed a little, and she dropped her fists to her side. "I appreciate your defense, but we have a lot more we need to discuss. You realize that, don't you?"

Charlie studied the floor, then looked into India's eyes. "Yes, we do. You are unlike any girl I have ever known. I admit I saw glimpses of your independent spirit, but it never occurred to me that the girl who insisted on attending a suffragette parade would follow us into marriage. I am having difficulty dealing with your ideals of self-determination. This outlook seems unnatural in a woman, even an American one."

India blinked a couple of times and tilted her head in thought. Charlie had put his finger on the crux of the issue. She certainly was not like any of the simpering debutants he had expected to marry. She was not even the same girl who had gone so obediently to New York with Mother. When India looked in the mirror these days, she sometimes wondered who looked back. The heiress being offered to an English title in exchange for refurbished social position? The grieving daughter marrying to escape the expectations of her family? The nascent suffragist? The bride who longed to be loved?

This could well prove to be the most important conversation of her life. The realization made her head swim. Fainting like an insipid schoolgirl would not do. Needing to sit, India gestured toward the fireplace. Charlie nodded and followed. They took their positions on opposite settees, facing one another across an expanse of worn, but still exquisite Aubusson carpet.

India chose her words carefully. "You are correct, of course. We hardly know one another. Let's be honest. You needed a fortune, and I wanted an escape. One might say we have entered into a merger rather than a marriage. For my part, I want a marriage. I want a life partner who will support me as I will him. I want a husband I can trust and confide in, a husband who is not only my lover but also my friend. I want the opposite of what my parents had. What I need to know is, aside from my money, what do you want?"

Charlie's eyes grew wider. He shifted his gaze to the west windows, then looked at her with a crooked smile. "I say, that is an honest, if somewhat brutal assessment. I said I am having difficulty adjusting. I did not say I wanted our marriage to end. Quite the opposite. As usual, I have expressed myself poorly. I am not accustomed to having to explain my actions or my motives. Will you allow me to try?" He looked at India with such yearning that she nodded but did not return his smile. "While I find your quest for independence surprising, even alarming at times, I also find it fascinating. If my sole purpose had been to marry a fortune, as you put it, there were several young ladies who would have suited quite nicely and with far less trouble. I admit that at first, I resisted the idea of you, but then I would have resisted any girl pushed forward as a potential bride. I was still too caught up in Annie. The more I was in your company, however, the more attracted to you I became. I admit I fought the attraction. My behavior has been less than gallant at best, at times ghastly. Please say you will forgive me." He rose and moved to her side on the settee.

India pulled her lower lip between her teeth while she considered his explanation. It was not enough, not nearly enough. "I suppose I can understand your confusion over Annie. What I need to know is how you feel about me. I need to know if I am first in your thoughts and in your heart. I have no idea what your true feelings are and it is very important that you tell me." She fixed him with an arched brow and serious expression.

Unexpectedly, a rosy flush crept across Charlie's cheeks. "We British are never comfortable expressing our emotions, but I will endeavor to make my case. Over these past months, I have come to cherish and admire you. I would gladly kill anyone who threatened you in any way. You are my countess and will be the mother of my children. Please believe that I hold you in highest esteem."

India's head and heart were on the verge of exploding. When she finally found her tongue, her words came as a shout. "But do you love me? Can you love me now or in the future? Dammit. I need to hear the word."

CHAPTER 42

Charlie's eyes couldn't have been wider if India had slapped him. His expression evolved with a succession of emotions - surprise, confusion, anger, contempt, and finally understanding. His usual reaction when he didn't know what to say would be to give her an ironic smile and say something he considered humorous. India crossed her arms over her bosom and glared at him.

Charlie cleared his throat. He took each of her arms and gently lowered them to her sides. He moved closer until their bodies almost touched. There was a softness in his eyes she had never seen before. First, he kissed her forehead, then her temple. Pulling her into a firm embrace, he pinned her arms against her sides. "My poor darling. I see how all of this must appear to you. What a bumbling mess I have made. To answer your question, I must first offer further explanation."

India pushed against his embrace, which tightened until she gasped, "Let go. You're crushing the life out of me."

Charlie loosened his grip but continued to hold her close. "Will you listen?"

India pulled back and tried to look at him. She could only catch a glimpse from the corner of her eye. "I'll listen, but you better be very convincing. What you've said so far falls short, very short of the mark." Although the day was not overly warm, perspiration popped out on India's forehead. She squirmed until Charlie released the pressure a little more.

He put his mouth close to her ear and spoke quietly. "The reason I went to see Annie in such a rush is that I feared the child was mine. I could not bring myself to speak of it until I knew the truth. If the boy had been a Westmorland, even one born on the wrong side of the blanket, I was prepared to do the right thing by him. I would have made financial arrangements for his care and education. I admit my feelings were in a state of confusion, but as soon as I was with Annie, they sorted. I knew the child wasn't mine, and I also realized where my heart lay. It was not with Annie. I care about her welfare, but I no longer love her. She is the past. You, my darling, are the future, the only one I want. You ask if you are first and the answer is a resounding yes. If our families had not interfered, if the matter of your fortune had not been such an issue, I might have seen the truth much earlier. My heart is yours. I love you body and soul. The thought of losing you is unbearable. Please believe me."

He gripped her shoulders and pushed her back so that they were face-to-face. His eyes were brighter than usual. All the tension and anger melted and flowed down India's cheeks. They stood with their arms around each other until the gong sounded announcing it was time to dress for dinner.

Charlie placed a finger beneath her chin and lifted until their lips met. His kiss demanded that her passion match his. When he ended it, he looked searchingly into her eyes. "What more must I do to prove myself?"

India tilted her head and pressed her lips together. A catalogue of possibilities ran through her mind. He could so completely forget Annie that he never mentioned or thought about her again. He could take her side against his mother. He could include her in decisions about how her money was spent. He could let her make the decisions about the improvements to the castle, starting with electrification and plumbing. She had seen the power station in Grassington from the train window and commented upon it. There were so many options, so many ways that he might demonstrate his devotion. As she ran the tip of her tongue over her lips an answer presented itself. It felt more important than all the others combined.

She did not smile. The situation was much too serious. "You have asked what you can do to prove yourself. Here is my answer. You can take my side against all who believe me unworthy of being your countess, even when I'm wrong." A little stab of guilt pricked her conscience. Even under present circumstances, it was an unreasonable demand, one at which he might easily laugh.

Without a hint of humor, he pulled her close again and whispered, "I will gladly slay all dragons regardless of who they are. No one will question your worth ever again."

She rested her forehead against his shoulder. His words touched her deeply, but she would be damned if she would start blubbering. Humor and irony made for good cover. Her voice trembled a little when she spoke. "Even with my questionable heritage?"

This time, Charlie chuckled. "You are not the only one in this marriage with familial skeletons. You have graciously never mentioned my father's perfidious squandering of the family fortunes. He was certainly no paragon by any standard."

India gasped. "I would never hold a person's parents' misdemeanors against them. We don't choose our relatives and a child has no say in what a parent does." India leaned back so that she could see his eyes. "You know, I think I would be better able to deal with people's snubs and slights if I knew exactly what they hold against me. I know it has something to do with my Ledbetter grandparents, especially Jane. Knowing what I am fighting would make it easier."

"And you shall know, my darling. I promise. If that is what it will take to make you completely comfortable in your role as my countess, we will one day discover the truth together."

"But when? We've only just left America."

"We will return to New York at some point in the not too distant future. No matter how much you may protest, Petra is your mother and you will eventually come to miss her. I suspect you will even miss that old battle-ax of a grandmother. When the time is right, we'll plan a visit. I understand Cunard is building a ship that is said to be unsinkable and will be the fastest on the seas. Once we get the necessary improvements completed here, we can plan a trip to America. What do you think?"

"That you have made promises I'm going to hold you to, so don't get any ideas about reneging, buster."

A burst of laughter filled the room. "Yes, My Lady. I will keep that in mind, but aren't you forgetting something?"

"I don't think so." He gave her the kind of look governesses give uncomprehending pupils. India frowned. "What? What is it?"

"I have stated without hesitation, well maybe there was some hesitation due to my British upbringing, but certainly unequivocally, that I am in love with the most beautiful girl in the world who just happens to be my wife. I'm a lucky bugger save for one thing." The humor drained from his face, replaced by deep solemnity. "Does she love me in return?"

India pulled away. "Do you mean you really don't know?"

"As you so eloquently put it, I need to hear the words, dammit."

Her fingers traced the outline of his jaw until they rested on the nape of his neck. Caressing the ruff of hair above his collar, she said, "Yes, I love you. I think I have for a very long time."

He picked her up in his arms and carried her to the bedroom door. Kicking it open, he crossed to the bed, lowered her onto the counterpane, and began unfastening the buttons on her blouse. "Dressing for dinner is highly overrated. I have a much better idea for how we might spend the evening." He bent and covered her mouth with his.

India broke away from a kiss that sent her desire soaring. "What if Aletha walks in on us?"

Charlie gave her a lascivious grin. "I left word that we were not to be disturbed and that we would take dinner here in our apartment. You are very tired from your travels and need to rest."

"Rather confident in your ability to charm, are you not?"

"Yes, but remember I have tasted my lady's charms, and I know her to be a passionate creature." He traced the line of her cheek with his finger. "I am the luckiest of men, a fact that I will never forget. I promise you that, my darling."

And he was right. He did have a much, much better idea of how they would spend their evening.

ABOUT THE AUTHOR

Linda Bennett Pennell has been in love with the past for as long as she can remember. Anything with a history, whether shabby or majestic, recent or ancient, instantly draws her in. It probably comes from being part of a large extended family that spanned several generations. Long summer afternoons on her grandmother's wrap around porch or winter evenings gathered by the fireplace were filled with stories both entertaining and poignant. Of course, being set in the American South, those stories were also peopled by some very interesting characters, some of whom have found their way into Linda's work.

Linda resides in the Houston, Texas area with her sweet husband and an adorable Labradoodle, Lulu, who is quite certain she's a little girl, not a dog.

NOTE FROM THE AUTHOR

Word-of-mouth is crucial for any author to succeed. If you enjoyed *The Last Dollar Princess*, please leave a review online—anywhere you are able. Even if it's just a sentence or two. It would make all the difference and would be very much appreciated.

Thanks!
Linda Bennett Pennell

We hope you enjoyed reading this title from:

BLACK ❀ ROSE
writing™

www.blackrosewriting.com

Subscribe to our mailing list – *The Rosevine* – and receive **FREE** books, daily deals, and stay current with news about upcoming releases and our hottest authors.
Scan the QR code below to sign up.

Already a subscriber? Please accept a sincere thank you for being a fan of Black Rose Writing authors.

View other Black Rose Writing titles at www.blackrosewriting.com/books and use promo code **PRINT** to receive a **20% discount** when purchasing.

Made in the USA
Las Vegas, NV
22 September 2023

77921996R00215